The Color of Blood

A Novel

Taylor Charles Hall

Print ISBN: 979-8-9945873-0-0

First Edition: January 2026

Cover design by Ken Oliver

To: you know who you are.

"Blood it must be — blood has peculiar virtues" —
Mephistopheles, Faust

"Of course, they're just warm bodies. That is, until they aren't."
— Anonymous

The sad whispers wander from the plains to the shore
Caw-birds yonder call my name as before
Watchers have discovered your sweet pain — a gift
Now the whistling winds plunder your torment — what a lift!

Blue. A Pretty Color for You.

1

Professor Peter Barton sat at his office desk reading over the graduate student papers that had accumulated over the past month. It was something that had needled him weekly as it grew worse, but he had finally felt that the time had come where he could concentrate on providing feedback to his seminar students of his Topics in Social Cognition course.

After four in the afternoon on a Friday, Blanchard Hall, housing his office in the Department of Psychology on the campus of University of Southern Florida, had little to no commotion happening around it. Even the residence halls were relatively quiet. With the exception of a moderately competitive ultimate frisbee game and the various outside loungers enjoying the remainder of the temperate spring day, many students appeared to be resigning themselves to the prospect of later nightly activities.

It was the perfect time where Peter could really make a dent in the stack of work, a time he not always saw as a burden but, in fact, looked forward to—relishing early flashes of genius from the words of his rising scholars. The truth was that the thoughtful solitude was a real haven for Peter—one that he couldn't enter upon at home with all the demands from his wife and son. That night, Peter knew they would be waiting for him with their routine modes of communication of "Peter do this" and "Peter give me that." That's why he decided to really enjoy his time—taking in the moment for meaningful contemplation—what he lived for—the very reason he decided to become an academic in the first place.

After some consideration of the work before him, Peter scrolled down a comment in the wide margin that he told his students to use—writing in his script cursive that had long been dreaded by grad and undergrad alike. Such comments commonly meant one thing by those who already invested a good part of their time in completing such assignments, that most dirty of words that suggested something awry, a lack, a deficiency, a wanting. Revision. And here was a case of no exception, for one thing Peter couldn't stand for in his position, something that sometimes unsettled him in bed at night, was a student who slipped through his fingers without an education. Thus, this student before him now was going to receive that excellent education that Peter had idealized from the very beginning even for himself—the one that equally required both the student and professor's very best effort.

A rap on the office door jolted Peter from his intellectual sanctuary. He saw Clint entering the room with a magazine under his arm and the same warm smile that welcomed him his first day at Southern over a decade and a half ago. But, there was something a little off in his demeanor.

"Appears that Eldridge has done it yet again." He began in his deep booming voice. "Only this time, he's made quite a splash."

He laid a magazine before Peter over the papers on his desk. It was the latest edition of the Journal of Psychophysiology Quarterly.

"You don't say," Peter said opening the Journal and browsing the article titles. While Peter had plenty to do, he always welcomed a distraction by his long-time colleague and friend, especially when the hyper-competitive egotistical nature of an interdepartmental struggle for publication came up. "A Genetic Architectural Basis of Phenotypic Ethnic Animus. Okay." He raised his eyebrows while flipping to the corresponding page number.

"Interesting, no?" Clint stood there holding the same sardonic smile that Peter had at first missed.

"At least that." Peter scanned the entry doubling over the abstract before his eyes slowly descended down the page. "He used Cognitive Bias Testing?" he asked rhetorically in a bewildered tone.

"Naturally. What do we even know Eldridge for after all?"

"I'm not really sure."

Clint chuckled. He gave Peter a moment further to consider the revelation.

"So…what do you think?"

"Well," Peter began before meeting Clint's gaze, "Did you read it yourself?"

"Yes."

"*All* of it?

"Yes, Professor." Clint's smile only grew.

"Good. And, do tell me, what did you learn?"

Clint comically put on a show of introspection. His imposing tall robust physique combined with his dark complexion really added to the act. He was the type of man who had the force of presence to draw the attention out of just about any room and whether Clint was in the lecture hall, cafeteria, faculty meeting, or even going on a double date with Peter and the wives to the cinema, there Clint was in all his majesty. And the voice only complemented it all. Speechless, Clint finally threw up his hands in a show of defeat.

"And just who is this?" Peter tapped on the second author's name. "Associate Professor of Biology Gerson Jersey, University of Southern Florida."

"*Intrigue.* No idea."

"But, do you know which of the faculty also know about this," Peter inquired.

"No, but I am curious of…who exactly funded this project? Why didn't we hear about it? And what exactly is meant by *peer review* anymore?" He laughed.

"Yes, who, indeed, are these *peers* anyhow?" Peter joined in.

"Eldridge knows he has none here."

"But, how did you even find out about this?"

"The most unlikely of sources, the university newsletter."

"I didn't know you read those."

"Emptying my mailbox today, I happened to see this firecracker on the front page. After class, I had to go straight down to the stacks and fetch the latest edition."

"Firecracker is right," Peter said opening his laptop. "Now let's see…" On the university homepage, he clicked on the Southern Florida Daily.

"*Holy* shit." He ran his cursor over one of the two headlines as he read aloud. "Professor Discovers Genetic Material Shedding Light on Possible Source of Racial Bias." Peter then sat there silently staring at the article incredulously.

"If that's a firecracker," Clint gestured toward the journal, "this may be TNT."

"Yeah, great, and now we are going to have every racist conspiracy peddling prophet from here to the Gulf Coast," Peter said absently.

"More than that."

2

The natural light receded from the small town of Palm Gate and the artificial light of the lamps illumined the pathways that crisscrossed campus. Quiet appeared to engulf the community with the exception of the occasional gust of wind that bristled the large elms that appeared to invade the neogothic architecture.

For the town of a large university near the southeast coast of Florida, Palm Gate had a rural charm with its woods, lakes, and walking trails. Mainstreet was lined with a variety of establishments to meet every need. There were restaurants, cafés, salons, ice-cream parlors, pharmacies, local bookshops, and even a rage room for tame thrills. Among these, Sally's Bakery was an especially frequented destination by locals and visitors alike, who couldn't resist the aromas of freshly baked bread and fudge.

Running parallel to Mainstreet was the university. This institution, being the hundreds of acres of broken latticework of brick buildings and bronze statues, had an inseparable history with the town. The University of Southern Florida had started as a boy's boarding school in the postbellum South whose land had later become acquired by the state. By the forties and fifties, it had already made a name for itself in the fields of the sciences and engineering—shedding its safety school status to attract many bright students from across the country and world. Nordrick Hall, for instance, the biological sciences building, was later named after one of its residents, Henry A. Nordrick, a professor who made a significant contribution to the study of Parasitology, including the life cycle of *Proorchis sapiens*, the ancient critter that has long been scourging humanity—clogging biliary systems from the consumption of raw fish.

The center of campus, also known as the park, had its own history—being a signpost of the civil rights and anti-Vietnam war movements of the 60s and 70s with thousands of students, along with university faculty, holding signs and shouting slogans in a fortuitous demonstration of solidarity and goodwill.

The university seemed to have only grown on a string of successes. Not only was it now consistently ranked among other academic centers of the state, including University of Florida and Miami, it had become a force in collegiate sports with a football and basketball team that each participated in three national title games. Therein developed a loyal following of local, national, and international fans that never failed to sport their USFL Titans regalia. There was a sense of belonging with publications revealing high student and faculty satisfaction with campus life annually boasted as being among one of the highest in the country and the good word only spread. And that good word is what drove many like the newly hooded Ph.D. graduate, Peter Barton, fifteen years prior, from the cold recesses of Ithaca, New York to the sunshine state.

3

Peter drove to his home in Preston Heights, a subdivision of colonial style houses on the outskirts of Palm Gate. Pulling into the driveway, he turned off his car which included the evening jazz station he had been enjoying. He sat for a moment listening to what sounds he could hear from the neighborhood. Only the trees whispered and hushed. It was a kind of melody Peter also enjoyed. That serenity was the determinative factor for why Peter had signed with Margery on the jumbo loan for the house in the first place. It had been a bit of a stretch financially, but his wife was immediately sold on the place. She wanted the ideal home where their son could grow up. Now, they both agreed that the only thing that the house was missing was more kids, and that was something they were going to let happen in due course.

Peter entered seeing Margery standing at the kitchen island with her favorite bottle of red on the counter. Coming over with a smile that said she was ready for business, she wrapped her voluptuous figure around Peter kissing him. Peter was ready too, but he knew that good things came to those who waited.

"How would you like it?" She whispered in his ear.

"Hard."

"Good," she agreed looking at him with hungry eyes.

"By the way, my day wasn't too bad." She laughed kissing him again.

"Roger's upstairs. He's been waiting for you to get home to play cards."

"Did you eat?"

"No. Are you hungry?"

"No."

"I already fed Roger. I'll make you a drink." He gave her a small kiss before she went into the east wing of the house where they had a mini bar.

After placing his leather briefcase on the corner table, with copy of the Psychophysiology article inside, Peter walked over to the balustrade calling down Roger. The boy immediately came running out on the upstairs landing.

"Dad! Can we play cards?"

"Depends." He gave his eleven-year old son a serious look.

"Did you do all of your homework?"

"Yes," Roger answered with equal gravity.

"And your grades?"

"All A's."

"So no C's?"

His son shook his head with embellished sincerity.

"Okay, I'll ask Mom, too."

Margery re-entered the room with a topped off whiskey glass.

"Roger's teacher make another call this week?"

"No. But, I called her, and she said he's been behaving himself."

In suspense, Roger waited for his dad's answer while Peter considered. This had been a recent ritual with his son ever since Roger rediscovered the deck of cards, one of his old stocking stuffers, and Peter taught him how to play Gin Rummy. Now the boy was hooked, and Peter was glad knowing that he and Margery made the right call in not giving him a smart phone too early.

"Okay," Peter finally conceded, "grab the cards." Roger rushed away in a flash.

Margery put the drink into Peter's hand. He sipped it. "Mmm…perfect. You know just how I like it." She responded with a knowing smirk walking over to the kitchen while Peter's eyes followed.

With classic Hoyle deck and pen in hand, Roger ran down the stairs, as Peter settled into his favorite button tufted living room chair.

Roger pulled out the cards with the folded paper inside indicating the running score. To complete the ritual, he plopped himself on the floor opposite his dad to separate the jokers and count out the deck. When he was satisfied that none were missing, he half shuffled the deck—not quite being able to complete the bridge at the end.

Peter gave him some pointers, as he made multiple attempts. "No, keep your thumbs there…release slowly…better…yes. Keep practicing and you'll get it every time."

Roger dealt the cards across the coffee table. Hunching over, Peter took them, fanning them out in his hand. After drawing a card, he discarded before sitting back again. "Your turn."

He knew it usually took a moment for his son to organize his cards and finish his play giving him a moment to take another sip. When his son discarded, Peter leaned forward again to draw.

"Dad?" Roger looked curiously at Peter. "What did you do today?"

"You know what I do. I'm a professor."

"A psychology professor," Roger added.

"That's right."

"That's what I mean. What do psychology professors teach?"

Peter eyed his son with interest—not knowing the source of the line of questioning. Sure, he had told him in the past, but something was always left wanting in the explanation.

"Well, Psychology is the study of the *psyche* or the Greek word for life, soul, or mind."

"I know. You told me. So what do you actually do?"

"We study how people think and act."

"So can you tell me how I think? What I'm thinking now?"

"I don't know." Peter took a moment to answer. "You're probably thinking that I don't know what you're thinking right now."

"That's right. You don't know what I'm thinking."

Peter laughed to himself at the precocity of his son's response. Taking the next card in his hand, he discarded the same. "And why do you say that?"

"Here's why." Roger shifted to take the king of hearts from the discard pile. Placing it down with the king of clubs and spades. "Thirty points for me."

The news of the study broke Wednesday evening of the following week. Networks were immediately gratified by the exploding ratings happening overnight as simultaneous pieces were released including on-site reporting from the university, aesthetically pleasing graphics, expert interviews, guest commentaries, panel editorializations, and the most suggestive language necessary to move internet consumers to their highest level of self-actualization. The shares, comments, and likes followed and replicated exponentially—each new engagement perpetuating the last. The phrase and picture factory turning out so massive of a response that most of the response lingered fruitlessly. And while some interfering participation quelled some of the tumult, many of the responses superimposed each other, even rippling to the far reaches of the cybernetic globe.

When he saw the coverage, Clint immediately called Peter. He told him of the network station where the co-author of the study was being interviewed.

Peter couldn't even be sure what was on his cable package anymore. Except for the occasional movie night, the flat screen in the living room was rarely used. Roger had always preferred the one in his room upstairs for watching his daily Syfy shows and while Peter and his wife never prohibited the use of the one downstairs, they were glad to have a relatively peaceful sanctuary.

"Dammit." Peter breathed rummaging for the remote through the TV cabinet's cables, electronics guides, and program package information.

"You may miss it by the time you find it."

Peter confirmed the channel before hanging up with Clint. He was able to enlist the aid of his wife to help him look. She soon pulled it out from the side of a cushion on the sofa.

Trying the channel number, using the interactive guide, and doing the old-fashioned flipping method were all to no avail.

"Well, we may not even have that station anymore," Peter told Margery.

"Or…" his wife thought aloud. Peter stopped flipping and waited for her to finish. "You could merely check in a little bit and it'll probably be posted somewhere online."

"Really? Where?"

She scrolled through videos on her laptop with Peter standing over her shoulder. Browsing the titles, Peter told her to stop—pointing at one.

"Study of Genetic Racism. An Interview with Professor Gerson Jersey."

"Posted only an hour ago," his wife added.

"Let's see it."

After having to watch ten seconds of an advertisement for a male virile power supplement, Propense, Margery clicked to skip to the video showing two men sitting in an LNN network studio.

"With me here is Professor Gerson Jersey, Professor of Biology at the University of Southern Florida. He is author of a multitude of publications including the book, The Genetic Personality, and Deviant Ancestor. More recently, he has co-authored a controversial new study in the prestigious journal, Psychophysiology Quarterly."

Peter choked out a scoff at the word prestigious.

"It's good to meet you Professor."

"My pleasure," grinned a middle-aged mild-mannered man who Peter thought looked familiar.

"Now, I understand that the co-author Professor Louis Eldridge couldn't make it today."

"Yes, he's been engaged, I believe, on a different network."

"Of course. You both appear to be extraordinarily busy people, and so I thank you for making it here." There was a slight pause but no response before the news personality continued.

"Let's delve right into it. Now, I am not a man of science so please forgive me if I don't understand something, but what I have gathered from the article itself and other sources is that you conclude, within the study, that there is a *gene*, if inherited, happens to instill the possessor with certain negative attitudes towards other groups of people."

Jersey waited for him to continue but was already looked to for clarification.

"That's not quite right. It is not as if there were one specific gene but more like a complex relationship involving a heritable collection of them whose manifold interaction exhibits a tendency or likelihood of group preference," he expressed holding hands together in the form of prayer before intertwining his fingers—squeezing them together.

"Heritable? Aren't all genes heritable, Professor?"

"Genes are heritable but there is some uncertainty about likelihoods of heritability, but this goes well beyond the limited scope of this study. I'm anticipating future research will shed more light on the matter."

"So, that—that may not be ascertained at the moment…but to clarify something else…" The interviewer waivered momentarily—checking his notes before starting again. "There is a likelihood for group preference associated with these…what do you mean by that?"

"All that can be concluded so far is that there is a probability of expression of these genetic markers—not a certainty. And that is not very surprising given what we know about other genetic relationships. Take genetic testing for susceptibility to types of cancer. These do not indicate that one will acquire that cancer, but that they have an increased probability. But there are other factors that cannot be precluded, expressivity and environment, for example—"

"But, what specifically is group preference here? Is that the kind of prejudice that we see in these deadly incidents between the police and the African American community or is it something less pernicious? Maybe I prefer dog-people for example. We like to walk our dogs around the neighborhood and take them to the dog-park, so I prefer their company than to non-dog people. That's my preference."

Professor Jersey gave a polite smile as if he heard a joke but withheld his laugh. He projected an air of patient self-possession with confidence and composure. His outfit added weight to every measured word. The azure-colored silk vest and pin-striped-burgundy tie kept drawing Peter's attention away from the professor's face. *Like a politician, he has had pre-interview practice*, Peter thought.

Jersey began again slowly, "While Professor Eldridge will better inform you to that part of the study, the conclusion specifically states that the carriers of these genetic markers have a tendency to exhibit an animus against those people independently identified as people of color and a preference for people not so identified. Thus, depending on how you wish to state it, it is really two sides of the same coin and preference and animus are used interchangeably throughout."

"Those mean quite different things, Professor. If one has a *preference* for one group, that doesn't mean that they hate or wish ill on the other or that they—"

"Not necessarily," Jersey cut in. "Think about how you just mentioned the police shootings. Preference for one person over the other makes a world of difference from the most serious of incidents, such as in the administration of justice, but even to the most seemingly mundane matters such as being chosen for a position, loan, becoming a tenant *et cetera*. In the former example, we see officers disproportionately shoot or arrest those unfortunate people compared to others. And what you see as those ten feet of difference completes the mile; it is enough to cost them their lives. The same can be said for all of the other ordinary pursuits in life. When an employer selects one person over another, that difference is enough to make both of their lives radically different in quality, as with attaining a mortgage or renting adequate properties. Like these, you may see a difference, but, in effect, I don't, and neither does Professor Eldridge, and I think…most people will who reflect on the probable implications of this research."

"So how do you know that these genes cause such dispositions? I think…that would be like trying to prove that a set of genes gave people an affinity toward the color blue. How can you even begin to show that?"

Jersey finally forced a laugh belted out in regular intervals. The interviewer smiled warming up to the professor—welcoming a moment of some levity. "I do wonder that myself," Jersey said suddenly recovering. "As you can see, I am very fond of the color blue…but in all seriousness…" He said straightening up before beginning again. "We have implemented a very advanced AI system called OperAnd that does a thorough statistical analysis otherwise missed by laymen and experts alike. It has built the genetic profile based on the two thousand participants of the study who, under controlled conditions, showed a statistically significant preference through bias testing."

"That is, a preference for people who are not considered people of color?"

"Yes, for those others who were universally agreed upon, by the participants, as people of color."

"Okay Professor, what now? If everything you conclude in the study is true, what do we do with this information? Shouldn't people be judged based on their actions and not on the contents of their genes?"

"Those are good questions, and I am glad you asked. I think I'm not the only one who would like to know what may perpetuate a certain vileness of humanity, that page of history, that we hope to turn one day. We will certainly still judge people based on their actions, but we simply cannot ignore facts. And perhaps if we understood ourselves even a little bit better with these facts, especially those who may possess such genetic markers, they could be more cognizant of their own behavior and the adverse effects they have on others who are different. That special reflection of those possessing such tendencies could start curbing those inhumane injustices in a big way."

"And I hope people reflect on their behavior whatever their genetic makeup…"

"Turn it off," Peter said as if his teeth were being scraped along cement.

Margery didn't have to hear him twice. She closed out the window.

"Okay, you saw it." She summarized after a deep breath. "Feel better now?" She asked sarcastically.

"No, I don't," he said flatly.

"A week ago, drinking coffee is healthy. Yesterday, coffee causes cancer. Today, genes cause racism. What's next?" She smirked to Peter trying to lighten the mood.

"I love you, darling," he said returning it.

5

Blinding colors from every direction penetrated through him. They were burning the very retinas of his eyes and radiating through to his head in a series of icepick pains. At first, nothing else could be registered—nothing could block them out. Even with closing his eyes tightly, the light made it through and so did the agony. There he was suspended in a timeless limbo being the force's helpless receptacle. *"Please…,"* he groaned to someone with no other recourse. The light didn't abate, but the pain did considerably.

A figure appeared. With crystal clear resolution, there before him glowed a table of hewn stone. Not only did he see it, but he could know its detailed history. And he comprehended the ancient slab that had been dimpled by countless fingers.

He found himself capable of rewinding and forwarding the stream of images associated with its surface. Every shining image that he poured over told a tale. There were meals arrayed with various cutlery, ritual sacrifices cutting the throats of bulls and calves, as well as a dead child laying motionless as his parents looked on.

Others were much different. In fact, there was a phantasmagoria of rapings, killings, whippings, and other horrifying events that sprayed the table with tears, semen, blood, and sweat. As a witness to these, his stomach curdled while his head still ached with each pulse of light that shown through. But, his curiosity won out. He kept cycling through more images wanting to know all the table's dark secrets. At times he even had to look away at the climaxes of these atrocities.

One of these moments afforded him the occasion to see another figure that beamed through the kaleidoscope of light. A giant toad, about the size of a backpack sat before him in a field. It seemed altogether uninterested, doing nothing with eyes closed. Its history was far less interesting than that of the stone. It was only days old and was a recent recipient of a smorgasbord of bug guts, corpses of toads and other organisms. He wondered if it was watching him but redirected his focus onto his original inquiries.

It didn't take long, however, before a putrid stench invaded his nostrils. At first, he thought it may have something to do with the altar, but he looked back to notice that the toad had grown much larger. It was now the size of a golf cart but still assumed a position like an unimposing paper weight. He fully turned fixing his gaze on it—waiting for what it would do next. It simply sat their motionless, but he knew the heart was cranking, its digestive system was flowing, its lungs inflating and deflating. *I'll elbow that fucker if it comes any closer*, he thought. *Maybe I could use the slab?* He envisioned himself being able to lift it and bashing the amphibian's brains in a firework of colors, but he decided that this would be too heavy an order. The animal didn't budge. So far it was a mere boulder of the landscape. He proceeded to walk around to the other side of the monolith to better keep an eye on the creature as he further satisfied his curiosity. While his playback of the altar's history resumed, it slowly drew more of his attention away from the rest of his surroundings. The toad began to bore him, and he felt complacent about its presence. Even though the perceived stink grew, what finally snapped him back to it was some perceived movement. The toad had begun pulsating, and in that short interim, had grown to the size of a car.

He stumbled back in terror at the sudden mass before him. He needed to get away and fast. Nothing that big would be sustained long without a constant source of nutrients, and he believed he could be the next coveted item on the menu. He ran from the monstrosity as fast as he could—spurning the desire to look. But, that's when the noises began. The echoes of the movement of puddling liquid in a cave followed by a striking whip. It happened a little to his left, so he angled more to the right. Then it was right behind him, so he tried cutting back. Like a pilot evading a bogey, he tried every maneuver to win some advantage. Finally, it landed a partial hit on his left leg. The sticky substance held him as he tried prying himself away with his right. He fully threw the weight of his body forward entrenching both his feet into the sandy ground as it tried slurping him backwards. The tongue peeled from his shirt and pants more easily than he thought the struggle would require, and with his center of gravity still so positioned, he fell to the ground.

Trying to anticipate the creature's next move, he swiveled his head around ready to dart in a new direction. But, just as its tongue had retracted in a flash, it shot back at him.

Witnessing the whole range of movement in the same slow motion he experienced as a car wreck survivor years before, the tongue struck him square in the torso. He desperately thrashed behind him with his arms—grasping with full knowledge the prospect of becoming the future refuse of the seemingly disinterested mass. This only made it worse as his arms also adhered to the giant gelatinous sponge. He came to realize that his little run was over. To struggle now was futile.

Out of his periphery, he saw the lazy eyes of the beast rolling out to catch a momentary glimpse of the morsel it was about to devour. And the next thing he knew, with force cracking back his neck, he was within the dark gullet of the frog's body soggifying— soon to disintegrate along with the rest of the particulate of its previous meals. That's when he realized he wasn't the only one. *At least, I'm not alone*, he said to himself. He somehow knew the bodies of millions of people—not bugs—had been its former victims. And they were all disintegrating within its stomach acid just as he was now. His skin was joining the others in being slowly singed from his body.

6

A space was open in faculty parking Lot A—a lot that was closest to Peter's office. Rarely, had Peter been able to find a spot so close, but he was early.

The night before, he awoke from the dream. He had laid in bed a while as thoughts pervaded his mind. From 4 a.m. on, he had already been up drinking coffee and composing a response to the publication. After multiple revisions, he was somewhat satisfied with the outcome, but he knew that there was still a piece missing. That piece would have to be reserved until he could speak to Professor Eldridge directly, and he knew that, if it was going to take place at all, it was going to be one uncomfortable meeting.

Professor Louis Eldridge earned a name for himself in the Department of Psychology at the university. He was privately known among his colleagues as Louis the Fourteenth or Little Louis, for what the faculty deemed as only acceptable behavior from a French monarch. Faculty meetings could be unpleasant affairs with his irascible temperament. He was overly sensitive to criticism and would lash out as if in the depths of biblical punishment.

He's a hard pill, Peter considered, grabbing his briefcase from the passenger seat. Given his uncritical dedication to implicit-bias research and the accompanying skepticism of the faculty, Little Louis was afforded no reprieve and always on the verge of his next explosion. Nevertheless, Peter, as well as the rest of the faculty, had developed plans of action to effectively deal with the prima-donna. A balancing act between direct criticism and assuring the integrity of Eldridge's bruised ego was what worked best in the past and the way he decided to proceed.

Walking in the crisp morning air along the winding paths to central campus, Peter was alone with his thoughts. When a problem of some weight came to his attention, it tended to excite the normal placidity of his mind. But his stomach soon interrupted as he passed Wilson Hall, one of the most frequented campus cafeterias, where he could smell bacon from the grill. Some students still in pajama bottoms crossed his path heading back to the residence halls with paper cups and doggy bags in hand. Not having had any breakfast since the witching hour, he thought of stopping for a ham, egg, and cheese biscuit, but instead fixing himself on the next easy cup of joe he could brew for himself in the office.

Peter pushed through the heavy double wooden doors to the backside of Blanchard Hall—one of the many long buildings skirting central campus' open area, the park. While the outside of the building consisted of interesting stonework, the austere interior left much to be desired and was subjected to a constant state of renovation. With the exception of the old leaky roof, Peter didn't know at what stage it was currently in or what was even planned exactly, if there was one. Qualitative improvement was yet to be seen, but work areas were at least demarcated.

Ascending the rust smelling staircase with partially corroded wrought iron railing, Peter noticed the flashing blue lights that subtly played against the old panes of glass. The police had positioned themselves on the road that ran along the far east border of the park. *They must have already anticipated some trouble ahead,* Peter thought peering through the blur.

Once he got to the third landing, he was winded and panted down the long corridor. It wasn't usual for him to go to that floor or enter the far east wing of Blanchard Hall. In fact, he didn't remember the last time he had, but he wanted to stop at Eldridge's office on the off chance that he was already there. No lights were on, however. No one was around.

Having looked up his room number just that morning, he was also curious of where such a man resided in relation to himself. How could Peter have been under the same roof for so long with a man who could bluster the faculty out of meetings and not know where he was? *Surely, that was a gross oversight to have such a loose cannon nearby.*

At the end of the hallway, few offices remained, some unoccupied, but on one had a small unassuming black plastic name plate containing white sans serif lettering, "Professor Louis Eldridge." Below the name, appeared to be a recently taped schedule of office hours which were very few. Peter reasoned that while they were far below the minimum requirement, which student would want to do themselves the displeasure? *Did he act differently around them?* Peter highly doubted that.

Even though there was no light seen coming from the bottom of the door into the dark hall, Peter decided to knock. No answer. As much as he admitted to himself that he was a little relieved, he also very much wanted to tie up this loose end. Just as Professor Jersey mentioned the evening before, Eldridge was now a very busy man and had most likely been slated to appear on multiple platforms—riffing endlessly on implicit bias research and probably causing untold damage to the public's scientific literacy. Peter knew he was just going to have to wait.

Back in the comfort of his office, he brewed one of his daily pots of strong black arabica. The whole office always smelled that way and when Mr. Coffee was on, the aroma permeated well into the hall outside confirming that the professor was in. It drew Clint that very morning who found Peter staring at his computer screen holding his token white mug with the faded red C. To break Peter from his reverie, he lightly tapped on the door. Peter turned without surprise. "Grab a cup," he said simply—no serious formality remaining between the two friends.

"Don't mind if I do." Clint took one of the two remaining mugs that read, "Drink about it." He poured it almost to the brim before adding the powdered creamer Peter kept on hand for guests. Drawing a wooden stir-stick, he blended the powder thoroughly before making a stooping sip.

"Professor Jersey didn't do half-bad," Peter told him still fixated on the end of an email.

"You found it?"

"My wife did online."

"How about that outfit?"

"Very nice…but I tell you what, I was even more impressed with how he handled himself."

"Have you met him before?"

"Never. You?"

"Nope, but do you know who has?"

"Yes."

"Eldridge."

"Yes, and I was wondering that myself. How do two astronomically different people end up collaborating together? But, well… it happened."

"That it did. And it was presented as science—science with a capital s."

"That's why I've written a paper to address concerns with it."

"You mean, you've already finished it?"

"Almost."

"Really?"

"I'm just reaching out to Eldridge as we speak to see if I misconstrued anything."

"I wouldn't even bother. Just write it and print it as soon as you can and stop this mess."

"So, I take it then, you saw the police outside?"

"Of course, they are stationed around the whole campus. It's hard to miss."

"I was here a lot earlier… I only saw the set up in the park."

Behind the computer screen, Clint started to notice the outline of Peter's tired uneasy demeanor. Placing the coffee on Peter's desk and sitting down in one of the small wooden armchairs, it was uncanny how it somehow accommodated Clint's large frame.

"You look worse than hell."

"Thanks. Couldn't sleep."

"It took a while to drift off for me as well."

"Well, I got to sleep but then I woke up."

"So you had a nightmare?"

"I woke up to *this* nightmare," Peter evaded.

Clint quaffed some more coffee before sitting back in his chair. He carefully studied Peter putting additional touches on the email. "Tell me," he interrupted after some thought, "Who are you going to send the paper to?"

"I've been thinking…" Peter faced Clint to gage his reaction, "Maybe I'll send it to Psychology of Today. They publish my popular work pretty reliably. I can usually depend on them…"

"The magazine? And they'll put it where? I suppose in the editorials?"

"Maybe," Peter said still thinking.

"Then that will be published in, say, what? a month? at least?"

"What are you saying? I should put it in the school paper then?" He laughed to himself.

"I'm saying you should put it out there right away. This is time sensitive material. This is damage control, Pete. Remember Wakefield's Lancet article about MMRs and autism? We're *there*."

"We're not quite there—"

"We're *there*," Clint corrected in his forceful bass. "This is it, and we have a chance to make this right early.

There was a pause. Clint had Peter's attention. "Okay, let's assume that's true, I don't want it to be, but let's say it is. Where should I publish?"

"You need to address people in the same way they are being exposed to this journal article. That's how you're really going to get the message out."

"The news media?" Peter sneered. "They don't want to hear what I have to say right now. It would ruin their ratings."

"Have you seen Professor Garretty ever comment for WNT?"

"No."

"There is a reporter there, Patrick Eggers, who's interviewed Garretty multiple times. From what I hear, he's fair. He's not afraid to really investigate and dig into the details of stories."

"Good. Then Garretty can tell him. I'm relatively sure Garretty has the same level of skepticism that we do about now."

Clint shook his head. "He doesn't want to touch this. Not with a twenty-five foot pole."

"He doesn't?"

"I spoke with him yesterday. Eggers reached out to him as well, but he doesn't want to comment at all…he knows it's potentially toxic."

"Potentially?"

"But, you could comment in his stead. I think Eggers would go with Garretty's recommendation and I'm certain he'd recommend you."

"Why don't you just do it? Maybe you're the one they really want to hear from."

"You're the one who wrote the review, and I'm sure your thoughts about it are already well articulated. If he wants, I can put in a word as well, but I know you already have your first book out, and I can't spend my time as a go-to commentator at this juncture, when I'm still writing my first."

"Come on. The book can wait."

"Pete, I've been steadily working on it every day, but I'm worried about falling behind and the pressure's been building for years. I mean, I'm still reeling over all this, but I need to focus. If you do it, I know at least that I couldn't have done any better. And I'd feel relieved if a friend, with the same view, with the same emphasis on academic rigor, is delivering the undiluted truth."

Peter listened sipping his coffee. "Okay," he said thoughtfully setting down his mug, "I won't say no, if he agrees to it."

"He will."

7

The campus buzzed with the late-morning bustle as students traversed across the park's freshly mowed grass. Other than the police presence, it could have been any other Thursday morning, as there was no sign of disturbance. Some curious students even removed their headphones to listen to student questioning of the police about what event was taking place. Unlike those students, however, after sending the email to Eldridge, Peter read the Dean's to the community. It addressed "viable" threats levelled at the university by "right-wing contingents" following the news coverage of the Eldridge and Jersey article. He was curious about the student reaction but already running late for his graduate course in the library, he didn't bother to stay and listen.

He entered the James Darcy Library on the Northeast corner of the park which held his specially reserved meeting room for his graduate students in his Topics in Psychology seminar. He preferred its facilities over any of the dated rooms that Blanchard

Hall had to offer, and with positive feedback from the students, he continued to reserve the space.

The students were already seated in the tall-cushioned chairs surrounding the long boardroom style table. He briefly apologized for his tardiness as he entered setting his briefcase down at the head that the students had unofficially reserved for him. Out of his bag, he fanned out on the table their latest papers marked with his customary, albeit sometimes unwelcome, commentary.

"Here are your drafts to take at your leisure," Peter started—bringing some quiet to the room. Two students in the back were still finishing their conversation, but he continued. "Now, for some, I am glad to see overall solid work. Keep it up. As for the others, I am going to have to remind you, to my chagrin, of the basic practices to keep as well as pitfalls to avoid in doing your analyses. I bring them up again because these aren't *small things*, rather, they're essential. Frankly, these are habits that should have been instilled or snuffed out in your undergraduate studies." He waited for the weight of his statement to settle in—now garnering the full attention of the students in the back.

"When writing your paper, you have to be as specific as possible, qualifying your language, and staying on point. I don't want to see conflation of concepts or overgeneralizations. You don't write "party" when you mean "celebration." A celebration can be a party while a party isn't necessarily a celebration. You have to be as concrete as possible or you're not really saying anything at all.

"Neither do I want to see you using a handful of special cases to conclude something about a broader population without good reason. This kind of mistake is a dime a dozen. And just think about that for a moment…which of you knows someone who is sort of a loner?" Reluctantly, a few hands rose. "Well, they're all mass murderers." A few reserved laughs followed.

"My roommate might be," someone added with a snicker.

"Don't fall into that trap. It just isn't true…Neither am I interested in topics that are outside of the scope of your research. I want these to be short and sweet. That means less than thirty pages. Everything else you can save for your thesis or dissertation."

Peter paused while he surveyed the room. The students' eyes all conveyed the same message. He was heard. These were the moments where Peter capitalized on the time they spent together—possessing a secret hope. Despite the odds against it, perhaps ten years from then, they could remember what their professor said. *Someone, just someone may*, Peter thought. And that was enough.

"Lastly," he cleared his throat, "I want to warn you of the very real danger of something we've studied extensively. And you may remember the constant vigilance necessary to weed out the intrusion of this wily germ that infects everything we do in our field. *Confirmation bias.* It is a *fact* and attested to by multiple independent studies. If you think you don't suffer from it, *you are wrong.* You need to work at ridding yourself of its influence. *Leave it at home.* Always look for alternative explanations and take them seriously. If you don't, then, hell, go home and start writing holy books because you are no longer interested in fact finding; you are only interested in preaching."

Peter stopped himself abruptly. Not liking his change in tone, he decided to wrap it up on a less personal note. Every year, to one class or another. He shared his famous Sigmund Freud story. This appeared to be the right moment. Squeezing the back of his chair tightly, he considered it before confirming to himself that he had not yet shared it with this one.

"I simply cannot stress this last point without mentioning someone who we should all be familiar with by now. And while I'm not sure exactly of what your opinion of our Father of Modern Psychology is…" This brought a smile to some of the students' faces. He was glad to see the change. "…I do distinctly remember, at the time, of what I thought of him in my own post-graduate studies at Cornell, and to be honest, I wasn't very impressed with his body of work. *But…*if there is anything that I believe you should take away from Freud, it's about what would, ultimately, cause his demise in 1939. You see, after many years of his daily regimen of smoking thirty or more cigars, Freud went to see his physician friend, a Doctor Felix Deutsche, about a certain painful mouth abrasion. He visits him with some concern, to show the doctor—informing him that he wasn't going to like what he was about to see, and as soon as the doctor sees the growth, he knows immediately that it's malignant and would certainly spell the end for the famous psychoanalyst. But instead of telling Freud, for what he believes to be in Freud's best interest, assures him that it's only benign. A surgically removable growth that shouldn't trouble him any. Of course, he then proceeds one night, in Freud's own home, to tell six of Freud's close friends in a vow of secrecy. (Not much to say back then about doctor patient privilege.) It's only years later that Freud finds out about this heavy secret that was carried in confidence for so long. The truth was—was that it was going to kill him whether he knew it or not. And what was his reaction to all of this? Well, he was *furious*. With what right could they do such a thing to him, to think that he couldn't stand the burden of knowing? And needless to say, he no longer spoke to Doctor Deutsche anymore after that. Deutsche had treated him like a child after all. Despite the paternalistic desire to shield him from this horrible fact that wouldn't have been of much help to him anyway, Freud had wanted to know it. He was willing to face it, whatever it was. And afterwards, when he sought a new physician to replace the old, he told him right away the necessary conditions of their relationship—what it was that Freud so highly valued. That is, he was *never* to withhold the truth from him no matter what the consequence. Because you see for all his faults, Freud knew something. He knew the potency of *fact*. And that no matter how ugly or how cumbersome that fact was, he knew that he both wanted to know it and accept it. Because it doesn't depend on anyone else. Real facts have power. Real facts mean pain. Real facts mean death. And in the end, they always prove themselves to be true, as they did with Freud—as they always do. So, if you should know anything about the man himself, know this: everyone should place supreme value on fact as he did. Facts are precious, divine, and the way we should approach them is with reverence and with the utmost humility. In our work, they are indispensable. So, the next time you write your paper about the state of the *facts*, just you remember Freud." Peter finished the story with a wry smile on his face. He always enjoyed the pensive looks that accompanied every telling. But, this time, he relished little. The story reminded him of his own uncomfortable facts of the day—of what remained on his agenda including his business with Eldridge and the pending interview.

"Now that I've said all that I wanted to say about Freud and the conviction with which I expect my students to undertake their work, I'd like to open the floor to any discussion."

"Professor Barton," spoke up his advisee and third year doctoral student, Johnny Pearson.

"Johnny, yes?"

"We were just talking about the article by Professor Eldridge and the impending student protest. We wanted to know what your take is."

"Impending protest? Well, that part is news to me—"

"Yeah, it's all over social media," Lindsey Cunningham excitedly added, another doctoral student just ending her first year. She was the one who always came into class in business attire. Peter always appreciated the professional sentiment.

"I see," Peter failed to match her enthusiasm. He had been waiting for the question about the paper. He just didn't want to answer it. He didn't want to appear that he had imposed his own opinion on his students in any way. He still believed that—that wasn't his job. To have them make their own informed positions was. But, now, everyone watched him with keen interest. "I can answer that, but first, I'd really like to know the views of my students. What are they thinking and why?"

"I think," Lindsey's eyes wandered off in thought, "they are mostly scared."

"Scared of what?"

"Scared of the right-wing groups. Scared of the university being under siege by them."

Johnny laughed. "Of course, they can't put the university under siege," he said rolling his eyes.

"I don't mean a literal siege. I mean like with hostile pressure. They'll stick around terrorizing everyone."

"And is that all that they're scared of?"

"No. They're worried about racists being in the university, too," Lindsey said ruefully.

"And are any of them worried about being called racist themselves?"

They all looked around as if no one had even considered it.

"Why wouldn't that worry them?" He searched the class for an answer pausing over the most outspoken students.

"Almost no one thinks themselves racist. So, they don't think anyone will call them one," offered Gemma Stanley, an aspiring Clinical Psychologist and frequent class contributor.

"Isn't that interesting? We assume the best of people and that they will judge our behavior accurately. Is that necessarily true?"

"Not even with my friends," Lindsey tittered nervously.

"But, what do *you* think, Professor?" Johnny persisted.

Peter knew he had to give them more, but he wasn't prepared to reveal everything. "What I think is that I'm stunned that everyone, including this room of psychology graduates, automatically accepts the conclusion of the paper as accurate without question. I mean, did anyone read the paper itself?"

The students sat there quietly, some more uncomfortable than others. Lindsey adjusted herself in her chair pulling her business skirt down. Peter waited for her to speak, as he knew she had something to say.

"I didn't read it," she finally admitted as though it were self-evident. "But, I do know that Professor Eldridge wrote it and that he knows what he's doing—"

"He *co-wrote* it," interjected Johnny.

"Yeah, there is also Professor Jersey. He's a Biology Professor," Gemma clarified.

"I know someone who took his class. He said that he is one of the best professors he's ever had. He has five stars on Rate My Professor," relayed Yash, another of Peter's advisees originally from Surat, India.

"Focusing on our side of things, let's talk about what he's doing, specifically, in the paper. What kind of research would prove his conclusion?"

Peter knew that this was no easy question. If they hadn't already thought about it, it could require some time. As he awaited a response, he finally pulled out his chair and sat down. While some professors were uneasy when it came to long moments of quiet, having to fill every instant of each class with speech, he embraced it as part of the learning process. One had to be challenged in order to grow was Peter's philosophy. The longer he gave them to think, the more the pressure built on them to pose some kind of answer.

Johnny was the one to soon end the silence. "To be honest, I didn't read the article, but I read other sources about it," he said.

"What do the sources say? What method did Professor Eldridge use to establish that a given group has a bias?"

"Implicit-bias research."

"Exactly, implicit-bias research. And what are we talking about here?"

"It's where respondents have to…categorize negative or positive statements along with various stimuli…most commonly photos revealing darker or lighter skinned people, as good or bad."

"Correct. And while Professor Eldridge administered these tests under more controlled conditions, has anyone taken such a test online? There are a number of universities hosting research sites with running tallies of test takers and their results."

Many of the students indicated that they had. "Oh yea! I did years ago," Lindsey resounded brusquely over the others.

"Okay, Lindsey, and what did you think?"

She awkwardly grinned at herself self-consciously. "It wasn't good. I remember it showing that I had a bias towards lighter skinned people."

"But, what did you think about the test itself. Was it fair to indicate that?"

"I don't know," Lindsey appeared to be thinking aloud, "I remember making mistakes that I didn't mean to make, but…I suppose if I have a deep-seated bias, I wouldn't necessarily be conscious of it."

"It said just the opposite for me," Gemma expressed emphatically drawing the attention of the room. "I remember making some errors, but I didn't remember what. I was so focused on winning the game, because that's what it seemed like to me, a game."

"So, it actually showed that you have a bias for darker skinned people?" Johnny questioned.

"Yes, at least, that's what it said."

"But, do you *feel* like you have an actual bias against lighter skinned people?" Peter reformulated the question.

"No, I don't think so. I don't really care about that."

"Then, what is another explanation for making those errors?"

"I think it was just that the test asked me to complete it as fast as I could, and I made some errors in trying to do that."

"I think that is quite possible."

Lindsey couldn't sit still at this exchange. She suddenly sat erect. "But, like I said before, that's why it's called implicit-bias. You think you made errors for other reasons, but in the end, there is a deep-seated bias prompting you to choose as you did."

"I don't think so," Gemma said dismissively.

"Well, Lindsey, that still remains to be demonstrated. I told you earlier that we should try to look for other explanations. Isn't that a much simpler explanation than what is suggested?"

"Um…*no*, Professor," she said as if surprised at his question. "Combined with the other research on cultural racism, it isn't a stretch seeing how it fits in with the other data."

Johnny sat back in his chair sneering at the new direction of the discussion.

"What other data?"

"Like justice system data."

"We can't be experts at everything, so we should try to at least be experts in our own field. That is a large enough enterprise to occupy our time. So, I want to focus specifically on this research, that should stand on its own merits, as it claims to do."

"I think it should be taken into consideration."

"The conclusion should be arrived at independently of information extraneous to the experiment itself. That's how science has worked in the past. Now, you can ask if that is a legitimate requirement to retain, and we can discuss that at length… but I want to go back to discuss something of what I believe to be more pertinent to the nature of your disagreement." Peter collected his thoughts in search of the right words. "To summarize, both cases, Lindsey and Gemma both appeared to be, I think it's fair to say, surprised at the results of their tests. They both don't consider themselves biased in any way. One thinks the test doesn't really measure bias. The other does. Have I spoken accurately so far?" Both women nodded in agreement. "Assuming the test is right, something remains to be explained…why… in, what, twenty-five to thirty years? Have neither of you noticed any sign of persistent bias? I mean, I think we are all reflective people here—people who want to study Psychology to be in the profession. Yet, this never occurred to you before?"

"I think it is unconscious like how hidden motivations are revealed only in a dream, and sometimes it takes time to realize why we do the things we do. The test helped me realize how I've acted in the past—"

"—Or the test gave you a story to explain away certain moments of your life," Johnny suggested.

"That could be true Lindsey." Peter pondered holding his chin in his hand. "It is odd, however, that when confronted with all of our daily decisions, we only first noticed our own bias when taking a test called an implicit-bias test. Doesn't the name of the test supply the answer to what is still supposed to be a question? Why don't we all just answer the test perfectly? If we don't, we are biased because we dislike a certain group—not that we made mistakes for other reasons."

"But Professor, as you know, racism is still a big problem everywhere."

Johnny sighed. "Racism is the biggest *deus ex machina* of our time."

Peter's eyes warned Johnny. He knew he could soon find himself in some hot water for even evaluating such a comment.

"Racism is a *big* problem. Anyone can see that from what happened in my country, too. It has a long history," Yash suddenly declared with some gravity.

"Of course, Yash, racism was a problem and still is. But that still begs the question. Who are the racists? This test may or may not answer that question. In fact, I think a more accurate indicator would just be to see what someone says to the question itself. *Are you biased towards a certain group?* Let them seriously reflect on their own motivations. I have never heard of a bigot where the truth of their own bias doesn't somehow come out in that conversation. If they are repulsed by the notion, it seems rather important enough for them not to be one. And isn't that terrific? Wouldn't it be more believable that they really aren't rather than for them to be considered as part of this covert association? It sort of reminds me of all the news reports of secret Satanists in the 80s. They were always supposed to be somewhere around in the shadows sacrificing and molesting children. But not in that order…okay maybe in that order." Some chuckled while others sat uncomfortably as if adjusting after pissing down a pant leg. "Every corner you turned, there was supposed to be another one. Where are they all now? Good question, huh? Why couldn't they all just be like the good Satanists of today and profess their loyalty openly?"

8

As the late afternoon lunch rush slowly died in USFL's five dining halls, the outside central campus area traffic swelled. Uncharacteristically for that time of the day, the park and immediately surrounding areas were now humming with activity. Students, locals, outside activists, and curious spectators had coalesced with signs, black attire, costumes, and even lawn chairs. Many of the signs had the same designs and slogans in a coordinated effort: "Racism isn't welcome here," "Colored lives matter," and "Titans don't back down" with a titan about to crush a swastika under its boot. Other signs had a more personalized touch: "Academic Freedom on 'roids" displaying the exaggerated veiny musculature of a giant curling a dumbbell," "Believe in science, not racial violence" with an image of Einstein contrasted with Hitler, and "For justice and peace, no campus police" addressing the corresponding magnification of police presence, who were already, unknown to the community, being borrowed from surrounding departments.

There were other unrelated displays. Frat brothers from Alpha Beta wearing green tights and feather caps were dancing in chorus lines with leg movements in unison ending in doffs of the hat. Another man was conspicuously costumed as Cupid. He wore a toga and two extra small winglets on his back equipped with customary toy bow and quiver. A friend was filming as he walked around pointing out people that he intended to shoot. A few couples even indulged him by a kiss at his suggestion.

Meanwhile, the news crews carried more equipment from the recesses of campus to capture the historic moment. All of the main line protestors were covered in high definition with wide angle lenses on all the major networks. While reporters interviewed a slew of participants, few were deemed worthy of viewership. Nevertheless, all were packaged as a part of the unified rally headlined, Knowledge over Hate.

Despite the dearth of local voices, personalities from around the country and globe—anchors, actors, athletes, governmental officials and other dregs from previous news cycles, were dug up to comment on the latest benefaction by academia to the cause of justice. There was already a prevalent outpouring sign of support for the scientific integrity and bravery of the Journal of Pscyhophysiology Quarterly and authors of its entry. "Science is the pinnacle of human achievement. It has run the gamut of history from its early fraught ineptitudes to finally lay waste to the burgeoning force of hateful ideology," a columnist at the Manhattaner Magazine was already writing a soon to be published draft. He continued, "In many ways, science was the last bastion for the archaic thinking of the past that impeded the kind of progress for which our time has continuously called. Science, however, can be resisted no more after this manifest injunction for the purification of the biased presuppositions that have heavily weighed on minorities for centuries. It has now risen above the enslaving contexts that, up to this time, it had preserved with gross complicity. Instead, it has been its own instrument for redress. It was the medusa that showed itself the mirror."

9

Clint adjusted his driving glasses in the late afternoon light. His phone loudly rattled in the cup holder of the car's console. He held it before him and glanced at the name of the caller. While driving, he usually let the call go to voicemail—why he never bothered to set up the car's blue tooth in the first place. Today was different. The more the day elapsed, the more his agitation grew, and he knew, this could be the answer to it.

"*Hello*," he emphasized with pleasant familiarity.

"Hello *yourself*," Garretty joked, both men sharing a laugh. "I stopped by your office and saw that you already blew the coop,"

"Yeah, had to make my escape early while I still could. I'm on daughter duty today, and I didn't know if I was going to have to start building a camp over there."

"You're right, this is turning into what I imagine Woodstock was like. I'm on my way out as well."

"So, anything happening?"

"I think more party busses have just arrived."

"More?"

"Caravans of activists of every strand. You wonder if they have a number they call when these things happen—one eight hundred protest or other. How could they have mobilized in less than twenty-four hours since the interview? It seems like someone knew something well in advance."

"Yeah…but what are they even going to do over there?"

"I saw that they have an agenda out with a list of speakers that runs well into the night."

"Let's hope that's all it is."

"One can hope when there is doubt."

"Yeah…I have my doubts."

"So, any news?"

"Pat Eggers of WNT said he is *really* looking forward to meeting with Barton. I gave him his number, and he said he'd reach out."

"*Perfect.*"

"Glad Barton has a piece ready for all this…I haven't had time to dive into many of the details of this particular study…do you know where he plans on publishing the article?"

Clint sensed Garretty's discomfort. He knew that his next line had better be reassuring and non-judgmental enough to end this line of questioning.

"Trust me, *I* understand. He hasn't decided on where to publish… he just knows it's important enough to reach out to a wider audience, so I'm just glad that you have a contact that can help make that happen."

"With what we're seeing, of course."

"I appreciate it, Tom."

"No problem. Barton has always been fair. He's bound to give the public a dose of reality about this kind of study."

"Are the doubtful conclusions of these studies anything new?" Clint wanted to hear Garretty reaffirm his own commitment to the opposition.

"Only for the public at large."

"Exactly."

"So, it's for the best—"

"Tom."

"Yeah?"

"Get yourself out of there while the roads are still open."

"Yep. Will do."

"Take care, my friend."

"You too. Best to the wife and kids."

Pulling into the driveway, Clint looked at his watch and sighed recognizing the hour and a half he still had before picking up the twins. With his wife, Jenelle, still at work, the whole house was his. It was time to get busy.

He unlocked the door, carefully unlaced and removed his shoes, and entered his study setting his leather briefcase on the room's recliner. Unsnapping the fasteners, he removed his pad of notes placing it on his desk already neatly filled with stacks of books, journals, and annotated printouts.

"Okay," he told himself after briefly looking over the resources he had accumulated. He sat down, opened his laptop, and pushed the power button. The driving glasses, he lifted from his head, were cautiously folded by his massive hands before being placed in his shirt pocket. With a double click, the text he had been working on opened. Meticulously, he began scouring it from the night before. Meanwhile, outside of his window, he could hear the birds chatting between the sounds of rustling leaves. In the distance, there was also a lawn service with a chugging motor throwing trimmings of the neighbor's yard on the sidewalk and street.

Clint swallowed down hard the little saliva he had left. His eyes had wandered over to the framed photo he had mounted above his desk. Though he couldn't see the image clearly, the silhouettes in front of the camera were well known to him. It was of him and his father with the family gathered around just after his Ph.D. hooding ceremony at Harvard.

The chair creaked being relieved from the great weight as he got up. He decided to peer at the photo more closely. Everyone looked happy that day, especially Dad. As he confirmed, his dad's smile wasn't the usual smirk he had worn from time to time at the typical family outings or on vacations. They usually said he'd play along even though he was tired—tired from another day of hard labor. This one was different. It was flagrant. It came out with no modest inflection of his facial features, even showing teeth as if he were going to break out into a full laugh. It said one thing and one thing only to Clint—*victory*. That was the image he never wanted to forget. While his degree was framed and sitting over his desk at the university, here was his true pride. Again, he gulped down hard with his mouth begging for moisture.

He entered the kitchen taking a cold bottle of water from the fridge before returning to the creaking chair. Already downing over three-quarters of the bottle, his eyes kept reverting back to his dad in the photo.

"Okay," he said to himself again, as if redirecting a child back to his school work. He scrolled down some and paused over the next paragraph. As he analyzed the text, his eyes began the process of deregistering. The evidence of the text slowly disappeared from his vision. He was now looking to the side of his desk at nothing in particular.

"Dammit," he finally concluded with some resignation. He closed the computer and left his study to the house's spacious living room. The TV clicked on with a pause in the surround sound system. He recognized the location that was being covered on the news even with the descriptors partly blocking the view. Loops of sprawling images of the university were being replayed as commentators discussed the mounting presence on campus.

"There's simply no end to the support," the tall skinny freckled commentator explained to the anchor. "Ya'know what a day this is for the history books…what a day for the black community…"

Yellow. Can't Suffer this Fellow.

1

To those living in the neighborhoods just north of frat row, there was nothing in the air that night to indicate what was happening in the less than mile distance that separated these homes from central campus. It was a Thursday night like most. The early-week partiers were still looking to repeat the glorious revelries that began their academic careers. The only difference being that these same gatherings were now appropriately recast as "watch parties"—drunken venues that would normally be reserved for away football games, but everyone was curiously thrilled to see what was happening to their university, good or bad.

As the large outside projector screen blared the ensuing coverage of the chaos on campus, Mark Dempsey and Deborah Haugh stood in the farthest corner away from the din.

Mark had his arms wrapped around his girlfriend knowing well what state she was in. He pulled back to look at her and saw the same silly inebriated grin that she had when they first met.

"One more drink for the road, babe?"

She pushed out her lips with eyes half-closed expecting his reciprocation. He kissed her sparingly.

"One more for me then," he said to her as much as to himself. "Be right back."

Mark was easily able to reach the keg. Most of the party-goers were now looking somberly on at what was then occurring on campus. He saw on the screen a blurred mess of protestors now battling with police for continued access to the park. By this time, the event had already been deemed an unlawful assembly and was required to disperse. Mark could make out the line of police and smokey tear gas that billowed all around. They had been pushing the throng back continuously, but the crowd put up a defiant resistance at every turn—returning fire—pelting the officers with canned goods, retreating before coming back for another round.

Tilting his cup slightly, Mark filled it with beer from the tap—thinking about what tonight's news would mean for them. *Would they go to class tomorrow? Could he and Deborah finish their sophomore year?*

Would the name of the university itself somehow go down in infamy from then on? He decided to forget about these questions, at least for tonight.

While he sipped some beer, he started back to the corner of the yard where he left Deb. She wasn't there. He scanned the sparse groups for any sign of her drunken conversation. *Was she laying down again—against the house? Not again.*

Many of the friends they had come with at first had since moved on and weren't around to help him look. He walked from one of the far corners of the yard to the other for any sign of the short-hooded figure in the light blue sweater. There was barely anyone left on that side of the yard. Worry began flooding in. *What if…?* Feeling for his phone, he was about to call her when the worry he had felt suddenly boiled into anger. On the other side of the party, he saw the back of her. There she was in the light blue hood conversing with some strange man near the entrance.

On his approach he heard her drunken giggling to whatever the man was saying. He couldn't quite make out the mumbles. He thought of waiting to see what would happen, but he already felt hot, and his anger drove him forward.

"There you are," he stopped beside Deborah, as she was bowed down laughing to some new remark. She looked up with arms folded around her torso still relieving the pressure.

She seemed to have forgotten he'd left. With her bout fizzling, she straightened grabbing Mark's hand. "This is Mark, my boyfriend," she told her new acquaintance. Now that Mark was closer, he could just register the thin face beneath the gray denim military style cap. If it weren't for the beer in the man's hand, Mark would have thought the man an undercover cop or drug dealer.

The man watched Mark from under the hat. The eyes said it all. He didn't want him there.

"This is Jack," she indicated to Mark.

"Jacques Junior," the man corrected—sticking out a hand that Mark took. Both shook with a forced smile.

"Sorry, *Jacques* was just telling me about another party where they're having jungle juice. Maybe we can go, too?" she asked Jacques to confirm that the invitation was still open.

"Is that so? Was *that* what was so funny?" He waited for Jacques to say something.

Deborah's look of discomfort shined through her alcoholic high.

Jacques smiled widely. "You're both welcome to come," he delivered with a slight Caribbeanesque accent—the word "welcome" being drawn out.

Mark tried to make eye contact with Deborah. He wanted to intimate his reservations about going anywhere with this man. In fact, he thought she was being especially foolish. But, it seemed apparent that she was falling for the man's cleverly designed pick-up game that had her bawling a moment before.

"I think we're going to pass," he said letting go of his earlier question. Her eyes connected with his and understood in a moment of stark sobriety. "I think we've had enough to drink tonight and we have classes tomorrow."

"Dunno about that," he resumed the same grin—taking a sip of his beer.

"You don't think?"

"No way," he said smirking to himself, "I drive the bus." He motioned toward the projector screen.

"You mean you drive one of the busses for the protest?"

"S'right."

"So, you aren't one of the protestors?" Deborah asked seriously.

"No, I just drive."

Mark and Deborah both seemed relieved. They, like many students, were conflicted about the whole event. They saw the protestors having a right to air their grievances, but at the same time, they weren't sure why their campus had to be the center of the movement.

"But," Jacques Junior added late, "I'm not going to say no to their invitation to party…" This time, his knowing smile was fully directed at Mark's girlfriend.

"Maybe we could just go and see?" She pleaded with Mark.

"And you smoke? They've got *weed*," he drew out the last word enticingly.

By the look of Jacques' bloodshot eyes, he decided that they probably did.

"And I want to meet some protestors," she reached for yet another reason.

As he stood there, Mark realized the predicament he was in. He wasn't about to go with Jacques who seemed all too solicitous towards Deb, but if he said no on behalf of them as a couple, it would welcome her resentment from then on. If he only said no for himself, at least it wasn't about *we* anymore—only you. The prospect of her going anyway was a certain risk, but in either case, he knew that both outcomes were unacceptable. He played it the best way he could.

"I'm tired. You go ahead if you want. I'm probably going home."

Her face indicated that that was the most undesirable possibility. She glanced between the two men finally resting on Jacques Junior.

"Thank you for the invite, but I've a paper I need to start early tomorrow anyway," she slurred.

"Sure? There's gonna be a lot 'a people there. And I'm sure my boss'd love to meet a smart young lady like you."

"That's okay," she put her arm around Mark, "enjoy the party."

When Jacques left, they shared another alcoholic kiss.

"There was something not right about that guy."

"I know. Take me home."

"Let me just finish this."

Mark took his time finishing the beer. He noticed that Jacques had already exited the yard but wanted to ensure that he had time to lose more interest and clear the area completely. In the meantime, the screen showed thicker plumes of smoke covering a wide swath of central campus. *Did he smell something in the air too?* A faint whiff like burnt trash at a land fill.

They exited the party and started their walk back. It was only four blocks to the shared house that Deborah rented.

Mark figured he would end up staying the night there as usual. He longed for their customary ritual of sharing a hot shower together only to commence with round two the following morning.

A young group of men came towards them with beverages still in hand. They disrupted the empty night with their laughter and antics. One even screamed the apparent bane of his existence. "FUUUUCK! COOOPS! FUCKING OINKERS!" The man almost dared them to be around the next corner. He did, however, interrupt his rant to politely greet the couple. "Hi," he said, considerately.

The group passed by taking their noise with them. Their echoes drifted and faded between the houses and trees of the street.

Finding themselves suddenly alone, Mark decided to look back. After the strange encounter with Jacques, if that was even his real name, he wanted to be sure it was safe. The man wasn't just being flirty. He remembered where he had found them. It didn't strike him at the time, but it struck him now. It was right next to the entrance to the party where he could lure her away quickly and alone. No. Jacques' behavior was outright predatory. It was fortunate he was with her. Things could have gone very differently on one of the nights they were apart.

The neighborhood was quiet. The only thing amiss was a moving truck parked on the other side of the street a block down with its lights on. He didn't remember seeing it on the way there. *Was someone moving tonight? Were they renting the truck for an event tomorrow? And who even gives a fuck?* Mark did. Something wasn't sitting right with him.

The truck slowly eased out of the space along the street. Mark guided his girlfriend back onto the center of the sidewalk to make plenty of room for it. *They could just as well be drunk*, he thought. "What is it?" She asked unaware.

Suddenly, the truck screeched to a halt. Two men got out slamming doors as they exited, one of them with a military styled cap. Mark immediately recognized him.

"Go!" Mark yelled pushing Deborah who was slow to recognize that the two men were running at them. There wasn't much time. Mark pitted himself between his girlfriend and the closest attacker. The one he didn't know.

Terrified of the sudden onslaught, Deborah shouted for help running to the first door she could reach. Jacques split from his companion and chased after her.

What Mark didn't anticipate was the man he tried to block, didn't stop. The stocky figure plowed right over him with his shoulder leading like a pro footballer. Mark left his feet, hitting his back hard against the pavement—the wind taken right out of him.

At the same time, pounding against the door of the residence, Deborah screamed in terror. The light was out. Prospects weren't good.

Jacques soon plucked her small figure from behind into a bear hug. She squirmed around as his thin muscles maintained a solid grip like a Nile crocodile on a zebra. Jacques' partner escorted the pair to the back of the Youhaul opening the latch and lifting the door to the storage area.

The front light of the house came on. A neighbor from across the street opened his door to witness the commotion as well.

The horrors of Mark's mind already started dancing. Still out of breath, he gained his footing and rushed to the back of the open truck where Jacques already had her inside.

In a coordinated effort, while his partner entered the cab and started down the street, Jacques quickly pulled the rope as he pressed Deborah firmly against him with his other arm.

Propelled by the imagined demons running in his head, Mark launched himself into the compartment before Jacques could close it all the way. The door banged shut as the rental careened down the street. With lungs still frantically collecting oxygen, he was quick to recover his fall. Now, he confronted her kidnapper.

Jacques was fast. He was adept at these contingencies. The spring-loaded blade was at the ready. It came for Mark while Deborah thrashed at Jacques' back. In a pulsing display of adrenaline, Mark threw himself forward as a last-ditch effort to tilt the balance in their favor. It didn't work. His fist merely glanced Jacques' thin face as the knife struck Mark's abdomen.

Mark reigned down fury on the smallish skull that fit the denim cap, but it wasn't enough to relieve the pressure on the knife. Instead, Jacques worked the knife through more of Mark's bowels ending the onslaught of fists in sheer agony.

As he applied pressure to his wounds—hugging himself, Mark's warm blood oozed out—ensleeving both his arms with an escaping fount running copiously onto the metal floor.

Deborah screamed with tears streaming, clawing and thrashing as best as she could against the relentless body. Now that Jacques was satisfied, he took out the knife and threw it into the corner. Having already spent much of her energy, there was little she could do. Jacques easily restrained her.

Consciousness was leaving him. Mark knew it. He had failed. As his vision faded in and out, he saw Jacques tie his girlfriend, arms and legs, to the sole cargo of the compartment—a bike rack, commonly found around campus.

Possessing no rush or eagerness, Jacques proceeded to cut off Deborah's blue sweatshirt. Already having absorbed much of her boyfriend's blood on it, he discarded it into the large red puddle beneath their feet.

The speed of the truck picked up, a turn slid Mark across his own blood into the corner. Pain was all he felt anymore. And all he wanted was it to go away. The warmth of the blood briefly sheltered his cold body as all hope evaporated.

2

The coverage was good. The networks were pleased with the viewership that evening. "What a spectacular panorama!" A WNT executive voiced his approval. "I like that tear gas-flare aesthetic," another chimed. LNN pieced together a highlight reel for the night that simply blew away the competition. They tended to every detail, knowing something as seemingly inconsequential as a transition between shots was all that separated themselves from a Pulitzer. They knew how to rouse the audience into at least a short-term commitment to consume more. Certainly, they must've been getting something right as everyone in media agreed. They'd all be having some more of that.

Yet, despite the profusion of eyes, what really happened was still widely disputed among witnesses of Knowledge over Hate. Did the police become overzealous in their enforcement? Was the unruly throng the first to ratchet up tensions? Many took that very disagreement as license to create or embellish.

What was not up for debate, however, was the damage. Numerous windows were smashed along the park including those of Blanchard. An emergency phone was throttled into uselessness with steel bats stolen from the storage room for the USFL baseball team. Henrich Hall, housing the Department of Languages and Literatures was raided. From its second floor, desks and other objects were hurled through windows into the park in a flurry of druggy exhilaration. Barely legible scrawls of graffiti were found tackifying the gothic architecture ranging from witty to ones of questionable relevance: "Titanic Pigs," "Diversity Now!," and

"Power Player." Symbols for anarchy along with the hammer and sickle were sprayed over the engravings of statues. The statues themselves, including the majestic likeness of Henry A. Nordrick, were de-bronzed with flat black over the hands and face.

To top off the night, a layer of garbage and debris were littered throughout campus as after a festival of successive rock concerts. The accompanying smell rising with the morning dew was the scent of piss and month-old yogurt. Despite the vigorous revolutionary sentiments of some of the visitors, the stench didn't fail, in the least bit, to sour the stomachs of the most stalwart Che-like activist, hanging in the air as if campus were a dedicated landfill.

In response, an early morning email sent from the University President, Dietrich Scott, cancelled Friday's classes. It stated that while the university wouldn't tolerate destruction of its property, he conceded the protestors had a right to express themselves. At the end of the email, he even made an open invitation for them to celebrate academic achievement in a spirit of togetherness. "Our body of students are diverse at the core, and they have called it home here. I hope that the protestors will be able to do the same."

His lie was immediately exposed by members of the media pointing out a seventy percent Caucasian student body hardly comprised diversity.

3

That morning Peter was taking no chances with his car. The President's message appeared to imply that the visitors hadn't completely left, so he had Margery drop him off on Mainstreet on the way to Roger's school.

Downtown Palm Gate was flooded with people. Patrons packed restaurants and cafes along the campus. In the distance, Peter could see Sally's Bakery with a line extending well down the sidewalk. He usually pined for their homemade French toast, but today he was nervous. Today there was the interview with Patrick Eggers from WNT.

He walked the campus like a disabused prostitute noticing that even the residence halls hadn't been completely spared. He frowned seeing that between the likeness of two prominent buttcheeks, "Enter here" was spray painted with an arrow directing traffic into one.

Following the trail of debris to its epicenter, he somberly observed the crews attending to the sealing of broken windows and disposing of the rubbish now resplendent in the morning light. Clubs, stones, bottles, cans, wrappers, cigarettes, signs, clothing, shoes, shit, and even the occasional needle and condom were some of the many laurels on display.

One student, apparently a member of a volunteer cleanup group, carefully lifted a rhinestone decorated bra—showing off their discovery before inserting into one of the industrial strength trash bags. The find would only be one of the many outré items that appeared to supervene the rally's cause.

The entrance to Blanchard Hall was already propped open when Peter got there. "Careful," a badged staff member warned Peter as he crunched over shards of glass near the entrance. From the look of it, unlike Heinrich Hall, the interior of Blanchard was preserved.

Peter ascended the stairs thinking if there was a reason for it. *With Mobs, thinking wasn't exactly as important as emoting—the little tantruming shits.*

A new email from Eldridge was waiting for him, "I'll be available for calls from eight to nine this morning," Eldridge deigned a response. Peter looked at his watch. His window was short. Taking a deep breath and gulping down more coffee, he dialed. He could feel his heart thump along intermittently between every ring. It was like he was prepping himself for an explosion.

"Hello?" a leery voice answered.

"Professor Eldridge, it's Barton."

"Good morning. How can I help you?" The voice expressed icy peevishness.

"Well, how're you?"

"A bunch of hooligans just destroyed much of campus. How do you think?"

"Yeah," Peter exhaled. "That's related to the reason I'm calling. I want to discuss the publication. I think it'd be helpful to clarify—"

"The paper speaks for itself. What people do in response to it is not in my control." Eldridge fired defensively.

"I understand—"

"I've merely arrived at where my research has led, and if it suggests something controversial, then so be it. I'd just as well do it again."

"Nor do I think you shouldn't if you think it's—"

"I never intended anything bad to happen to the university—"

"*Professor?*"

"Yes."

"I'm sure you are incredibly busy at the moment. I just wanted to address some questions. Would that be alright?"

"Why not? But I don't see how anything could be misconstrued by a colleague."

"OperAnd."

"The AI algorithm. Yes, what about it?"

"From what I understand, it detected the genetic similarities creating the profile from the implicit bias testing data."

"Yes, it's incredibly sophisticated. Aepoch Systems developed it to use machine learning in order to penetrate into the complexity of genetic combinations. It analyzed the data of both groups at a very high level and in a relatively short timeframe determining the specific markers that compose, what we have since coined, the Chromagen makeup."

"*And…*only about eight-two point seven percent of those with the Chromagen profile are determined to possess actual bias?" Peter interjected.

"*Only* eighty-two point seven? It's a scientifically significant result." Peter could hear Eldridge's irascibility flaring.

"I'd agree, but it does make you wonder about the other seventeen point three percent"

"Professor Jersey and I do think environment does factor into it, but one simply cannot ignore that level of association."

"Is it causation or correlation?"

"Of course, we think that it does play some role."

"I'm not sure that I'm going to have to tell you of the great difficulty in establishing the proposition that genes determine a general racial disposition."

"Doesn't it just confirm a long history of struggle and hate that has long since called for a reason?"

Smiling to himself, Peter decided to resume his inquiry— thinking better of taking on Eldridge's glaringly fatuous question.

"Within that eighty-two point seven percent that you determined to have a bias, only one question answered incorrectly tilts the test into indicating that such a bias exists. Am I understanding that correctly?"

"The test is incredibly easy to answer. If a mistake is made, it is highly indicative. However, if they make a mistake in favor of bias and then one with a contrary bias, no bias is determined…You should try to take it yourself and see what I mean. And in the end, either way, I believe the results are reproducible to a similar percentage of predictability."

"From the sound of it, it's like taking a keyboard test where making one typo indicates that someone can't type. That's a dangerous test when the result of one error categorizes someone as racist."

Eldridge's reply was surprisingly measured. "Having put it that way, with serious stakes as those, a non-biased respondent should put forth the maximum effort possible. They don't want anyone to think of themselves as a racist, even their own opinion of themselves is on the line when they are informed of the results. On the other hand, if they don't care, that suggests that they are more likely to have active bias."

Peter wrote a note to himself on a yellow legal pad before him. "Okay…So you agree, from your response, that there is no real difference between being racially biased and racist? Could you have used the words interchangeably in your paper?"

"Sure. Is there a difference anymore?"

Peter's object wasn't really to argue. He only wanted to be thorough. Jotting down another note, he inhaled before delivering his final question. The best was saved for last.

"Unless I missed something…what really remains to be explained in all of this research is what made you and Jersey even decide to use OperAnd in the first place. Why did you create a genetic profile? Was there something that *suggested* genetics actually played a role in bias?"

"Asked and answered. We felt that this could explain the long history of racism…"

Something snapped in Peter when he heard what form the answer was going to take. A feed of the chaos that ensued streamed through his head and a glimpse of the future to come. *How ridiculous it all was. How goddamned stupid to pass this off as academic.*

"It's bad science. You felt? Well, I feel that women who live alone have the genetic material that causes a propensity for cats. Why not put those data in OperAnd next? Maybe there is a seventy to ninety percent cat-lady association."

No sound was heard from Eldridge's end. Not even a breath.

"What other genetic associations should we come up with? Let's try every single profession. Let's try plumbing profiles. What about those who hate clowns?! Let's try those with a distaste for cilantro. I bet we can come up with countless significant associations. What do you think? What does that *suggest* to you?"

The words that finally came out of Eldridge were said carefully and quietly, but the manner in which they were expressed portrayed a decisive rancor in the emphasized enunciation of the consonants and a rolling over the vowels.

"You sound worried. What is it? Do you have something to hide Barton? Take real care."

The line clicked to dial tone.

4

Clint laid in bed as the sun poked through the blinds down on his face. His head ached and his mouth was parched. He was reticent to lift himself off the mattress—not only because of residual effects of the alcohol but from the knowledge of the previous night's events.

Early that morning he was still monitoring the news coverage long after Jenelle and the kids went to bed, as if being a witness somehow kept the horde from further surging out of control. The bottle of scotch that he opened kept him company near the couch as he bounced between the sofa and the fridge—clanging some more ice into his glass before gurgling more brown relief inside.

He felt like shit, and now with his neck strained, he forced himself onto his back. Clint laid there a while to see if he could doze off again, but it wasn't happening. Despite the canceling of classes, he knew he had to trudge on. There were emails he had to attend to, and he wanted to be ready for Peter's call. Then there was the business of the book. But, he knew as far as today was concerned, it had to wait.

Dragging his body off the bed while trying to keep his neck straight was at first unsuccessful. He groaned as the already strained muscles retightened. He was able to dangle his legs over the side of the bed as he sat there erect in preparation for his next move. After drawing in some air, he propelled himself upward with his legs and arms in unison resulting in what he thought could be his whole enterprise today. *Minimize the pain.*

In the kitchen he took two NSAID tablets from the cabinet and washed it down with a glass of filtered water from the fridge. He went for seconds and thirds until he was able to rid his mouth of the medicine's bitter taste.

The bottle of scotch was still on the coffee table with an unfinished glass next to it. Nearby sat his mobile—still reserving the spot he took up the night before. It contained one missed call from Jenelle. He already figured she had a message for him. Her decision to leave the bottle and glass out were part of that message. It was: Dear husband, Get your shit together. That was a conversation he just had to get over with. The sooner, the better.

The phone rang once before Jenelle picked up. She had been waiting for his call.

"Good *morning*," she impressed upon him.

"Hey," was his only response as he waited for his scolding.

"*Hey?* That's *it?*"

"I mean: *Hey* Love of My Life."

"Yes. So you wanted to tell me something?"

"Not really."

"*Really?* I think you do. All you did last night was drink and watch the news with barely a word…"

"You've seen the news."

"Who cares? There is always going to be people like that. You know that. The only thing that matters is that we're all okay. Better than okay. The girls are happy and healthy. We have a nice house in a great community. Whatever happens at the university, it'll pass."

"You're right," he said staring at the black television screen before him.

"Aren't I?"

"I know," he expressed, scorning the thought of turning the twenty-four hour news cycle back on.

"Well, if you already know that, then why are you still letting it bother you? Huh?"

Clint didn't want to get into it. He thought of the quickest way to end the conversation and chose it.

"It's all a lie, hun."

"Of course, it's a lie. Even some of these people probably already know that."

"Even so, I don't want my profession tarnished by those selling snake oil."

"That's what you've been so mad about?" She laughed as if it were such a small thing. "You can speak out. I'm sure you've criticized papers like these in the past. So do it again. Tell them they're wrong. Tell them why."

"Peter is doing an interview about the entry with WNT today."

"That's great. Peter is always so well-spoken. I've been meaning to call Marge and have them come over soon."

"Sounds good."

"But, what about you? What interviews are you doing?"

"Peter and I happen to have similar views. I'll let him do it. I told them if they want me to follow up, I will."

"You'll follow up?" Her voice took an overtly suspicious tone.

"Yeah, I didn't want to be repeating the same points. There is already too much exposure for this rag already."

"Can I speak to Clint please? *Hello* is my husband there? None of this sounds anything like the man I married. The man I married was all too proud for any of this…"

5

"Pleasure to meet you, Professor." Eggers reached his hand out and met Peter's in a brief firm shake.

"You can call me Peter."

"And you can call me Pat. But for the interview, I'll be calling you Professor Barton. That okay?" He wasn't really asking.

"Of course."

Pat directed the cameraman over to the far wall that contained a long bookshelf of academic titles. He asked the crew for their input before deciding that it was the best place to stage the interview.

"It'd be alright to take two chairs over here?" He motioned over to the ones in front of Peter's desk. Again, he wasn't really asking.

"Sure."

"Let's talk over here for a moment while they're still setting up." Peter followed Pat to the corner of the room, considering his level of pushiness. The truth was that he didn't mind so much. Pat's assertiveness was always implied, exhibiting a certain level of tact that stirred no resentment.

"I know we talked briefly the other night, but I just wanted to reassure you that if at any moment you don't feel like you answered a question to your satisfaction, don't panic. We can always do another take. The important thing is that all of your concerns are heard, and even if I disagree with something, I'm not going to try to put you into an ugly light. I know why some of us deservedly get a bad rap, but I'm not at all interested in doing that." The way the message was delivered—looking Peter squarely in the eyes—expressed a certain warmth and sincerity putting some doubts to rest about the man's integrity not so much in what he said, but in the forthright manner he expressed it. Peter just had to believe that such people were still around even in the greatly sleazified business of mass media.

"Believe me, my colleagues and I are just grateful to have our voices heard. Thank you for doing this. As you can already tell, I don't imagine what we have to say is going to be too popular." A grin formed on Peter's face.

"Now we wouldn't want too much of that otherwise people would simply stop watching." Pat countered with his own capricious smirk.

"One more thing I'd like to add before we start…" Peter listened as if he were caught suddenly with the legal disclaimer. "Try to make everything as simple as possible."

"Certainly."

"I mean layman of a layman as possible…our audience demographic largely do not consist of professors of Psychology." Peter wasn't sure what was meant by his smile that followed, but he nodded along in agreement.

"Also, try to say everything in such a way that you cannot be reasonably misunderstood." Peter looked at him with some seriousness. "You must already know that many from here on out will only try to misunderstand whatever you say." He looked away nodding, recognizing his own naïve assumption that his coming forward could only promote other good faith conversations. Having seen the aftermath on campus, however, that was comically preposterous. The fact is that no rational discourse would be able to rattle such convictions. *How one even shakes a belief system is still largely a mystery.*

Other doubts flooded his mind while Pat inspected the crew's setup. No. He didn't want to go through with it. Maybe there was time to still back out? There just had to be someone better for the job. Despite his steady spike of blood pressure and the sweat building under his arms that would have surely been red-flagged on a polygraph, but one recurring memory gnawed at him.

There was an unassuming boy at the back of the class in the tiny desk with his backpack next to him littered with the different colored racecars. He remembered packing the racecar lunch box that year. The boy had had an outright obsession with them. And there he was half turning around in his seat to give a big smile to his dad. How exciting it was for him his first day of school. More salient than his first trip to Disney by far. And as a professor, the significance wasn't lost on him. But, there wasn't only Roger's excitement. There was something else in that look. Roger was checking that Peter was still there. That his dad hadn't left yet. Not yet. And he was so glad to be there to remember a moment he could never forget. And here he was.

Pat returned to Peter. "So all set. All ready to go?"

Peter was a dam ready to burst, and he took the plunge.

6

A unified police force mushroomed by late afternoon setting check points around campus even building a temporary operations tower on the park that looked like a toll booth propped up by scaffolding. A nine o'clock curfew was issued for the university and Palm Gate.

The governor of the state even offered reinforcements to President Scott who declined in a mid-afternoon statement. In it,

Scott derided the detractors of his earlier speech. No, he didn't apologize for the perpetrators of the damage done to campus. He merely asserted their right to protest. He also called for calm—denouncing the reported violence that followed last night's events including the witnessed abduction of two students, Mark Dempsey and Deborah Haugh. He encouraged anyone with knowledge of their whereabouts to report right away.

Palm Gate was closed to vehicles, but its foot traffic increased. It was a festival mixed with idle undergrads and pockets of outsiders. Containers were openly carried and hand rolled intoxicants drew little attention or concern from cops.

According to the media, the gathering crowds were a sign of unity and respect for diversity. To the students on campus, however, it was more an event to alleviate boredom and watch zoo animals roam around. On the surface, there appeared a certain comradery of fellow partiers around the same ages, but there was something hidden on those brows, the corners of their mouths, and in the exchanging of words that sometimes provoked raucous bursts of laughter. The unkeen eye failed to see a nascent antagonism by the future alum.

Unknown to most demonstrators and students, those who did possess the rare sight for subtlety were also watching and noticed. They understood those inputs that could motivate most into doing almost anything from the most menial task to even putting on a most elaborate performance. They knew that in the end, such machinations weren't really too difficult to affect in this subspecies of ape. The vast majority of humankind were controllable as bees are controlled to produce honey. Maybe not as easy as a puppet was moved by a puppeteer, but perhaps as one blows the seeds of a dandelion into a direction that one so desires. Those being blown only knew of the wind.

7

Deborah's eyes fluttered between unconsciousness and pain. A quiet sound of rending metal snapped her firmly into the present. Naked and cold, darkness surrounded her. Her wrists and ankles firmly bound by metal bracers. Her breasts, back, and stomach tissues, cut and torn, stung with unrelenting fervor. *When can it end,* she thought. *What's the point of this? Please let it end.* She had begged and begged but was given no reprieve as Jacques had inflicted yet more damage to her body.

While he did it with a smile, it was done without mirth. It was done almost systematically with scientific indifference. But, she had sensed they weren't alone. Someone else was watching and seeing her suffer. That appeared to be the whole point after all.

Tears poured down her chaffed and dried face stinging old wounds on her chest as they came. *Mark.* That is who she grieved now. Despite all the horrors she faced, his memory helped her continue—helped her withstand all wounds. Nothing was more precious now than those last moments they shared together. His kiss. His eyes in hers. His brave attempt to save her. He wasn't going to just let her go. And now she was possessed by the idea— an idea to which she commended herself. Along with the dim hope of rescue, she hoped he'd still find her yet. Dying not only couldn't prevent that but was the very means of that reunion. This she simply had to believe as she was now catapulted ever closer to that ultimate destination.

Her ears perked up as the sound of mechanical failings continued. First it sounded like the bowels of a steel haul against the pressure of a raging sea. Only the storm worsened and the sound grew louder. Either that or it was getting closer. She couldn't be sure. Whatever the sound was, it paralyzed her with fear. And she was right. It was no rescue.

"Oh God please. God please." She prayed in a whisper. *Let me go fast*, she added in thought. The metal screeched in the pitch blackness nearby as if the malfunctioning machine was dollied there. "Help!" she yelled at it as much as to God. "Please stop this!" The noise continued before shutting off suddenly as with a switch. The echo now only permeating throughout the cavern. An engulfing silence ensued.

Her limbs shook with fear within the bracers in anticipation of whatever it was that had approached her. A cold sweat dripped down her face and formed around her wrists and ankles. The imaginings of her mind sped through a myriad of possibilities and made her skin crawl with whatever was to bite at it next.

She knew her end was coming. She pictured Mark there waiting for her—trying to console her. "It's okay, babe." He grinned at her with that suggestive smile. "Everything's going to be okay. Just a little bit more and nothing will ever hurt again."

The defunct metal stirred. This time further away to her right. Her thoughts fixed on Mark and his grin. *That grin.*

Those events that she saw that expression sprawled across Mark's face played before her. She decided that there was something else to it. A certain levity. In fact, she determined that she didn't like it at all. *Just what was so amusing? Or was it sheer lust? After all, she wasn't the only one he put on that look for. There were others at parties that he flashed that smile to. Other women. That look. It wasn't so loving after all was it?* And now that doom was rearing its ugly head, her breath was taken from her like a carpet ripped from underneath. *What if Mark never felt the way she did about him? What if he'd lied? What if he never really loved her?*

The tears flowed anew and her belabored breath drew at irregular intervals. Her head bowed forward as the heavy drops splatted on the cement floor. She battled the new revelation within her. Everything that she knew contradicted it. Her experiences were witnesses. *Why would he even try to rescue her in the first place? WHY DID HE PUT YOU IN DANGER? He didn't. He appeared cautious and protective. WHY DIDN'T HE ENSURE YOUR SAFETY? That doesn't make any sense. He put everything on the line for me — even his life. HE WAS FIGHTING OVER A PIECE OF MEAT. That can't be true. People don't do that except for the ones they love. ANIMALS DO. He loved me. IF HE REALLY DID, HE'D HAVE SEEN TO YOUR SAFETY. HERE YOU ARE.*

Through blurry eyes of despair, she finally noticed to her left the two inanimately glowing points of crimson suspended in darkness.

8

Peter sipped his watered scotch as WNT stole away to a men's razor commercial. "You looked so good, honey," his wife's head had been laying on his shoulder on the sofa before she proceeded to twist squeezing hard against him as he tried to balance his scotch. She pressed her warm lips to his and then to his neck.

Overall, Peter had been pleased how the interview turned out. Eggers was true to his word. His answers weren't trimmed as to lose the sense of what he was saying. The questions were all relevant and important. Outside the pressing him on his motives for his *keen* interest in the matter, the questions were pitched underhand. His wife, from the feel of her body in the night gown was also pleased.

Roger sat on the carpet Indian style playing solitaire before the TV. He was strangely quiet during the whole interview—not like his usual Q and As that would occur during any major televised adult event. Instead, he dealt himself his cards, placing some here or there pausing to gawk up at the screen whenever his dad would start speaking again.

"Hey Roger," he called to check in, as Roger combined two rows with another. He waited as no answer came.

"*Roger?*" his mom called to him more fervently. With a puzzled countenance, he faced his mom who was laying back on the couch. He stared as if awaiting instruction.

"Everything good?" Peter asked. He shook his head in agreement. "Did you understand what was being said in the interview?"

"Perhaps," he said returning to his all but certain Solitaire win. Margery chuckled at her son's use of the word.

"Well? What was it about?" Peter further queried fishing for more insight into what his son knew. After a moment of quiet, Peter wasn't sure if he had lost Roger's attention yet again. His son only sat with back turned analyzing his cards.

"Psychology," his son blurted laconically back at his parents. The answer seemed to tap into Peter and Margery's funny bones for a good long laugh.

"Mom?" Roger interrupted her dying giggles.

"Yes?" Roger appeared to be placing his final cards into one of the four stacks from the long columns.

"Could I have some more spaghetti?" He was referring to the leftovers in the fridge from their dinner hours earlier.

"Okay," she wiped her eyes and lifted herself into sitting on the front of the cushion.

She looked back at Peter with a playful expression. "You want some too?"

"No thanks," he said touching his wife's back as he swigged some more whiskey. She pushed herself up and headed toward the kitchen.

"I won." Roger finally said showing the four stacks of suited cards.

"Nice man."

More commercials played above Roger as he shuffled the deck for yet another round. Peter was relaxed. His nerves eased—not only from the whiskey—but he knew he had done the right thing in the end and was at peace for the moment.

In the background, one ad showed diverse couples popping gum in their mouth with audible satisfaction on a scenic hike together. This was followed by the young woman's enigmatic smile making Peter's mind wander.

Peter's phone buzzed from the couches' accent table.

"You nailed it," Clint rang excitedly into Peter's ear.

"It wasn't really me. Who would've thought there was an honest journalist left somewhere?"

"I know it," Clint said with the same energy.

"I mean, he just asked me relevant questions then I answered. Then it was aired almost untouched?"

Clint laughed.

"Garretty called me right after just to say that he was also impressed—that he couldn't have done better himself."

"Tell him thanks. I may just have to try to steal Eggers away from Garretty for a future book."

"Not if I do it first."

Peter paused to drain the rest of his whiskey including crunching on the few small pebbles of ice.

"So, what do you think? What's the reception going to be on campus?"

"Don't know really."

"Me neither…What if it isn't any good?" He murmured in state of drowsy intoxication.

"Well—"

"What if it results in violence?"

Seeing Jenelle still cleaning up in the kitchen, Clint spoke as quietly as his booming voice would allow on the way to his study. "If it does …I don't think you should feel bad about it. How they react is up to them."

"I tend to agree, but I guess it's different sitting in my position now…I don't think the message will be well received."

"Why do you say that?"

"Because people that feel threatened tend to lash out," Peter sounded almost as if in some sort of trance.

"You think they feel threatened?"

"To think that a good number of those out there have been passionately fighting for nothing…well…that just won't be acceptable."

"I think that they see sowers of doubt as the very proof that their enemy exists."

"Sure," Clint stared at the photo of his father on the wall starting again slowly, "maybe you can't reach the true believers, but I think there are many others who'll start to question. Who knows? Maybe they were already questioning but they just needed to know that there are others out there who aren't afraid."

"*Clint.*"

"Yes?"

"*I am afraid.*"

The TV continued to echo voices in the room flashing the spectrum of colors in the dark as the sound of forks hit ceramic.

Peter had poured himself another and drowsily sank further onto the sofa while Roger and Margery finished off their plates.

"Police say that the night of the Knowledge over Hate Rally, Deborah Haugh was taken against her will after a fraternity party on Laughlin Street, only a few miles from the police barricade. Eyewitnesses say that after a struggle with two men, Deborah was forced into a Youhaul rental truck. From conflicting reports, it is not clear whether Mark Dempsey, her long-time boyfriend was an accomplice in the kidnapping. Activists from the rally have since rejected any suggestion that it had anything to do with the largely peaceful demonstration. University President Dietrich Scott urged the university community…"

"Oh, turn it off already!" Margery said wearily.

Peter hit the button of the remote lying next to his foot and they finished their meal in peace.

The sun beat down on Peter's long brimmed hat causing sweat to pour from his scalp onto his face. Using his forearm, he wiped away yet another wave before uprooting more of the thorny weeds invading the bed of blue salvias. With both hands, he yanked sproutlings adding more to the two sizable wads that, if not for his garden gloves, would be feeding blood to the soil.

He inserted the fistfuls of plants into the trash bag then stood up to survey his progress. It didn't feel like it had been that long ago, but his garden was already knee deep in overgrowth. In any case, he decided it had been long enough since he could enjoy a day like today. It felt good to be outside in the sun taking in the scents of the rich earthy soil and the tangy green foliage.

A faint ringing soon eroded his reverie cutting through the buzzing of the flying insects and the intermittent breezes. After a couple more high-pitched cycles, he realized it was the house phone that his wife had wanted to keep for emergencies. Now with Margery and Roger out shopping, Peter was just going to let it ring. *If it were important enough, whoever it was could try again.*

He waited for the ringing to cease before returning his attentions to the task at hand. The landline wasn't often used and it being on the no call list, he wondered at the possibilities— imagining on all the old forms where he had written the number. *Who knew what people could still find it if they had a mind to look?*

Before ending this train of thought, there it was again. The ringing resumed. Instead of ignoring it this time, he desired to put his curiosity to bed. Removing his gloves one by one, he made his way into the house. Taking the phone from its cradle, the caller ID indicated a private number.

Peter pushed the talk button and listened—waiting for the anonymous caller to reveal themselves. All he could hear at first was some shuffling around as if someone were organizing some papers on a desk.

"*Peter Barton?*" The voice shot through the speaker as if the young man were desperately making a point to assert himself.

"Yes?"

"Black babies, black babies, why you wanna kill black babies?" The man rhythmically spouted into the phone with a hint of manic exhilaration.

"Excuse me?"

"How does it feel to be a *fucking murderer* prof?!"

"Murderer? I think you're confused…" Peter knew the caller could be reacting to his interview, and while he could have just hung up, he took pity on the impressionable young man.

"You don't know what you've done?"

"Well, I certainly haven't murdered anyone."

"Eichmann said the same."

"What are you talking about now? Adolf Eichmann?"

"We weep for the deaths of our brothers and sisters, but we'll celebrate when your threat comes to an end."

"Who is this? Do you know who Adolf Eichmann was?"

"Are you ready for your final solution?"

The caller clicked off to reveal the dial tone leaving Peter in a lurch of dumbfounded concern.

10

Peter struggled to maintain focus as Yash made his final paper presentation before the class. Since the call to his house on Sunday, he had been able to think of little else. The disturbed young man was not only working at a different wavelength but appeared to be working within a whole different history of the world.

The other gnawing prospect was that despite the congratulations on an interview well done by his own students and some that passed him on campus, the caller may have also been a student at USFL—a threat that existed a little too close to home—too close to his work too close to his family. And if this man had his home phone number, there was a possibility he had his address as well.

Soon comes your final solution. Who says that? One moment he compares him to Eichmann and the next he proposes to take a page from Eichmann's journal. He already predicted that there were some out there beyond his reach. *Black babies, black babies, why you wanna kill black babies?* But, he didn't quite know how far.

Then came the business of telling Margery. Up to this time, it had been his burden alone—his to assess the threat and act accordingly. He didn't want to disturb Margery's peace by something that amounted to only a prank. But, now, he knew that that wasn't right. He had to tell her just in case—just in case things got worse. She had to be prepared.

Yash periodically looked to Peter as if for approval in further advancing his paper's thesis. The students by and large appeared engaged preparing for the usually active Q and A that followed. Johnny absently stared at the wall behind Yash while Lindsey sat astutely jotting in a journal.

Checking his notes, Yash proceeded to read his conclusions one by one. This he had directed at Peter but still couldn't help being distracted by something through the glass. This happened a few times before Peter himself had to turn to look. Not many students usually hovered around this corner of the sixth floor of the library, nevertheless, just outside the door was a man perusing the stacks. The brim of the patron's military-style denim cap tightly covering his eyes as the late morning sun generously poured through the windows at them.

11

Lindsey sat in the chair across from Clint reviewing the feedback that he penned on her blue exam booklet. This was the usual ritual for her. Following any marked assessment, Clint would anticipate her showing up during his office hours, and like clockwork, there she was. After addressing a series of, how she put it, "clarifications" that she had prepared in her notebook, she would go over all the essay questions once again just to be sure that nothing had been missed. This was the phase she was now in, and Clint almost smiled to himself at how well he knew her routine.

Overhearing two, almost spectral, figures idly chatting as they fleeted by his doorway along the old corridor of Blanchard Hall, he waited patiently as he witnessed her eyes scanning each page of content. Clint knew that there were other pressing tasks on his agenda including an unfinished email—his response to another student—still open on his laptop pending final touches, but he found that he could rarely concentrate on such matters with someone around.

Reaching the end, she closed the blue book's cover looking up at Clint smiling with a hint of mischievousness.

"So Professor…" Clint glanced over to the door as if to verify it was still open. "I was wondering if you're speaking at the rally Saturday." He paused for a moment, surprised, maybe even a little offended by the nature of the query. Picking up on his displeasure, she qualified, "I didn't know if they might've asked you to say something…"

Clint saw the adverts around campus. Only they didn't label it a rally this time. *Black Victim Memorial*, they called it. It was supposed to be held in solidarity with others around the country including a march around the Capitol to the Lincoln and Vietnam Memorials to commemorate the unjust deaths of members of the black race, or something like that.

"No," his mouth transformed into a grin to replace the grimace, "I don't think they want me speaking, as they wouldn't like what I'd have to say."

Now Lindsey firmly wore her own expression of unease as if she had just contracted it from Clint. "Why not—? Shouldn't you— don't you…support—" She stared off searching for the right word.

"Miss Cunningham, why are you asking me this?" his voice boomed a little more than he wanted, coming off briskly, accusatorily.

This further unsettled Lindsey, who was already regretting her presumption. After a long pause she started again. "I thought that since you're a member of the department…ya know? Home of the faculty who published the article…"

"I had nothing to do with the article," he looked at her very seriously but developing a softer tone. "And as I see it, the only virtue of being a part of this university—being connected to the same department—is having a sense of shame and responsibility. I don't feel the need, normally, to comment on bogus papers."

"But, it is really about victims in the end."

"I don't need them to remind me about *black* victims. Frankly, I have a pretty good memory already. And I, especially, don't need to go to any memorial where no one is better remembered or exalted than themselves. No thank you. Hard pass."

Lindsey's attentions shifted around the room indicating to Clint that she was still processing what he said. After about a year of getting to know her, he was used to this sort of behavior, but what he was not used to was the accompanying gloominess that soon darkened this exchange.

There she sat with her eye shadow and lipstick fastidiously applied that morning highlighting the loud blue eyes upon the very unimposing, petite frame. And here he was, sitting across from her, a middle-aged patron of Big and Tall sabotaging the beliefs of this impressionable young woman. In fact, Clint could hardly see much of a difference between her now and one of his teenage daughters—really just starting to lift off the runway of life. And like the time he told them about the fascinating mythos of Santa Claus, he started to feel really bad for her. On the other hand, unlike his daughters, he knew that his job wasn't to shelter her from facts. Despite this relatively recent issue of controversy on campuses, on the nature of a professor's role, he frankly scorned the idea. He got his doctorate to discuss big ideas—not follow the dead-end fancies of adolescents.

"Professor, I don't know what your experience is, but I can't imagine anyone doing a memorial for someone who would have some ulterior motive other than respect. I mean, who even does that? And whatever the merits of the paper itself, it brings important issues to the forefront. So, this can't all be that bad."

Clint's face grew to the proportions that experience dictated were one of the rare times a teacher had to demonstrate a garishly held absurdity to his pupil. "Miss Cunningham, people *lie*."

12

Coming to as being launched from a cannon, Peter stared at the bedroom ceiling listening to the sounds of movement downstairs. Margery was home.

He remembered coming back after his mid-day class deciding to lay down. What followed was a feverish roller coaster of a nightmare featuring all the torturous devices that his mind could muster. Hideous faces, tall scarred surgical malformities with seemingly sewed on smiles and impossible cheekbones chasing him down endless shadowy corridors at breakneck speed. He managed to evade them for a time with his yet unknown athletic ability. At one point, it even helped him clear a starry abyss in the floor many body lengths across. But before his relief could set in, another face emerged at an intersection reaching at him with long boney arms and pencil length spindles covered in custom white leather gloves. He managed to get free with his momentum but was now subjected to the incessant prodding of the feelers at his back that sent chills through his spine.

At the next intersection, he ran in a new direction without losing much speed, but to little effect. He somehow knew it was over from the beginning. Something had him in its grasp, and there was nothing he could do. *Just submit.*

The hand penetrated into his spinal cord, incapacitating his legs. Its associates joined with the tingling prodding fingers covering his body, investigating, searching.

Feeling as if he were laying in a box of exposed wires with some charge to them, one hand finally poked its long fingers through his abdomen like five syringes. When they stopped, it yanked at something that pulled his whole body forward. Slowly, the fingers came out with something unseen in its grasp. When it took what it needed, it disappeared with the rest. Emptiness ensued.

Peering down the long empty hallways, there were certain things he knew. He was alone. His family was gone. He flung his whole body forward. No tears. A dry bawling of pure despair. It was a long cold agony that his body tried to release. On and on he went that way—trying to cope with his loss. Endless pain. After a time, the questioning would come. Were his wife and son ever real? His loneliness was a vile thirst he couldn't quench. Then he awoke.

He wiped his face with his forearm and sat up on the comforter searching his thoughts for clues to the genesis of such manifestations. *The creatures were a nice touch, Peter.* "Where'd you get that from," he said to himself rubbing his stomach in relief. There was a murmur from downstairs. Margery was telling Roger something that he couldn't quite discern. *It's time*, Peter concluded. *She has to know the danger.*

Peter lifted himself off the bed and made his way downstairs.

13

Kristi Connor was driving her accord with Yunnie Lee north of Baltimore. It was late and her steering wheel was now dampened by her palms. She was nervous. This would be her first-time meeting Mr. Simon Ray, the billionaire financier and philanthropist, founder of Ray Foundation where she had been working as a lead organizer for the past few months along with her assistant, Yunnie. Despite being so close to the Black Victim Memorial Rally in D.C., her direct boss, Marcus Levy, head of the foundation, called her that morning saying that Mr. Ray would like to meet them both right away.

Kristi knew that there was a lot riding on the coming event and was hoping to make her mark with her first true test as a leader. It was enormous pressure that could be felt throughout their headquarters in D.C., but she welcomed it. Her only fear now was that her power would suddenly be taken before her big debut, and for this, much of the afternoon, she had spent practicing her response to scenarios in front of the bathroom mirror.

"These are some big estates," Yunnie said eyes roaming from one house to the next. Kristi didn't say anything, but Yunnie continued as if in the same thought. "Why do you think he'd have us come way out here?"

Kristi kept her eyes on the road. "I don't know. To *charm* us?" This caused Yunnie to break into a chuckle. Kristi only smiled.

"Well, *I'm* charmed," Yunnie added.

"Says the lady charmed by the pizza delivery boy," teased Kristi glancing over to gauge Yunnie's reaction.

"Boy? Come on. He was at least twenty," she giggled followed by Kristi. Once the giggling died, Yunnie resumed looking out the window. The large groomed lawns of the colonial style mansions passed by in the night.

"What do you even know about Ray?" Yunnie asked seriously. "I remember not finding much online except the most basic info."

Checking her phone in the cup holder with the next Wayz app direction, Kristi saw that the turn was coming. She waited for the audible instruction before signaling and veering right at the intersection.

"To tell you the truth, I don't really know. He's been extremely successful with his investments at Atta Capital and other firms, very well connected and very generous both here and internationally."

"But no kids? No family?"

"I also know that he is a very private man and details like this aren't forthcoming. I wouldn't ask unless offered."

"No," Yunnie looked decided, "of course not."

They turned onto a driveway with an eight-foot cast iron gate connecting the brick walls lined with razor wire surrounding the premises. Kristi poked her head out of her window and noticed the large posted camera that now monitored over them as she reached out to push the call button. A moment went by before being addressed by someone on the speaker verifying their identities. The gate slowly pulled open and she followed the illumination of ornate lampposts.

The estate was exceptionally big compared to the houses in the vicinity possessing two more recently added wings matching their older colonial style base. The façade of the structure portrayed it as one inhabited by a prolific family. With the exception of the wall itself, it appeared from the outside warmly inviting.

Kristi passed the garage to the main entrance, followed the roundabout parking behind the familiar white Lincoln SUV.

"Is this who I think it is?" Yunnie queried.

"Mmhm."

"I didn't think he'd be here too."

Kristi didn't think so either. *He must really be shitting his pants about right now*, she thought.

A man greeted them in front of the portico wearing a white collared shirt, light brown dress pants and dark blue sports coat. While polite, he didn't strike her as possessing the mannerisms of a butler exactly. He led them into the foyer that revealed the unexpected extravagance more reserved for a museum than living quarters. The place was exquisitely lavished by canvasses reminiscent of sixteenth century nudes and sculptures of the Greco-Roman world.

"It's wonderful!" Yunnie paused as her eyes were dazzled by the works.

"Yes, he's quite an admirer," said their host already leading them into the next room.

Kristi thought better of taking offense of him rushing them along. Who knew what kind of schedule a man of Ray's stature even kept?

He led them through a long library filled with books encased with glass from floor to ceiling into a smaller sitting room where her boss, Marcus Levy, was laying more in a couch than on it.

"Here you are. Have a seat and he'll be right with you," said the dubious steward leaving as soon as they arrived. Upon departing, Kristi noticed the grip of the automatic jetting out from the shoulder holster within his coat. She should've recognized it from the first. The man was more security than anything else.

Marcus eased himself off the couch. "Glad you both could make it," he delivered with drowsy intoxication.

"Of course," Kristi forced a smile knowing that there really wasn't a choice.

"Sit down and put your feet up," he said lifting his nearly empty crystal glass from the cherry table. "Can I make anyone a drink?"

They both politely declined taking armchairs straddling the couch. Marcus returned from the mini-bar to his place with his glass refilled. With Yunnie looking to her, Kristi opted to fill the uncomfortable silence first.

"So is Mr. Ray occupied with something?"

"He stepped out for a moment."

"I see."

"That's okay," Marcus said crossing his legs. "It gives me a chance to ask you how things are going."

"As a matter of fact, *great*. We have everything set to go with our speakers and equipment, transportation, social media outreach, contingency plans…" Kristi tried recalling what she practiced in front of the mirrors, but it wasn't readily coming. "Weather's looking good. I think everything indicates there will be a large level of participation…likely a day for the history books."

He paused as if waiting for some more details to be offered, further wracking Kristi's nerves as she waited for comment. She was glad that this was only a practice session before meeting Ray. Maybe that was the whole point of Marcus' exercise, as she had already updated him earlier that day over the phone.

"Perfect," he finally said taking a sip of brown liquid. She was partially relieved as Marcus transitioned to making his customary inquiries about family, but before long, the apparent captain of security soon swooped back in.

"He's ready to see you both now."

As they rose, Marcus remained where he was seated smiling knowingly at Kristi before taking another sip from his glass.

The guard took them to a staircase with a balustrade featuring a rich ironwork of flowers surrounding the stoical visage of a Greek goddess. "Gorgeous," Yunnie said in tow admiring the work on the way up while Kristi refused to look too closely, already being overstimulated by the previous works and now on a mission to have this meeting over and done with. She speculated if they could still arrive back in D.C. by midnight. *Perhaps I can even manage a good six hours of sleep,* she told herself hopefully.

They reached the second story revealing a dim hallway only lit by the painting viewing lamps that shined from above. "Right in there," said their guide indicating an open door before leaving once again. They entered a massive study that appeared to be the product of tearing down multiple walls of the house.

"You gotta be fucking kidding me," Kristi said under her breath as she entered the gymnasium sized room filled with art, books, and other curiosities. The room appeared unoccupied with a large desk and set of comfortable sitting chairs. An old brass telescope stood near one of the large windows behind it.

Yunnie was immediately drawn to a five-foot obelisk lamp lit from the base that shot beams of colored light in surprising directions around the room. As she continued to survey the room, her eyes stuck on what she first had mistaken as a bulky piece of furniture next to the entrance. What she had come to realize caused her heart to jump. Ray was standing right there.

"Hi Mr. Ray," she floundered.

"Oh my God!" Yunnie burst out after turning to see the man standing at the door.

"Good evening, Miss Connor and Miss Lee. I've startled you," he said in a deep soothing voice.

"That's okay," Yunnie returned as if it were a question.

"I'm sorry. I didn't see you at the door," Kristi expressed reaching her hand out to shake the giant's. His mitt of a palm met hers with surprising softness. "Nice to finally meet you."

Yunnie walked up to do the same. The trepidation still seen on her face looked hard to conceal as they shook. The shock was still wearing off. Her "nice to meet you" almost didn't come. Kristi could understand why.

Ray was an imposing figure, easily over six feet tall and wide at the waste. His face that now wore a tranquil smile was full with accompanying square jaw meeting the top of an unusually conical head. His whole shape from the front struck Kristi as almost triangular. *He must have a hell of a tailor fitting him in that black suit,* she pondered.

"My lamp interested you," he directed at Yunnie. She straightened in anticipation of a question that never came.

"Yeah…" She turned to further inspect the strange piece.

He gave her a moment then offered, "Within light always belies a mystery."

She took in the shimmering colors, as if in a sudden trance. "It's really nice…How did you find something so, unique?"

Steadily making his way over from the doorway, Ray paused before the lamp looming over Kristi's small assistant. Even Kristi's gaze appeared to be drawn by the obelisk as Ray studied it.

"I can't really tell you, you see…my collection has been accumulated over decades."

His stare became vacant as the lamp continued shooting shafts of reds and golds onto his head. They played their game distorting his features—appearing to transform them into someone else's.

"You have a lovely home," Kristi commented—not liking how it sounded as it left her lips. *Home? From the inside, this didn't appear to be anyone's home.*

"I'll show you more if that's what you'd like?" While his demeanor was pleasant and inviting enough, he held a statuesque expression like some of the sculpture he possessed.

Kristi started forming the image of a very stoical man with eccentric tastes. She was now convinced that the man had no family—being a rich philanthropist with more money than he knew what to do with whose idea of going on a splurge was breaking down and adding a Cezanne to his collection. The story had a certain charm to it.

Kristi and Yunnie both agreed to his offer.

"Good. We can discuss events as we walk."

He stood at the door to the adjacent room. "We can start here," he said waiting for them to enter first. Kristi hesitated at the doorway. The room was still dark.

"Go ahead," Ray insisted. "Don't worry about the light. It'll come."

Kristi forged ahead with Yunnie close behind. She could tell that the room possessed a certain depth like the last. Dark centers of shapes populated the space with the outside house lights barely illuminating it through the windows.

Still, the light didn't come until after Kristi felt the ridiculousness of the situation. Why exactly was she bumbling around in the dark to trigger a faulty motion sensor, she couldn't say. But, before she voiced her discomfort, they heard the click and found themselves in another exhibit of Ray's collection. Marble figures and paintings from the same periods occupied the room—only now in a greater concentration.

"*Wow*," Yunnie sounded.

Kristi didn't agree. *Once you saw a few works like these, you've seen them all,* she thought, as Yunnie studied a chest up bust of a feminine form.

"Take a look around and see what catches your fancy," said Ray monitoring from behind.

"Cleopatra?" Yunnie queried.

"I had it commissioned in marble based on an ancient depiction."

"Ah." She acknowledged.

"A great figure." He spoke as they gazed on the matriarch who appeared indifferent to her spectators.

"How so?"

"Look at her here now over 2000 years later…Living at a certain crossroads can be enough."

The bust stirred Yunnie's imagination. *Could it have captured something like the queen smiling at the arrival of Antony's ship? Or did the slope of the cheeks indicate that her initial impression was incorrect?* An empty look of despair—even something like her last moments alive? Somehow, her heart told her the latter. In fact, she began to feel as if she were her in the moment.

Ray left Yunnie—striding over to Kristi, who was now meandering around the gallery trying to appear more interested than she was.

"You don't really like my art, do you?" his voice softly purred through the space. It startled her—both the sound of his voice and the abrupt question.

"No, I really—"

"You know there are other historical works of art, *per se*, that I think even you can admire."

"It's not that."

"This coming rally can, by all definitions, be deemed a work of art. It has all the elements that compose a masterpiece. It has a rich background—the very seat and beacon of one of the oldest democratic governments in the world. It has an organic color of struggling people in the foreground yearning for upheaval. And all of it will be memorialized in a world rife with cameras. Angle after angle being saved for posterity with generations to stew over and digest."

Here it was. At this point, Kristi was listening intently. She had known this was coming. Ray was trying to tell her in so many words that this matter was of consequence such that fucking up just wasn't an option. And in so many words she was supposed to say: 'I won't fuck it up. I'm worth my salt.'

Ray continued almost unbrokenly, with only the slightest pauses for breaths, "All of the material is there. The only thing left that it needs is the artist to make it all happen. It needs you, to put its pieces together so that the people will have more than just a protest—many will now be a part of the very symbol that will continue to perpetuate itself in others until change really happens—a nuclear level change that no one has yet seen before."

His eyes were locked onto hers. His expression almost plastic in its presentation. For a moment, she felt fear gripping her as she shook her head to agree to whatever this inanimate thing was telling her. But, Ray severed the connection. He paused his monologue to direct his dark unfocused eyes behind her.

Kristi saw Yunnie standing nearby appearing as a witness to something disturbing. She was glad that she wasn't the only one who noticed. *How accurate was her initial impression. Eccentric is right.*

Before the uncomfortable silence could really settle in, however, he started again softly. "Now I realize that this is less like a painting or sculpture than these here, but as the organizer, you are in control of the focal point which it all hinges and evolves from. And much like formal art, even here, if the artist loses focus, its quality quickly diminishes. Sometimes the distinction between a masterpiece and an average piece of humdrum is a momentary lapse." Here, Ray's piercing dark eyes ended up back on hers. They weren't so much waiting for her answer, but rather, searching for it.

"I believe it's shaping up just as you envision it—a masterpiece in the making," she expressed confidently.

Gradually Ray's lips pulled up into a grin. Kristi was relieved to see that at least something about her pleased him.

"Terrific," he said summarily.

Turning to Yunnie, who was still standing nearby exhibiting body language of someone who has been violated in some way, Ray asked, "Are you liking my art?" While Yunnie's features were stark, it appeared Ray decided to ignore them.

"Really nice," she tried sounding upbeat. Her eyes passed to Kristi to gauge her reaction.

"Good. Then we can check out my next collection if you're still interested."

Ray led them to the far door of the gallery and across the corridor to a room in the front of the house. Yunnie reluctantly followed behind.

Kristi could now only guess where the actual master's suite happened to be as surely yet another bedroom had been turned from its former use. *I suppose there are still plenty of rooms left to choose from.*

This time, the light flicked on immediately as she crossed the door's threshold. More paintings lined the walls with a large marble work at the center.

"Now I'm sure…" Ray spoke still directed at Kristi as a continuation of their earlier conversation. "There must be some questions or concerns that I could address before the big day?"

Transfixing on the central piece, Kristi identified the likeness of the statue, as of a pregnant nude sitting on a bench.

"I think everything is really falling into place," she said, again quickly losing interest in the room. But, realizing that not having any problem about the details was also a problem for such an event, she offered one. "I think the only thing is the matter of Senator Dembier. She's supposed to be the one speaking at Lincoln Memorial, but we've repeatedly reached out to her office for confirmation with no response…." Ray walked beside Kristi seemingly unphased by what could be construed as a major issue. "On the other hand, Marcus did inform me that you've already gotten her assurances?"

"Marcus is right. You have no need to worry about Susan making her slot. She is a long-time friend. We are in touch on a daily basis."

"Oh. Great." She said, feeling stupider now for bringing it up.

"Miss Lee," Ray now addressed the assistant who had been hovering around Kristi seemingly distracted by some of the works. As if snapping out of a dream, she turned to Ray. "I understand that you have done some coordination of your own with social media groups occurring in several cities?"

"Yes," she said composing herself. "We have organizations in San Francisco, Seattle, New York, Houston with an excess of eighteen thousand RSVPing that they'll be in attendance for the rally."

Ray said nothing, so she took it as her cue to continue. "In San Francisco and Seattle alone, we have about thirty-three thousand and twenty-five thousand marchers in attendance, respectively."

"That's wonderful," Ray declared absently.

A quiet fell over the company and seemingly the whole house. While Kristi knew that Marcus was still downstairs and Ray's guard was likely somewhere in the vicinity along with residents of the greater Baltimore area, she felt that they might as well have been in the middle of a forest in Alberta. Something about the situation gave her a heightened self-consciousness and increasing gratitude of having a reliable assistant come along.

"These paintings…" Yunnie tried penetrating the eerie quiet for her own comfort.

"Yes, one of the collections I'm most proud of."

"Who is the artist?"

"An Italian painter. You may have never heard of him. His name is Enzo Benucci. In my opinion, he's one of the workers of some of the most compelling art composed in the world today."

"So they're contemporary," Yunnie answered her own question.

"He has perfected the rendering of the pregnant nude form, a major theme in all his works."

Kristi glanced around the room curiously. Everything had been marked by a nude in a late term within different settings of nature. *Had eccentricity turned to fetishism?*

"Everything but the center piece is his, which I had specially commissioned to bring the room together."

"I'm sure he is a really interesting person to meet," added Yunnie, her eyes wandering.

He is a man very devoted to art for art's sake. In fact, most of the money I give him, he gives back to charity."

"Wonderful."

"Do you really like it?" Ray asked her.

"Of course." There was no doubt that she did.

Kristi weighed the question as she was caught by another painting displaying a solitary nude bearing the full weight of a looming childbirth. The woman was exiting a water hole that was encapsulated by a den of trees all lying within a open field. While it appeared to possess a certain Rembrandt quality to it, it also made her feel uneasy. There was something wholly indecorous about its perspective. One could even speculate that it bordered on the perverse.

No, she decided. She felt violated just in the looking. It was as if she were the very woman being exploited by the shameless appetites of a nearby voyeur. It made her skin crawl in revulsion, and to avoid the discovery of her whole body's uncontrollable outward rebellion against the work, she quickly turned to something else.

14

An ocean of people rippled before the steps of the Lincoln Memorial. Live broadcasts interrupted local stations to show Senator Susan Dembier of Wisconsin speaking from the small podium just below the throne of the sixteenth president's likeness. The following was properly soundbited, disseminated, and promptly lodged at the Library of Congress.

"We always knew, despite what some had tried to tell us, other pseudo-scientists, that racism isn't real. (boos). Isn't happening when we knew it was happening. Denying our very experiences of it. Well now, *we know*. (cheers). Now, we know what lengths they will go to. (cheers). Yes, we do. We knew all along. And you see what they are trying to do to us even now? Can you believe it? They are even trying to silence the very science itself that shows what we have been trying to say from the very beginning. (boos and hisses). That every meagre look and every false smile. Every subordination or slight that we have felt was that evil creature, still rearing its ugly head, plain and simple. (cheers and boos). So nothing's changed.

For four hundred years. *Nothing has changed.* (boos). Now let me ask you. What are we going to do about it? Huh? What? I'll tell you what. *Fight.* We're going to fight. (cheers). *You. say it.* (*Fight!*). That's what we're going to do. And fight we must. Every person of color around the country must. You see? I'm not asking you to become an activist. No. I'm not asking you anymore to make signs and come out here. No more. That's not what I'm asking. What I'm asking for you to do is to simply *live!* (cheers). To survive the white flood (cheers) programmed to annihilate us from the face of the *earth!* (crescendoing cheers) AND I'M URGING CONGRESS TO TAKE IMMEDIATE ACTION IN DRAFTING A BILL TO PROTECT US AND TRUE SCIENCE FROM BEING DISTORTED!"

Across the country, the reaction to the speech was electric. Black neighborhoods ignited the streets with chants and fellowship. Quotes of it, appearing in feeds across social media, headlined every mainstream news outlet. Even coverage of other protests took a back seat compared to the analysis and editorializing of the young senator's remarks. A partisan panelist from WNT noted, "Finally, a speech that spoke truth to oppression." The American Broadcast Network aired a live discussion prompting a contributor to share, "This is the seed change needed that will make white people everywhere face just what it is that they do to blacks." But, one of the most oft repeated lines of the day was from an interview of the singer and activist, Larry Dreisner at LNN who was quoted saying, "When she said, 'white flood,' I was chilled to the bone— knowing that's how we are. That's *exactly* what we are."

In the weeks following, scientists, who early voiced their concerns, declined to comment. Unlike the time at the release of the study, however, conservative media would no longer be quiet. They mounted their first major counter-offensive. "[Senator Dembier] appeared to be having trouble recognizing her position as a powerful senator in her whole racist world narrative," wrote the editorial board of the Washington Daily Journal. "I've never seen such venom, especially, as it is glitzily being paraded as an antidote. Who knew that racism could be resold as a way to liberation?" conservative commentator and comedian, Jim Herbert asked his audience after playing the clip of the senator. He continued, "One industry in this country that perhaps hasn't been lost to globalism is marketing. And *boy*, do we still know how to resell something—repackaging manure with a nice bow."

These diatribes, as usual, did little to quell the excitement of the opposition—being largely dismissed or ignored. "Jim Herbert meets Jim Crowe," scoffed one online personality. Another even referred to such shows as "klan meetings redux." It was all working out quite nicely for those who delighted in the status quo—just the way that those who had already chosen their side wanted it. Again, the world of knowing who was right and who was dumb was clearly demarcated—an unambiguous bliss. At least, that was until something altogether adventitious and unacceptable occurred. The WNT segment with Eggers questioning Barton took the internet's interest. How could this be? How dare it be!? One of their own networks and, presumed people, were being disagreeable? And just how were they supposed to press this very equitable piece into their very savory board? It was all simply too much. Unpalatable. A redressment was due—a redressment to make up for all those bitter years of living under the yoke of the other.

15

Resting his head in the living room armchair with his laptop closed on the coffee table, Peter processed recent events with the quiet necessary to do so.

Things have changed too much or have they really? The past few weeks, while the situation on campus has calmed following the Black Victim Memorial, he has still been the target of particular incidents. Even with nothing happening to his person directly, his car had been vandalized. Large dents had been kicked into the sides and "heil nazi" spray painted in red just below the driver-side window. And if that was it, perhaps he wouldn't be sitting here now considering his options. What happened yesterday changed things. In the lawn and garden section of the Cooper's Hardware store with Roger placing mulch bags into the cart, he saw the same man stopped behind them that he'd noticed many aisles before. Every proceeding aisle, there he was with his empty cart. The direct glare removed any doubt.

Wishing to pre-empt the situation, Peter asked the stranger if he needed help. To this, the middle-aged man grew a sickly smile.

"No, none needed. Thank you."

"Okay, let us know. I even have a helper today," he said indicating his son.

When Peter turned to go, the man added, "Now, what a kindly white man! Thank you so much!"

Over his shoulder he saw the strange fellow resume his attentions toward them. The depraved smile told him all he needed to know. Roger and he were leaving.

They left the cart and walked out. Peter vigilantly looked in his rearview mirror on the way home.

Peter didn't tell Roger why they left. He didn't end up telling Margery either, who already knew about the vandalism to the car and threatening calls. Since then, he had been wracked with anxiety—trying to determine how to proceed. *Maybe if things got worse, Margery could stay with her parents in Tacoma. Yes, maybe that. But, what would be considered sufficiently worse? Someone harassing him on campus? Someone entering the house? Would it have to end up coming to that?*

With a shiver through his spine, Peter envisaged the man from the hardware store peering with that foul grin into one of the front bay windows. The expression revealing one at the brink—any moment the verge of chaos.

Peter went to the window and peered out. No one was around that he saw peering back. The street was quiet. Some neighbors were home with a car passing, but little else happening.

Peter surveyed the area. The garden stood empty. *Today was not a day he would be able to get his hands in the soil.* He reserved those days. He liked to take his time.

Across the street was the Shanwell's home with their gas guzzling Hummer in the driveway. He wondered if Jack's wife was also trying to get pregnant or were they just wanting plenty of space for guests in their five thousand square foot home. Even now, Peter thought how empty his own house was with only a fraction of that space used. But, with the soon to be revealed surprise on the way, Peter could finally sensibly fork over the large payment at the end of the month.

Up the street, Peter noticed a moving truck parked against the curb. He hadn't seen it there before and neither had he seen anyone moving. People didn't often leave Preston Heights, as even now, after all the recent happenings, Peter didn't really want to have to either.

The loud jangle of the landline ruptured Peter's pensive state causing him to blench. This time faulting himself for being a grown man, he straightened before hesitantly picking up the receiver.

Nothing.

"Hello?" Peter said to the quiet.

"It's about time."

"What?"

"For racists to die," The hushed rasp blew into the phone.

"Do you know—!" Hearing only the dial tone, he slammed the phone back onto its cradle in a burst of anger. *How about that? Even after changing the number, they were back at it. Someone from the university with access must have leaked the new number.*

Squeezing the landline insert and removing it from the wall would have to do for now, but he already knew that Margery and Roger may have to leave Palm Gate, at least for a little while, that is, before new bait could be thrown to the zealots and things escalated further. For a face in the window staring at his family would be hideous. Imagining it being there even now made Peter reevaluate everything. To put his own neck on the line was one thing. Seeing such a threat come to where they live—where Roger does his homework—where they sleep at night—would be far too late.

Green. Witness of the Obscene.

1

"Roger, they're here!" his mom called to the top floor from the bottom of the staircase.

"Coming!" he yelled back.

Clint, Jenelle, and their two daughters were welcomed in—exchanging their customary hugs. Clint drew out the two cigars peaking out of his front shirt pocket.

"Perfect." Peter smiled taking one of the two that Clint presented him.

"I figured you could appreciate it about now," Clint added.

Peter read the label and smelled the sweet rich aroma—breathing out with satisfaction.

"Yes, thank you. Just what the Professor ordered."

"Now, I wasn't sure that I should give you one… I've seen many a good Cornell man knocked on his ass from this firecracker."

"Well, if a Harvard man can do it then, by God, we gotta follow."

They chuckled their way into the living room as they heard the sound of the kids thundering up the stairs.

"I believe I have just the right accompaniment for this here." Peter meandered over to the mini-bar in the east wing with Clint behind.

"Single malt?"

"Please."

He popped the top of the bottle and poured three fingers into two glasses.

"Ice?"

"Neat's fine."

"Me too."

They clinked glasses and sipped.

As usual, before he would smoke on the patio, Peter would check in on his family to avoid doing it in front of them. He poked in Roger's room to find the kids playing B.S., a game the girls taught Roger. It didn't look like he was doing too well now possessing a good third of the deck. He saw that the girls were still teasing him about the size of his hand, but he just smiled. Losing never bothered him too much.

Downstairs the wives were already talking over events in the kitchen in hushed tones. Peter could smell the spinach dip and cheese nachos baking in the oven. Margery was multitasking—preparing the macaroni salad with cobbs of corn boiling on the stove as Jenelle chatted at her at the counter, glass of wine in hand. That was usually how she liked it. With most of the cooking, she usually liked to be the solo act. Only with barbecues, Peter knew he had to do his part too.

From the fridge he took out the patties and hotdogs using his elbow to shut it, all the while, adroitly, holding onto his glass and cigar in the other hand.

"Look at this man," Jenelle said with a smile.

Peter sipped his scotch winking at the both of them. Margery turned pecking him on the cheek.

"Very smooth." Clint said.

"I think I've seen Clint do it with two," Jenelle laughed. Clint didn't.

He opened the door to the patio allowing Peter through who twisted with the finesse of a young tennis star.

"Impressive once again."

Setting everything down on the outside table, Peter proceeded to uncover the gas grill.

"I never told you?"

"What?"

"Truth be told, I waited tables."

"Really? A Cornell man who had a real job once?"

"And what does a Pilgrim know about it?"

"Hey. Ya'know—just asking."

Clint laughed along with Peter undressing the large steel capsule.

Clint emptied his glass then fished for the cigar cutter and zippo in his pocket. He clipped the end then circled the lit zippo around it, drawing in the flame with his breath.

"Everything going alright then?" Clint asked curiously as Peter ducked down to turn on the tank's valve.

"Well, not really," he said frankly.

"Seriously? And what now?"

Before continuing, Peter turned to confirm that the back door was shut.

"I got another call today."

"Another? Even after—?"

"Yes, even after I changed numbers."

"But why always the landline?" Clint asked before taking in another draft of cigar.

Peter adjusted the temperature knobs, feeling the heat out of the top of the grill with his palm.

"I don't know. Does it even really matter why? They found a way."

"Yeah."

"And it was as gross as ever."

"What did they say this time?"

"Let's put it this way. I had to make a call to the police again just before Margery and Roger got back with the groceries."

"Another threat?"

"He said that it was time for racists to die," he told Clint plainly.

"Naturally."

Clint stood for a moment just smoking, pondering what it would be like to have a death threat against himself, Jenelle, or the girls. It was unsettling and imposing another side of reality on this otherwise pleasant day.

"What are you going to do about it?"

The question lingered. There was a long quiet. Clint started to wonder if Peter was going to answer it at all. Before he could change the topic, however, Peter started again slowly, quietly.

"After what happened yesterday, the car, and this now, I really don't know anymore."

"I understand."

Clint handed Peter the lighter again.

After a long exhalation of smoke, Peter added, "And I can't really say that anything appears that it's going to get better. I mean, did you read President Scott's letter to the community?"

Clint chuckled, "*His reach out to the nearest people of color* was something else."

"Absurd."

"It was like he was calling on people to help those with some malformity."

"And that he was already picking a side. Eldridge and Jersey."

"It's good publicity for him. It falls in with the times."

"You bet. He's absolutely loving it."

They both watched the grill stewing over the new world in which they now found themselves. *It didn't seem that long ago when the academic world was different*, Clint thought with his next inhalation. It was still fresh in his memory when he lost a letter grade after changing a conclusion by omitting the word *likelihood* from his paper. He couldn't forget his grouchy developmental psych professor, Hart, on that day when he approached him after class.

"Mr. Dumfries," he said with a scowl, "If you are going to make jumps in your reasoning, you may as well just go ahead and jump yourself right out of university. I expect a lot more from you sir." *What happened to that world?*

2

Everyone was able to sit outside at the patio table. Their plates now stood virtually empty save for Roger's who loaded up again with two burgers. One of which he was munching on when Margery stood up.

"Thank you so much for coming today. Peter and I wanted to celebrate and share the good news with our close friends."

"We're finally getting a pool?!" Roger asked excitedly, mouth still full of burger.

This cracked up the adults, but the twins still sat curiously waiting for Margery to finish.

"No, Roger," she said after composing herself. "You are going to have a baby brother or sister."

"Oh," he replied.

Jenelle, Clint, and the twins each stood up giving Margery a hug—congratulating her on fulfilling her long expressed goal of having a second child. Peter stood finishing his third scotch, knowing that this was only a formality. Of course, Margery had already told Jenelle and he'd told Clint. They held the secret at least in telling their kids, but it was more of a celebration than anything else. When they were done, he kissed his wife.

"*Well?* Which one is it?" Roger asked still a little surprised by the news.

"What?"

"Boy or girl?"

"We don't know this soon, Rog," his dad answered.

"Well how about *I* choose?"

This got everyone roaring including the twins.

Daniela mouthed the word *what* to everyone as they belted out their hee-haws.

Roger only smirked.

"And which do you prefer?" Jenelle posed with the laughter dying down.

He hesitated, not knowing if he really wished to share, but he decided to continue anyway. "I'm good either way…but in the end, I hope for a brother, I guess."

"And why is that?" Jenelle immediately followed up.

"Because…I guess…ya'know, we can talk guy stuff."

"Guy stuff?" Daniela snickered.

He looked at Daniela. "What? Guys have stuff they want to talk about too."

"You know if it is a boy, he's going to be a lot younger than you," Jenelle pointed out.

"Yeah, but we could, at least, one day, talk guy stuff."

His dad folded his arms play acting his part. "*Hey*, now what is all this *guy stuff* that I'm hearing about?" he said in his best disgruntled parent tone.

"Dad, you know. Guy stuff. I'm sure I don't have to tell you."

"Well, if you want to talk *guy stuff*, can't you talk to me about it? I mean, *I'm* a *guy*." Peter inflected with his best macho voice he could do while shaking his head.

"No Dad, guys have to talk to other guys."

This caused some pause in the group—losing the audience on some aspect that took them down some rabbit hole of their own.

"So Roger, let's see if I have this straight," he said with his own undisguised masculine voice. "You need to observe the *guy* rules by speaking with another *guy* to talk about *guy* stuff other than your old man, who is a *guy*?"

Everyone listened to the voice that seemed to demand attention. All were quiet despite the farcical manner in which Clint expressed it.

After a moment's pause, Roger answered with the inflection that said it was all obvious enough. "*Yes.*"

3

The kids ended up demolishing a whole apple pie. Each had a large warm slice with a scoop of ice-cream before running off. Roger asked his dad if the twins could borrow both his parent's bikes, as they all agreed that they wanted to take an evening ride through the neighborhood.

Peter said that they could so long as they stuck together and stayed in the area. He couldn't blame them for not wanting to stay in. The outside breeze blew the mid-afternoon heat away— invigorating those bodies who ventured out.

The couples each had a small piece of cherry pie that Margery topped with whipped cream. She also brewed a pot of coffee to take the edge off the intoxication.

Now that the kids stepped out, they took their time eating and drinking peacefully as one of those rare moments that adults could let a little off the throttle—time they could finally exit the itinerary, at least for a little while.

Of course, also when this happens, sometimes, one simply can't relax. Sometimes, one is merely afforded that leisure time to worry, and unfortunately, this time, that was the case for Peter. His piece of pie sat largely untouched as he stared off lost in his own thoughts.

Margery, noticing, reached her hand out to touch Peter's that was clasped around his coffee mug. His hand met hers—squeezing it to show that everything was fine, even though the rest of his body said that it wasn't, even though, she knew it wasn't.

"So Peter," Jenelle had appeared to be forming something in her mind for a while now, "after that impressive interview on WNT…"

"*Impressive?*" Peter laughed.

"*Really*, it was," she affirmed a little surprised.

"Thank you Jenelle, but I don't think I'd call it that."

"Peter's all about playing that false modesty card," Clint gibed.

"I'm afraid that, after watching myself, I'd have to objectively disagree."

"How *could* you have you done any better?" Margery queried as if the answer were preposterous.

"Don't get me wrong, I think that what I said in the interview was on point. I kept my answers as short as I reasonably could realizing my audience. But, the one thing that was sadly missing was, well…charisma."

Clint and Jenelle both laughed but Margery didn't. She sat stone-faced. It was one of those atypical moments that told him he was dangerously close to being unable to share a bed with her in the near future.

"*Honey,*" she said with that special gravity that meant something dire had happened—such as *honey, the house burnt down* or *honey, your father died.* "That's just not true. You were very charismatic. Frankly, I've never seen you so attractive in my life."

Peter realized that this was going into uncomfortable territory quickly. His remark had even caused a personal affront to his wife, who took enormous pride in the man she married.

"All that I'm trying to say is that someone could have done it better than I." At this point, even Clint and Jenelle looked a little peeved. *Just where was this going,* their faces read. Peter knew he had better explain and be quick about it.

"I mean…you've seen some of these popular figures out there now? These internet personalities are the people who really have the influence. They have their wit and charm…In fact, it doesn't appear to be at all about clarity or cogency or even honesty anymore. People are all about following someone likable—I mean, someone—very likable—you know, who really catches their eye."

"You have someone else in mind then?" Jenelle asked half jesting.

"Sure. How about WilliStacks or DreamPiper? I'd take either of them, with their millions of followers who, not only receive the message, but act on it—commenting, liking, subscribing, sharing their videos. If we had one of them in our corner making our case, I think it would be a game changer."

"No—" Clint began.

"Hey, if I could've had some young charismatic influencer to argue my point with *memes, roasts,* what have you, I would've done it. Almost no one watches these news shows anymore except those in retirement or those who want to clip them to be put in the most negative light possible for their own purposes."

"I don't think so, Peter," Clint resounded through the company. "In fact, I believe your interview right now is making positive waves."

Gauging Clint's face, *no*, was all that Peter could say to its seriousness.

"It's true," Clint confirmed picking up his phone off the table.

They all looked on curiously as he scrolled. Their phones almost melodically buzzed and dinged in perfect unison upon receipt of his share.

Peter looked for himself. It read, "Brave Professor Doubts Science of New Racism Study." Clicking the link to the video revealed the enormous amount of traffic that it drew with an impressive ratio of likes to comments. Just how could over two million people come to appreciate a professor ramble on about the details of an entry in a journal of Psychology? He thought he may have had some insight about how the internet worked, but this proved to be the contrary.

As the video started, he muted the sound still wondering at the details of the post, even venturing into some of the comments section.

Margery shared her screen with Jenelle, watching the video intently with the sound on low—seemingly more interested in appearance than substance. Meanwhile, all that Clint could think to do was add, "I thought you'd already know about this."

As he put his phone down, Clint waited to meet Peter's gaze with a smile. *Told you*, it said.

"*What?*" Peter snickered at Clint.

"So?"

"The comments are largely against me. I think it's because I've mostly pissed people off—anger junkies getting their fix."

"Let's just go by the comments section then," quipped Clint.

"You looked so handsome," Margery inserted into the conversation, as she just finished satisfying her curiosity about the video.

"But not anymore?" Peter joked.

"I'd have to agree with her Peter," Jenelle observed, "I just don't see the problem."

"Look," Clint said, wanting to conclude this line of inquiry as quickly as possible. "If someone more charismatic happened to do it, I think the effect would be marginal at best. And that is to assume a lot. That's to assume that it was executed with precision as well as wit. Otherwise, the message could be compromised—being considered as entertainment value only…"

"But—"

"And even at the end of that, with someone like DreamPiper, they could just pigeonhole them as a non-authority."

Peter scoffed at the prospect before resuming. "But, I'm more concerned with reaching the youth. Considering the age group that is all up-in-arms about now, I think hearing it from a middle-aged man has its limitations…I even wondered if a follow-up interview shouldn't rather be done by someone more relatable."

Something in what he said perked Jenelle up in her seat.

"I don't know if relatability will do much of anything. If I were to venture a guess, I'd say that content dwarfs relatability almost every time."

"Have they approached you about doing another interview?" Jenelle asked with added interest—ignoring her husband's response.

He hesitated, looking over Margery as a gauge to decide if it was too soon to talk about it.

"Well, as a matter of fact, he called me the other night to see how we're doing, and to ask if I'd be willing to do another, given the controversy of the first."

"Really? And you didn't say anything?"

"Margery and I have been discussing if we want to go that route. As of right now, the jury's still out, but for all that's been going on, it has crossed my mind more than once to hand over the reins to someone else."

"Yes, it's just awful what they're doing."

"It's a surprise the news media has kept off your property so far."

"Yeah, well, that could change quickly if we draw anymore attention to ourselves. I think they're just keen on keeping their biological fascists alive long enough for follow-up headlines."

"I thought they wouldn't be interested in doing Biology stories anymore."

"They'll do a story, Biology de-Mythologized," Peter cracked.

"Oh, they'll say yes to that."

"Of course, anything with Bi in it."

"Anything with a porn sounding headline."

"That's their competition."

"May as well look at the porn. Could learn more."

"Ok that's enough! Gentlemen!" Margery sounded, still letting out a chuckle.

"So, when are you going to have to decide?" Jenelle pressed for details.

Peter looked to his wife. "I don't know…"

"Can't tell you what to do Peter, but you know at this point, if I were you, I'd just as well do it," Clint spoke looking at both his wife as well as Peter.

He wanted to make it clear to her just where he still stood, as she appeared on the precipice of insinuating his further involvement.

A little surprised at his friend's importunity, Peter asked, "And why do you say that?"

"I understand why you want out, but it would just look bad, especially now that no one wants to touch it. If we build a respectable opposition, what you're facing now won't be as much of a problem."

"Why don't *you* just do it then?" Peter smirked.

"Agreed," Jenelle chimed in, "I think my man can take care of it." She pressed her hand on his enormous thigh.

Clint adjusted himself uncomfortably maintaining his own smile. He knew why he didn't care to be the figurehead, but he didn't like the sound of any of the answers. Nevertheless, he went for it. "You know I'd do it, but I'm black."

This caught the whole company off guard. Peter bit his lower lip. Margery sat uncomfortably staring at the table before her waiting for them to move on. Even Jenelle didn't know what to say. It was as if Clint's blackness now being made apparent got in the way of their entire friendship.

Finally, Peter answered him. "Yes, so? You're black."

"You see how this interview would go with me, don't you?"

"Um…yeah, I can imagine."

"Well, it isn't going to be so much about my expertise so much as *this* guy is black."

"Sure."

"The questions will be about how I feel as a *black* man or coming from the *black* community." Every time he said the word black, it was emphasized like a slap to the face.

"And what's wrong with that?" Jenelle said, a little indignant.

"It quite limits me as a human being, doesn't it?" Peter thought aloud, "Yeah, I see your point."

"You can answer the question."

"Yeah, but should I even have to?"

"I'm sure Eggers would do you the courtesy to not ask you anything demeaning if you explain it to him," Margery offered.

"It's going to come up. It has to come up and if it isn't him, it'll be someone else."

"Not necessarily," Jenelle pushed.

"Look, it wouldn't be as good as it is with your video just gaining popularity. I'm okay to do it, but I want to build off what you started. I don't want to argue using their identity game. I want to be seen as one concerned professor of many against the study because of how poor it is—not because my skin color is crying out from the wilderness. To play their own game is to lose. Pure and simple."

4

As the sun conveyed its last message for the day, Roger trailed the girls up the street practicing his no-hands steering. His bicycle careened left then right with his body movements. Only able to do it five seconds at a time, it was far from a straight track, but after much practice, he was now proud of himself for how long he could sustain it. Too bad, he felt that the girls took no notice, as they sped past the curated yards of the grand residences.

"That's why Jeffrey is not into Estel anymore."

"You mean, they've already broke up?"

"Yeah. I think, it's obvious. He's always paying attention to Jeanie."

"Dayum that's cold. She shouldn't've let him go all the way with her."

"He went all the way?" Roger interrupted innocently, trying to ascend into a new echelon of teenage gossip.

Daniela glanced back to see that he was still there. Her mouth slowly turned into a silly grin.

"Don't worry about it," Giselle imparted to the straggler, "this is a private conversation and you're too young."

While Roger felt a little hurt, he did wonder at the privateness of yelling a conversation through a neighborhood.

"Yeah," Daniela agreed. "This, what we're having here is girl talk. You can go ahead with your guy talk somewhere else."

"*Gal* talk," her sister corrected.

"*Gal* talk," she repeated—looking back to gauge Roger's expression wearing the same smile. Roger felt better about it with Daniela. It was a simple tease.

"There's also guy *and* gal talk. Guys and gals can talk to each other, ya'know, diplomatically." Roger felt a little proud of himself earning a giggle, at least from Daniela. She was always the one he liked best of the twins, and also the one closer to his age.

A catchy K-Pop jingle soon interrupted their exchange. Giselle pulled over on the side of the street to produce the cell phone that was tightly wedged in her jean pocket. It accelerated her heartbeat just to be able to make use of the sleek device, as her parents had restricted it to only calls and texts. However, her excitement was short-lived when she saw that the call was only from their mom.

"Yes?"

The others stopped nearby. Daniela listened intently with a countenance suggesting someone's recent passing.

"They're here…not far. Okay."

They waited for the official news from Giselle.

"It's time to head back," she sounded, a little disappointed.

"But you know what this means?" They waited for Daniela to finish. "Rat race!"

"*Rat race?*" Roger asked.

"Yes, whoever is last is a scurrying rat."

But before Roger could question further, "Ready, go!" she shouted hightailing it down the street. Roger chased her in hot pursuit.

"She sure is the strange one," Giselle told herself—setting a moderate steady pace back.

Roger gained on her quickly despite the late start. He was fast but so was she, and even more than that, she was sneaky. When they were nearly neck and neck hugging the curb, she swerved far to the outside to ward off his passing. From her expression, she took this maneuver partly for the sheer glee of it, laughing chaotically out of breath. The ruse didn't work, however, as Roger cut in closer to the curb, determined to achieve victory now, after such a surprisingly treacherous tactic.

Daniela wasn't out of it yet though. She corrected course screaming out her battle cry and sense of frustration as she kicked the bike back into gear—cutting the curb as close as she could. Roger knew that she could overtake him with her speed at any moment, and with the scream projecting from behind him, he looked to finish the last few hundred yards as error free as he could.

Passing the last few cul-de-sacs before the driveway, Roger saw victory within reach—only one minor obstacle lay ahead—the long Youhaul rental truck parked curbside. Not taking any chances losing to someone who'd never cease exercising bragging rights, Roger steered within inches of the truck's carriage. It only took a moment to clear before he realized that it was going to happen. Indeed, he was going to win this ad hoc gender bender for whatever it was worth. A glorious smile was already plastered across his smug face.

After reaching the driveway, his bike squealed to a stop as he squeezed hard on the hand brake. Almost immediately, the fetid smell of something nearby hit his nose full blast. He threw his bike to the ground coughing as it began invading his mouth. It was as if a circus had died in a sewer. He stumbled around as Daniela pulled up too.

"I let you win! I…" Her face quickly soured.

"Ughhh! What the fuck is that smell?" she asked as she too dropped the bike and bolted out of the immediate area.

Roger looked around as the smell failed to abate. There was nothing—no fertilizer—no dog droppings—not that they would explain this. He finally looked at himself. A dark oily streak ran up his jeans from his ankle to his thigh.

"Disgusting!" he exclaimed. The sight now in conjunction with the scent greatly unsettled the contents of his stomach.

After seeing the culprit on him, Daniela found the same on her own jeans. "Shit, shit, fuck," she rang out in frustration.

Both huffed some more before Roger sighted a clue to the vile ooze's origin partially circling the rims of their bike tires.

As Giselle made her relaxed finish, Roger tried waving her away. He yelled and pointed to the street but to no effect. She calmly maintained her pace like a soccer mom who was casually tracking her daily outing.

"What is it?" She halted before what appeared to be the aftermath of an attack of hornets.

"Look!" Daniela held her hands out like she wanted a hug. When Giselle just made out the lines of substance in the dimming light, she broke down laughing.

"What?! It smells worse than shit!"

Giselle got off the bike and let it crash as her fit evolved into deep belly laughs. She crouched into a fetal position with her face in her arms while Roger and Daniela only glared.

Between her bouts some words came. "I saw…it on the street…and just went around."

"What did she say?" Daniela asked Roger who just stood there dumbfounded.

Giselle tried again, "I saw it…and rode around."

"And what's so funny?" Daniela asked indignantly.

"You had…no idea…what…hit you," she shielded her tears with her arms, sputtering on.

"Where did you see it?" Roger asked.

"The truck."

"What?"

"Next to the truck."

Roger walked to the back screened-in porch to tell his parents what happened. Peter took out the garden hose and filled a couple of buckets with suds. He let his son use the scrub brush to go at the stain while Jenelle assisted in scrubbing at her daughter's.

Peter pulled the hose over to the bikes adjusting its nozzle to jet the water at the gunk on the tires.

"That's something awful," Clint said surveying the stain.

"Yeah, the association will have to inspect the sewage and drainage system."

"The bad news is that Giselle said it came from over near that Youhaul. If you ask me, too close for comfort."

As Peter continued spraying, he silently pondered, studying the tired, abused body of the rental that continued to blot the community's aesthetic. The news reports had railed on about the continuing investigation of the kidnapping of a local university student. Of course, just coming to remember that her boyfriend carried it out using a Youhaul truck didn't give any credence to it being related to this one in his neighborhood now. The fact that thousands of these trucks were being rented out daily was no grounds for suspicion, but it was a basis to fight against his own biases. And that's just what he was doing now—warring to overcome his base instincts.

"I'm going to take a look," he told Clint, absently.

They proceeded to the sparsely lit corner of his property—approaching the truck that looked even more beat up and forlorn than from the driveway. Peter paused to initiate the flashlight feature of his phone before potentially ruining his new white tennis shoes in the mysterious goop—prompting Clint to do the same.

Proceeding with caution, he spied the unremarkable cabin and the surrounding pavement while Clint rounded the truck in the other direction. The storm drain retained its contents with no back-up, as it hadn't rained for days—neither was there any indication of illegal drainage. On the other side of the truck, however, Clint smelled the ungodly spillage before spotting it—a thinning line running in accordance with the street's slight incline backwards to the curb.

"Found it!" Clint said from the back of the truck. "Source of the Nile."

When Peter came around, it didn't take long for him to do the same. The substance was leaking from the bottom crack of the door to the storage compartment.

"What in the hell could that be?" he asked Clint bewildered at the thought that someone could be moving the sludge around town or from God knows where—the plate indicating the vehicle at least originated from Pennsylvania.

"People are moving around everything with these now…" Clint snidely offered.

"Yeah," agreed Peter inattentively—too preoccupied with what to do next. With the padlocked door preventing his next obvious move to satisfy his newfound concern about the nature of the rental, the next would be to confer with his neighbors, hoping to come upon the user of the shit-wagon. Given the patent contravention of public health interests, however, there was only one course left for Peter to take.

The police arrived to the neighborhood promptly. Peter could only guess that with the details of the location, the type of truck in combination with the malodor coming from it, deemed the call high priority. The blue lights from three police cruisers played across the flower beds, bird baths, and artisanal stone-work of the otherwise serene properties of Preston Heights. The lights, in themselves, could have signified the presentment of any festive spectacle in the community—a party, fundraiser, or concert. But these only menaced the residents with long forgotten doubts and fears drawing them away from their ignorant comforts.

The first officers on the scene asked Peter the basic questions—the when and how of his discovery. They could see the what. It was coming out onto the street. While they didn't say anything in front of Peter and Clint, they gave each other chilling looks after examining the oil slick with seeming zoological origin. Other neighbors soon joined including Jack Shanwell and his wife. It was a wonder to the officers how no one had really inquired about the truck until then. They all simply assumed one of the neighbors had been making use of it despite no one having seen anyone in or around it since first appearing three days before.

As they waited for the officers to complete their investigation, more people came. *It was really turning into quite the block party*, Peter thought. Not that such things normally occurred in Preston Heights. The crowd even seemed to draw Roger and Daniela back to the source of their recent degradation. That was before Peter and Clint told them to return to the house.

"But, I want to see what's inside."

"Back to the house, Rog."

"I think I should know—"

"To the house."

"I'm the one who noticed it first!"

Peter kept his stern look to make it clear that in this case, he was adamant, and nothing was going to change his mind about it. Roger knew of these rare instances and that more pushing on his part would be frivolous. He dawdled—trying to catch another clue before he fully made it back to the steps with Daniela—each glimpse meeting another full face from Peter.

"How's it going?" Margery texted—keeping abreast of the situation while they waited for Daniela's jeans in the dryer.

"They haven't really said what they are going to do," Peter sent back.

"Tell Clint that Jenelle wants to leave as soon as the dryer is done."

But, looking to Clint, he knew that he wasn't prepared to go— not just yet. He wanted to know more, like the rest of the concerned citizenry—what was it that stained the curb—that threatened American families not far from their doorsteps.

The next set of police arrived on the scene. They chatted momentarily before popping the trunk to their cruiser. With a full view of their hardware, Peter comically entertained the idea of them blowing a hole through the Youhaul's door with a pump action shotgun. Instead, they handed out a two-foot long pair of bolt cutters to the Sergeant who he'd talked with earlier. This appeared to excite the gathering and they were more than willing to make the hole to the vehicle that the officers requested. But, after letting him through, one could sense their disappointment as the other officers forced them all back.

Peter was not content to be kept in the dark either. He had a right to know, as he called it in, and as a resident of the neighborhood, dammit, he had a right. The sergeant torqued and clipped at the padlock multiple times before another gloved officer casually removed it from its seat. With one officer illuminating the door, another unhooked the latch launching the door skyward. As they did this, Peter slipped passed the guarding officer, who was also more interested in the contents of the compartment than anything else. There was a screech and a wave of stink that assaulted Peter's nose full blast. There was nothing to do to quite prepare himself for what followed. No officer bothered to detain him as they all gaped at the trunks of bodies and fleshy accoutrements that littered the steel box. Peter saw toes, arms, intestines, with a mound of mammary glands that must have piled up next to the door. All of it taken in without judgement—pure stimulus upon confrontation of utter shock. What it was that brought it to an end—that tipping point—when neither Peter's nor the accompanying officer's stomachs could take anymore—was when that gelatinous conglomeration of parts and byproduct that had accumulated against the door avalanched into the street below—splatting like tossed out porridge. Peter drew back enough in time to avoid the brunt of it, but not enough to avoid bearing the shrapnel. The *fait accompli* was a general mass purging where even the strongest of stomachs gave way. If not during the first wave, it was after the partially-digested dinners added to the mix.

Straightening himself, through watery eyes, tangy regurgitated barbecue still tinging his tongue, he saw the aftermath. It was pandemonium. The crowd dispersed everywhere to enact that vital purge—trying to release them from acute infirmity. Even the experienced crime-scene officers, performed their bodily functions. There was no escaping this infection that laid dormant for so long. A certain innocence was lost as it broke those already fragile bonds they had once called community.

5

"Because she doesn't work here anymore," Marcus levelled with her.

"Oh," said Kristi standing before her boss' desk feeling a little stunned.

Yunnie and her had been close and she rather looked forward to their exchanges. When no agenda was set, around nine every morning, they would have their breakfast club of two, a *coffee and danish session*, as they called it, in the conference room. That hadn't happened for the last few days. She simply hadn't shown for work and didn't return any of her calls or texts. *So that explained it*, Kristi thought. At least, that was the simplest explanation. But, she was more than a little disappointed that her friend wouldn't have confided in her immediately after her firing. Instead, she imagined she was probably holing herself up in her apartment draining bottles of chilled white wine and shot gunning some series with the Devil as the protagonist. While she thought that Yunnie shared her emotions pretty openly, whether others felt uncomfortable or not, perhaps that's just how she was after being dealt such a blow—shutting down and taking some time off-grid.

Witnessing the sour look, Marcus had been waiting for Kristi's *why*. Instead, all that followed was quiet. That was the last thing he wanted. Give him some yelling. Sure. Give him some cursing. Okay. Even give him some pleading—yes pleading. But don't give him quiet. Anything else would do as it was the one thing he didn't know what to do with except to pre-empt a response. And while it didn't always work out, what followed this time, even surprised himself was what rolled off his tongue in all its buttery comfort.

"Sorry to spring it on you like this. It was nothing personal against Yunnie. She's a terrific woman with many admirable qualities… But, the stakeholders agreed that while the protest here did great, others across the country simply didn't meet their expectations."

"And how's that? The numbers were there. I don't ever remember thinking we'd have such a showing in…I mean…San Francisco had estimates of over fifty thousand! Who could've expected that?!"

Marcus paused after her expostulation. As in all things, he was going to control this conversation. That's what was needed of him now. He knew he had to silence her doubts. Doubts didn't breed good subjects—only good questioners.

"I'm sure I don't have to tell you after the meeting with Ray. Expectations are high—enormously high. But, the positive out of all of this is that we succeeded. You succeeded here. What was something largely seen only in the national spotlight has been buzzing internationally. BBC, Sky News, RT, Al Jazeera all about Senator Dembier's speech." He systematically placed a hand on each article as he said the outlet's names aloud—her eyes drifting from one headline to another. "You see? We are on the verge of real lasting change. We are—" He stopped himself. While what he said moved her, he saw that it wasn't enough to turn her mood. He stood and circled around the desk in a maneuver that he wielded thousands of times without fail.

"*Kristi*," he said delicately—embracing her around the shoulders. Some unchecked tears rolled down her cheeks quickly as if fleeing hopeless incarceration. They surprised her, but at the same time, affirmed how difficult it all had been. With pressures of politics, fundraising, and logistical quagmires along the way, it was all coming to a head. And through all the late sleepless nights, she had her friend Yunnie to keep her going—to keep the optimism and spirit of why she took this job in the first place—that someday, somehow she could create real positive change.

"You should've asked me first about Yunnie." She hugged back. "That was my call." She said it not so much as a form of argument but as of acceptance.

"I know. I know," he divulged to her ear gently. "But it couldn't be helped."

"I think I'm going to see her in the conference room, but she's not there."

Kristi fixated on Marcus' classical style painting near his desk of a woman walking solitary along a beach. She wasn't sure what to make of it. The face wasn't discernible among the drifts of sand.

He thought he played the role as a compassionate confidant quite well—a trace of a smile now imprinted his face. How important Yunnie was to her wasn't so clear before. Kristi wasn't profiled as the sentimentalist type, but such was life. One had to simply roll with the punches.

"Yes…I know how much she meant to you. But, now this is bigger than that. This is bigger than any one person. It's even bigger than us," he whispered airily.

"And I haven't heard anything from her. She's not even answering my calls…" Kristi continued inattentively—staring at the woman's flowing white dress in contrast to the orange hue of the late afternoon sand.

"It's okay. People come and go in this city. I've been here a long time, and that's what people do. I can't tell you why, but they come and then go."

Something in his reflection disturbed her reverie. She snapped back into herself as if from a strange dream that was hurtling into a nightmare. Just what was she doing here exactly? Why were they hugging? She needed to see her friend.

6

With the largely melted ice sloshing around, he drew on his glass of Wild Rooster yet again striving to wash away yesterday's events that were still lucid in his mind. The leftover McClellan's he had when he came home that night wasn't quite a potent enough numbing agent. That's when he selected the much higher proof elixir from the back of the cabinet. And now here he was, still in his pajama robe working on the bottle—consciousness coming then going.

The way things were going, Clint felt too ensnared in emotion to finish the work that he had already cut out for himself. The contents of his desk were even starting to develop noticeable dust and he stared at it all now powerlessly—so powerlessly. With the unfolding of recent events, his hands, those titan gauntlets that both wrought his dissertation and had held his two baby daughters like wrapped troll dolls, didn't want to cooperate. The only thing they wanted to do was to grab a bottle. It was either that or the neck of whoever it was that prevented his forward progress. And with them not being around, the bottle would just have to do.

At least, his wife's pesterings became less and less. She'd wake him sometimes in the middle of his naps before she left the house or to simply check in—asking him for more details, as last night's findings were then all over the news.

"Jenelle, I said that I told you. *Last night,* I told you." he asserted the third and final time.

"Everything? Did you tell me *everything?*"

Clint didn't say a word out of exasperation. Of course, the night prior he told his wife what transpired. The only details he managed to leave out as nonessentials were the exact contents of body parts and his accompanying dry heaves. Soon after that, as his wife already knew, the police shut down that area of road. Residents of Preston Heights would have to drive around, and according to Peter's texts, authorities proceeded to tent the area with a crew donning hazmat equipment under tall prospector lamps.

"If you told me everything, then why are you like this? Huh? *Hun?*" Clint sighed heavily sounding like either a hibernating bear or a man whose lungs were filled with gelatinous fluid.

"It's not about that," he partly lied.

"Then what is this about?"

Sighing again, he knew that he opened himself up to this question—one he didn't want to talk about. Nevertheless, he now had to give her a satisfactory answer—an answer that would at least buy him a few more hours alone.

"Much the same as last time. The constant fingering of our race. The whole ridiculousness of me trying to explain some of it to our friends…Will we ever hear the end of it? I'm so goddamn sick of it—"

"*Honey*," she halted any further utterance. "That's what this is about? I thought we talked about that. What is it to us, really? People are ignorant and nothing's ever going to change that including you sitting here wallowing away."

"I'm not wallowing." He wore his best reassuring grin.

"Whatever you want to call it. Either way, the drinking hasta stop."

"I know."

"Your daughters have been asking about you but know not to disturb you in here. Go and see them."

"I will. I'm just going to close my eyes a couple more hours."

"Well, go to bed then. I'm sure our bed is a lot better than that chair."

He slowly stood up in a haze of inebriation—following his wife out. It wasn't easy for a man like himself to do what he did. What he had told his wife was almost all true—not to mention the unfinished book. It's just that what he said about last night wasn't. The fact was that he had never seen anything so unspeakably vile in his life. The humans reduced to inhuman remains were treated worse than cattle feed. And to see them slop onto the street like that was causing his whole world to stall. It was as if he was at forty thousand feet and now it was all crashing down. First class ticket or not, he was crashing and his whole body was teeming with gloom and fear.

Or-anger.

1

The university's Artsy Satyr was a publication that courted controversy. As an independent student paper, it retained some staying power for its nearly twenty-year history. Over that time, it had published volumes of poems, stories, and essays from the university community that both drew a range of critiques from high praise to sheer vitriol. The former was garnered for pieces such as the essay "From an Anonymous Source" that criticized the overbearing response of the university administration for alcohol related offenses on campus. The piece was such a success that word of it even reached President Scott's desk culminating in a revision of policy. On the other hand, some later criticism had the opposite effect—reaching such a fever-pitch as to lead to calls for the administration to terminate its on-campus operations. One piece that came closest to such a result, entitled Fagasus, caused such an uproar that the campus' Christian community united, even the Catholic and evangelical groups banded together in an unlikely ecumenical capacity to draft an open letter to the community both urging action to have the paper immediately shut down and the poem stricken from its record. And while many students supported these calls with actions such as boycotts and holding protests to block the entrance to their offices, the paper and its record of submissions remained intact. And to most, this was not at all a surprising result. The administration was rather consistent on these matters. SFLU was a public university after all, and that meant being a space that allowed for the exercise of one's First Amendment rights. Thus, short of there being anything illegal, namely, viable threats and libel, the administration tried to distance itself from these issues as much as possible. To do otherwise, would be an unwise impediment to basic democracy, at least, according to legal scholars at the time. "And without this provision, just how could we be discussing this issue at an institution of free inquiry," one administrator carefully elaborated to local media at the time. The principle of it all was nearly unanimous among academia—unanimous as well as resolute. Just what was resolute about it? It was firmly held until something changed without notice. That something happened from an unusual and, as many now admit, unlikely entry finding its way into the monthly page that followed Knowledge over Hate. Attention to it, however, only came weeks later, when it appeared that some zeal for the movement was dying away. The mysterious nature of the work including its merits, as it appeared pretty dry and hum-drum, was what really had the community talking. Over a week's span, word spread such that the Artsy Satyr's site drew a record million viewers in traffic. Just what were the student-body supposed to make of it exactly? What form was it even in? Was it an essay? Was it a poem? And what was its purpose? Was it serious? Was it parody? To whom or for whom was it written? Was there a hidden meaning? Everywhere people were weighing in on the mystery piece whether it was in classes, cafes, or message boards, an opinion about it was heard. The controversy reached such a fever pitch that the author's contact info was requested by local media so they could clarify what it was really about. Someone just had to be answerable to the community's offense. They had to be held accountable for the words as well as the anger. But as the paper admitted, the author's stated name was merely a pseudonym. Its creator wanted the passage simply to be taken as is. And that is as follows.

What is racist?
By Joshua Rhodes, Senior, College of Engineering, SFLU

It is the belief that racial differences imply the superiority of one race over another.
It is the belief that one race should dominate over others.
It is the oppression of a racial identity whether it be social, economic, or political.
It is any system legitimating a society filled with racial inequity.
It is any system underpinning such a society.
It is any treatment of individuals of a given race that results in disadvantage.
It is the use of any racial slur in order to belittle, malign, or show contempt for a person or people in reference to their race.

It is the use of any racial slur with the deceptive intent to belittle, malign, or show contempt for a person or people in reference to their race.
It is the use of any racial slur.
It is speech that consciously and intentionally makes use of racial stereotypes.
It is speech that consciously but unintentionally does so.
It unconsciously but intentionally does so.
Any articulation that both unconsciously and unintentionally makes reference to a racial stereotype or any racial implication of inferiority.
It is any speech or act that, whether consciously or unconsciously, intentionally or unintentionally, explicates or implicates the differences between races, positively or negatively.
It is the belief and or articulation that one is not racist due to *de facto* positive relations with person(s) of another race.
It is the covert belief that one is not racist despite racist or racialist tendencies.
It is the covert belief that one is not racist without perceiving one's racist or racialist tendencies.
It is, despite not perceiving one's own racist or racialist beliefs, thoughts, or tendencies, not to openly confessing to them thereof.
It is the express denial of seeing any differences in race.
It is the internal or external denial of witnessing racism in people, places, ideas, animals, or objects.
It is disagreement with a given political system, person, party, movement, or ideology that purports to stand in strident opposition to racism.
It is inequality.
It is someone genetically determined.
And what is not racist? They are those dutiful commissions outside the wrongful acts and illicitly born persons that, notwithstanding other probable decisive conditions, are precluded from the above.

Many critics couldn't exactly disagree with the specifics of the piece despite ardently accusing the author of harboring veiled racism. The paper itself was called out, at least, as an enabler if not the very center of racist propaganda on campus. What was truly adventitious about the whole episode, however, was that the paper had virtually no defenders at all. The Campus Conservative even agreed with those on the left—blasting it as racist albeit for a different reason. It stated that the piece was "part and parcel of the whole racist platform concerning itself with redefining concepts—instituting meanings that wrested yet more control from the public." Community leaders agreed with the same conclusion, so what did the details really matter? Something from the administration had to be done.

President Scott didn't venture a defense. He issued a letter assuring the community that proper measures were being taken to see if the Artsy Satyr committed any violation of the university's Code of Conduct. It was enough to spur the protesting forces back to life as their presence immediately perked up on campus. They appeared to amass outside the main administration building of Peckhart Hall—a castle like structure at zero degrees of the park that is featured along with many university logos as a symbol of institutional prestige and posterity.

Its chants grew over the course of the afternoon piercing into some of the classrooms and lecture halls that surrounded it, sometimes drawing praise and other times the ire of those ill-informed.

2

"God, the fuck is it this time?" Johnny asked Yash as they cut through one of the dining halls that abutted Peckhart.

They both scanned the crowd of protestors who impeded their way—partially chanting with a young man in a black hood on a megaphone. He was short and skimpy enough who, if not for the studded face and confident soundings, one might think a minor. The cadence "What are we here for?!" "Down with the racist cour-i-er!" was being repeated ad nauseum and whenever it appeared that the chant's fervor was dying out, the boy's voice carried louder to stimulate the like response.

Yash formed a conjecture after picking up on something in the crowd that hinted at the nature of the matter. "Something about a racist article?" he offered—noticing Johnny's embittered scowl. He appeared fixated on one section of the crowd. Next to the sign "Justice for Deborah" was one that simply read "Genetic Testing Now."

He started slowly, quietly until his voice crescendoed. "What in the actual fuck?!"

3

His haw reverberated down the long corridor of Blanchard. "I love it," he expressed eyes watering. After the recent atrocities, he thought he needed a good laugh. "You may only know Him by what He is not."

Professor Garretty looked at Clint with inquiring eyes.

"Why, it's absolute nonsense of course," he clarified.

Garretty maintained his expression of bafflement. "Thomas Aquinas," he answered, as if that settled it.

"This student *has* some wit, engineering himself quite an amusing tract. I'll give him that."

He could feel his spirits lifted even after only a few days following the horrible scene in Preston Heights. He and Peter hadn't seen each other since then as if doing so would only remind them of the horror they experienced.

Of course, the papers covered it which drew national attention, but Clint didn't read any of them. He wanted to soon forget, and hearing about this new development unfold on campus appeared a good diversion from the run-time inducing error he saw last Saturday.

This afternoon, he brought the question to Garretty, who he ran into on the way back from Dorfman Hall after lecturing his undergraduate Abnormal Psychology course. Now, on his MWF schedule, he often paused before the scaffolded repair on Heinrich due to the most recent enthusiastic work of protestors. Giving a cursory inspection of the damage with his tongue working on a starlight peppermint candy, he cough-laughed at the irony in overhearing the new protest only a few hundred yards away. When he was satisfied, he turned suddenly—startled to see his colleague patiently waiting nearby.

"Tom!" he quickly recovered.

"Sorry to have gotten you unawares," he said with a grin.

"Believe me, you didn't get me anything," putting on his own.

The renewed campus presence came up in their chat on the way back to Blanchard. Garretty did his best to explain to Clint its significance.

After reentering their offices, he even brought over an article that still had the blasphemous work embedded in its body. It was the newfound source of Clint's mirth.

Garretty stood nonplussed while, at his desk, Clint read on. His feelings about the protest and its cause were unequivocal, but he wanted to wait and gauge his friend's reaction sufficiently before a trickle became a gush. Finally, Clint forced the issue.

"You look like someone walked over your grave. Everything alright, Tom?"

"Maybe…but…uh am I the only one who finds the work just about as boring as hell?" Clint noticed a certain beleaguered strain written across his face.

He played his friend's reaction off with a sense of levity coughing out a few more laughs. *Besides, what did some angry people on campus really amount to in the end? What were a few smashed windows? What was it all in the face of bodies being poured out onto concrete?*

"I think that's part of the point, Tom."

Garretty proceeded to give Clint what appeared to be a thousand-yard stare. It nearly wiped the remaining smile from Clint's face upon seeing his true reflection. But, before it slipped completely, he held it—appearing as one of those smiles worn on faces of those supposed to be about as happy as a surprise birthday party for a senior with Huntington's.

"These buffoons," Garretty finally grumbled looking away. "They're making a mockery of an important democratic tool— making it all dull—so dull." He was speaking as if in a daze. Clint wondered if it was a sort of safety mechanism that allowed him to enter an altered state to quiet his anger.

"Worker's rights, Vietnam, Wall Street bailouts…and then this piece of flimflam…So let's tear down the whole fucking university already."

"My friend, why don't you tell me how you *really* feel?" He tried a last-ditch effort to lighten the mood.

"Perhaps that's the only way," he ignored. "The way to make them stop…Multiply the offenses. Make it so boring no one will listen. Make them so ridiculous—so silly that no one wants to be around them anymore."

"I don't know about that," Clint thought aloud. "What if that's what they want? More aggravation. More stimulation. What gets certain people more attention than that in an age where nobody has time for anything?"

Seeing Garrety's sudden lapse into an uncanny placidity, Clint thought he may have finally struck a chord. He continued, "No. The only evil considered to be out there anymore doesn't seem to be what is ugly or cruel or disgusting, faux-art and what not. It's whatever's leftover. Those matters that remain entirely…unremarkable."

He surprised himself at where his mind wandered to. This time his lips paused before his train of thought reached its terminus. His mind began working out its implications before he decided to share it after the extended silence that followed.

"It's whatever leads to no engagement—no comment or opinion…and I think that's what this is coming down to. If no one is listening, you got to be loud. You got to be in their face. The more absurd, the more ridiculous, the more commentary. And that's a good thing, right?"

When Garretty left, he sat almost completely still at his desk. Without his realizing, his breathing became irregular. His pulse shot up. The South Florida Monitor's headline was the first to materialize. It read, "Six Butchered Bodies and Counting." He tried to stay away, but he just couldn't anymore. Rational sense had to be made. More details were necessary even if those details had to additionally haunt him. Clicking the article, he slowly began reading—weighing every word as if possessing some strange masochistic desire.

4

Kristi rapped on the door for the second time. She did so with more gusto than the first. It didn't seem necessary. Yunnie's apartment was only a seven hundred square foot one bedroom.

Kristi had visited countless times since they became friends. She remembered her frequent rendezvous after work coming to

Arlington and having a glass of wine or two before going out, or, just as equally satisfying, staying in and watching what they had come to know as their *cocomfort* movies (enjoyed with hot cocoa on occasion but mostly alcohol). Laying on Yunnie's sofa with a blanket, every so often sitting up to sip a chilled glass of golden chardonnay—a perfect setup after a long stressful week of organizing.

And the last movie they saw…Under the Tuscan Sun—a form of therapy. The hope of seeing a single woman striking out on her own and still achieving something that approximated success made any baggage from the week easily forgotten, at least, until Monday. This type of film always brought tears to their eyes.

"Are you sure you don't want the sofa?" She had asked guiltily wrapped up in the warm blanket.

"No, I'm fine. The love seat is very comfy for me." She remembered Yunnie sounding so sweetly innocent at the time. Still, she wasn't convinced. That was something about Yunnie. She would always put others before herself.

No one answered. The hallway was quiet and neither her friend nor anyone else was moving around as the one o'clock hour ticked by. *Was she out? Did she leave town?* It was quite possible, but she decided to give it another go for good measure. The third rattled home. It sounded different than before. She thought that it almost sounded as an alarm. It wasn't only a knock but the sound of a worry. And the sound was true.

She lingered by the door debating with herself if the use of Kristi's spare key was justified in this case or not. That morning, she remembered taking it with her as if it were only an afterthought. Of course, she couldn't really use it without Yunnie telling her to, but she took it anyway. Besides, if Yunnie found out that she entered her apartment without permission, wouldn't she be angry? Kristi wouldn't be upset if Yunnie used the spare she gave her. But, then again, everyone was different, and a friend giving it to you didn't all of a sudden waive their right to privacy. Did it?

Kristi walked a couple of doors down, stopped and reconsidered. She pressed her fingers against the ringless copper that she took from her purse. *And so what? What if she were mad? Be mad.* Kristi was already mad. And someone she thought was a friend, could've at least told her that she would disappear like this. *Who even does that?*

She thought it over some more. Come to think of it, Kristi knew a lot of people like that. They were everywhere these days. But not Yunnie. If there was anything she learned about her friend, she wasn't one of them. She knew this. Her anger wasn't really at Yunnie at all. What it was that really incensed her now was that her friend was gone. She needed her and couldn't do a fucking thing about it. Even as the boss, what did she do? Nothing. *What kind of fucking friend was she?* She was really hating herself right now.

That will change. Be okay and that will change. I promise you, Yunnie. I'll go in there tomorrow and demand Marcus that we keep you on. If they don't let you stay, I'll leave. I don't care anymore. I'll leave. Please be okay. The more she thought about it, the more she thought that she wasn't.

The bolt clunked back into the door with ease as she shifted it open. No one seemed home. The lights were out. The empty wine bottles on the coffee table that she expected, weren't there. Everything appeared to be clean and in its place, just in line with her friend's normal *modus vivendi*. There was no aftermath of a crisis here.

As she made her rounds into her bedroom, her closet, her bathroom, peering into the fridge, everything was just where it should be. Kristi felt herself a ghost witnessing all these details— floating from room to room, but almost unreflectively—like it was a dream.

She pulled out her phone and opened her texts with Yunnie. She scrolled over her messages again—many now unanswered. The last she received from her was the night of the rally. She said she youbered home a little drunk, and sorry that she didn't say goodbye. It was all typical Yunnie—even laughing about it. Only she didn't know that this goodbye could really be that. Like, sorry, never see you again.

She repeated her hauntings numerous times more before finally sitting on the sofa where she often sat—where her friend often gave way to her own comfort. She eyed the large flat screen against the wall now off—blank, empty. That was the way she stayed.

5

The jingle of the ice in Peter's glass slightly stirred as he brought it up to his lips staring out at the command tent that now sat where he had seen the remains of all those bodies—dismembered women. At least that was what he remembered seeing parts of—the parts he could distinguish. The news stories had managed to leave that part out so far—except to speculate on one of its contents being that of Deborah Haugh. He was surprised that they hadn't yet confirmed or disconfirmed that yet. *Perhaps they did already know but were still holding out details a little longer to build a better case.* God, he hoped it was true. Sometimes all one needed was an explanation, a place holder, no matter how ugly. For some reason, Peter was the type that it took some of the edge off.

The overfilled glass spilt on his shirt as he lost concentration of what he was doing. His hand let go of the blinds, as he assumed a better balance. This time his sip was more steady as he sought to empty his glass to a more manageable level.

"Shit," he said to himself seeing not an insubstantial amount of whiskey on the floor. *God, I'm turning into a sloppy drunk,* he thought. *Was there any other kind? Margery won't be able to take it.*

He went back into the kitchen with stomach gurgling. It wasn't from hunger. That was clear, and his recent diet didn't help, mostly consisting of straight whiskies and highballs, but it was still sitting better than solid food. Ever since the night of the community's human soup potluck, almost nothing stayed down well. And the tent out front was a testament to his recent dyspepsia.

Peter doused a couple of paper towels in water adding a dash of soap to one. He went at the spill with the two-punch method with alacrity hoping that Margery wouldn't come upon his mess. While in the course of their marriage, this would be rather a small matter, but with all the recent going-ons, anything small was becoming monstrous.

The night of the neighborhood spill, he told Margery all that happened as there was no use trying to hide it. She could read it all over his face. When he told her the pertinent facts, she cracked. It wasn't like her, but she did. The tears started slowly enough, but by the end, they had formed two great rivers down her cheeks. The weight of it all was finally too much. The calls, the vandalism, the effects of the on-campus drama, and now a sheer obscenity laid right before their eyes in their own neighborhood. It was like some twisted gift—the dead thing a cat brings to one's doorstep. That last part was what worried him most. If it was that serial killer descending upon their town with a rage against women, it would surely be a tragedy—one that has occurred in other university towns in the past. Awful, yes, a surprise, no. *But, what was this? With all that was happening to the country, university, family, was it all just a strange coincidence?* He threw the paper towels away and drew down the last few fingers of his drink. That night was when they decided. It was time for Margery and Roger to leave Palm Gate. She would stay with her parents in Washington and would have Roger finish out the remainder of the year at school there. Peter would come out in the summer, and they would wait for things to calm down in their once cozy little town. At the end of the week, they would drive the four days to Tacoma. A frog formed in Peter's throat at the thought of seeing them leave.

Placing his glass down on the kitchen counter, he could hear Margery upstairs knocking about in their room—prepacking for the ride north, as they discussed. Roger was in his room reading some Terry Brooks novel. And here he was thinking about having another drink, but the stickiness of his hands from the spill nettled him. He ran them under the warm water of the sink.

6

Even with the cloud cover's distortion, the sun would have its day. The garbled morning light, seeking structure and definition, had found it once again.

The park's earthy smell that brought the anticipation and excitement of summer plans for many an undergraduate pervaded the surrounding buildings of central campus. It was a sign that final exams would soon appear and be over and the four or so years would culminate into all the rights and privileges earned at its completion. It was the sign of new beginnings—the sign of a future.

This day, however, had other signs as well. The signs of anger, malcontent, and disgust. The righteous sort of signs shown on the faces of students and faculty alike who stood behind Peckhart beholding the great anathema spray painted along the curved stone bench that surrounded a memorial statue, as the old university codger peered indifferently beyond.

Clint joined the others observing the red letters splayed playfully on the scene of yesterday's protest. Amidst the open venting and taking of photos to be shared with the world, Clint quietly ruminated over it. The hastily scrawled word, while not technically a slur, its intent was another matter.

"Disgusting." Peter had caught up to where his friend stood.

"You could call it that."

"*Well*," Peter sounded with a shade of irritation, "what else would you call it then?"

After taking a moment, Clint was decided. "I'm going."

Peter followed Clint in the direction of Blanchard listening to him make the call to university services about the graffiti. His voice was clear and calm, and at the same time, stressing the urgency of having the word removed, or at least, covered for now.

"Just in case," he explained after hanging up. Peter understood him—*just in case* any more damage could be avoided. But they both knew that the brunt of it had already been done.

"What did they say? They give a time?"

"Already know about it. No time."

They walked on to themselves. Peter was hunting for the right words, but they weren't coming. This was going to be awkward no matter what, but something had to be said, so he settled on some.

"I'm sorry you had to see that. It's heinous and shocking. I can say I never thought that kind of thing would happen at a university anymore…especially here."

"It doesn't surprise me given what we are in now."

"Racism like that doesn't surprise you? I'm beginning to think…Maybe I shouldn't have done anything. Maybe I should've just let all the academic drivel go. Ya'know? Just let them lie. Let this incident snuff itself out. Who knows?"

"What're you saying?"

"I just don't want to be responsible for even partly sparking back to life some actual racists."

Clint snorted at this—not quite believing the direction his friend was taking. "You didn't. And *nigglers* is not a racist word. Some of the campus community just had enough."

"*Not racist*? You know what it is that they're trying to do."

"Sure. Get attention. Lash out."

"People are not going to interpret it that way—the world isn't."

"Right. It's giving the activists more of what they want."

"And they're going to blame me," he huffed as they continued back at a brisk pace.

"*Pete.*" Clint looked over to make a quick study of his face. "Everything alright?"

The question struck Peter off guard. He paused before answering. Not wanting this to be a pity-party, he proceeded with caution. "Yeah…even with… as you know… Margery and Rog starting to Tacoma Saturday…while I wouldn't call that bad…it's not ideal. But, hey, we're healthy. Money's okay. We've got extended family. We have options…"

Clint took time to have Peter process what he had just revealed. Every second that passed made him feel ever more uncomfortable with his wavering—now not knowing how to save face.

Finally, Clint broke in, "Naturally, it's bothering you, and as it should, because what you're saying doesn't sound like you at all."

"It's not—"

"But now saying that having stuck your neck out for academic integrity and it's somehow your fault that some idiot sprayed graffiti? I mean, come on."

Peter could have continued his initial protest but instead stared out into the distance. Traffic now building along the walkways and lawns, the campus just wasn't very familiar to him anymore. How fast it had grown. The once grassy patchwork was being converted into new halls ever faster with their matching layers of brick like setting in a new 3D jigsaw piece. Only this puzzle, while it had a beginning, it would never be complete—its expansion virtually endless. Even after years of his tenure, Peter saw it as almost unrecognizable—almost a formless mass with no center anymore. Was that what he was a part of now?

"Maybe you're right in a way," he breathed out in resignation. "I have no fear putting myself out there for my beliefs—including what people start associating with me. But that doesn't mean I'm not afraid anymore for my family. If I do something that harms them even in a roundabout way—even in sharing my last name…I've realized I'm not so willing to do even that." The words rolled off his tongue, he knew, sounding like hogwash—just something trite that anyone says such as how *I have no regrets* or *I don't hold them any ill-will* but he, at least this time, sincerely meant them.

"Our families certainly won't be safe if we let them have their way. So, yes, *you are* looking out for your family, and you know that there's nothing you are going to be able to do about these agitators…If the inquisition here already doesn't like you—it doesn't really matter—they'll take the thinnest and most improbable of associations and try to make them stick."

"Yeah," Peter said preoccupied, "I know."

"But look." Clint halted before Blanchard. "I am sorry about Margery and Roger having to leave, but under the circumstances, I understand why. Right now is…with what happened last week…that was enough to even get me thinking of taking an extended sabbatical next year." He forced a chuckle at this last part.

Peter listened stoically—surveying the long gothic façade before them.

"But, remember, all this is just temporary… summer is about here anyhow… and in the meantime, whenever you want, you know you can stay with us. We have the spare room…and some of Jenelle's home cooking." He smiled at the last prospect giving Peter's shoulder a squeeze of reassurance.

"Thanks," Peter said. A disquiet of his stomach had steadily grown worse. He felt that it could have been the bagel he munched on his way out the door. That wasn't it. His mouth now dry, everything was telling him that things weren't well.

Their footsteps disturbed the mausoleum like lobby of Blanchard with the walls dishing the sound back. Taking the old staircase, sweat exuded from under Peter's arms and forehead. When they reached the second floor he wiped it with his sleeve slowly catching his breath as they made their way along the corridor. It was as empty as usual for this time of the morning. Many of the professors headed straight to class and students didn't come to office hours until much later. All that Peter wanted to do was put on a pot of coffee—not that his stomach needed it—and reset in the twenty or so minutes before he had to make his way to class. Before reaching his door, however, an apparent apparition—a tall man in a blue blazer came out into the corridor from the psych department's main offices. It was so suddenly that it startled him. If

Clint was phased, he couldn't tell. Registering Eldridge's face softened the initial shock but only a little. It looked gaunt, sleepless, older. His baggy eyes were securely fixed on the staircase down.

Peter and Clint both did a double take as if confirming that they'd both witnessed the same thing. Of course, that wasn't all it said. It said, "What the fuck?" It said, "What's next?"

7

"Now how did it strike you?" Levy asked Eggers whose attention was momentarily taken by the painting of the solitary beach goer.

He put on a smirk as a show of amusement. He was not amused.

"Interesting question. Let me ask you just how it was supposed to *strike me*?"

He returned to that same confident smile that met him at the entrance to conduct the interview. "Most are surprised to say the least—if not appalled by the results."

"Why was the study done?"

"You first. Really, I'd like to know—"

"As a journalist? Personally? What?"

"*Any* or all of the above." Marcus reached for his bottle of water on his desk to lubricate what sounded like a virus-infected throat. His dark bushy eyebrows betrayed any sense of discomfort, however, with their cocksure exclamation.

Eggers had left his bottle on the desk unopened. Even with the constant barrage of personalities that he was accustomed to running into due to the nature of his job, Levy still fell outside of this range. He was not at ease with this man and that was saying a lot given the totality of hot-take interviews of all manner of celebrities, politicians, and criminals. At one point he even entertained a party with the muse that he would perhaps still feel comfortable in his own skin interviewing an Ed Gein. Sure, Ed Gein, he had no problem questioning since whatever lay hidden, much could be revealed. But here he doubted he was going to get much of anything out of Levy. There was just something about a true pro-bullshitter in their face. He doubted Levy believed anything of what came out of his own mouth. It was just an exercise—a procedure—one that he didn't want to waste his time with. He felt there was only one card to play—the top bower.

"To tell the truth… what struck me is that Ray Foundation has its hand in bankrolling this type of research. Research whose results could cement the importance of its ongoing mission of addressing racial injustice."

"*Bankrolling*?" Levy maintained the same smile with a hint of mockery. "We were cited as one of the organizations funding the study, as you read. So does it look like we are trying to hide something?" he chuckled and paused for a response. "There is no conspiracy. The study was done, and we didn't have any prior knowledge of the results—knowing they'd be released no matter what."

"So, you had *no idea*?"

"Well, *no* idea? Others already had a feasible theory that there may be a genetic component to the question of why racism is ingrained in our society. That is exactly what we thought merited further exploration."

Eggers check marked a bullet point on his yellow legal pad before meticulously recording Levy's answer.

"Isn't it disingenuous to have an organization that seeks to establish what it already presumes to be true? Isn't it like proposing a cure for a disease whose existence is still in question?

"Mr. Eggers, I'm not liking this form of Q&A."

I guess that just makes it unpleasant for the both of us then, Eggers thought.

"You deny that racism is a disease in our society? Racism denialism is simply a non-starter. We all know that the disease already exists. The only question is who's part of the infection and who part of the cure?"

Eggers paused. He already had a follow-up question in mind.

"Come on now. How's about you write my response on your pad there?"

"I am." He proceeded with his pen dutifully—not at all bothered by the barb.

"Let me ask it this way," he began again. "The study itself, the way it was set-up, that was dubious at best, wasn't it?"

"*What do you mean?*" Levy made a playful confounded frown that ended as a question.

"You may already be aware of the many problems in methodology that Eldridge's colleague, Professor Barton, pointed out in our last interview…"

"Look, neither you nor I are qualified scientists prepared enough to have this discussion really—"

"That doesn't mean—"

"So I'm not going to pretend to have the extensive training and background knowledge to be able to address Barton's claims…"

But, of course, you want to address them anyhow, Eggers anticipated.

"But I'll just say this. Professor Eldridge and Jersey are coming with more than *twenty* years of experience from multiple disciplines and now with a slew of award-winning academics praising their work—"

"*Others* are not." Eggers curtly inserted jotting down Levy's response.

"I know a lengthy list of pre-eminent scientists who are already convinced by the study's claims if you'd like to see it. I can bring it up," Levy said reaching for his computer's mouse.

Eggers followed by reading from his pad. "Are you familiar with *Devon Genetics Research Lab* at UCLA?"

"No," Levy replied still intent on bringing up the document.

"Michael Gillespie, Chief of Research, claims that Chromagen is like finding *animals in the clouds.*"

"Is that right?"

"He is not convinced it amounts to much of anything. In fact, saying that…" he read from his notepad emphatically and incisively. "*They indeed make the presumption that the genetic profile must necessarily include the profiles of only, what are considered, Caucasian people, but looking at the sequencing, I find that highly dubious and would expect it to include multiple races, even those considered to be African American.*"

This time Eggers could see the effect in Levy's expression. He gave up on showing the list. There was a ripple in his steel façade.

"Like I said, you and I are not scientifically qualified to say anything. *Therefore*, I can't speak of the merits of what this or that scientist says. Nevertheless, I do know that Eldridge and Jersey have thought through their research very carefully and have an answer to these concerns. Some may disagree, but many other scientists do accept their methodology as straightforward and honest." *But we both know you aren't* was the look that Eggers directed at Levy.

"*Mr. Eggers*, like I said, there simply is *no* conspiracy here." Levy's grin again blazed with that supreme confidence and sincerity of conviction that must've engendered some kind of positive reinforcement in the past. "Now the time is ripe to let the authorities in the field to sort these questions out and accept their much-needed expertise."

Eggers let the tension of the conversation ease as he penned the response. It occurred to him that he was largely just going through the motions now. The rest of his questions were merely dotting i's and crossing t's. But, he was hungry—having already seen a chink in the armor, he wanted more.

"Since… I know that you declined the option to record this interview, have you—"

"Sure—*sure!*" Levy immediately cut-in as if he knew exactly what Eggers' question was going to be. "But first, allow me to establish something for the record."

Eggers waited for him to continue, but when he didn't, he almost dared him. "Yes?"

"Why are you so one-sided on the results of this study? *Really*, what is it about it that bothers you? Is there any point where you would begin to ask a difficult question to the skeptics on the other side? Could it be that you're too afraid? And why would that be?"

This time it was Eggers' turn to smile. The bait was laid out for him, and he knew what Levy wanted to imply by the question. It was a label that could, in effect, dismiss all prior rational inquiry. It could all be supplanted by a simple and scurrilous header—all too frequently utilized, yet still effective.

"Because you don't get to do that."

"Do what? Ask questions?" he said with a smirk of presumed triumph.

"I mean to scare up an everlasting choir based on a false premise."

"Scare up… wha—?"

"Don't you see how people of other races see this? How they'll constantly be getting a fever without an infection?"

"*What?*" Levy's boyishly puzzled face appeared surprisingly genuine.

"In other words, could it ever not be racism when everyone is wondering whether another person's genes makes them a nazi?"

The follow-up failed to clear Levy's face of confusion. It was at this point, Eggers wasn't sure if he should try to press on. Should he let his question linger or take another crack at breaking the program? He chose the latter.

"How is this not going to look like just another discussion about the viability of eugenics?"

Something registered on Levy's face. The look that remained—a pursing of the lips—appeared bitter—a flash of contempt.

"Does it really matter…?" His mouth almost imperceptibly formed that faux-confident grin. "If that's just the way the cookie crumbles?"

"But, that's just what you're assuming." He was hating this man—not sure why he even responded except as perhaps a natural reaction, as a journalist is wont to do.

"Just leave it to the experts." Eggers couldn't help a chuckle while Levy took another sip of water.

8

Death. It would be sweet. This had entered her mind again and again— not so much as a thought but as an instinct—a basic need. Hanging there didn't provide a good opportunity for thought. It was just existing in hell. And in this hell, it wasn't an auspicious time for repentance.

Her wrists were bound from a high ceiling in a cavern that reeked of a charnel house. The putridity of which she only added to with her own vomit and other bodily substances she's contributed since the day of her arrival.

Images of the past days flashed through her mind as confused glimpses in a feverish dream—a swirling motley of chaos. *Were they real? Did it matter anymore?* They were nothing to the flaccid suspended mass.

It was the pain that mattered. Sheer pain streaked through torn muscle and ligaments. Shoulders both pulled out of her tiny frame. The rawness of the flesh on her back contained the spikes of a metal flail still embedded—left hanging as an ornament of despair. The once smooth back now appeared in different hews of red—a detailed topographic map with the one solitary torch below illuminating its gruesome history.

Yunnie, at some point, accepted her fate. But it took a series of choices that would bring her to ruin—not all of which were hers.

She had lain comfortably across her sofa not far from where her friend sat days later. It had been a long night following their victory coverage of Knowledge over Hate and word from the others across the country. They met at Rafferty's Bar to celebrate. Kristi, Levy, and the other office crew were in high spirits. There was a champagne toast followed by shots. Two were shots of Patron. And the third was the final one. Bacardi 151, she remembered. *If that's the case, why am I still awake? I'd be sleeping by now.* She peered around dazed. Things didn't quite add up. What happened with that third shot? She was sitting at the bar chatting with Levy feeling buzzed. Levy said something that she didn't like when the tray came back around. Levy offered her a drink from it, and she took it. She hadn't remembered it at first. *Oh, fuck.*

It was on the way to the restroom that she began to hold onto the wall—trying to keep herself up—but couldn't. She stood and then squatted down repeatedly. Her legs were too weak to keep going. She didn't know what was happening. Was she that drunk? Some strange medical ailment? The easiest explanation didn't occur to her at the time. A comforting arm came from behind. It helped her and she let it. It wasn't just that she had no other choice. She needed that arm—desired it. Everything was blurry. It guided her to the back. She remembered walking out onto the street then stepping up into a vehicle. Then as soon as her body hit the comfortable seat, she fell over and passed out. That was where she was now. Asleep.

Groggily she came to with a fright—awaking into a nightmare. She was riding in the back of an SUV with her arms bound behind her. A Velcro like strap snugly grated the skin around her neck. A pill boxed size apparatus over her throat and chest. She wanted to get the uncomfortable device off of her right away, but her wrists wouldn't budge. Indeed, they hurt from how tight they were wrapped together with something hard like a cable.

A stranger sat next to her. The whites of his teeth splayed in a monstrous grin in the still darkness of dawn—only the ambient sound of the car bumping down a rural road played to their viperous dance. She whimpered in fear but tried to compose herself. The eyes of the man menaced her with a vulgarly high look. "Hi sweety," it voiced foreignly without perceptible movement of his mouth. She saw the light from his camera phone pointed at her.

"What're you doing?" She said weakly. It seemed a rather inane question but it was what she really wanted to know—voicing her thoughts aloud without filter.

"She speaks?" The voice narrated ignoring her question. The phone still hovering before her face. It was more than just the flashlight function, she knew. She was being recorded. The phone pivoting ever so slightly to catch the details of her position. *So this was an abduction? Would her parents have to put up their savings to have her returned?*

"Who are you?" her voice reverberated through the cabin. The side of the driver could be seen in the darkness but made no reaction. Neither did the man with the phone pointed at her.

The pain was biting in her wrists and her fingertips had a slight tingling as the blood flow to them wasn't at all optimum. She tried aligning them to make for the least amount of resistance, but it was still far from pleasant.

"Listen. Could you please just adjust this…on my wrist? I don't care what you want…I'm losing feeling in my hands." Her plea again rang out to seemingly deaf ears. The man continued his recording as if what she said was as meaningless as a dog barking at a mailman. *What the hell? The man didn't appear to be narrating anything anymore. There was a meticulous documentation to what he did. What was the point of any of this?* With the feeling of being trapped and no abatement in sight, she had no recourse. Her panic mode set-in.

"Get this off my fucking wrists! Pleassse!" She squirmed and twisted her wrists violently despite the pain, in a desperate effort for relief with a thought that they could loosen. They didn't. Her fellow passenger only pulled back a little, still with phone aimed. "Do you fucking hear me!!! I'll do what you want, just—!" She tried standing even though her ankles were also bound. She tried kicking the restraint off but her body collapsed back onto the seat, frozen with pain. It shot especially through her neck, wrists, and ankles. Her chest burned from the electricity coming from the device. Her whole body went rigid—muscles all tense. Time stood still until it stopped. She wasn't quite sure how long she had been zapped but she really hoped she would die in the middle of it—that her heart would just give out. Sadly, it didn't, and it was still ticking as it would hanging from the cavern. Holding the remote in the other hand, her captor then warned her but not directly.

"This beech should really know better what happens if she misbehaves," he chuckled into the phone." A tinny metal sounding scratched from its speaker.

There was no escape. She complied knowing it could all be worse. And the man broke her countlessly more times. The thought of any kind of living relief was lost—now in her suspended state. The hope that some merciful hand could still free her— release her from her suspension—to let her touch the earth once again was also lost. Her feet were already separated from her. It happened hours prior. An oxyacetylene torch did the job easier than a knife cutting through hot butter. It was almost too easy— anti-climactic; it was as mundane as two overly ripe avocados falling from a tree onto cement. Her feet now just sat there beneath her corpse lifelessly glimmering in the dim light of the torch with two flickering orange orbs nearby.

9

The fifty-eight-year-old gaunt white man in gray suit stood at the podium ready for the latest parley with the community and nation in only a relatively short period of time. He could feel his blood pressure up—something that his doctor recently upped his dose of Lisinopril to get under control. It didn't bother him too much right now, however. It was all necessary. In fact, the attention is exactly what he craved; it tended to bring his worsening bones to life. His dream of a late political run wasn't all dead. Now if he could only handle the helm of the ship in the storm, everyone would see his true leadership potential.

Running his fingers through his salted hair, he thought he looked the part through his phone's selfie camera. The logo of USFL showed unobstructed behind him with the shaded silver lettering and red background exhibiting the desired effect of pomp and prestige that a media relations room was designed to project. Yes, he was president of this over one hundred-year-old institution and, yes, he was standing on the shoulders of giants—meaning, of course, he was even bigger than all those who came before.

President Scott put away his phone and tweaked the shape of one of the mics. The cameras were all set. This was it. He was going straight into the university address in one live shot. The hours of initial damage control, preparation, and practice post-incident were now all leading to this. The countdown commenced with the room seemingly devoid of any other sound. All he could think to himself was how surprisingly calm and composed he felt as a cold dribble of sweat ran down the side of his abdomen.

"Good afternoon to the university community—students, faculty, family, friends, trustees, and alumni, as well as to a concerned nation. This morning an incident was reported to university police that an act of graffiti had been committed in front of the Peckhart Memorial Statue." He made a prolonged pause peering up from his prepared notes for emphasis before continuing. "When the area was inspected, it was determined that the nature of the graffiti indicated that this was in fact no petty crime. It was a *word* whose very incidence involves an historical regime of oppression against a defenseless class of people—a *word* that seeks to further burden the downtrodden and divide our university as well as our country and abroad." Again, he let the message sink in now slowing on his delivery. "*I* will not say the *word*, as it has no place in a modern university setting devoted to diversity and inclusion, and *I*, as its representative, have a responsibility to not contribute to its perpetuity. I even question whether some words, as these, are so negatively charged that they should be duly retired from history—their very utterance being an affront to human progress—an affront to us as an institution—progress' beacon. We simply can't let our mission be upended by hate…and we won't…*This* matter will be resolved. The person or group responsible will be found as it is now being investigated by campus, state, and even with the support of federal authorities. Yes, the President, himself, called me this morning to kindly express his own support and to offer investigators from the FBI to assist. So let me assure those stakeholders of the university community as well as the nation. No quarter will be given to those trying to impose a hostile existence upon the most underprivileged of our community—no place safe to rest their head for those who hate. *This is certain.*"

He felt the wave of exhilaration at how it was all going. He knew it was no time to fuck it up, especially now with the crucial part— the part that he took immense pleasure in delivering. "What I do want to caution against, on the other hand, are those taking matters into their own hands. I understand the pain. I understand the frustration, but that outrage should be expressed productively and that is by showing trust in our authorities to do what they do best in utilizing the most advanced methods and resources in law enforcement. We should at this time rather build the love and support to those most affected here at home—not to cause them further pain by mindless destruction. In light of recent news, that *that* is working at cross purposes should be clear. Surely, what this incident has proven is that the contribution of our world-renowned faculty is turning heads. Someone feels threatened. And I believe that is a testament to how far we've come—shaking old ways of thinking because, as we all know, all progress is provocative.

"USFL now leads the world with pioneering research— courageously carrying the very torch to illuminate the origin of these evil artifacts of history. We are uncovering more and more about their cause which will enable us to resolutely and utterly close this chapter of history once and for all. So, while these backlashes against progress are ugly, they are also good, as they are a sign of growing pains. They are signs of a sea change shaking these racist institutions to their core—breaking their very foundation. That is why every effort must be made to protect academic integrity—to protect our storied university. So, in addition to the efforts of law enforcement, I'm also calling for stakeholders of the community to come together to tackle the disparities that led us here and how to navigate our way forward. I'll be voicing our proposals in the coming days seeking the input of our community with humility, openness, and understanding. In the meantime, I have a simple request of all of you. All that I'm asking is for us to come together now. There is no solution of the individual here. The only way out of these complex problems—the only way of the future is with the resolution of the public—a public that I continue to proudly serve. Thank you for all of your thoughts and kind support."

10

Peter nervously carved his way through the sea of mostly black that continued to amass on the park. A clamor of voices sounded off different rumblings in a storm of zealous outbursts of rage. Peter held his leather briefcase close to avoid collisions as much as to shield his own person. He realized too late that his usual route to Pressman Hall was a mistake this time, as it ventured into a rapidly building torrent—running too close to Peckhart before the turn. It was his last lecture of the day, and as much as he wanted to cancel it, he also wanted to set a good example to his students—never humor tantrums.

He cut early between halls Richert and Vossman failing to curb his anxiety as an inflow of more groups of protestors were pouring to the park from the other way. He was now like a fish swimming upstream with piranhas swimming down. Only in this case, he didn't exactly know who the piranhas were, but they were around. *Black babies, black babies, why you wanna kill black babies?*

His pulse shot up when his whole path suddenly went from a brackish mix to quickly becoming a dark gulf. He found it difficult to find the right holes through—roughly mirroring the student in a grey backpack just ahead of him passing mask after mask, shadow after shadow—figures flashing by like a maddening zoetrope. He sensed their anger—their aggression—their sweat. Sometimes he even felt a stricken face linger on his. In an instant, he braced himself as he saw one set of eyes flash a vicious hunger at him piercing with bloodthirsty odium. A jolt pierced through his spine in anticipation of an imminent impact as the eyes floated uneventfully away.

The coming intersection brought a lighter mood and crowd. Peter began breathing a little easier at not having been confronted. That's just not what he needed right now—to be affected by any more lunacy—the lunacy that was, in fact, breaking his family apart.

He stood a moment to leer back at the macrophagic mass. He'd seen them before yelling, marching, parading, acting even before coming to town. But, only recently was when he really opined about them. Now he judged them. *What were their motivations exactly? A sense of justice? A need to believe? Money? The euphoria of lashing out? Did it really matter? It was all so small, pathetic really. Maybe on the exterior it looked heroic—it appeared as noble as an old oak, but he knew, as others with any sense of what true bullshit is, that inside it was a lot of rot. So they were angry? Well fuck them. He was angry.* If their message was to breed hate, then he was one who bore them fruit.

Having his pulse approach back to normal, he continued to the door of Pressman. A scant number of students were now going through the double doors. He hoped that the coming protest didn't turn his students away from campus—away from their right to be there. *Could classes be cancelled already?* He had to check when he was inside. Just as he reached the threshold, Yash was exiting followed by Gemma and Johnny.

"Professor Barton?" Gemma expressed as if there were some doubt to his identity.

"Good afternoon," he managed to smile at each as they stepped before the door.

"And look at this shitshow," Johnny said, as he looked over Peter's shoulder at the flows of protestors. Yash only stared on as Peter turned too.

"Oh God! It's worse," Gemma added lamely. Peter turned back.

"I don't remember seeing you over here before?" he said wanting to inject a sense of normalcy back onto campus.

"Professor Garretty had class relocated with the news this morning," she answered.

"And I'm glad he did," Johnny furthered—his demure eyes still not breaking from the crowd.

"Won't somebody do something, Professor? The administration? I mean are they just going to let them destroy campus again?" Gemma sounded with distressed frustration.

Peter wasn't sure how to answer. He wanted to stay positive but wasn't going to lie. He began to imagine what a campus decimated would feel like—the smell of the smoldering ruins of the brittle bricks and the vast wafts of black smoke spreading for miles and miles, the James Darcy Library exploded open with book guts littering part of the park, campus statues disappeared—the only evidence breaking the surface of Duck Pond. *But what then? A rebirth of sorts? Modernistic structures perhaps? Buildings designed with avant-garde geometrical shapes to demonstrate the progressiveness and forward thinking of the admin? Buildings almost all dedicated to addressing the immortalized issues of race-science and equity?* He shuddered at the possibility.

"We'll see."

11

Clint was busy scrolling the area map on his phone, as the deluge continued at the center of campus. It hadn't seemed that distant before he started, but now he knew that the walk to north campus was quite the trek. While he enjoyed taking in the fresh air, the anticipation of the sudden ad hoc meeting clouded his mind.

The email about it arrived late, but it didn't surprise him one bit. President Scott needed to cover his ass after all, because as events started to unfold, the trustees would want to know that he was doing all he could to pacify the mob. It was indeed a funny thought. *Pacify the mob—what a silly business. And it would do to have another black on some committee, wouldn't it? Wasn't that the whole reason that they reached out to him over others?* They just couldn't stop reminding him precisely what they thought of him. In any case, he was going. Someone responsible had to be there after all, and he didn't trust them to invite anyone else that fit that description.

After passing Nordrick, he entered a part of campus that he'd never gone to before. It was a more recent addition, and while in the same neo-gothic style, it had more frills. There were larger windows and classrooms decked out with a much more technology friendly environment than their earlier analogues. And while their accessibility also appeared to have improved, new sidewalks, handicap ramps, elevators, it was strange to see it all empty, especially with what was happening just south of there. The dearth of people spelled out a completely different story—the feeling in the air was of a stale foreboding—feeling more like the empty facilities of a suicide cult right after drinking the punch than an institution of higher learning.

Clint glanced in the direction of the tumult. All he could make out from there was the view over Duck Pond with the layers of buildings that obscured his line of sight to the park. That something big was happening only a few hundred yards further, no one could really tell.

He made it to the auditorium doors of Turner Hall. There was a muffled sound of a voice speaking from inside. He was late. Not waiting for a pause, he pulled the door open finding himself beside the speaker. Many of the attendees judged the late arrival as he marched up the steps to an empty seat. The speaker continued.

Sitting on the edge of the aisle, he left his legs there as there was insufficient space for him to comfortably fit between his seat and the next row. It irked him greatly and combined with the whole reason he felt compelled to be there in the first place, his irritability had only gotten worse. When he started to listen to the speaker's message, he reached boiling point.

"…so President Scott took the time to suggest a list of possible approaches that could produce a positive impact…" The speaker began addressing the list of bullet points on the screen. "The hiring of more diversity staff conducive to a multi-ethnic perspective could help accommodate students of all backgrounds as well as symbolically project a positive presence. Alternatively, Student university representatives could help infuse a more active role for minorities creating stations on campus for them to better address the needs of the community—being a more bottom-up approach promoting campus belonging and ownership that has seen much success at University of…" Clint scanned to the end of the list—impatient for the finale. *Diversity admissions coordinator. Mandatory race conscious orientation. Minority exclusive safe zones.* It was all too much for his stomach to take. The amiss feeling caused him to recall the human slop he experienced spilling out onto the street only days earlier. His ears heard but didn't listen as if an automatic shut off valve had been triggered. The thought had occurred to him to just get up and leave, but a part of him wanted to see this through—that he would regret not having at least tried to stem the insanity.

When the speaker had finished, it was time to pass around the mic. A lot of hands were raised as his assistant made the rounds to those who wished to comment before the resolution vote. A bespectacled professor with red matted hair and aquamarine shirt of embroidered dolphins was the first.

"Professor Riley, Life Sciences. Thank you for the presentation. I appreciate President Scott for taking the time to piece this together even at this late hour." He chuckled irreverently. "But, ya'know, better late than never," he said clearing his throat. "I really want to thank my colleague, Professor Jersey for bringing this issue to the forefront…" To Clint's surprise, the man indicated with his head toward a Jersey whose arm was draped over the back of an empty seat. On his other side was the long thin face of Eldridge with accompanying snout that should've been a dead giveaway as soon as he came in. But then again, the hall's attendees were too numerous to give an account of all the personages that graced it.

"…I think the idea of doing a freshman orientation with some kind of unconscious bias testing would be greatly beneficial. They could recognize their own prejudices and adjust their behaviors accordingly, creating a much more welcoming campus—an extraordinarily friendly one to minorities. This is the realistic route to go because the other way, would of course…" Another arrogant snicker escaped his face. "It'd just be undoable…I do want to adjure, on the other hand, about a more, as you said, bottom-up, grass-roots approach. I suppose it's all good on paper, but this university needs to take more responsibility for what happened last night. To delegate it to the ones most affected would reject this newfound commitment to bridge the racial divide. Someone just spray painted perhaps the most hateful, destructive word right at the center of campus. It really beggars belief at the sheer audacity to threaten our most vulnerable…"

"*No sir.*" It couldn't wait. The fire in Clint compelled him to stand. His body towered down over the audience and speaker. The room, including the professor with the mic, stared back up at the giant with the striking voice. Even Eldridge and Jersey swiveled themselves around to take note of the imposition. "Let's not pretend, Professor Riley, that the graffiti is something that it's not," Clint thundered.

"I'm sorry…Mister…"

"Professor Dumfries, Psychology." The *mister* felt like an intentional snub from the petulant weasel.

"Professor Dumfries, it is not your turn to speak. I'm—"

"I'm afraid that it is. Someone has to establish the record before we can continue. I have had some trouble listening to mischaracterization of the present situation that we now find ourselves in, and I believe there is no time to continue humoring this pathetic game."

"What? You deny there's a problem?" There was that laugh again.

"Just not the kind of problem we're treating here."

"Have you taken a look outside recently? There are a lot of people that would say—"

"Let him talk," the presenter at the center of the theatre broke in. "We should agree on the extent of the problem before we try to resolve it. Professor Dumfries, please continue."

Clint waited for another protest from Riley, but the man only sat there.

"As I see it, this matter is over a graffiti artist. A criminal act that must be punished but has happened countless times in the history of this university—sometimes being from some football rivals of other schools—a local Palm Gate teen—what have you. As far as the *young people* flooding the campus right now. That is the real problem that we are humoring here—thinking that if we appear to do their bidding, they will be in any way satisfied and leave our campus alone. That is not going to happen."

"What do you propose to do?" He heard the same haughty voice speak into the mic.

"They have already done enough damage to our campus. The police should make them leave and cordon off the area. It's as simple as that."

This caused a clamor through the lecture hall. Disparate voices expressing their own protests and outrage. Shouting was heard for Clint to shut up or get out. Meanwhile, Eldridge and Jersey sat there passively as if their only purpose were to witness—their eyes simply following Clint's every move.

"What about the next day or the following? What if the police injure someone? It'll be all over the news." Riley was already standing again—cutting through all the noise with the mic.

"That's always—always a possibility!" Clint slowly overpowered the din. "But, I'd say it's worth it. This university is worth saving."

"And what of you making so little of the racist slur assaulting people of color—threatening our very way of life?" The rowdiness of the audience cooled. The original speaker hadn't moved— appearing to give up his moderation role. They all waited for Clint's answer.

"I saw the word. Did you?"

"Everyone in the nation now knows it."

"Even if it was the word, let's not *pretend* even for a *minute* that it somehow offended *you* or *your* sensibilities."

"It's atrocious."

"It's *celebrated*. Blacks across this country use it. Every popular rap song uses it." At this, the audience appeared to freeze. Clint gave an impassioned stare at his interlocutor almost daring for him to continue as the man reluctantly gazed back through his glasses.

"How is this helpful? You're going to tell those outside that?" A woman a few rows ahead of Clint came to the man's aid—her voice sounding like a scolding grade school teacher.

"I don't need to. They know it's not about what the word does *to* them; it's about what it does *for* them."

"It doesn't make you sick?"

"Frankly, yes, it does. But, you know what? So does this, right here. The campus is being wrecked, and no one appears willing to put a stop to it."

"Wrecked? I agree, by, among other things, *racist graffiti*. That's what we're doing here. We're trying to get to the root of the problem.

"Okay then, let's stop *all* those destroying our campus. Let's have President Scott tap the authorities now to prevent any more damage."

"Don't you see? The authorities are *part* of the problem," she offered him mystified at his own ignorance.

Clint stopped himself. Something in her look gave him a special moment of cognizance. In nearly all those turned to him now was that same disquieting trace of something broken. Like in the face of a man yelling obscenities into thin air on the street—a look that was worn defiantly, proudly like they all reveled in some special form of knowledge, and merely to possess it, was sufficient enough to save you. In this context, her words made more sense. All of it did. They didn't form a statement to be evaluated. They were more of an incantation, a wish, an ode, or outward sign of homage. Words devoid of action—denuded of value. That's when he decided on the absurdity of the present situation. How ridiculous he must look in engaging these people in an argument. Nothing would come from being here.

"I can't continue this…anymore…with those willing to trade our campus for a word game."

"No one's holding you!" the mic rang out drawing coughs of laughter. The chamber waited as Clint took his time stepping down to the hall's exit. A light applause followed his departure—its sound biting. The feeling of emptiness ensued at the futility of it all. The thought had occurred to him that it was nothing that a drink wouldn't fix.

His steps through the hallway to the outside door made a faint clattering echo. He was almost hypnotized by the sound—ruminating on his own thoughts. Giselle and Daniela came to mind. What a world they were growing up in now—a world on the one hand speaking loudly for justice and the good of humanity yet allowing for destruction—for parts of mutilated women to spill out onto a street. How could he let his daughters live in such a world? What choice did he have? All that he did to get where he was—the obstacles overcome only to have enlisted professional grievers rhetoric him out of a room. Jenelle would surely scold him tonight. With dejection creeping in, before reaching the entrance, he turned at the sounds' irregularity. Eldridge was approaching him fast from behind.

12

With her heart pounding rapidly through her chest, Kristi came out of her office toward the pair of dark police uniforms that had entered Ray Foundation. She stopped mid-approach seeing them escorted by the secretary to meet Marcus.

She remembered calling earlier to report on Yunnie's disappearance and now was scared to see them actually come in the flesh. With still no answer from her friend and the updates concerning the Youhaul Murders fresh in the news, she knew she had to act even if it turned out to be her own insecurities causing a great inconvenience.

She wasn't quite sure why she was especially nervous now, however. Was it the fact of the police's presence, incarnating her worry or was it something else? The thought of them going back to see Marcus seemed to scare her. Would he feel betrayed? But, then again, why should he feel that way?

Recalling their last meeting, Kristi felt she had a reason to fear. The way Marcus handled Yunnie's firing was one thing, but the way he explained her departure is what really gave her a cold shiver. It was how easy people live and leave a place that didn't comfort her at all. On the contrary, it hurt her. It's what she imagined of herself one day. It was as if this city would suddenly swallow her up whole without a trace, and no one would care. Who would even know? With all the powerful people around, how would anyone notice the disappearance of one of the plebs as compared to a senator? When she thought of a figure like Simon Ray, she knew that in the end, she amounted to little more than a peanut stand at a circus.

13

After dismissing the few students who showed up, Peter called Clint. They both had the same object in mind—a strong invigorating drink before heading home. Where? They weren't sure. Mainstreet probably wasn't safe to move around and the police presence was already closing roads down. Recognizing that Clint wasn't far away in passing Wilson Hall, they agreed to meet for the rest of the way to Lot A and make a decision of where to go next.

Peter exited Pressman making his way west. The groups in black diminished as he moved further from the park, but sightings of students were scantier. *Where had they all gone?* Peter didn't like it. He felt something bad was about to occur and wanted to get out of there fast.

With virtually no one around, it wasn't hard to spot the familiar giant with tan oversized coat nearby.

"So was it that bad?" Peter asked, picking up the conversation where they had just left off.

"Don't ask," Clint said eyes warily remaining on his surroundings. "At least, not until I get a drink in."

"Where to?"

"Flannery's?"

"Good. Kilkenny on tap."

"Look at this mess here."

They came upon Lot A now largely emptied of cars. In their place was a continuous maze of busses. There were only about two dozen recent arrivals—positioning masks and donning backpacks. With his own gear already in place, a sort of foreman was making his rounds in seeing to all their needs.

Clint got a good look at the bloc as they passed. The view on his face was clear. They weren't welcome. Peter shared the same sentiment. He saw his car not fifty yards away when Clint suddenly stopped. It was enough to make Peter's heart jump seeing the indignant face.

Off in the distance, he saw the buzz. The foreman was handing out the long dark metallic shafts of what appeared to be Maglites, one to each activist. It was quite a good bit of organization for what the news portrayed as a scrum of ragtags whose sole interest was justice. What he didn't know was that Clint was homed in on a different detail, namely, the one thumping its steel head into his other hand. The crinkle in his mask was unmistakable. The feel of the blunt force slapping onto his palm seemed to be just to the thug's liking.

"Hey!" Clint erupted, marching in their direction. The sound blast surprised some in their group whose heads turned right away.

"What're you doing?" Peter quickly sidled his friend—as an urgent plea for him to discontinue.

Like a force of nature, Clint wouldn't listen. He felt as if he were in the middle of a valve turn to release dangerous pressure.

"Gentlemen, now what are we doing with those?" he indicated with his hands to one who hadn't yet secured his in his pack's netting. The question was heated yet constrained. Peter was glad, at least, to know Clint hadn't completely relinquished his composure, as he almost imagined him trying to confiscate the flashlights and manhandling bodies every which way with his massive frame.

If they were surprised at first, they weren't the least bit now— nor were they intimidated. They ignored his question. Some were still securing equipment while others slung on their packs. Eyes, however, tended to gravitate back toward Clint, as if they were assessing the danger of a feral animal.

Peter, not far behind, called to his friend. "Let's go. This is useless."

Clint burned a hole with his glare, as he watched the group finish their preparations. A young man returned it.

"Is there something I can assist with over here? Really? How can I help you with that? What do you need?" Clint pressed.

The young man appeared to take no interest in Clint. In fact, he pointed out Peter to the comrade next to him, saying something through his mask.

"We've done all we can," Peter implored—noticing the unwanted attention. He put his hand on Clint's back. It was enough to break Clint from his trance. This battle was already lost, and he knew it too.

Breathing deeply, Clint turned back with Peter. *What got into him exactly? He didn't know.* All that he'd seen and heard lately had caused him to do things that he never saw himself doing. He knew there was nothing that a confrontation would accomplish, but he did it anyway. He acted like the sight and smell of guts were just about around every corner. He'd see more saccules of a large intestine once owned by a person, and it was enough to put civilization on hold. It was enough to unleash his worst.

While making their retreat, the members of the crew talked. One of them even poked the foreman in the back who was busy cutting open another box of supplies. The message he had to convey couldn't wait.

"Barton?!" They heard someone shout after them. Peter turned with Clint to see the foreman and the rest now following. *It was only a matter of time*, Peter thought, *before he got burned by someone recognizing his face.* The interview he did must've really left a mark. Now he knew there was no time to dally. His pace quickened.

"Yo! Stop!" they heard, but with the car no more than twenty yards away, Peter ignored them and so did Clint. The group, however, would not be denied such an opportunity, as they entered into a full run.

Peter rounded the car, unlocking the door with his fob. "Get in!" he told Clint whose dark blue Buick was still a ways down.

They swung open the doors and slammed them shut. Peter pushed the start button. Nothing happened. The error message appeared. "Push the brake, fucking idiot," he whispered to himself as he did. The car started just as the foreman and his team surrounded it.

Clint still had the presence of mind to hit the door lock while Peter slowly edged the car forward, but this met with stiff resistance, as the group in front refused to budge. Peter stopped as what sounded like a fierce volley of hail showered down on the car from multiple directions. The options raced through his mind, as the intensity of the kicks grew. *Did he want to be the professor that ran over a protestor? Would they ever let him out of prison? One thing was for* sure—it would certainly end his career. But, perhaps they'll just get tired. They'll stop.

"Whatever you do, get that nazi out!" The foreman yelled his encouragement to the others.

Clint saw the man from earlier in the rearview. With Maglite still in hand, he was banging it with great effect on the trunk. Soon it found its way to the rear window at first bouncing off with a good vibration before plunging through—causing a spray of glass pebbles and shards to launch through the cabin hitting both passengers.

"*Drive!*" Clint roared with certitude. "*Drive!*"

But Peter couldn't. He had imagined running over some twenty-year-old kid. He couldn't bring himself to do something like that. He just couldn't hit the accelerator.

Meanwhile, the Maglite bandit swatted away most of the remaining shards from where the back window once was. Another soon found his calling getting up on the trunk and stepping through the opening.

"Go!" Clint reaffirmed to Peter with his body turned toward the immediate threat. The inside man soon reached back to receive the gift of the holy weapon that allowed his entrance. Its light now beaming on due to the ferocious blows that it already dealt. His crouched swing with the Maglite nearly struck true. Peter felt the glancing blow to his neck from the long shaft, as Clint tried catching it mid swing. Despite the adrenaline, the pain through the fat of his neck was intense. From sheer instinct Peter slumped forward as if to dodge the next round causing his foot to slam the gas. The car ripped forward thumping some bodies aside and bouncing over a foot.

The man in the backseat was flung back at the initial jolt.

Peter sat up to turn the wheel just in time before hitting a parked bus.

"Get us out! Get us out!" Clint yelled as if Peter had anything else in mind. They flew through the parking lot hitting air on each speed bump.

"Stop the car!" The man with the Maglite held it as if threatening to strike again.

Instead, the car screeched through the turn to exit Lot A, as Peter put as much road as possible between them and the campus.

The lights of a police checkpoint flashed up ahead.

"I said, stop the fucking car!" The young man hit the back of Peter's head rest with his still illuminated steel mace.

Catching the man unawares, Clint's long arm shot out toward him getting a huge palm around the weapon, and with a jerk, yanked it free with relatively little resistance. The skinny frame of the man tried to immediately retake it, but Clint placed it at his feet wrestling the man to get him under control.

Peter drove straight toward the checkpoint—the south gate of the campus. Clint, predicting this last move, had other ideas.

"No. Down here. Right here," he indicated already having the mele well under control. There was one turn off to a circle with a small park, a pond, and an old historic house. Peter trusted the voice of his friend and made the turn.

They rolled through the trees up to the pond and skid a little to a stop on the dirt drive. No one was around. As Clint knew, it was already closed. The old well-preserved museum house with the newly painted white siding stood before them eerily. The man in the back seat tried his passenger door, but Clint had already triggered the child safety lock. He then tried to jump out of the back, but Clint caught hold of him again.

"Here help me," he told Peter who nervously looked to his friend as if he wanted no part in the crime they were about to commit.

"We just want to talk," Clint said, reassuring the young man as well as Peter.

Peter unlocked the car and then got out to open the passenger door. Clint still had control of the man's arms at his sides, who had appeared to have given up the struggle for now. There was blood flecked all over coming from multiple wounds on the arms of both men. In clumps it dotted the seats, doors, and console like the night sky. The backseat was awash with glass. There was no way they could sit him down in it in good conscience.

"Okay, he's going to let you go in a second," he calmly told the man breathing heavily through his black mask whose eyes shot around still in a frantic state of survival. "Don't try to run. There's a lot of glass here. As he said, we just want to talk. We're not going to hurt you."

"Even though you tried to hurt us," Clint added catching his breath.

The man didn't say anything, so Peter proceeded.

"In three seconds, my friend here is going to let you go, so be careful as you exit the car."

He made the count and Clint released the man who fell without Clint's balancing force. He put his hand out to prevent his fall into the seat.

"Fuck!" he said as the glass bit into his hand.

"Careful," Peter repeated. He offered the man a hand, but it was refused.

Clint opened his door brushing off the glass and inspecting the damage to his arms as he came around to assist. They both made room for the man to exit who appeared to take his time due to the injuries he sustained. But it wasn't as it first appeared. As soon as the man hit the ground, he tried to bolt kicking up dirt in the effort. Clint was prepared for the ruse and caught the man's foot with his. The man stumbled to the ground and slid through the dirt. He walked over and grabbed him from behind, and with some cooperation, stood him up. Slowly, Clint guided him back to the car—leaning the man's back against it.

"There," he said surprisingly affably after all that occurred. He proceeded to drape his arm over the man's shoulder as if they were both best friends posing for the camera on a camping trip.

"We're bros now, right?" He chuckled, as his thick bloody arm weighed down on him.

The man's mask was now around his neck revealing the scraped boyish face that lied beneath. It was something that Peter was not expecting. That the kid was nigh twenty, wasn't a surety; however, the stunning wrathful defiance in his face was.

Peter had 911 dialed but refrained from pushing the send button. Seeing the boy's face, suggested to him why Clint wanted them there. What it offered was normally an impossible opportunity to understand what this was all really about. Something that the news wouldn't write about—what the police were powerless to stop. He'd be back out on the street in no time and no one would ever know anything about him. Not only as a victim who was just assaulted, but also as a psychologist, Peter needed to know.

"You got your wish," Peter said lamely—better assessing the outside damage to his car. In addition to the window, the dents were everywhere and massive. *They simply don't make cars like they used to*, he thought. "Next time you need a ride, just ask."

"Shut your fucking nazi mouth!" the kid shouted at Peter without the smallest inkling of humor. Peter couldn't help but laugh. Maybe it was partly the adrenaline high. He sensed that Clint felt it too. Just what was so funny? Perhaps it was that the boy didn't at all look like a happy camper despite the set-up, but it was also at what he thought of next.

"Welp, I'm afraid the Hitler-wagon is out of commission." This had Clint rollicking back and forth which caused the boy to move with him. As they both belted out a good long laugh, the activist looked the worse for wear. But as the visible resentment grew, the funnier it became.

After a while, Peter wiped the tears from his eyes. Here this kid was about to murder him only minutes earlier and now they were having a good joke at his expense. What an extraordinary thing life is—where all is on the line and at any minute one's fortune turns on a dime. If there's a small moment to enjoy, Peter figured one needed to take the opportunity.

"Look, I think we started off on the wrong foot," Peter began again. "My name is Peter. What's your name?"

The kid didn't answer. Rather, he rolled his eyes away from him in disgust.

"I'm originally from Rochester. Where're you from?" He waited for some response or sign of interest but soon continued when there was nothing. "I have a son and a wife. What about you? *You* married?" His pauses grew longer, and as they lingered, the young man appeared to grow more irritated. "Yeah married about ten years. It's quite something how life changes…" It was almost as if Peter were talking to himself, nevertheless he figured that there had to be something the young man would latch on to.

"I remember when I was as young as you. I too was looking to fight the good fight—helping those more unfortunate—"

"Just shut up."

"What?"

"It's nothing like the time when you were growing up."

"You don't say?" Clint snarkily perked up.

"How's that?" Peter asked seriously.

"We're opting out."

"What?"

"The petty gains—the subservience of peoples to the little game you play. The very foundation of this country."

Peter's eyes met with Clint for a brief moment. There was a confusion that was shared.

"You call me a nazi."

"And you all are."

"Who is?"

"This country."

Peter began wondering if this was a good idea after all. Further questioning just felt like abuse. This person was not well.

"So," Clint wanted to probe further, "who organizes your group? The only anti-nazis around?"

The kid held his silence.

"You consider yourselves anti-nazis?" Peter sought clarification.

Here was the young man's own turn to laugh, but it was more of a snort—a weaselly pompous sort of expulsion of air.

"Well, isn't that nice of you?" Clint asked sardonically. "So, only out of the kindness of your hearts have you come here to teach us your anti-nazi ways. Paying your own way for your chartered busses and brand new gear…all to send us a message…and for what? For free. Because when you were offered money, you rejected it, of course. What a *petty gain* otherwise. Am I right?"

The young man stared off sucking his teeth, as if he were not comfortable enough to discuss this further.

"So he's right? You were teaching us a lesson in anti-Nazism?" Peter followed.

The man kept his eyes a ways off. "Is that what this is or isn't?"

"It's revenge," he said to Peter's face before firing a gob of spit right into it.

14

It was past six thirty, Kristi's nerves settled down a little even while the conference room's TV screen showed the escalation of the protests at University of Southern Florida. So far, the police stayed out of central campus with minimal incidents—only a few smashed windows and occasional graffiti, but all in all, pretty tame.

The news even had Senator Susan Dembier commenting that she was frightened for the students who faced "radical currents" on campus. She suggested that the university take strong action to address both extremist dogma and the inherent racial inequities persisting in education. When asked specifically about the protestors, she spoke auspiciously. "It is *their* campus. They paid for it, and it's time to take it back. My message for them is that…" She turned to the camera with an endearing touch. "I want you to know our prayers are with you—even though we are many, we are in fact one spirit and hell or high water, won't keep us down."

Kristi watched passively as she worked away on her laptop. She had decided that her office wouldn't do on a day like today. No one would bother her here. Yunnie and her both valued the large quiet space as opposed to their small, cluttered offices always drawing the observance of a passerby. Their privacy, from day one, ceased to exist until they found this refuge. When asked about their work at the long wooden table, no one appeared to see the value in it anymore. No one seemed to understand women's desire for privacy or even the concept itself. Even now, strangely, in the last number of days, with Kristi completely alone, she felt the attraction of eyes multiply.

Marcus slipped into the room from the far side. He walked toward where Kristi now sat with a gentle smirk and lazy bloodshot eyes. The closer he got, the more unsettled Kristi became at how his face presented in the sun's late afternoon light. It appeared almost menacing if not for the other signs of recent stimulation. *Was he in fact drunk?* She didn't know for sure, but his silence was a weapon used against her. The ambient sound of the TV was the only ease to her discomfort.

He sat to her right, and the grin sat with him. *Why didn't they speak? Was the opportune time closing?* She went back to her laptop. She clicked around at nothing in particular trying to avoid her building sense of fear. She decided to continue the silence. In fact, she was intent to wait to the ends of the earth for him to speak first.

After a moment, she made a furtive glance over to him who was now comfortably laying back in his chair staring up at the screen. The coverage of the protests continued unabated. The stylish panoramas presented them as if already a commemorated flashpoint of history. Everything was positive. Nothing could be construed otherwise.

The broadcaster narrated over the shots as if giving his benediction over the whole enterprise. "What a powerfully clear message of hope and a promise we yearn to see fulfilled, if not for us, at least, for our children's children."

Marcus' grin grew. She heard him whisper something to himself. What was it? She thought she'd heard 'Thanks en Benhen,' but she wasn't quite sure what he was saying. As the segment went to commercial he cleared his throat and turned to her.

"How's it going?"

"*Good.*" She tried sounding upbeat.

"No," he said plainly, "I don't think you are."

She refrained from answering. She knew what was coming.

"I spoke with the police."

Again, she said nothing. She wanted to hear him say it all.

"They told me about the investigation into the disappearance of one of our late employees..." He made eye contact with her as she looked up from her screen. It was enough to bring the tears. They gushed down her cheeks. He swiveled over to hug her.

She hated him, but she was helpless.

"It's okay. It's okay."

After a time, he pulled back only keeping her hand. He squeezed it.

"I thought we talked about that."

"I know," she said emptily.

"If you would've just told me more of your concern, don't you think I would've helped you find her?"

"Yes."

"I'm sure she'll turn up. She's a smart woman—a fighter."

"You're right."

"But now you know that the police are involved, it puts a black spot on our whole organization. It doesn't look good for us."

"I—"

"It's okay. She was your good friend. I understand completely."

He squeezed her hand a bit more but not too much. His thoughts burned in his brain. *Stupid fucking cunt. If you could've only fell in line.*

15

Peter called the police and gave them their location. They decided to have the kid sit in the passenger seat while they waited. It wasn't long before he proceeded to kick and break the dashboard. Clint tried to have him stop, but Peter told him to just let it go. The car was already destroyed.

They both had a chance to call home to tell their wives. Clint was forthright with the details, Peter was more reserved. He wanted to tell Margery face-to-face, and even then, he wanted to break it to her easy. He decided that she had been through quite enough and so did he.

The light was fading, and despite the circumstances, the little park with its pond was a peaceful reprieve. Well after the banging and screaming within the car had ceased, one could hear the frogs and crickets make their little stirrings as the plop of a small fish jumped here and there to earn its evening meal.

Peter yearned for a place like this. He could imagine all of them living in the house. Roger would be skipping a rock over the pond while Margery held the hand of his sibling who was making some of his or her first steps followed by a yip of excitement. It was enough for him, but things weren't so simple. Not a mile away, there was a campus being overrun by whatever ailed this young man. He wondered if Roger could be afflicted the same way but quickly banished the thought. He didn't think his pleasant reverie should be so readily abandoned. Nevertheless, it soon had to be— the area being immersed in blue light accompanied by sirens.

The police took a good look—going over the details multiple times: the dented car, the broken window, the injuries, the flashlight, the IDs, and the statements. In the meantime, the young man screamed his indignation at being held against his will. He explained they had kidnapped him and took him there. When asked about the damage to the car, the pitch in his voice increased describing a desperate struggle to contain him where he eventually used the flashlight to break the window to escape.

"And did you also make the dents to the outside of the vehicle?"

"What dents? I was trying to escape! Are you going to arrest them or what?!" The distress of his voice only grew. It was as if the sheer display of emotion itself was cause enough to take them in.

"Sir, I need to know. Look, it's okay if you had to make some of them. I'd understand…"

"I may have made some of them."

"How many? Five? Ten?"

"I don't know. I guess like five."

The young man was arrested. He fruitlessly fought against being cuffed as they brought him to the ground. His ID indicated him as a Felton Cross of Chester, Wisconsin. The youthful countenance burgeoned with red as he launched his last retaliatory acts of insults and obscenities before being put into the back of the squad car.

It was getting late and even after being informed that they'd be part of a further investigation, Peter and Clint felt a relief that it was at least over for now. When the officer heard that Clint's car was still on campus, he recommended not going back for it yet.

"Things aren't looking too good," the officer offered in a moment of candor.

16

The smell of burning filled central campus. The noxious chemical odor assaulted the nostrils and lungs of anyone in the vicinity or downwind. It was a deceptive scent—more akin to what is expelled from a factory than a simple building ablaze.

Henrich Hall was the first they tried to set fire to—seemingly intent on finishing what they started doing from their last flutter, but when that was thwarted by a line of police and a fire hose on the crowd, they managed to do it to Porter, housing the History and Classical Studies departments.

Smashing out windows, they lit and hurled a Molotov inside that quickly caught the furnishings and spread. The police stealthily mobilized their lines of soldiers in full riot gear to capture and secure the area. Volleys of various projectiles rained down on them: rocks, bricks, bottles, trash bins, and fireworks connected with vests, helmets, and shields without much hinderance to the police's advance.

It was when they came to a seemingly benign unguarded wall of debris made of desks, shelves, and other broken sprinklings of lecture hall fixtures, that would ultimately come to define that night—and to unequivocally denote a man in uniform.

As they started their crossing over, a huddled down runner from the shadows threw his lit zippo onto the pile drenched in accelerant—igniting a wall of fire. The resulting explosion sent officers hurtling, burning through the air like residual embers of a firework display.

With the unit divided, weakened, the protestors sprung on the separated officers still recovering from the conflagration. The small melee weapons wrecked havoc on their bodies. One was mercilessly bludgeoned in the helmet with a steel tire club while still on his hands and knees as another kicked him in the abdomen. The body soon slunk back to earth unable to support its weight, as they mercilessly continued to ravage him.

Another officer had more success against the oncomers—one wielding a tire iron and another, a flashlight. He shielded himself from the first, felt the blunt force of the second on the shoulder, before bringing his club across the activist's face—sending him sprawling back.

"Fuck you piggywiggies!" "Donut time!" a pair taunted officers across the gulf before chucking two firework mortars over. Stunned or not—this was the tipping point. It was enough to propel a number through the fire—striking out at the offenders with a fury that defied all prior restraint and training. Other officers joined their rally with a new morale—emerging from the other side largely unscathed—striking protestors indiscriminately from the aggressors to the fleers—face, groin, neck and back of the head. One even left the ground with a cop's baton to his throat gurgling and spewing saliva as he struggled helplessly to break free, as onlookers further demurred.

As the sky flares ignited along the ground in massive blooms of sparkling white and yellow burning officers and others, WNT's drone camera along with other media outlets' mobile units homed in on the stunning imagery of the mayhem caused by the men in blue.

WNT's Don Waters from its New York studio broadcasted over the violence with a controversial oft-quoted message: "We think we've come so far in the twenty-first century. But to see these graphic images of our supposed protectors try to snuff out those making a stand against racism at a revered institution of higher learning no less, is almost self-parody. It reveals the stark reality for all the skeptics out there of institutionalized racism becoming flesh."

His quote was well heard, but the way the video itself spread took on a life of its own. Shots of that night's aftermath rapidly snowballed over the internet. Multiple hi-def zooms of activist bodies completely immobile gorged the public's hunger for some time. It did something that nobody dared admit. To see the grit, the raw brutality that society has only tried to cover up in civilized times, ignored the sieve that had been depriving some of a largely missed nutritive source.

17

Peter pulled into his driveway with his headlights meeting a darkened house—scarcely a light on. He wondered if Roger was already asleep. It was only nine fifteen, so it wouldn't be the usual. Margery wasn't, to be sure, especially after his disturbing check-in. Still, they probably had been packing the car and would be drained. He was starting to rethink if bringing Clint there was such a good idea. They were both tired and had been through a lot but were more intent than ever on having that drink together.

It was okay in the end, he thought, pausing before getting out of the car. It sure as hell beat anywhere else at that time, especially given the news over the radio about the riot and road closures. Besides, while he knew he needed time to fully tell Margery, he also wanted some time to process it, and there was no one better to do that with than with the friend who was there with you. Clint and he had sure shared a lot in the last couple of weeks, and as ugly, dark, and frightening as those times were, he felt that they had never been closer than now, as if they were of the very same blood.

He opened the door to see the flashes of light from the TV screen play off the walls in the dark and heard the murmur of network news coming from the living room.

As Peter stepped out into the TV light ready to meet Margery, he found only the evidence of her on the sofa with its pillows arranged just the way she liked them to relax. He imagined, with events being as surreal as they were, himself being that character of the movie just coming to realize that he was hallucinating it all—that none of it was real—that his wife and son, in fact, never existed. Absolute hell then a hard cut. In contrast, this brief thought made everything seem a little better than it was.

Motioning for Clint to follow, he made his way to the mini-bar in the other room. If anyone was sleeping, he knew he could always bring company there to talk, especially when things got a little louder with immoderate drinking. But before Clint continued, he stopped—catching sight of the live coverage of events unfolding on campus. The fire in Porter glowed over bodies seemingly gone haywire on the streets and walkways. It occurred to him right away how unnatural their motions all seemed.

"What in the living fuck?" he rasped to himself numb and exhausted. The images raced by as he stood there almost out of time and space. It took a moment for him to reorient and find Peter.

Peter was just re-corking the single malt he finished pouring. It was at least a couple shots worth in each glass. Without prompting, Clint took his and downed it in a gulp.

"Cheers," Peter chuckled before draining his own.

Clint put his whiskey glass back onto the bar. "Round two?"

Peter set his glass down. "Pour'em," he said on his way out of the room. "I'm going to check on Marge. Be right back."

"Peter?" He looked back to Clint whose hand easily palmed what looked like a toy bottle. "It's all over the news…it's ugly."

As he walked by the TV, Peter's eyes only passed over the coverage. He was intent on making it to the stairs and on having even just a moment of peace with his family.

Reaching the landing, Peter heard Margery talking on the phone on speaker to her mother. He looked down the hall to see Roger's door closed but the light still on.

"Maybe it's best they burned the whole gawddam thing down, ya'know?"

"*Mom!*"

"I'm just saying…maybe the roof will cave in on at least some of them."

"That's awful."

"You don't say?" Peter entered their room with a forced smile. Margery stopped folding clothes with a sigh of relief. She went to him. They hugged and kissed, as her mom pattered on.

"…It really is unfortunate. All those homos to go on living that way with…You only hope they can be put out of their misery," she explained in her New England accent continuing on by herself for a time before Margery cut in.

"Mom?"

"Yes?"

"Peter got back."

"Oh *gooood*. Hi Peter!"

"Hi," said Peter trying to iron out the disgust in his voice.

"How are you?

"Not bad. You?"

He gave Margery the look that she knew well. He didn't need this right now.

"Really? I'm seeing this news and its so gross. I can barely watch—"

"*Mom?*"

"Yes?"

"Peter and I need to talk. So, gotta go."

"Okay, I understand you gotta tawk about all that. Drive safe tomorrow, okay?"

"I will."

"Peter, you be safe too. Don't let them make you get out of your cah. You shouldn't have to do that. You can just—"

"Bye *Mom*!"

"Okay bye sweetie. Love you."

"Love you."

She hung up.

They stayed in each other's arms.

"You didn't tell me what happened, but I'm certain you can't go back," she said this into his ear. "You have to come with us now."

Peter knew this was coming and even with that foreknowledge, the words delivered a potent pang. Despite all, he loved living in Palm Gate. He loved teaching at the university. But, most of all, he didn't want to retreat from the enemy. He didn't want to give them power, but he knew now that that's just what he had to do.

He then told her all that had happened that day from passing through campus crowds to the police, recounting at how their Nissan, now sitting in the driveway, had become destroyed. She listened confused, almost incredulous at the rapid escalation and at the apparent dearth of police from campus early on. Her questions kept coming and Peter eventually ran out of answers.

Holding his hand against her abdomen completely still, she smiled.

"Nothing?"

"You can't feel her, but I can." They couldn't yet verify the gender of the baby, but for some reason, both had been referring to it as a girl, as if they knew that's exactly what the universe wanted for them in the end. In fact, whenever Peter imagined the baby, as he did now, that's precisely what his mind had fleshed out—a beautiful baby girl, who he already loved dearly.

"Really? Already."

"Yes."

He held her from behind like that for some time lost in thought. Finally, he broke their moment. "Where's Roger?"

"In his room. He helped me around the house a lot today. I think he's still reading."

"I'm going to check on him and then head back down. Clint's probably done with the bottle by now."

She gave him a serious look.

"What?" he asked as if she voiced her concern aloud.

"Let me know when he needs a ride home."

"I'll take him."

"I smell the booze."

"I only had one, so I'm still good."

She looked up at him quizzically.

"Let me take him. You just finish up," He pleaded soothingly.

"No more drinks for you."

"One more," he smiled putting up one finger.

"Okay," she smiled back, "just one." She put her finger to his lips as if sealing his promise with a ritual.

Roger's light was still on peaking out from under the door when Peter tapped on it. There was no answer so he cracked the door cautiously—remembering his son recently protesting about his need for privacy. On top of his comforter, there he saw Roger's head plastered in a book, body expanding and contracting in deep breaths of sleep. He laughed at how comical it looked. He remembered how easy sleep used to come in youth. The chaotic sprawl looked rather uncomfortable but perhaps the adult anxieties of life blocked such freedom. What a blessing it was for children to be free of their snare.

He slowly inched the book from under his head. It was clearly another one of the magical fantasy books he loved so much now lining his shelf in shiny graphic covers with worn creased spines from frequent use.

While the movement caused his son to stir, he proceeded to auto-adjust to the soft mattress underneath. The covers were much easier to get from under him and over his legs. A peaceful sleep uninterrupted. Nothing indicated anything like the dreams Peter had been having. Perhaps he was a part of one of the adventures in his books, where even in the fantasy world, it retained its own internal rationale.

Peter found the bookmark on his nightstand and stuck it in the place he left off. He closed it seeing the cover of prominent adventurers overlooking a mysteriously befogged town below. It was called The Billows of Rimwood. The description mentioned a strange smoke plaguing the hometown of one member of the party of adventurers consisting of two elves, two humans, a dwarf, and a half giant as characters of a long running series. Peter wondered at how stories like these had been written for ages and would likely appeal to ages more. The internal psychological implications were fascinating if only he had the time to read them for himself.

He switched off the light and stood there waiting. He imagined his son still awake. Roger would give him a hug and tell him something ordinary about his day. After all that had happened, he really wanted that. A memory to hold onto when things got hard. A moment that he knew was fleeting as boys grew older and shared less and less.

He descended the stairs hearing the familiar jingle indicating an LNN breaking news report. A correspondent was broadcasting in front of the familiar statue of Henry Nordrick that Peter knew was an area well north of the park. A crew were directing questions at him from their Atlanta studio. It appeared to be a quiet, peaceful evening, at least in the dim light around the graffitied figure.

"I spoke to the police chief who demanded reporters leave the area immediately due to concerns about their safety. When asked to what danger he was referring, he only mentioned the fire and protestors."

"Did he say anything about the measures of force the police were taking? If we should be more concerned about the kind of clearance methods being implemented?" a studio personality queried.

"Repeatedly," he shook his head in assent, "I voiced the concern over the use of violence hindering the valid right to protest. The police chief's response was that there was quote *nothing valid about what's going on here.*"

"Unbelievable."

"Useless," Peter said to himself turning off the TV before leaving the room.

Heading to the kitchen, he saw the illumination from the back porch light. The soft sound of smooth jazz poured through as he opened the sliding glass door and slipped out. It was in the careful way he closed it, quickly and completely, that suggested he was going to protect those inside from something and it wasn't from the sound of piano and xylophone.

Clint had his head in his hand scrolling something on his phone with his glass partially filled and a new bottle of TJs—a brand Peter considered to be lower shelf.

"Peter, I owe you a bottle."

"Don't worry about it."

"I got you."

"You have my glass?"

"Sorry. It's inside."

He retrieved another glass from the kitchen and sat down with Clint at the patio table that they had just used the night of the cookout, that was, before the truck incident occurred. Only a couple of vehicles now remained on the street from the subsequent forensics and cleanup crew, but it was still all too fresh in their minds. Peter figured that this was, in a sense, a reversion back to sanity for Clint reminiscent of a time before where neighbors could still just meet and share a drink—those moments where liquid bodies didn't flood residential streets and where the youth went to learn at university—not destroy it. Of course, it could also be that, despite the events transpiring a few miles away, it was a pretty nice night to be outside with a steady evening breeze coming from the east.

Peter took himself a good pull of whiskey after pouring himself another. The music from Clint's phone was soothing and while they sat quietly that way for a good moment, it wasn't enough to dislodge what was really on his mind.

"Eldridge threatened me," Peter told his friend frankly.

Clint looked up from his phone with glazed eyes. "What? *When?*"

"I remember talking to him about the study over the phone. Remember? Before I did the interview?"

"Yeah?"

"He said to take *real* care and… I've been thinking on that."

"Wait. You think Little Louis is above petty, empty threats? I mean for the amount of time we've known him, I'm not at all astounded." Clint laughed at the thought.

"I didn't say it was empty." Clint's expression turned serious. "I didn't much think about it at the time, but now, I keep asking myself, why he felt he had to say that of all things. *Real care.* Instead of just insult me, he chooses those words, and they are said…well…calmly."

The episode was taking more of Clint's interest. It looked like his mind had caught onto something. It was filling in the steps to his own conclusion.

"I believe he wanted to tell you to fucking die already."

"It's not typical Eldridge. He may have taken a course in mindfulness, but I think he's still resorting to toxic behavior. When he feels threatened, he simply lashes out somehow."

"You think he really believes in his own research?"

"No. What I think he really believes is how useful it can be."

"Why do you say that?"

"He told me himself."

"How?" asked Clint furrowing his eyebrows.

"When I asked him why he ran the numbers trying to link genetics to bias in the first place, he suggested that it was simply an answer to a query and a satisfactory one at that. His answer appealed to usefulness rather than evidence."

Never had he thought so much recently of the man whose unofficial department epithet indicated how small he could be. In the past, it had been better not to think of him at all, but now, so much more was at stake—so much he did affected the university community and well beyond.

"I think you're right," Clint finally spoke. "You know, I was going to tell you. I thought it was nothing, but I saw Eldridge today."

"Oh?

"He was sitting with Jersey."

"So they're close?"

"I don't know. What I do know is that after I said my piece and left, he caught up with me on the way out, engaging in what I thought was small talk at first, a friendly gesture after a heated exchange, but now I doubt that. He came up personably enough, asked me how everything was. When I made reference to the meeting, he passed it off. *You'll see*, he said. *Everything'll be for the best.* Then followed with a strange analogy."

"Being?"

"Something like: a fellow horse may not like the ride, but soon enough, they'll be pasturing together."

"What?"

"Sounds benign enough—prosaic."

"Not to me."

"I thought he simply meant something like: hey we're all in this together or some other trite bullshit to say when there was nothing really to say, but now I think of how bitter the medicine one has to swallow—the hard ride. In other words, maybe he was saying that he knew the meeting was all nonsense, yet, still, the ends justify the means. It was all done for a purpose—not that what was done was any good."

"He's lying," Peter proclaimed with disgust. "He's lying and he knows he is. The study is bogus, but he knows how powerful of a lie it could be."

"Sure, it could bring the untold fame and attention he's always craved."

"Influence."

"That too. It could."

"As a psychologist, he doesn't have to look too far for those data. There are already pigeons worth of peer reviewed studies there…No…this has always been about him."

"Them."

"Yes. Them."

"Jersey, too."

"God, who knows all those wanting something from this?"

"But you don't know he's really lying—not for sure, anyway."

"I don't know, but you know what? I'd wager my whole career that he is."

"We'll probably never know will we? So what's the use?" Clint delivered with a sigh of resignation before sipping from his glass. The wicker patio chair made a straining sound as he proceeded to lean back in it.

Peter drained the rest of his glass before reaching for the bottle once again. He hated the feeling of helplessness. They both did, as they sat there listening to the chords of a piano reach out to the next one in infinite space. What was happening to the campus was in the fore of both their minds, but neither had wished to be the first to enter in on the subject. *What these impressionable kids were being fed couldn't be believed. It simply wasn't true. Of course, they were trying to feed it to him too, and what the stomach rejects had to somehow be expelled outwards.*

"Do you think," he started with a discernable slur of intoxication, "Blanchard is safe tonight?"

Clint drowsily sighed an answer, "I'd imagine."

"Are you sure?" Peter pushed.

"Yeah…" Clint looked at him in wonder. "I'd think there are too many buildings for them to ransack first. It's, at least, highly unlikely."

"So, our offices will be safe?"

Here Clint sounded with an edge of agitation "*Yes.*"

"Well, I'm not so sure."

Clint now sat up. "You honestly think that someone is going to break into our offices?"

"I don't see…why not."

Clint laughed. "I really wouldn't worry about that at this point."

"I'm not worried," Peter said with calm as his friend sounded more rattled. "I mean you were at that meeting today. You also heard the president's speech. Why do people think they're doing this? What does this violence have to do with their message?"

"Message?" Clint repeated dubiously. "Perhaps these *are* simple protests, as some would have it, and given specific experiences of large enough crowds with disparate elements, they tend to spiral out of control in the aggregate, projected by a form of mass hysteria brought on by the interactivity among the elements."

"Right. And that would be a perfect blanket explanation. Little investment necessary. At least a good place holder for any doubt."

"People also recognize that others have a tendency to blow off steam. That when people are unable to rein in the chaos of their own lives, they wreak havoc upon things or people inside of their control. The results of economic uncertainty for instance, but—"

"And what explanation do you favor? What do you *really* think?"

Clint hesitated, eyeing Peter curiously. "I think you already know."

"Just say it."

"You saw what they had: the busses, the equipment, the platoon lieutenant, whatever he was. Hard to see how this is not somehow coordinated, well-funded."

"That's a conspiracy theory, right?" Peter accused.

"Okay Peter, I don't need to be a part of this tract from Plato right now," Clint vented seeming to have reached his boiling point.

"At the end of the day, most people will probably think, as they are trained to, that if they had a new avenue of destruction, it'd be because of one of your first reasons, which I believe is reducible to one simple idea, the mob. Even more elementary is that it is just what stupid does. Stupid people do stupid things even outside of their own direct interest."

"So?"

"So no one would really think too deeply about what destruction or chaos they cause on campus. That defines itself. The last thing most people are taught to think now is that there is a deeper reason. They know that a conspiracy, for instance, is a loaded term and would be laughed out of a room if they brought it up."

"Okay, but where is all of this going? Get to the fucking point, *please*."

Peter knew that he had tested his friend's patience, especially at this juncture with all of the recent stresses culminating into the moment, but he needed to show him how he'd arrived at what was called for. He knew that the only way to convince him was to go down this gradual circuitous path. A more direct approach would only look reckless and impulsive. The fact was that Peter saw this as anything but. It was simply necessary, as this may be the only opportunity to act before things permanently devolved.

"If someone broke into Blanchard tonight, no one would really question why. With all that is happening, I doubt they would do more than pass it off as another target of mob violence—another unfortunate casualty of a maddened crowd's misdirected anger."

"So?"

"That's where Eldridge's office is."

"Yes, *and?*"

"That's where I'm going tonight."

"To do what?!"

"Break in."

18

Her bed was soft, cool just as she liked it, but tonight she felt that it was somehow working against her. She tried every position, but sleep wouldn't come. Of course, she knew that it wasn't her bed at all, whose mattress she had even spent a small fortune on. It was the thought reel that plunged her into yet another deeper more unpleasant rabbit hole keeping her awake. Up to now, she had thought about taking that sleeping pill in her medicine cabinet. That would surely do the trick. Only she didn't want to feel strung out in the morning. Besides, at these times she found that she was able to think—to really think about everything—about her job, her friend, and her life still tied to both.

She speculated now whether Marcus was really who she thought he was. There was something about his behavior that went beyond just the feigned sympathy—something altogether despicable. *What was he about? Why did he behave so passive aggressively? Was it because she went behind his back? Maybe. But how could he not see Yunnie was important to her—firing her so callously like that? And why didn't he seem to care about her being missing? It almost seemed like he had something to do with her disappearance.*

Yeah, right. Now you want to entertain a nutty conspiracy theory, Kristi laughed to herself. *Maybe in the near future you could just leave the NGO world to find work on some crank podcast discussing Bigfoot or the faked moon landing. There is a niche for that.*

Laying there, now with the image of Marcus' stupid grin gnawing at her, sleep felt hopeless. She usually knew how to banish such unacceptable images—how to manage a potentially sleepless night. If she sensed the mood she'd be in, she would come home and take a long scorcher of a bath before watching TV, something noncommittal, a run-of-the-mill drama that she could pick up again anytime: Sherlock, Vampire Diaries, or The Crown while eating something sweet. And that's precisely what she did tonight: a big bowl of strawberry ice-cream after a bath with an episode of The Crown playing with her feet up on the ottoman. It wasn't too long before drowsiness came. She felt it along with the unusual gloominess of being alone in her apartment with no good friend to turn to anymore. It should all have been more than enough to zonk her out. But, tonight, it wasn't. Tonight, her thoughts weren't all that peeved her. It was that some part of her felt inexorably wrong. Sure, it was a diminutive part, but one that coarsely brushed up against the rest of her—a part that appeared to demand the respect of the whole.

Hours passed rolling around in her bed with her invisible foe. Images rushed through her mind unabated with no end in sight until a click chirped through the dark. The sound was short and muffled through her bedroom door yet enough to perk her ears up bringing her into a terrifying present state of consciousness.

Someone is opening my front door, she imagined. Completely still, she listened the way a deer does its stalker in the woods. But unlike the creature, she resorted to immediate disavowal of the instinct. *The neighbors. It's them. Mikel and Barbara coming home from another late-night drunken jaunt,* she tried to calm herself. It didn't work. She stared at the doorknob, knowing that someone must be standing on the other side. *Was it moving? Yes, it was. This is no theory. This is really happening.*

The door opened a crack with an almost imperceptible whine that she wouldn't have noticed if she were asleep. Her heart thrusted through her chest with such a gusto that she felt it gave her away immediately. She was awake. She was helpless, and she was the soon-to-be victim. All she could think to do was to stare from her side, half fetal, at whatever menace was violating her space.

Another moment the door inched open fully. A skinny shadow stood at the threshold. It loomed there as Kristi beheld it. They were both completely still. Both regarded the other under the veil of darkness. It was that period of quiet, that absence of objection, that seemed to give it license to proceed, easing through the door carefully sliding into the room as an anticipatory chill coursed through her body.

She squinted her eyes as it approached her bed with the glint of a long implement projected before it. The outline of a face could almost be registered beneath a tall cap as it creeped closer. Her eyes were almost completely shut as it stooped over her feigned slumber.

Despite her heart rate, it didn't seem to notice how she was fully awake and aware of the monstrous design it hoped to commit unnoticed in colorless night.

When was she going to move? She didn't know if she could. Her limbs were in a state of paralysis. *How could she just lay here and die? She couldn't, could she?* Any second she imagined the feel of her murderer's slender tool plunging into her soft flesh—probing deeper and deeper—to solve this strange malady called life. It would only be a matter of minutes before it'd be over. *Maybe she should just let it. What was all of this for anyway? Life was a cold lonely place only for the cruel. And what was a better end? Wasn't murder just as natural as birth? It happened every day.*

Time seemed to stand still. The stab didn't come. Instead, the figure crouched down before the bed producing something new in its hands—a small rag and bottle. It was the kind of flask a priest would fill with holy water to carry to the sick and homebound.

The figure spun off its top carefully emptying some of it into the rag. The strong aroma of grass clippings immediately filled the room and her nostrils. Its initial potency flushed her body with a warmth that brought new life to her limbs and resolve.

In an instant, she rolled to the other side of the bed screaming with blood curdling ferocity—stunning the figure momentarily. She yanked the drawer of her small night stand open which jetted fully loose without the due weight she had anticipated. Its contents of condoms and birth control spilled out onto the floor, but not the gun. Her .22 caliber long rifle Ruger was missing.

She flung the drawer at it from its handle with relative success. It grunted as the thin wood broke apart in making contact with its head. She unlocked the balcony door and slipped out scouring for a means of escape. She first tried the doorknob to the living room and cursed at how reliable she was in locking it. *Could she jump down to the next floor?* Seeing the slim possibility of landing there, she preferred dying with a fight, implicating a murderer, rather than suicide.

The figure followed through the blinded room into the light of the city revealing the arm with the slender blade followed by the gaunt face of a man with blood streaming down from under his hat. *She must have caught him with the corner of the drawer. Good.*

"You one mouthy beech," he expressed to her with a foreign tongue. The face was crazed like in the visible rage of a tweaker. It reminded her to keep screaming, and so she did. *Maybe someone would hear and help. Mikel and Barbara?*

The smile her attacker wore showed no mirth as he came at her to the far corner of the balcony. This was it. All would be decided now.

Picking up one of the twin aluminum chairs, she swung it at her assailant as hard as she could, but he caught it with his free hand and pulled. It almost slipped from her grasp as she hugged onto it for dear life. Instead of relinquishing it, she pushed her weight into it as if she were a mother oryx against a lion. The surprising reversal thrust him into the other side of the balcony against the metal rail. The knife clanked to the stone, as he endeavored to hold himself up.

In trying to force him over, she expelled a primordial war-cry but felt her control slipping. She knew he was steadily gaining the upper-hand. Instead of waiting for this hopeless denouement, she abruptly abandoned the chair—reentering her room making haste to shut the now half-open door and lock the intruder out.

She heaved all her weight into the effort before a shuddering crash into the frame of the chair that he managed to insert into the doorjamb. She threw her body repeatedly against the chair bending its aluminum frame irredeemably, but he soon seized control pitting his body against hers on the door itself.

She took the initiative again of another strategic retreat. She flew from her bedroom and living room through her now unlocked front door.

In the hall, she echoed her continuous imprecation for help, knocking at all the neighbors' doors, all the while, eyeing her door at a distance—awaiting his emergence from her apartment at any second to continue the onslaught. She wailed for two endless minutes seeing no one come to her aid.

Finally, just as she started to doubt herself what had just occurred, her attacker came brazenly into the bright hallway light— the denim revolutionary cap sitting snugly over the frantic façade that she had only glimpsed before. She ran back further in the long corridor assuredly piercing the sleep of many with her now operatic vocals.

He stood there unmoved, as if considering continuing the pursuit. No hint of the smile anymore, which was obscured by the shadow cast by his hat's brim. A door between them opened. A shirtless man in boxers, revolver in hand, saw her before seeing the thin man at the other end make a dash to the staircase exit. As he left, she saw her closet duffle bouncing from behind his back.

19

Peter and Clint drove down Main Street. In the night, it looked like it could have been a ghost town for some time, as many of the businesses were securely closed up. The owners of Sally's Bakery made the place look like a military bunker having bolted down all of its steel shutters that it usually did only in the anticipation of a hurricane.

Peter believed their leaving was the right decision, even though this was no hurricane. It was worse. He just hoped it wasn't too late to do something about it.

They pulled into a small empty visitor lot just abutting campus. This would have to do. There were police checkpoints everywhere and if they got any closer to the park with the car, they could have even more problems to contend with. The plan was to get in and get out without being so much as a blip on anyone's radar. So far so good.

Switching the ignition off, they sat there quietly in the dark. Their uneasy look suggested it was still way too soon coming back to campus after their earlier encounter.

Clint took in a deep breath and exhaled. They were both thinking but not saying what was on their minds. But the fact was that there was nothing much more to talk about that hadn't been said. They had both made their decision.

The point of contention hadn't been that something should be done, even something drastic. Every day the university they once knew was slipping further into madness and, what was more, it may even take the rest of the country with it. The real question, rather, was whether Eldridge did have something damning enough that they could obtain without getting caught. Peter believed he did and that they could, but Clint wasn't so confident.

"If things trend the way they are now, I don't think I could forgive myself for not trying when an opportunity like this presented itself," Peter had explained to Clint.

"You think that Eldridge is just going to leave something on his desk? *Come on.*"

"I think that you give Eldridge too much credit. But, no, I'd imagine on his computer."

"Computer means password. You and I are not going to be breaking into any encrypted system."

"*We're* not breaking into it."

"What do you mean?"

"I'm getting help from a friend."

"Who?"

"Paul."

"Paul? Paul?" Clint looked dazed.

"Paul Kemp."

"You're drunk," Clint shot out eyeballing his friend from across the table.

"Not true." Peter stared back unaffected by the outburst. "I've never been more sober."

Clint laughed off the response before downing the rest of his glass.

"No," Clint refused, knowing exactly who he meant.

"He's—"

"He's not coming with us to—the fuck are you saying?"

Peter sighed resting his eyes on his friend—deciding to slow down to give him a chance to catch up.

"Paul can do it…" Clint looked in wide eyed amazement at what he was hearing. "We'll take the desktop. Make it look like some members of the black bloc got in. Like we talked about, I don't think anyone consequential will think twice about why it happened. Who knows how many buildings they've already breached and for what good reason?"

Clint sat there silently in continued bafflement. Peter even surprised himself at what he had just said. Even now through a cloud of inebriation, he recognized that he was acting quite selfishly in trying to have Clint come at all. There was no reason to drag him down too.

"Ya'know, you're right," he suddenly concluded. Clint looked thrown off by the remark. "You don't have to come."

"What?"

"You don't need to. I can do it alone…You have a family and a future here. I'm already one foot out. I've exposed myself too much. You haven't."

The giant sat there unmoved. His demeanor portrayed an agitated deeper reflection going on. *He wasn't coming*, Peter thought. *But he'll still try to convince me not to go.*

"I imagine this Paul's the same techie you've told me about before?" He finally said, surprising Peter by the inquiry.

"My old roommate."

"He still doing shady jobs?"

"When the cause is right."

"Well, in this case, is the cause right enough for him?"

"Exposing lies as big as this. Nothing better."

With his hand over his glass swirling it around—jingling the tiny shards of ice as he looked on, Clint spoke again. "Say I go…" He put the glass down before him. "We get the computer. Your old college roomie scours the hard-drive and finds nothing remotely untoward on it. What then? Oops? My bad?"

"A big boo-boo," Peter offered sarcastically. "I suppose we are going to have to get a lot more used to the idea of being where we are right now. That is, working under the new academic order."

Peter's face now captivated Clint. The fixed austere mask didn't bat an eye to what it heard.

"Hey, they may even call on us to give our own ode to the movement," Peter continued. "Who knows? Psych professors administering anti-racist freshman orientations, new course offerings, degrees. Hell, your name may come up to preside over entire conferences on the matter. How fun that'll all be?"

Clint sat there unbemused—imagining the unpalatable flavor of the hypotheticals. The possibility of the sheer presumptiveness of such a request was what really roiled him. That was something he couldn't at all stomach.

He stirred in his chair again compressing the wicker with his bulky frame. When the creaks settled at last, he summarized where he stood.

"Right," he said.

Peter cut up his old black Pink Void tee. It wouldn't be missed and neither would the old neglected Pirates and Nike caps found in the hall closet. These, in addition to the hold-over winter coats and gloves from his life in Pittsburg he thought would be sufficient disguises for that hour. And they almost worked perfectly. The only catch was that the coat he gave Clint was almost unwearable— snugly hugging his chest only after his arms ripped up the inner stitching. It would still have to do.

The last elements they needed were the hardware. This, Peter had covered from his tool bench in the garage. There he loaded up his hiking pack just as they had witnessed the protestors do earlier that day—only Peter's equipment was the inferior. He took two short plastic flashlights, two hammers, a standard claw and hand sledge, and one three-foot long crowbar. When Clint saw the latter, Peter thought he perceived alarm flash across his friend's face, as if he didn't understand the full magnitude of what they were about to do until then.

In fact, Clint's stomach did fall at that moment, as if on a carny ride drop. The thought of damaging anything on his beloved campus was a lot for him. But, in thinking of what was happening there now, the use crowbar was dwarfed by comparison. If this tool was only used sparingly, on Eldridge's office door for instance, to preserve the very integrity of the institution to continue on, he knew he'd have to come to terms with it.

Peter came to see Margery sitting up in bed reading. He told her where he was going—to take Clint back home—leaving out their impending illegal adventure to campus first. She looked tired. It had been a long day after all—for him too.

"Peter," she said holding him with eyes closed.

"Yes?" He kissed his wife.

"Don't do it." Peter's heart skipped withdrawing to see what she was getting at. Her expression wasn't giving anything away

"Do what?"

"Don't drink anymore tonight, okay? Come straight home." She opened her eyes to measure his reaction which softened.

"I won't."

The silence was finally broken by Clint's movement. Peter saw his friend tremble with the bag in the backseat. With someone else, he may have mistaken it for a sign of fear, but he saw his friend earlier that day at a time he'd never seen him—at his peak. This was not a man so much afraid anymore as invigorated by a purpose. Peter couldn't be sure, but perhaps that was part of his reason for coming in the end because here he was too. What they both witnessed in the neighborhood that day not only hardened their resolve but provided the impetus of a new energy reserve that they didn't know they had. And now it was their time to expend it. It was their time to try to set things right—to assert control.

They started across the lawn grass with the stone wall containing the sizable USFL insignia etched into it. The well-groomed hedges and flowers surrounding it almost seemed unreal at their being untouched with all the defacement going on. The yelling and fireworks popping off in the distance certainly lent a strange ambiance to such a welcoming and prestigious image. The thought of prospective students and their funder parents patently raising their objections to attending at this point caused Peter to chuckle. But then seeing Clint's giant figure parading across campus with a Nike cap and tight coat that was more of an untucked shirt started Peter rollicking.

"What is it?" Clint stopped to look back unable to see his friend clearly as Peter tried to expel less air in every burst. Instead, it came out as a whimpering choke. The improvised neckie concealed the smile well.

"Your coat—" was all he could get out through the laughter.

"Are you serious? You *are* drunk."

The comment only compelled Peter to laugh more as Clint responded with his own coughing boffs. The mood quickly changed, however, as they proceeded. A faint scent of smoke that was at first tolerable took on a biting pungency—a reminder of the looming insanity just beyond.

20

The city lights of the dark early morning flashed past Kristi's unseeing eyes. Officer Calvin, who was driving her home, didn't get much out of her since her request to turn down the AC. With "Mmhm" and "No" being all of her subsequent responses to his small talk, he decided to take a hint. Not that she was being rude, but she had already done a lot of talking and now needed time to think. The questions they asked her at the station opened something akin to a vortex in her brain with all firing neurons leading to the same place. It had become undeniable that whatever happened to Yunnie, almost happened to her.

"Your one special lady Miss Kristi," said Detective Gonzalez's round jovial face just after she recalled her attack. She didn't like to be called Miss Kristi or Miss Connor for that matter, but the man possessed a wealth of warmth that was most welcome at a time when the world felt so cold. "I can just imagine his surprise to see that the woman under the covers was a force to be reckoned with!" He laughed a good belly full while Kristi politely smiled. Some of the effects of shock were wearing off, especially now on her fifth cup of gritty bitter coffee.

Another man from the force was there with them, Officer Brennan, who had originally accompanied Gonzalez into the room. "My God, John," he shared Gonzalez's fit of laughter but to a more reserved degree than his bearded, bald colleague. "Why would you want to be involved in politics Miss Kristi?" Gonzalez's chuckle petered out. "We need someone like you to do the trainings for crime prevention. What do you say to that?" he asked in short abrupt spurts. Kristi just continued smiling not sure if he was joking or genuine this time.

"Can I get you anything else Miss Connor?" Brennan asked, who had been standing against the door seemingly waiting for the opportunity to offer further assistance.

"No—well I," she was almost in tears from how much attention they were giving her and was touched even though she knew it was part of their job. "Could someone please…take me home, so I can…I won't feel safe there." She anxiously laughed out the last part afraid to tell strangers about her insecurity. The fear of that man, however, had won out.

Gonzalez reached his hand out seeing the advent of tears. He waited for her to take it which she did. It was big and its heat was comforting. It said, *we got you.*

"Of course, Miss Connor, we're going to have someone take you back so you can pack a bag and stay somewhere for the night. We'll be collecting some more evidence," Brennan said.

"What do you think we're barbarians? We're going to keep you living, Miss Kristi. You're a rare one." Gonzalez smiled and winked at her, and she was honestly flattered.

Kristi took her hand from Gonzalez's to wipe the tears from her eyes before taking tissues from the box that Brennan offered. She dabbed away at her damp face as Gonzalez and Brennan both waited attentively. She supposed she could have a better cry alone without others watching and was soon able to hold them back regaining her façade.

"I think it's best now that Miss Kristi has some much needed rest," Gonzalez told Brennan as much as reassuring Kristi herself. Brennan nodded.

"Ma'am, we have all we need from you for now. We're going to get back with you as we gather more information," Brennan explained. "We're going to look at cameras and talk to more witnesses. In the meantime, make sure to lock all doors, try not to go to places alone, especially at night, tell people where you are, because, in this city, you never know."

Kristi stared at him incredulously. "But I did lock my door. It was locked—deadbolted." She couldn't believe, at this point, that he dared assume such a thing, as if he should know that ever since she was a babysitter watching Unsolved Mysteries at age thirteen, she saw it as her religious duty to do so.

"Yes Miss Connor. I'm only saying to take precaution—"

"But, you don't understand. I lock my door *always*. How did he even get in?"

This time Gonzalez chimed in. "We don't know yet Miss Kristi, but people forget things all the time. In this city especially. We have parents leaving children in the backseat in the hot sun. Purses missing from restaurant tables where they were left. My uncle…he even forgot to put his truck into park when we were kids. It just rolled down the neighborhood street while we tried to jump back inside to stop it." He laughed upon further reflection. "It ended up crashing into a parked car setting off a neighborhood feud lasting to this very day."

Brennan pondered this story over before proposing his own formulation. "It could have been any number of things Miss Connor. People swore they locked the front door when they didn't in one moment of absentmindedness. I even recall doing it in a mad rush to take the kids to school before traffic—" He stopped himself as she adamantly shook her head at his suggestion.

"And sometimes it's the *balcony* door. Happens on occasion," Gonzalez spoke gently.

"No. No. As I told you, all of those things were locked. I checked the balcony doors later. Nothing—"

"Tell me ma'am, have you been going through something lately? Times of high stress can induce forgetfulness in a lot of people."

"Stress? *Yes.* I told you. My best friend has gone missing. Of course, I'm stressed about it."

"Yes, that could factor in—"

"Maybe this has something to do with that?" Kristi murmured aloud hesitantly.

Both officers, at this point, looked at her and gave each other knowing glances as if to say this conversation was going off the rails.

"While that is possible," Brennan proceeded cautiously, "it seems improbable when missing persons is a very common occurrence—without a crime happening at all."

"He was there for me—not for money. I pretended to be asleep. Why would he do that?"

"But why would he bother to go out of his way to take the friend too? This appears just a crime of opportunity. He saw a way in. Someone was there which he wasn't counting on, but in the end, he was set on taking valuables and that's what he did." She recalled the man taking her duffle bag. Only after reentering the apartment did she understand why—finding drawers frantically pulled open and her jewelry box missing. *Wasn't it strange for a burglar not to bring his own bag?* She knew she didn't have to be a professional detective to think of it. Still, one irksome detail she remembered stood out over all the others.

"I'm sorry to hear about your friend," Gonzalez added, "but I'm sure she'll turn up before long."

"No, no, no," Kristi ignored Gonzalez. "It doesn't make any sense. My gun was missing. I had it in the drawer next to the bed. Remember? I went for it first and it was gone."

"Or you may have forgotten where you put it."

This time Kristi was the one to laugh with acerbic breath—losing all patience with the officers. "You don't understand. I never move my gun. Ever. It has basically lived in the same place since I bought it…he must've taken it before he came in!"

"Ma'am let's wait to see what happens with…"

The trauma of the struggle had dampened her reasoning but now she had regained some clarity. Her momentum of off-the-cuff thinking started to rapidly bring events together that could have been written off as sheer coincidence, but then again, a coincidence wasn't that until it could overcome its own burden of proof. Her eyes widened exposing her deep blues as the latest revelation fleshed out in her mind. "He took my spare key. From Yunnie! He took the key I gave to her!"

Again, Gonzalez and Brennan looked at each other but no longer as before. There was a piqued interest and concern. Gonzalez pulled back out his notepad, as Kristi elaborated on all the details. She relayed what happened chronologically from how Yunnie was fired without notice to the strange behavior of her boss earlier that day. Gonzalez documented all studiously as Brennan only listened, this time, without comment.

As they approached Sarde Villa number two, Kristi's fear hadn't left her. Envisioning the face of her attacker impressed with sheer warped ecstasy, she didn't think she would ever be comfortable in her apartment again, new locks or not. While she recognized that she was still suffering the effects of her encounter, she also knew she would be unable to retreat. The part of her that wanted to quit her job and leave the area, was only a part. The rest of her never backed down from a challenge to a conviction. She owed it to her friend to see this to the end. In a world where everyone was an island, Yunnie, she realized, was what really mattered. *Friends matter. Ray Foundation didn't come close.*

Officer Calvin pulled in behind a police cruiser parked adjacent to the lobby entrance. He paused before exiting hearing Kristi's breaths become longer and deeper. "You're going to be fine. Nothing's going to happen with us here." She didn't respond. She knew she should feel safe now, but her body was the one that was working itself up. "I'm ready whenever you are," Calvin answered her silence patiently. She did a couple more reps of breathing exercises before pulling the door release. Calvin followed.

She proceeded to the entrance removing her key fob from her purse while Calvin had gone up to the window of the parked officer and exchanged a few words. Before pressing it to the access panel, she waited for him. The door released and they entered.

The hallway leading to number eleven forty-two wrapped in police tape, was enough to make her hesitate. It was like she was suddenly thrown back into the nightmare. *Were they sure he left? Did anyone check the cameras?* Now, she wished she'd asked Gonzalez more questions. *There was almost no price to afford peace of mind and what in the end was inconvenience? How could he even enter the building without someone's help? Maybe that someone was still around?* She debated if she were the only one asking these questions. In her experience, to believe in others' due diligence wasn't necessarily a slam dunk.

Calvin routinely opened the door with the key and flipped on the lights. She was surprised to find no one inside watching the place—unsure what the typical police procedure was.

"Try not to touch anything other than the necessities. Just pack what you need for a while. They usually don't take long…but you never know." She nodded before flicking on her bedroom chandelier.

The room was in the same disarray she left it with the balcony door still ajar, chair just inside of it, contents of her side table spread across the carpet. Rubbers spilled from the box she had were now shining in the artificial light. On the other side of the room, the dresser drawers were open—partially ransacked with a couple of items thrown out including some belts, scarves, and letters she saved as well as a pocket New Testament gifted to her. It all just looked like a show to her. The jewelry box was missing of course. It was in the most obvious place of all. First drawer on the right. She didn't bother to hide it and why would she? In the unlikely event of someone entering the building and having the key to her apartment? It was probably the first thing he saw.

She busied herself with her packing reaching for her big roll away on the top shelf. Unzipping it on the bed, she went back to the dresser to start with the clothes. Pushing back the first drawer, there, laying on top of the next pile of clothes was the dark metal of her .22 caliber Ruger. "What the fuck?" she said staring wretchedly. "What is it?" Calvin called stepping into the bedroom. It sat there looking back as if mocking her—telling her never to trust her own senses and intuitions again. *What was she? Stupid. A veritable mad woman? Someone may have thought so, but she knew better.*

21

With the view of Blanchard now unobstructed, Peter was optimistic at seeing this through. He had considered that there could be an opportunity to abort if the circumstances drove them to it, but now that he saw Blanchard's long gothic façade, he felt confidence building.

Any protestor action that remained appeared to be on the far side of the park toward Peckhart. Through the smoke and flashers of police and emergency vehicles, he could only make out shadows along the ground. A helicopter was spotlighting, and the tinny voice of a megaphone rang out over other disparate creaturely sounds. The words "area" and "arrest" were all he could decipher, and neither Peter nor Clint cared to stand still long enough to listen intently.

They cut across the open grass avoiding the areas illumined by the campus' extensive system of lamps. The relative quiet, in contrast with the far side, along with the light producing a smokey glare gave Clint the impression that they could've entered a purgatorial state skirting the edge of inferno. The heat from wearing the coat only added to the torment—causing him to hemorrhage sweat.

"God," he mouthed to himself, "get me through this" longing for a shower and a deep sleep on his German pillow.

They emerged in the light briefly crossing the only two-lane road and sidewalk that separated them from, what they once knew as, their second home. But as they approached, it towered over them as an eerie unfamiliarity—a mysterious mass. It was enough for Peter to momentarily forget where they were, as he slowed his pace to have a better look. The structure's outline could've been mistaken for a derelict freighter in hopeless need of repair rather than a proud testimonial of academia. Its hulkingly sad state practically yearned to be put out of its misery—to sink into the abyss rather than go on as something it could no longer claim the name of.

Clint chugged ahead. "Over here," he said unable to whisper, as Peter dizzily redirected course following him to the side entrance.

At the door, Peter slung down his pack that clattered with the tools inside. Clint watched him nervously as he set out the flashlights, hammers, and the long shaft of the crowbar along the ground. After a cursory inspection of the doorjamb, he reached for the latter only to turn it over in his hands as he looked on.

Clint's mind raced. *They weren't really going to follow through with this part, were they?* When they came here out of a sense of duty, they did so to preserve the university not to destroy it. And now that they were here dressed up as a couple of goons with their own prepared packs, it was hard not to feel disgusted at becoming exactly what they reviled. There simply had to be a better way than to desecrate the institution they both loved.

"Wait." Clint put his hand over the bar. Peter looked up at him curiously, waiting to be told another way. His friend reached back pulling out his wallet, as Peter puzzled over why he brought his billfold in the first place. He watched as he removed a key from inside one of its compartments.

"No, that's not the point," Peter started.

"We'll leave a window open," Clint said with a knowing smile.

"But—" Peter began before reconsidering. Was it really that simple? He used to have classes on the first floor near the main entrance. While the windows facing the park were usually locked, they could be unlatched. A student could easily have undone one without anyone knowing for months. Building staff were already a skeleton crew and seemed to never be around when people needed them. Peter felt almost embarrassed at the simplicity of it all. *Why didn't he think of it?* Receiving Peter's nod of assent, he inserted the key and turned back the latch.

The interior was dark, so dark, in fact, that it reminded Peter of the ghost tour he took with the family in New Orleans where one was given a flashlight in a pitch-black plantation house. Only those locales appeared all contrived. In this case, he thought that Blanchard could be the genuine haunted article. Most days, though he would never admit it, experiencing a ghost traversing its long hallways is exactly what he expected. Seeing one come out now, however, he was pretty sure would be far less frightening than someone of flesh and blood.

Using the flashlights, Clint and Peter ascended the stairwell to the third floor. Both were out of breath with clothes drenched in sweat. Clint thought of removing his mask and coat but thought the better of it. *Who knew what unknown camera could be hidden?* Besides, Eldridge's door was close, and all he had to do was help Peter get in and out. He figured five minutes to get in, five there, and fifteen back to the car. *Twenty-five minutes max*, he told himself. *So just hold on.*

The beams of flashlights tracked along the patterns of the old terrazzo floor until they gravitated toward their terminus, an old scratched up mahogany board. Peter noticed the same black name plate with the drab sans-serif lettering, the door's only adornment. Now, with his office hours' sign absent, it appeared to fit Eldridge's personality exactly—not that he expected to honor them if they were still posted. There was simply no student important enough to block the limelight that Eldridge had long craved. Even now, he was probably getting his beauty sleep only to wake up in a few hours to make his rounds on the television and podcast circuit. More commentary was needed after all. For when one was the arsonist starting the fire, might as well roast a few marsh-mellows.

Peter again set down the bag, as Clint shined the light on it in anticipation of him fishing for tools. He hesitated, and Clint said nothing as he felt the same as before. Here they were again, having a crisis of conscience. Who were they even kidding in the end? To think they were going to just come in, pry the door free and hammer through, was just ridiculous. Maybe with the alcohol still coursing through them they would reconsider, but with the door before them now, they couldn't do it—not even lift a glove.

"I can't," Peter finally admitted piercing the silence.

Clint didn't respond. He didn't expect him to, as he wanted no part in vandalizing the place either. Instead, they stood there a while in thought. Without knowing what else to do, Clint gloved the doorknob and turned meeting no resistance. The door creaked as it ingressed into darkness.

With reticence, they both entered flashlights crossing Eldridge's desk honing-in on the computer perched on top. *Too easy.*

How could that be? Eldridge forgetting to lock his door? But he wasn't about to question it now. He didn't want to be there longer than they had to.

He was moving around the desk focused on the task at hand when something caught his attention in the corner across the room.

"The fuck?" he said, aiming his beam towards the sound. The sight caused Clint a shock, stepping back from the body laying on the sofa, quietly breathing. Eyes were opened there, regarding them both—Eldridge's eyes.

22

Eggers was slumped forward at his desk shirtless in his jockey shorts with the blue light from the computer screen creating shadows off the well-formed bags under his eyes. He had been up for twenty-three hours now covering everything related to the USFL protest, and as with the prospect of much needed rest slipping away—the sun rising in only a few hours, he couldn't bring himself to lay down again. Realizing how fruitless such an endeavor was with his mind still humming like a jet engine, he conceded defeat. His consolation was starting up his Keurig with the rich tones of a French roast filling his nostrils. *Maybe now, I can actually figure this thing out*, he told himself.

A question had been haunting him from his earlier interview with George Bishop. The crude styled right-wing radio personality and conspiracy theorist was to be asked his opinion on the events quickly unfolding on campus. At the time, he thought surely there had to be a better story than to quote some hot-take from an out-of-touch idiot, but he reluctantly agreed to do so as a favor and because there really hadn't been much available. By the end, out of the drivel, the force of the question in context struck him and wouldn't leave. *What if you're wrong?*

"Excuse me? *Prioritizing criers over buyers?*" Patrick remembered asking.

"Absolutely. Activists crying over trivial or imagined outrages while the students are there paying for it all—buying a degree—a worthless one, might I add." George spoke with his usual token hoarseness as if he had been karaoking Pavarotti the night before.

"Well, I think that's an oversimplification."

"I really feel bad for them, ya'know? The state has put their seal of approval on indebting them for the rest of their lives when they could've simply accessed the local library."

Eggers laughed out of frustration. George was making too many claims at once and he knew he needed to slow it down.

"But, that's not how this works. You want an engineer building a bridge with only a library education? That's insane."

"What's insane is the cost of a dumbed down education. At one time it made sense and was worth the time and money. Now it is watered down to appease rich liberals who lack for nothing."

Eggers wore the skeptical smile as if to say, *so this is the game we're going to play.*

"What *do* they want then?"

"Among other things, for their friends to see them as paragons of goodness, of course, instead of what they really are."

"Being?"

"Morally bankrupt."

"Okay, I see…*And* who would these rich liberals be? Where are they exactly?" It was hard at this point not to sound mocking, but Eggers felt George didn't leave much room.

"Simon Ray. Ray Foundation. The main player behind this multiplication of activist groups and coordinating these protests even now."

The name mention surprised him, stirring an interest he was still pursuing. While he never really thought of the possibility of Ray being behind the protests themselves, it intrigued him. Off the back of a largely fruitless Levy interview, he was ready to listen to any insights on one of the primary organizations funding Eldridge and Jersey's research.

"Simon Ray? The philanthropist? I don't think that there's any evidence to suggest he or his foundation is involved with anything…of what we're seeing now, at least directly." His skepticism came out, as was his usual course when presented with something novel.

"They're paying protestors to go out there with signs, buses, maps, weapons…An agenda to cause chaos and destruction. And look at them out there, they're loving it! Acting out. No consequences."

"But, how do you know this? I don't imagine you're one of them," Eggers said with a humorous smile.

"Some are speaking out—making confession videos online…"

"I see," said Eggers as if to say that's all he needed to know to dismiss it.

"They had previously been hired for jobs by people from the Foundation and came out now to call these shams for what they are." The confidence in George's voice didn't diminish despite the reaction from Eggers.

"So, someone online told you? I'm sure you'll also find someone saying the exact opposite."

"The facts are there if you look and read carefully."

"Clearly."

"You can even find that the Foundation was a major contributor to the study. A study about racism science. Something that would be well in their interest to validate for future donors. So, if you think about it, it makes a lot of sense."

"But it doesn't."

"It wasn't enough for them to have such a study done because many aren't ever going to read it. You have to make it mainstream, and that is what the protestors are for. They had to get the message out by getting everyone to look at each other around the country wondering if somewhere deep down, in their very genes, they're some racist asshole. That's better than any billboard."

Eggers let him finish, not at all surprised that right-wingers had already spread the word about the source of the money behind the research. But, he wasn't buying the overall story. The Foundation didn't need to be paying protestors to get the word out. News media had already done that. There was just too many cumbersome details to work out. It sounded too close to well-known conspiracies like Jewish blood libel or a secret government cabal.

After a pause, he summarized his thoughts. "I don't think so," he said knowing his producers probably wanted him to move the interview along anyway.

George studied his face for a moment without any sign of negative emotion. It didn't look like the face of someone playing a game anymore. "What if your wrong?" he asked with a moment of genuine concern uncharacteristic of such personalities.

The whole impression caused Eggers' stomach muscles to weaken before answering with a suppressed chuckle. "I don't think so." He meant for the response to sound confident and decisive, but it came out unconvincingly. The doubts somehow managed to leak through. He sensed it. George sensed it. The crew sensed it, and he imagined the entirety of his viewership.

Despite the blunder, he managed to finish the interview composed. His feeling of embarrassment at what his audience likely witnessed, however, endured for a good part of the day. Only later had that feeling turned into what he felt now—a much more constructive feeling. He was pissed.

I'm wrong? Eggers now asked himself. *What if you're wrong?* He wanted to ask it at the time, but he knew that was just the kind of rhetorical theater he despised. "It's nothing—really nothing," he repeated to calm himself to focus on the task at hand whenever the image of his failure came to mind. But the replay would keep coming up again and again. In all its excruciating detail, he would have to relive the moment. It was only when he reminded himself of his own humanity that it quieted down some. The acceptance of the fact that the doubtless man he wasn't nor could he ever be him. It was an important step. That was just the part he sometimes played for the public. But why should he even malign doubt in the first place? Why did people hate it so? Though it was something of an imposter looked down upon, cast out upon the first inkling of its existence, it really got a bad rap. To have a doubt was indeed a good thing. It was a sure sign that its bearer could recognize something wholly outside of himself, a reality that Eggers had perceived as something much more surprising, dazzling than its bearer could imagine. It was holding the true story in the highest respect of its power and the very thing he hunted for now.

So, on he went with his most noble task—taking notes watching all the online confessions he could find, which up to that point only amounted to two. Next, he had to try to make contact with them, and perhaps, if he was lucky, even interview Ray himself.

Even though there had yet to be any aha moments after this many hours invested, he found himself more compelled—drawn into the story of videos and internet chatter. And though he never said more to George than that he thought the story false, he also didn't impart the fact that he wanted every bit of it to be true.

23

"Get outta here schlubasses!" Eldridge barked at them suddenly. "You're not s'pose to be here! You've no idea wharerya…" The stunted voice trailed off in a string of indecipherable obscenities that couldn't be parsed. Meanwhile, both Peter and Clint were still shocked into place. The idea had occurred to them that perhaps it was time to run but both couldn't move. "Can't you dimfuckingwits listen?!" Eldridge proceeded to follow with a groan raising himself up.

The moment for fleeing was passing as they both continued to regard their clearly boozy colleague, their flashlights staying on him—not only as a center of curiosity—but as a defense against him identifying them. As he struggled to pull himself up with abdomen expanding and contracting in deep heaves, both appeared to wait for the other's next move.

Eldridge managed to rise shielding his face seeking those who had so rudely awoken him. The sudden shift was enough to cause Clint to take another step back as a wave of strong-smelling vapor had managed to reach him. *My God, if alcohol could piss*, he thought, *it would smell like that.*

With his eyes drifting from one light source to the other, not liking any of it, Eldridge appeared to resign himself to the situation ceasing the yelling of profanity and waiting for what was next. When neither Clint nor Peter divulged as much, he felt compelled to ask the unnecessary.

"Who areya? Whaddya want?"

Scenarios ran through their heads. *What could they ask? Alcohol was a truth serum of sorts after all. They could still discover something about what they came for.* Clint gave it serious consideration before deciding not to say anything. There was simply no way Eldridge wouldn't immediately recognize the distinctly strong sound of his voice.

"You're here to steal my research? That it?" Eldridge guessed the very object running through both of their minds. "Why I invite you to try to make me talk!" he threatened the two masked figures interpreting their silence as a confession of guilt.

"No, we're not here to steal your research, Professor." Peter took off his mask and stepped before Eldridge.

"Wha?" Eldridge peered up in confusion at a face familiar but unrecognizable for the moment. The quantity of liquor he most recently consumed was greatly affecting his vision. It took a moment to put a name to it and then still he doubted, as if this were all just an alcohol-induced hallucination.

Clint's heart rate spiked. *What the hell did Peter think he was doing?* All they had to do was leave, but now he envisioned the arrival of police. He imagined the headline in the Palm Gate Courier reading something like: Masked Professors Join Rabble. The girls would see an unappealing photo of their father wearing a jumpsuit holding a serial number. At least his father wasn't still alive to have to see it or he'd feel responsible for the heart-attack that killed him.

"We came to campus to check Blanchard."

Eldridge appeared to freeze while Clint held his breath. He now saw what his friend was doing and was unsure where it would lead them.

Eldridge's mouth finally turned into a smile expelling air in an almost sickly cough at its zenith. "Barton! Yes, of course," he laughed.

Both men stood there unsure how to take this apparent moment of levity. It was clear that the man was almost mad with intoxication, but at the same time, the recognition portrayed an element of lucidity.

"And Dumfries? That you over there then?" he asked looking in Clint's direction. Hearing the sound of his own surname felt like being shot by a paralyzing dart to the heart like he was already hearing it at a summons or in a prison roll call. The feeling of shame of being caught behind a mask was almost as much as the time he was caught by the principal for skipping music class to read

Hardy Boys' books in the library. But he knew that there was no going back now. He had to trust Peter's improvised plan.

"It's me," he removed his mask with one hand fighting off any quavering sound of fear.

Eldridge made a wide drunken grin that was more than a little unnerving.

"So let me get this straight," Eldridge slurred, "you came in the middle of night dressed as hooligans to check your office…"

Peter didn't bat an eye. He answered, "that's right."

"Then you came here to the third floor, out of the goodness of your heart, to check my office too?" The voice poked at the absurdity and almost dared him to answer in the affirmative, and Peter didn't disappoint.

"And why not? Our livelihoods are all going to hell on a Harley. But, you want to know the real reason we're here?"

"What?" Eldridge asked with his sleepless bloodshot eyes fixed upon Peter's.

"*You*. That's why. We're here because of you. You caused all of this. This wonderful party we're having here on campus tonight. And hey, maybe after they're done, they can erect another statue, but of you, because of what *you've* done. And they can put it right over there in the quad. Won't that be nice? That is, of course, before it too is defaced and destroyed by the next mob."

Eldridge listened, not seeming to miss a detail of what Peter said, all humor had completely vanished from his face being replaced with an embittered twitchy glower.

"Fuck you!" he exploded. "I had nothing! Nothing—! I despise those people! I want them all dragged to the middle of the street and shot! I'm not responsible for how they act! Neither for all those others who are too monumentally stupid to understand research! If I knew what they were going to do I'd—I'd've released it all!"

Am I really hearing this? Clint's look to Peter said. Peter didn't see him. He was too wrapped up in the moment by the latest revelation.

"Released what?"

Eldridge stared at Peter as if he didn't understand the question, so Peter asked again.

"What would you have released?"

Snickering, Eldridge looked away at the wall, but Peter wasn't buying this act. He couldn't believe that he suddenly was too drunk to understand when he perfectly did before.

"Eldridge?!" he asked with the heat now apparent in his voice.

Eldridge's response was to take the vodka bottle just below the couch's arm unscrewing its cap.

"God, stop that," Clint sighed.

"You think you had enough?" Peter judged seeing as how only one fifth of the bottle remained.

He took a solid swig anyhow, slobbering some over the bottle's mouth then wiping his lips with the back of his arm. He then extended it as an offering to both of them.

Clint shook his head. Peter took it when it was his turn, but just before taking his own hit, refrained setting it down nearby.

"Isn't this comfy?" Eldridge pointed out before laying back on the sofa feeling complete after venting his diatribe. This in conjunction with the drink, immediately caused him to start to fade. The whites of his eyes flickered from pupil then back again as he just managed to stave off sleep.

While he questioned if Eldridge would even remember this exchange, Clint knew that Peter had only moments to extract the information they both sought. Now with too much serum entering into his blood stream, their strategy was soon to fail.

"Professor, Professor!" Peter snapped his fingers suddenly to have Eldridge come to momentarily. "You were saying something about releasing it all. What did you mean by that?"

"Ahhh-I…" he murmured shutting his eyes again continuing into a doze.

Clint finally stepped in putting his hands over his shoulders in a gentle touch to try to resuscitate the spent frame. It was just enough to bring him out of it and Peter took his chance.

"The raw data, Professor? Are you talking about the raw data?!"

The body now held itself up from the backrest under its own power with eyes open seemingly aware but barely.

"You're talking about the raw data. There were other participants? Right? Am I right? The sample size was actually bigger. Yes?" All he wanted was an affirmative, but as was usual in the world of academia, it wasn't the response he received.

Eldridge breathed deeply holding his arm again as if calling for the bottle.

"No—no more. Please answer his question as the university is riding on it!" Clint pleaded. "….for Godsakes Eldridge, would you just do the right thing for once!"

His head turned listlessly as if Clint's message had been heard, but to what extent wasn't clear. He groaned before responding.

"For the sake of yourself and your family," he eked out.

"What?!" Peter turned his head to lend an ear to the barely audible voice.

"For the sakes of you and your families…don't look into this…not anymore."

"Why not? What about our families? What will happen?" Peter shouted his question at the crumbling man—a man with tears starting to well in his eyes.

"He'll observe them. Corrupt them. Destroy them. Death…"

"Who?"

"No—"

"*Who?*"

He closed his eyes again reaching his hand back out curling his fingers—begging for the bottle one last time.

"And what about the university?"

Nothing.

"*Eldridge*, what of the university?!"

The last response came from the back of the throat almost like a growl of an agitated feline. "It's. too. Late."

In-die-go.

1

Kristi felt hungover without drinking a drop the night before. After checking into a Radicon in Falls Church, she awoke only after a few hours and couldn't bring herself to go back to sleep no matter how exhausted she felt. The only thing she knew to do was to turn on the news and percolate a pot of coffee with the room's complimentary maker.

She then sat up in bed viewing the images from the protest the night before. Running on a continuous loop with ample commentary, she watched as the officers beat protesters mercilessly with batons. But it was nothing compared to the highlight of the night. Nothing could top the raw brutality of the strangulation. The back and forth sudden whiplash motion of the protestor's head really turned her stomach. She winced every time she saw it, even seeming to feel the crushing force on her own throat followed by the deprivation of air as the baton locked around the cords of the young man's neck torquing it backward.

Along with fear, nausea ensued. Blood began rushing to her head and her heart leaped through her chest. Suddenly, there she was experiencing last night all over again. The killer's bloodshot eyes and deranged smile were coming for her as she swung the chair uselessly, waiting any moment for the long thin blade to open her flesh—to be the end of her—to decide that her experiences, thoughts, hopes, dreams, and anyone who cared for her didn't matter.

Just as the replay had shown on TV, so did her mind rerun those events beginning to end lingering on the same details, the aroma of freshly mown grass, the doped face, the foreign seasoning of his voice, her body virtually floating with terror. It's as if she had been on autopilot, not an actor but merely a witness, and if it weren't for the soreness in her arms and legs now, she could almost believe it was someone else. It was hard to accept, but she had enough fight and luck to be here now. Despite his apparent planning in removing the gun and entering when many would be asleep, she escaped. She had faced a predator and survived. *How many victims could've done the same? How many people out there, people like Yunnie, didn't?*

Tears formed on the narrow bridge of her nose. She wiped them, trying to turn her thoughts to prevent any more from coming, but it was too late. More welled and gravity did the rest. She knew it was only a matter of time before the floodgates opened. She muted the TV and sat there for some time letting out what she had been holding in.

Could she imagine Yunnie's suffering? Could she see the knife plunge into her friend? Yes, in fact, she could, but she refused to conceive too much. *What kind of hell on earth would have to persist to allow harm to come to one as her? How could funny Yunnie, kind Yunnie, beautiful Yunnie be untimely prized from it? In what depths of existence possessed such a monstrosity to take away such a gift? Perhaps this was it, of all possible worlds, this was it. And what was more?* It just entered her head as she saw a new headline glide across the bottom of the screen. "Violence Against Women Surges." *The fullness of this hell was still being created.*

She tried to retain hope telling herself that nothing was certain—that Yunnie could really still be alive. She knew that was what Yunnie herself would try to do. She would hug her and gently remind her of what she didn't know. All could still be well. But Kristi wasn't Yunnie. She accepted what she was a long time ago— a cold realist. And after what happened, she knew where the facts stood. She knew now that Yunnie was really gone—gone forever. The only substantial hope that remained for her wouldn't change that fact. Nevertheless, she believed that the hope that remained could still dry some tears, at least for the present. That hope was ruthless to its core, more ruthless than what she thought almost happened to her. Punishment. She would have liked to call it justice, but that's not what it really was. To her mind, it far exceeded a tempered response that most would associate with the word. She wanted whatever man whatever agency splayed out and skewered. And the same inner realist told her where to find this agency. No amount of Marcus Levy's hugs, assurances or perfect white toothed smiles practiced in the mirror would cause her to overlook the common thread between these crimes, that is, Ray Foundation.

Kristi composed herself and called Marcus. She knew this part was important. Not making the call would indicate a possible suspicion and the way she sounded on the phone could be revealing as well. Helpless naivety was just the sound she was looking for—just what Marcus sought to allay his fears.

He picked up the phone only after a few rings. No sound of anything untoward at all in his voice. *Was he really so innocent? Nothing was unexpected from the little psycho*, she decided. Just as she had to put on her little play that all was well, so did he.

To be convincing, she just let the words flow allowing some of the accompanying emotion to spill out, acting as if a close confidant was on the line. He listened with quiet reserve as she poured forth her recent brush with death during a home invasion only expressing a word of surprise at each new turn of events. Every time she heard a new word from him, she thought she could detect it—the pretense—the Pinocchio trying to act like a real man. *Just shut the fuck up already.*

She wanted to yell at him. She wanted to scream the foulest of curses of what she knew—something empowering to name him for what he was, but as satisfying as that could be, she knew it would be too short-lived. She would get no lasting satisfaction from it. Instead, she had a plan and knew to stick to it for Yunnie as much as for herself.

She finished her narrative with the visit to the police station which was the only part he had questioned her about.

"Do they have any idea who this man could be?" He asked as she smiled sickly at his sudden curiosity and at what she thought predictability.

When she answered in the negative, he left it at that—only expressing his sympathy and an offer to help in any way he could. It was just the cue she was looking for in his digression. She didn't hesitate to make her request frank. "I'll be needing some time..."

His sound of relief was probably more than he wanted to give away. "Of course. Take as long as you need." The timbre in his voice cracked at the end.

"I'm going to need a few personal things from the office."

This brought him a moment of pause as she thought it might. *Who'd want you still around after just trying to have you murdered? It was just too much of a liability. If he thought that she was a risk in speaking to the police about Yunnie, how much more of a risk did he think she was now?*

Proceeding cautiously, he countered. "I could have someone take them to you."

"No—no, I'll be fine. It'll be easier if I just get them. That way I can also say bye to the office for a while."

He hesitated again, but this time was a little quicker on the response. "Yes, do what you have to do. In any case, I won't be there, but I'll tell Vivian to arrange for your absence. In the meantime, take care of yourself…"

"I will."

"…And notify us if something comes up."

To this she didn't make a further reply, and instead of concluding the call, he took her silence as a prompt to make additional offers of assistance and what she considered further plastic statements of sympathy.

She pictured her horror of being attacked just the night before as he prattled on. Through it all, the sound of breathing—her breathing as if she had been in labor. Her respirations were like thrashings into a cliff while falling—genuine gasps of survival. How different were these sounds here now that she was having to endure utter tripe—the sound of his artificial air.

"Thank you," she said with some finality if only to make his grating voice cease for only a moment. "I think I'll be okay."

When they hung up, Kristi breathed a long sigh. The dirty business that had to be done was over. She had acted the part and to all appearances, didn't think she raised any red flags. *Taking the leave of absence should have helped with that. But to what extent was she still considered a loose end? Who knew?* At least she thought that it had to be a good sign that she wouldn't have to see him at the office. He didn't find it necessary to have to oversee what she was about to do, and while she believed she could lie to him over the phone, face-to-face was a different matter. She believed that all he would have to do was make eye contact with her and see exactly where she stood. Once he saw the fiery glare mixed with repulsion and fear, being looked at as if he were a de facto human leopard, he would be able to see into her mind as clearly as into a freshly squeegeed pane of glass. *He would see that she knew exactly what he was.*

And at that point, who knew what kind of novel measures he could be driven to given what he'd already done?

She took up her handbag and started removing its contents feeling deep between the crevices of fabric. She found months of old receipts, change, and an old stick of gum before finally feeling the nylon grip of her steel key chain underneath them all. In taking it out, she remembered why she removed the awkward ornament from her keys soon after it was regifted to her by her aunt. Not only was it bulky and awkward, but every time she reached for it to open a door, it was as if making a proclamation of her own insecurity. Like using the club on a Hyundai Elantra, it was as if she was grossly exaggerating the actual risk. In resurrecting it now, however, she sensed the true irony at how that danger she only recognized before, skeptically, now seemed to fully occupy the space it always had.

She traced her fingers along the tempered metal forming a rough semi-circle. While it was small consolation in a world of guns, it had the type of comforting weight and engineering of the machine shop. And like having the feeling of security in possessing her automatic, it brought some release to the nerves. For even if she lacked any training to speak of with such an instrument along with the fact that God knew she was no pugilist, the indentations set into the direction of impact would certainly not leave the other party with anything minor save a glancing blow.

Opening her key ring, she slid off the mini napa valley wine bottle keychain she had picked up on a trip in her twenties to replace it with the defense curiosity. She carefully threaded the piece the whole way around until it snapped securely into the loop. "Better than I remember," she said to herself in closing her hand around the nylon grip. She lifted it swinging a few times weakly as the keys jangled from the bottom.

Going through the motions, she could imagine circumstances hitting her assailant. She pictured the attack from the night before going differently. She could see that face—a glimpse of that shit-eating grin retreating even for a moment—a suddenly deflated look. That was what she could envision on Marcus' face too—a sudden change in that smiling gob of false confidence. Despite the way he always presented himself, she'd like to see him try to maintain it, after what she was about to do.

2

Only a few hours after taking Clint home, Peter's wife had awoken him after another unrestful nightmare. This time catapulting through space toward an endless hole of the blackest void, he thrashed trying to swim his way out feeling progress was being made at first, yet turning around to find the big gaping mouth suddenly about to engulf him. And for some reason, he knew what was going to happen. The facts about the force were laid bare. It wouldn't kill him. No, worse. Once he entered the cavern, he'd somehow become the same as it—a nothing. It would snuff him out so utterly as if he had never been, as if his son had never been—being both just the dust of potentiality. But Peter wouldn't accept that; he yearned to be. He struggled against it, with practical futility, desperately thrashing and screaming, as it took him closer. He was virtually touching the black soup when a voice called out for him. "Peter, Peter," it said. The hand on his shoulder, his wife's hand, delivered him back into the world.

With Margery standing over him dressed to leave, his memories came flooding back into consciousness. The obscene calls, the smell of rotting bodies, the physical violence of a crazed protestor, Eldridge's veiled warning, and now, worst of all, his family departing their home. *Why was it that things only seemed to get worse? How could they stand to get better?*

"Honey, you were moving around in your sleep again," she said with some concern.

"Good morning," he greeted her groggily—not ready to enter into any discussion of the abstract world of dreams.

She put on a weak smile for him. "You got back so late…Where did you guys go?"

"Yeah," he readily admitted. "We had a long talk when I took Clint back," he said dismissively.

At this, she gave him an uncomfortable look—a vulnerable one. He wasn't sure if she could see him lying or was apprehensive about the coming transition. It was enough for him to feel the pain he was trying to ignore—a pang at his very core that his letting them go alone wasn't okay. It was unsettling; it was wrong.

"When are you leaving?" he said sitting up in bed.

She sighed before answering. "After a few more things…breakfast and packing the car… In an hour I'd like to be on the road…"

"An hour?"

"Yeah."

"Good."

She gazed questioningly at him after his blunt response.

"That way I've got time enough to pack."

She looked amazed, almost offended by this new revelation.

"To go *where?*"

"To Tacoma with *you* of course," he expressed with due levity that had been noticeably missing from their marriage lately.

"What? You're coming?"

"Yes." He put on the confident roguish grin that he believed got her into bed with him the first time.

"Oh." She leaned over to kiss him. "Honey…I'm so…happy," she said kissing him between each word. "But, what about the university?" She furrowed her brow at the cost of his coming—still wanting him to explain how such a move could make rational sense.

"Well, it's a family emergency. I think they'll have to understand, and with all that has happened recently, I don't know how they'll say no."

"Really?"

"There really isn't much to do anyway except administer finals which I could have a TA do. I could offer office hours via video call."

"That's wonderful," she kissed him again. Her wet tears dewed his cheeks.

"What's wrong?"

She wiped her face and sat on the bed next to him.

"I just had a feeling…"

"What?"

"Like I may not see you again…"

"No—"

"The way things are going."

"No, I am not going anywhere without my family."

She smiled. "I'm so happy now."

"Me too."

And he was. Just like that, the shadow they had been living under felt a little lighter. Once his choice was made decisively, the ensuing peace of mind, so priceless, momentarily rendered so many of their other worries powerless.

It was about eight, with the Sun having burned away the morning dew. After parking the defunct Nissan in the garage and loading up the bags in the back of his wife's Honda SUV, Peter was ready to roll—ready for whatever lay ahead so long as it was with his family.

Roger had come outside carrying a couple new Hoyle decks with space and fantasy themes while Margery took a little longer checking on the status of all the appliances.

After making sure everything was off, she exited through the garage as Peter watched the sun's light dance over his wife's body on the way to the car. In the early morning light, it was strange how it bent about her figure, accenting both the curves of her waste and blonde hair. It struck him how gorgeous she looked that moment. It reminded him of the spritely young coed he met fifteen years before at a mutual friend's party. Even though the pregnancy wasn't exactly noticeable, he wasn't sure if it could at all explain what he was seeing now—her whole body was emitting a certain glow—a glow of new life.

"What?" she asked noticing his regarding silence at her taking her seat beside him.

"You look nice. That's all." She kissed him in response almost suspiciously before she looked at Roger in the back seat.

"Well, Rog, did you take everything you wanted?"

"Yes," he murmured distantly absorbed in the practice of his card shuffle.

"Alright. Well, we aren't turning around, so I hope so." She half waited for his reply but it didn't come, so she pressed the button on the garage door remote and buckled up.

As they pulled out, Peter and Margery both sat in a silent shock at how fast it all occurred in leaving their dreamhouse. Margery gave it a quick survey lacking the same sparkle in her eye that she had on the day of their first viewing with the realtor. It was strange. Could negative energy spoil the good memories of a place or could they exist compartmentalized? In other words, could they ever return by choosing to remember the good?

As for Peter, he couldn't help having to look back at the spot on the empty neighborhood street. The thought of the images there almost beggared belief. The irrevocable stench distinctly imprinted on the mind. The rush of liquid human dregs dragging over his shoes. At this point, he wondered, wherever they ended up from here on out, if things could ever return to a more innocent time.

3

"Nice of you to join us," Jenelle remarked from the kitchen as she saw her husband slowly make progress into the living room. Giselle didn't find it as noteworthy as her mom. She sat laxly at the bar quietly scrolling on her phone. Meanwhile, the television was airing people in a panel discussion weighing in on the events from campus the night before. It blasted with voices—not that the people were shouting in argument; they were all in agreement. Jenelle usually upped the volume considerably to be able to listen to it from the kitchen.

In place of complaining, Clint prudently turned it down with the remote as he sat back on the sofa. It was past ten in the morning, and he still felt exhausted by last night's outing. The sound had eventually awoken him reeling recent impressions unpleasantly back into the conscious present. Like Jenelle, they were nagging at him. He had tried to put them away for a while, to return to sleep, but he couldn't be rid of them as they begged for adjudication.

On top of all this, resentment was brewing. Sure, he was bruised and cut up, looking out for the future of the university and ultimately his family, but his wife still had a need to give him a hard time in waking up late. It was grating hearing that sarcastic inflection in her voice that lingered well after she spoke it, and it was almost a forgone conclusion that this would have to develop into a full-blown argument the way these things went. It didn't take long, however, for the TV to garner Clint's full attention— seemingly sapping all of his energy for marital conflict. While the negative feeling still burned in his chest, it shifted and transformed undivided to the man standing at the podium—the man he held responsible, whether fairly or unfairly, for failing the entire university apparatus. After what happened, Clint had a hard time taking anything he said seriously anymore. He had no more wanted to listen to him than to a monkey accountant trying to communicate a discrepancy about a stockpile of bananas. The first time was dizzying enough, yet here was President Scott making another go of it.

"Turn it up! I want to hear that!" Jenelle yelled over to him as the press conference promptly began. He reluctantly complied, overcoming an urge to turn the damned thing off. The last thing he wanted to hear now was that the tragedy unfolding on campus wasn't the problem it really was.

After last night, he had an idea what new dimension the protests could take. Their genesis didn't have to only be attributed to the lack of appeasement in the cause of anti-racism on campus anymore. He knew that now, almost anachronistically, the police could take an equal share of blame. And why shouldn't they? The cause was everything—having a quenchless thirst to be bolstered by all things useful no matter how weak the buttress, even speeches by people like Scott.

He thought about escape. Perhaps he could move to the chair in the study or even back to the bedroom? It was a good enough idea, but for all the willingness, he didn't move. The soreness in his body didn't let him. His last options were before him, and he was decided that rather than igniting an argument with his wife by turning the channel, he had to take his punishment by battening down the hatches—steeling himself in the face of Scott's feigned superior intellect and condescension. And in the end, he was glad he prepared. Scott's speech was all he'd thought it would be.

It wasn't until sometime after that Jenelle decided to go into the living room where her husband was. Having overheard a strange voice not coming from the TV, her curiosity was piqued in hearing what sounded like a drunk man daring someone to make him talk. She came upon her husband by himself sitting on the couch absorbed in his phone as much as Giselle was into hers. His wide-eyed expression, however, said it was more than just a passing fancy as the media played on.

"No, we're not here to steal your research, Professor," a familiar voice continued, as Clint appeared hanging on every word. It took a moment before he jumped, seeing Jenelle standing quietly nearby.

"What is *that?*" she asked, scoldingly.

He pressed pause and took a breath sitting back on the sofa again. The thought didn't occur to him that she would end up overhearing Peter's improvisation, but he supposed playing it out in the living room wasn't ideal even with the background noise of the TV. Either way, it didn't really matter. Though he preferred she didn't know about it yet, he wasn't about to lie.

"From last night," he spoke reservedly.

"Blanchard. That was where you were last night?" It was one of the last things heard on the recording.

Clint took the remote and finally ended the torturous broadcast before answering.

"Yes," he confessed, as if that were all that needed to be said about one of the most remarkable days he'd lived through.

"You were on campus? What the fuck *are* you doing?" She lowered her voice at the f-bomb looking to the kitchen to see if Giselle was listening.

"We're trying to save the university," he said forcefully, indignantly as if he suffered mistreatment by her accusation.

"I thought you were out drinking with Peter after…what happened…my God…," her voice softened wavering recognizing the misplaced anger at her husband who she thought had been wasting the night away in some bar as his family waited for him to come home. Her eyes teared up as she held her hand below to catch them.

Seeing his wife's carapace now broken under the weight of the truth, Clint grunted forcing himself off the sofa to comfort her. He wrapped his big arms around her and didn't try to explain more.

"I'm sorry," he whispered to her simply, as more of her tears poured out. She put her hands on his arms, and they held each other that way in the first uninterrupted silence in some time. They rarely had moments away from screens anymore, and despite the distress of his wife, he was happy to be present with her here in one of those all too fleeting winks of time.

In moving her hands over his arms, she soon discovered the scrapes and scratches, souvenirs of the car struggle the afternoon before. She followed some with her fingers before pulling back to have a better look at what she was touching.

Her eyes surveyed the damage along with Clint. Small, jagged markings worked around his arms' curvature with varying patterns that Clint knew were mostly consistent with the contact of glass between him and the zealot in the car. She then explored his eyes with sympathy as she gave the knicks on his biceps a comforting rub.

"You know my back feels worse," he said with a playful grin. She smiled and reached her thin arms around his torso rubbing with more pressure covering as much area as she could.

After some attempts, his smile grew saying, "I'm thinking a deep healing massage…"

She laughed, "Maybe later…if you stay home tonight."

"I will."

"No more fighting in cars or going to riots."

"No."

She stopped and stood on her toes to give him a couple pecks on the lips. He reciprocated knowing very well what these two kisses indicated. She wanted something from him—something she attached due enough importance to feel the need to soften her husband up. And so, he dutifully awaited for her to go through the motions, anticipating the request that he knew was coming.

"Tell me what happened," she began softly. "I want to know all of it—every detail from the car to that recording…no matter how bad."

Clint nodded with the measure of respect that such a direct demand deserved. He expected nothing less from Jenelle, and after checking to see if they were still alone, did just as she asked— imparting everything, unvarnished.

4

Eggers sat at his office desk with his trusty yellow legal pad. His computer was shut—his mind temporarily free of the unnatural noises of the world.

These were the essential moments for him. This was his time to write down his thoughts—the pad being an extension of his mind. Any promising idea was written and scrutinized. After a time, if it withstood his own criticism, he would asterisk or underline it, if not, he'd strike through it all with one definitive line.

Although every pad had one primary subject, anyone reading his notes could find themselves quite at a loss due to the scattershot nature of his thinking. There were lists of possible interviewees, locations, diagrams, and scenarios, but all with one distinctly invaluable product that he wanted them smelted into—true narrative. And while normally he had some confidence about what that was, the content on his page now had no asterisks or underscores at all. The page was largely a blank as much as the person in question was. Based on the little he could gather, Mr. Simon Ray was almost a shade of a man.

Eggers surmised that despite naming his own foundation after himself, Ray was someone who greatly valued his own privacy—clearly going through some enormous lengths to not have more of his information disseminated. In fact, most of what he could find online amounted to little more than conspiracy theories. Was Ray really involved in a child predator ring? Author of a CIA psyop or even a card-carrying member of the Illuminati? It was all there. There were little reliable facts of note, but fortunately for Eggers, certain things couldn't possibly remain hidden no matter what kind of influence one had. The tall heavy market manipulator who, by some estimates, had amassed a fortune of over fifteen billion dollars just wasn't so easy to disappear from the public eye.

As far as the narrative was concerned, emerging from the fragments, Ray appeared to be the picture of an American success story. An emigrant arriving in Newark twenty-four years prior from Trinidad and Tobago, it wasn't long before Ray made a name for himself, at least, in the financial world circles—contributing to the significant gains of a slew of successive up-in-coming hedge funds.

It was only when he founded Atta Capital in 2010, however, that he really started turning heads—making nearly a billion dollars alone in the short sale of Swedish Krona with the Bank of Sweden nearly going bust over the matter. This was the event that he was known for—the event that precipitated the Financial Times eventually writing a piece about the seemingly unscrupulous move and the man behind it. It was in the same article that Eggers was able to cross reference much of what he learned about Ray including the inception of Ray Foundation happening only six months before.

The inclusion of the article's discussion of the foundation itself was what appeared to temper the host of quotable irate voices speaking out about Ray. Rather than him being a "grifter in a ten-thousand-dollar suit" or a "insufferable leech on humanity," others highlighted his philanthropy through the foundation. One wealthy donor cited in the article, a Tom Cross, CFO of Imex Group, commented on all the negativity surrounding Ray. "That's not what I'm seeing. I mean, young women are already being lifted out of poverty from schools he's built outside of Nairobi and other parts of sub-Saharan Africa. I just don't see how that comports with…he doesn't have to do that…Look, what happens in the marketplace is dictated by a predetermined set of rules, and he plays by those rules the same as anyone else. No, he's a good man to do what he does." Paul Barrett, CEO of Rydel Tech appeared to make an even greater appraisal of Ray. "The Simon I know is a very thoughtful, considerate man. He has no equal in those qualities."

Of course, while this latter commentary piqued Eggers' interest greatly, they, like other avenues of inquiry, proved to be fruitless, as both men were no longer chiefs at their former companies and unreachable for comment. Neither was he able to garner anything from following up with the additional sources referenced who only admitted to knowing the effects of Ray's actions in 2010 and never claimed to know the man personally. Again, there was no story that wasn't already run over a decade ago. *Who was this rich man exactly? Why was his organization funding race research and what could he possibly want from it? More money? Validation?* Of all things, it didn't seem that Ray was the type of man wanting in either.

Interestingly enough, while Eggers, to his mind, hit a roadblock in stewing over where he would go next to develop his story, events were rapidly brewing—the unfolding of which sometimes happen so effortlessly and so coincidentally that it's no wonder that people to this day believe in some concept of fate. It was exactly at that moment while Eggers was pouring over one of the only clear images of Ray he found online—a round giant of a man— intimidatingly so—looming over his office staff on the steps in front of his foundation, that a figure coming from the same building was already making an inquiry in WNT's waiting area. It wasn't long before the call came, and so did she—someone whose destiny, they had no way of knowing, was so inextricably tied up with Eggers' own.

After her stop at Ray Foundation, Kristi hesitated before going to WNT's D.C. Headquarters. The thought of the possible repercussions of her next move really put her on edge.

She tried to reason with herself—tried calming her fluttering heartbeat. *Just what would they do to her when they found out she went to the press? Hadn't they already tried to have her killed? Could they do worse? There was no doubt. Money can do all things. Mammon has a tendency to miraculously make the seemingly unimaginable, a sudden possibility.*

What other options did she really have though? Even if she laid low and hoped to disappear from their radar (which she knew she couldn't do for Yunnie's sake), they already demonstrated that they didn't tolerate any liabilities. Indeed, the fact that they saw someone like Yunnie as a threat at all proved to her how cheaply the decision to murder was undertaken. *Their service and loyalty meant nothing. And if that were the casual way in which they dispensed death, who was even safe? Who could even stand to stop them? The police? What a false faith that was.*

As nice and reassuring as Detective Gonzalez had been, even hoping on the outside chance that they would get to the bottom of what happened to her and Yunnie, she just knew they weren't going to go far enough. If she had thought that, she wouldn't have been any good at her job. She wouldn't have known how the politics surrounding her functioned—the politics that Ray Foundation relied upon. The power of a politically well-connected organization like RF rendered a police force toothless. To stand a chance at all, she knew that the only way forward seemed to be to catch enough attention to garner some political backing. She needed to reach people from the other side of the aisle who she didn't know at all. And what other way to do that than to draw the attention of their constituents by putting her and Yunnie's story out there?

She pushed herself forward, despite the jitters in the parking garage, despite the feeling that the man with the denim cap could at any moment pop out from behind a car and finish what he started with that unsavory smirk—that empty bloodshot discernment. She plodded on.

Ignoring her flight instinct and not knowing exactly how to proceed, she went through the necessary motions. And now following the office intern rounding the corridor past the busy staff, she barely registered her luck at being seen by someone right away.

Kristi was shown into another hallway with a row of offices off the main newsroom. After two raps at a door midway down, "come in," a muffled voice inside indicated.

Standing behind the desk, awaited a welcoming Patrick Eggers. His handsomely symmetrical face with genuine piercing blues and warm smile stood in contravention to many of a D.C. face pull. The effect had an immediate calming influence over Kristi's tense features.

When he introduced himself offering his hand, she finally was able to peel her own sweaty palm from the leather handbag she'd been clutching since the garage.

"Nice to meet you, Miss Connors."

"Thank you for seeing me," she responded timidly.

He looked to the intern and gave his thanks before her departure then gestured to the chair for Kristi to sit. She did— giving a once over survey of the room of which happened to be in a more disordered state than what she pictured an office at a major news network to be. There was a mishmash of books and papers over the desk among a number of framed pictures of who or what she couldn't exactly make out from that side of the desk. Some unknown news awards also lined the wall behind Eggers dating to the early 2000s giving her the impression that he really needed this next big break. *However it was, at least,* she told herself, *there was no indication of some piece of avant-garde art haunting the walls as they did at the foundation.*

For a moment, sensing her jumpy disposition, Eggers let Kristi's eyes wander. Receiving the call only minutes before, he was at first skeptical of what reliable information Connors would provide him. While a quick Google search of the RF website indicated the position she still held there as Lead Organizer, he was still wary after his talk with Levy of what someone from the foundation could try to feed him. But, what at first sounded almost too good to be true, that face in the doorway started to make him a true believer. The information she had didn't at all seem like something she wanted to divulge. Rather, it was something she felt she had to and with great fear. In his experience, that was the kind of source he knew he could rely on—unclad truth that had to be professed begrudgingly. It was the other ones, all too chipper to share, the type to instruct you in patronizing intonations, that one had to be wary of.

"Sorry for the mess," he said seeking to cut through the silence now that she was more settled. "I don't receive visitors often enough and on such short notice."

"I—"

"Of course, I'll make an exception in your case. Miss Kristi Connors, of Ray Foundation?"

"Yes, I was…am." she admitted slowly, the words attached to her name sounding so ridiculous now.

"That's interesting that you came in here today. In fact, as you may have gathered, I'm doing a story about your employer. The one who brought you here, my intern Tessa, and some of the rest of the office staff know of my interests and were right to check in with me about you. Did you know of me or my work before you came?"

Instead of responding, Kristi had a sudden impulse to stand up and walk out with no further damage done—not poking the tiger anymore out of the sole desire for self-preservation. The rush came in a tormenting wave, but after some deep breaths, it subsided, and she reminded herself, *I'm okay—I'll be okay.*

"Miss Connor?" The darting eye movement registered to Eggers right away. That moment he was afraid of exactly what Kristi had a fleeting mind to do—escape. The concern entered his voice as his mind raced to find a way to put her more at ease.

"Can I get you anything? Water, coffee, tea?"

"No—no," she breathed out deeply. "I'm okay."

"Do let me know if there is any moment you feel uncomfortable about something. I don't want you to answer until you do."

She nodded her head in agreement before continuing to answer his original question.

"I've seen you before sometimes. I don't normally read or watch WNT, but I've seen you on while flipping through stations. And no, I don't really know of your work."

This last part was a surprise for Eggers, even a little disappointing considering how big the Barton interview appeared to hit the internet. In any case, he realized perhaps that it shouldn't have been so popular, despite his own vanity. The reality was people tended to bubble around the same echoing megaphones of their ingroup no matter the quality of the content. WNT appeared to attract the more conservative end of the spectrum and with one brief look into Kristi's background, she didn't appear to fit that demographic.

"So why come here? Why WNT?"

"I don't live far from here," she murmured not looking him in the eye. "I'm coming from Arlington." She stopped suddenly if that could explain it all.

Eggers waited for a full silence to come.

"But that's not why you're *here.*"

She shook her head before a word. "No," she uttered.

"Miss Connors, did something…happen at Ray Foundation?" he said noticing the tears welling up midsentence. When they poured, he opened a lower desk drawer and handed her a package of tissues. She wiped her face trying to pull herself together and show some dignity in front of this stranger, but in recalling the thoughts and feelings that brought her there, it abruptly became overwhelming.

"Take all the time you need…Just know that we're only two people talking. That's all. Right now, I don't even work for the news. I'm officially on my own time. Nothing said here has to be known by anyone, ever." What Eggers said in the moment, he meant—no longer seeing this woman as a potential story to cash in, but as another human being like himself that had been through some ordeal.

"But, I want you to," she said stemming the tears. "I want people to know."

She had thought at first, before coming there, that she would be more selective with what details she would provide, but once she started, she ended up holding nothing back. Like the tears, the whole truth had to come out. She at first supposed that she just needed to tell someone what was bottled up so badly that she spilled it to the first person who was *really* willing to listen. But that wasn't nearly the full story. The crux of the matter was that what she was doing here now in really opening up had always been a tall order for her. The sharing of deeply held experiences—the ones exposing one's naked vulnerabilities was something reserved only for a select few people in her life that were no longer with her. The last person she could really talk to about anything was Yunnie—a testament to how much she really missed her friend. But that was Yunnie who wasn't just anyone.

The first time Yunnie and her met, she knew how special she truly was. Everything came easier than it did with other people. And now while the content differed, it was almost deja vu in how she recognized something similar about Eggers as well. Some quality in him reminded Kristi so much of her and she seized upon it—pouring out her heart to him as if to make up for the lost time.

In listening, Eggers felt compelled, touched by every turn in this woman's story—soaking up every utterance, as if it all was happening to himself in real time. It was not at all what he was expecting to hear. That the foundation was corrupt in some way was already likely to him, but that they were involved in some murder conspiracy was more than he could believe at the moment. He just thought there could be a more reasonable explanation. Levy being a cold-hearted-bastard insensitive to his employees' wellbeing wasn't a stretch to see given his interaction with him. He may have played the part of a human, but it was a poorly acted one at that.

After conveying what was largely weighing on her mind, she took small sips from the bottle of water that he offered from the mini fridge behind his desk. In that interim, he searched for the right words. There really weren't any, but he knew he had to say something. She was counting on him.

"What you're going through is a lot—"

"You're not going to believe everything that I told you," she cut-in reading him perfectly.

Eggers hesitated before speaking.

"I believe that you believe everything is as you say, but I think the police are going to have to figure much of the rest of it—" He stopped himself short by her distraught look.

"But the way—the way he treated me that day just before it *happened*?" She was almost asking herself the question as much as Eggers.

"I know…it's disgusting…but while callous, it doesn't amount to being homicidal."

Her eyes widened. "You think I was wrong to come here? Isn't there a story from all of this?"

"There's only part of a story. I don't think you're wrong to come here. I'm actually honored that you were able to share your experience with me as you did, and I'd like to know how everything turns out after the police do a thorough investigation."

"The police are *shit*," she said with a sudden flare of anger, inducing a look of surprise on Egger's face. "When's the last time something like this was discovered by a simple police investigation?" she asked.

He didn't answer—knowing her point was quite valid.

"Can't you investigate? There has to be something?"

Eggers decided on his words carefully before answering. "I'm investigating Ray Foundation over an entirely different matter," he sighed. "Honestly, I don't know how I could help with this."

"You're investigating ties to this research at University of Southern Florida. I'm aware of some of the buzz that's going on…" she explained.

His reticence to mention it appeared silly at this point. With all that she had shared with him and with nothing much to go on anyway, he realized he had to put his trust in this woman. It defied his usual rule of keeping a lid on it until the beaches were stormed with a story, especially with a member of the organization in question being investigated. Everything about their interaction, however, told him this time was different.

"Do you know why they funded it?"

"Of course, everyone does, equality is in our mission statement," she remarked curiously identifying with the same group that wanted her dead.

"What I mean is that do you have any first-hand knowledge of why the study was backed?" Eggers clarified having no expectation that she did.

"No, I don't," she put simply. "As Lead Organizer, I was never really apart of those discussions…which I'm sure happened long before I even took the position there."

Eggers again sighed—realizing after the asking how high the bar to penetrate this story was.

"But, I'm sure this'll interest you."

His face responded with an inquiring expression as she proceeded to open her hand-bag that she'd clutched so tightly earlier.

With trembling hand, one by one, she neatly stacked the various colored thumb drives on the desk.

Eyeing them and the door warily as if each one were yet another incriminating bag of heroin, he walked over pressing the door's button lock to set himself more at ease.

After taking her time to rummage for a couple more stray sticks, by the end, she had assembled four rows of five thumb drives each.

"These are all the documents from the shared cloud, internal memos, and emails I could get before leaving today," she said as he beheld the treasure trove of data. "…I would've gotten more but…I didn't have any more space left on the drives."

The realm of possibilities started playing through Eggers' mind. He imagined the dirty little details that could abound from getting down into the muck of it. He imagined wiping off Levy's fake fucking grin again—this time, permanently. But, before he got anymore carried away, he checked himself. *Don't get your expectations up now,* he told himself, *you're putting the cart way before the horse. First thing's always first—the responsible thing.*

"I hope you know this is—" he started.

"What? Illegal?" Kristi cut-in again, sensing the patronizing tone. "Could get me in trouble with the NDA I signed before being hired?" She gave out a whimper of a sardonic laugh. "These fuckers…what they did to me…what they did to Yunnie…do you think I care anymore about that?" she posed querulously.

"You mean Levy. You think Levy did these things—not Ray?"

"From what I know, there is no major decision made by Levy that doesn't go through Ray first."

She said it just as Eggers had thought it. Levy was a disingenuous sort because he had to be. That was his job to get things done. Do X at whatever cost. Meanwhile, behind the scenes, a person like Ray did whatever he wanted through puppets like him. It was the way of the world to have someone to dissociate you from the residual excrement resulting from your actions.

"And what do you want me to do with them exactly?" he asked with a pretty good idea already, but not wanting to take them if unacceptable conditions were attached.

"I downloaded anything and everything that I could—not knowing if it would be useful. I wanted to leave it to someone—

someone in investigative journalism to look into them, and if there were something, find a way to get the story out."

"You want me to investigate if there is evidence of a murder conspiracy of you or your friend Yunnie? You think they'd just leave something like that out there?"

"There's a lot of data here. I'm sure with your reading between the lines, you'll find something incriminating…with their willingness to murder…there's bound to be something. Whether that's about what happened to Yunnie or to do with the research, I'll leave that to you."

Eggers pondered over what she said with eyes gravitating back to the drives. "And what is your expectation exactly? What's the end of all of this?"

"Justice."

"*Justice?*"

"The real kind."

6

There was something about driving that put one's afflictions behind you. The more road one rolls over, the more fields, bodies of water, and Podunk towns passed by, the more therapeutic the result, as if going over the distances were like bridging the very gaping wounds inflicted by life, sutured together by an imaginary needle and thread. And just as this was only the beginning of convalescence with wounds still needing time to crust over and develop into the mystery of new flesh, so was this only a beginning for Peter and his family.

He wondered at the topic as he drove down I-75, Margery in silence and Roger passed out in the backseat. He wondered at the frontiersman crossing the plains by wagon. He wondered at the new arrivals to America from the old-world crossing by ship. *Is this what they felt? Did traveling those weeks of endless plains and sea start to mend what was broken? And what could possibly be chasing them away from the familiar safety of the known to unknown?* To this last question, Peter had an idea. That particular recess of his mind, with the specifics of his recent past, was not to be broached, however. He could do without them, at least, for now.

Not ten miles on the other side of Ocala, Peter was no longer willing to be burdened by such memories. After an uncomfortable call earlier to the college dean to explain the situation, there wasn't really anything pressing left on the agenda for the day except the road. He felt good—not too tired and having a mind to make it to Pensacola before thinking about a room for the night. He was dialed into an easy listening station maintaining a speed over the limit but still without drawing the interest of the occasional state trooper. It was a meditative state—a state of recovery from overactive thinking, and looking over to Margery, she now appeared to be at peace too, fast asleep. It was nice not only to be in this tranquil existence but to know that there were many hours ahead of the same.

"*Peter?* Are you alone?" Clint's deep hollowed voice entered the earpiece almost as soon as the call was accepted.

"Hey, I'm on Bluetooth. Everything okay?" he answered registering something distressful in its timbre.

"She *knows.*"

"*Who* knows *what*," he said quietly, trying not to wake his family.

"Jenelle about last night."

"Oh," he said, casually as if someone told him that rain was in the forecast.

"I had to tell her."

"Yeah," Peter assented despite their agreement the night before to keep mum. He was surprised how un-angry he was with his friend. He supposed he expected it to come out eventually just not this soon. But at the same time, he could feel his heart pound almost in unison with the bumps on the road. *Does this mean Margery would find out today?* Whatever the case, he knew they would have an argument when she did, and he'd have to weather another storm. *Would she understand? She'd have to.*

"How's it going with you?" Clint broke the quiet in a voice of resignation. *Hey, what's done is done*, it said, *so let's move on.*

"Good. I'm on the road with Margery and Rog now."

"You decided to go?"

"*Had to.*"

"After last night, I know why you did."

Here the two men were in complete understanding. The value of their families was of fundamental importance and certain convictions had to be ceded to their own well-being. If Clint happened to call saying he shot a man during a home invasion, it wouldn't have phased him at all either. That's what a husband does. That's what a good man does. That's what this was all about in the end. Who was a good man and what would he do for his family? What would their future world have to look like if others imposed their twisted version of the truth on them? Who would turn away in this game of chicken when a more immediate threat became apparent?

Quiet ensued again. They both hesitated to continue knowing there still was a need to dispense with the business at hand—to make the next rational move with the best knowledge available.

"So, have you thought any about what we talked about?" Peter went straight to the heart of the matter. With all the options they discussed the night before, weighing on his mind in a dizzying fashion, he was almost willing to entrust the entire judgement to his friend at that moment rather than have his mind chug on about it.

"I think…the recording should be given to a member of the media."

"Okay, but like I said, Florida is a two-party state. Recording someone without their consent is illegal."

"Yeah, I know, but they will protect their source."

"I suppose we could let someone from the administration listen to it…"

"No—"

"And that way, they could be advised at least about some threat to the university."

"*Peter*, they won't listen."

"*It's too late.* Isn't that what he said? Sounds like a threat."

"They *won't* listen. To listen would be to admit that they are somehow in the wrong. That would make them look bad when right now Scott's on such a high."

"I don't know."

"Think about it. I have. This is all just a form of entertainment. Universities have been stagnating for years—irrelevant in normal people's lives, taking up the banner of something as vile as racism in all things is not a fight for freedom against injustice like a World War II fight versus Nazism, it's just fun. Scott knows this. He has no interest in whether it happens to be true. And now he just has to come out of this looking good. Nothing else matters to him."

Peter's brow furrowed at the mere possibility that his friend could be right, but he immediately scorned the idea. After what happened, he could believe a lot, but when it came to people in leadership in the American system, he still wasn't willing to give up the idea that they were generally good people. Did they possess foibles? Of course, they did like anyone else. Could they run off the rails? Sure, but rarely, and the system tended to self-correct. On the other hand, a derangement of the magnitude Clint suggested, at a prestigious institution no less, was just something he didn't want to entertain further. Up to now, his whole view was that these people in power were mostly good faith actors, mistaken, but striving for the best outcome possible. For in the end, such an outcome could only be to their benefit. And it was the liberal ideal that people like Peter, Clint, other academics, and stakeholders could help them see a better way forward. Therefore, as he saw it, there was still much to do short of the destructive force of outright rebellion. He wasn't willing to concede just yet that Scott was totally unbecoming a president. For if someone like Scott could so easily be rotten to the core, when it was supposed to be a rarity, what did that say about many others? What did that say about the entire system? Could it be rotten to its very core? Of course, that could also imply that someone, being a part of it, was also part of the detritus. That was why with Clint's marked cynicism, he could only respond with what he perceived as a healthy pushback.

"*Entertaining?* I don't think anyone could find this, remotely, entertaining," Peter said with annoyance.

"Yes, *you can*," Clint countered emphatically. "I've told you before of how attention is a scarce commodity these days, and these people are *dying* for it."

"Scott's misled like others."

"So, you're willing to confide in him with an illegal recording?" Peter's silence prompted Clint to continue.

"Even if he's simply misled, which I don't see how that's possible with all the recent blessings he gifted our beloved campus, you're assuming there'll be no fallout…that's why I think the media is a better route…we can get the message out. Let the people be the ones to reject this corrupt new science."

Peter looked over to see that Margery had stirred in the passenger seat. He noticed her eyes were now open. She had quietly been watching him talk into the headset. She smiled at him putting her hand on his knee.

It was time to get off the phone. It was time to do what his instincts told him to do before the conversation began, that is, to trust someone truly deserving of it. Clint could be the one to take the lead on this one. He should be the one to decide what's next.

"Okay," he exhaled finally. "Tell me what you have in mind."

What he assumed he was leaving was ground zero of what he could only conceptualize as a mass infection of the mind. For if it weren't an infection, what could one call it? It certainly spread like a contagion, and if it weren't a sickness, why did it attack so virulently? What other thing could compel the young man, who he'd never known before, to attack him with such vitriol? What kind of program had to be uploaded to be willing to beat a stranger to death (as he had no doubt would've happened) over a perceived ideology? A scourge? An infestation? A virus? Whatever it was, it imposed a heavy burden upon its laborers—the judges who were required to mete out harsh penalties over a possible misunderstanding of words. Who could've predicted such progress?

While the phenomenon could be described as an epidemic, possibly isolated to certain vicinities of the country, this was false. Peter would soon have to recognize after leaving, that it wasn't confined to locales such as the sleepy town he once knew. The United States as well as a swath of the developed world were soon found to be infected too, as waves of global violence soon boiled over following the university riots.

Around the world, people of nearly every demographic, demanded their governments to recognize the Eldridge and Jersey study and take action against racism. The argument was relatively simple. Racism no longer remained in the domain of an ethereal concept of feeling alone. It now was recognized as hard science ingrained in the very biology of people. When it came to dispensing justice before, such people could remain in the shadows committing their heinous crimes with impunity behind a veil of uncertainty about their motives. Their racist actions could almost always be refuted with a plausible deniability—a deniability that created a safe space for their persistent offenses. How fortunate then was it to live under the banner of progress. The arc of history, being irreproachable in its forward direction, rendered denial no longer an acceptable defense. Science dictated otherwise. It verified and outed the very enemy that had been blighting society since time immemorial. The only question that remained was what was to be done about these people. With no reason left to try to change minds of a being's nature, what non-drastic measure was even possible anymore? Debate flared in academia while tempers flared even more so in the streets.

The news covered the flashpoints of unrest around the globe. Viewers could watch protestors, vandals, thugs, and looters picket, deface, brutalize, and steal on the twenty-four hour news cycle—terrorizing places like Parliament and Ajaccio Squares, The Royal Mile, the campus of UC Berkeley and Boston Common. Police fought back trying to prevent or, at least limit, the damage, but little could be done with the great numbers of dissidents seemingly metastasizing through communities.

Under the auspices of making yet another sacrifice to that insatiable god of progress, the university system was the first to cave to the pressure of reform. USFL, Brown, and Stanford paved a new way in announcing separate disciplinary committees to decide whether a student had violated racial norms spelled out in their new respective codes of conduct. The controversial policies share provisions that emphasize reporting—an obligation to come forward for any act that could be perceived as racial animus. USFL outlined examples of such behavior that were not limited to any "slur, conversation, assignation, or work" that could imply any attribution of worth based on race or racial characteristics. Any person that the committee finds guilty under this mandatory reporting policy is faced with permanent expulsion and ban from all university affiliated activities.

Naturally, as with any extreme, much of the press lauded the new reforms. It was an improved era of civil rights. Even the outlets that wrote negative pieces were counted as positive PR by drawing more attention to the new innovative policies.

One controversial piece, "The Coming Eugenic Storm," an op-ed by Brent Allen, on the editorial board at the Strand Journal even predicted the advent of genetic testing as a coming requirement to enter institutions. "To do otherwise," Allen reasoned, "would both invite swaths of future race-based lawsuits, and more importantly, undermine institutional authority. For, after all, when the mighty Jupiter hath spoken, the earth shall tremble," he summed sardonically.

President Scott was one of the first to try to quash such "conspiracy theories." At the ACE annual meeting, he expressed that "it was neither ethical nor realizable to implement [these policies]." Furthermore, such speculation, he denounced as "setting a dangerous precedent, undermining our indispensable institutions and welcoming the actions of radical extremists." His statement was soon parroted in the media with like personages following suit with their own reassurances, even painting Allen and some secret group of unidentifiable rabblerousers as willfully ignorant. What remained, despite the discussion, however, was the continuing pressure of an oncoming tide of newly converted activists.

Almost three months later in October was the same issue really brought again to the forefront. By that time, as some speculated, with discontent and the looming pressure of midterms staring unpopular politicians in the face, the Minority Protection Act (MPA) managed to pass the House of Representatives. The bill sponsored by many special interests with the enclosure of their corresponding pork allocations, included the provision that OSHA require testing for the Chromagen makeup be performed on any persons involved in a managerial capacity for the "benefit and safety of the employees subject to them." Proponents of the legislation were apt to point out from the get-go, pre-empting the opposition, that this putatively large pill to swallow would be fully enacted only after a year's time to ready employers for costs of testing. Additionally, they relegated the working out of further details to happen after the initial passage and Senate review.

The bill's banner woman in the Senate, Susan Dembier, was the one to really make a splash in the social media rounds with her shared address to the opposition party. In her time slated to discuss the merits of the bill, she brought to the podium a copy of a study published in the Scientific Inquirer entitled, "In Review: Eldridge, Jersey et. al. A Scientific Consensus." From it, she read its summary conclusion that an astounding ninety-five percent of the scientific community agree racial animus is strongly associated with the genetic makeup identified as Chromagen. She then proceeded to lament the ongoing phenomenon of science denialism and the duty of government to protect those most marginalized in the community.

"What member of this chamber," Dembier started again in the loud pitch of a patronizing lecture—like a preacher bringing down the wrath of God on a well-known sinner, "would risk inflicting untold damage on even one laborer. *One* possibly being abused in the workplace? Suffering an unwavering torture merely for the way they were born? It's….a *disgusting* thought, isn't it? What other place do Americans spend a great deal of their lives in just trying to squeeze out a living? Who needs modern slave drivers casting a further yoke on our already overworked people of color? Now, I don't want to be curt, but, I'm going to have to be curt. A vote against this bill is a license for these practices to continue. A vote for it is the only way to keep known racists from perpetually infecting our system. I don't think I have to tell you what you already know. That is, a vote of no is another way of saying, *no, these aren't real people. No, they aren't deserving of dignity.* In other words, a vote of no is, I'm sad to say it—it's really a vote of yes, as in, *yes, I'm really a racist.*"

The speech turned out to be a resounding success. Not only was it a trend—extoled in legacy news outlets, but it was also shared throughout social platforms like Readit and InstaGrat. A slogan of support for the new legislation, Protect Minorities Now, or PMN, appeared everywhere—profile pictures, updates, comments, vlogs, live chats. Virtually overnight, so many appeared to echo the three white block letters on solid black background. Even a popular video of an elementary teacher instructing her classes of how to form the letters with their fingers made the rounds. "P! M! N! P! M! N!" the class chirped enthusiastically while shaping their fingers as if casting a magical incantation.

It was so simple. In fact, who wouldn't want to protect minorities? That's what the letters stood for after all. How could there be anyone against something so just, so righteous? What kind of intellectual philistine would block true progress—to choose a path other than the only moral choice?

Nevertheless, they were out there. And their numbers weren't insignificant.

War proceeded in both the chamber of the senate and the public forums of the world abroad. Was it not better to make one small sacrifice for the common good than to let tyranny have its day? Or was that sacrifice not so small? Was that itself the tyranny? Many people had already made their decision along with most of the Senate—deciding that they were willing to make that sacrifice, and at the same time try to browbeat the opposition with the word "racist" before they even had time to make their case. But, a case was made. An academic paper was produced.

"A Declaration of Concerned Scientists" was brought to the floor by Senator Christopher Norbert of South Carolina. It was a statement posted online and electronically signed by over one thousand seven hundred scientists of the world concerned about the premise, methodology, and implications of the Eldridge and Jersey study. To a largely empty chamber, Norbert quoted the declaration at length.

"Many of my colleagues have shared that one must not fall into a scientific denialism," Norbert peered over his spectacles at the sparse audience that remained. "I agree, but then the question still remains of which scientists one is listening to. Here I have one thousand seven hundred of the world's preeminent scientists calling into question the study at the center of this new legislation. And here's what they conclude—"

A heckler screamed, "PMN" just on the inside of the senate chamber. Norbert paused for the man's removal. The slogan faded into the background, echoing through the vast structure. Norbert continued.

"The study does not only fail even with the loosest definitions of what the scientific method is, it fails the sniff test as to the motivations of its authors when the conclusion is so powerful in itself that it appears to overcome all objections by sheer emotional force alone. Anyone that is found to question its veracity is automatically accused of what it purports to prove. They are expressing the racial animus that their genetic makeup imposes without fail, which is no surprise, as an estimated fifteen to twenty percent of the population are likely to possess the very same sequences." At this point, Norbert removes his glasses making a serious point of emphasis as he squints his wrinkled eyes above his otherwise remarkably smooth face. "Fifteen to twenty percent of the population," he said slowly in a befuddled tone. "Not only do they not think the study doesn't hold water under scientific scrutiny, but they estimate a good portion of the population has this Chromagen profile. And we are supposed to give this fifteen to twenty percent the shaft in leadership roles and perhaps ostracize them because of it? Simply outrageous. It may not pass a scientific sniff test but add a constitutional one at that."

Despite Norbert's address, some Senators as well as pundits parried his points by dismissing the declaration calling it not only unscientific but racism denialism as well. That fifteen to twenty percent of the population may have racist tendencies proved an even stronger case that the legislation was necessary to prevent discrimination in the workplace. And if these people wanted to be in leadership roles, there were still ample opportunities in independent contract positions that didn't require employees to work beneath them.

Whether or not these addressed the objections was beside the point, the Senate soon passed the bill under a threat of filibuster that was bypassed by cloture. It was sent to the president's desk and signed into law with a twenty-three pen ceremony.

Many analysts questioned how a government so seemingly dysfunctional happened to force through such expansive legislation on the entire country. The threat of violence and caving to popular voices were considered part of a broader movement that demanded the government take a more active role. A poll was cited to confirm that opinion where fifty-five percent of the country wanted the federal government to intervene more often when it came to their daily lives.

Needless to say, the very same poll caused a lot of pushback for those suddenly scared of democracy—prompting an article from the libertarian publication, ARN, that referenced the poll's results to question if it was time for certain liberty-minded individuals of the country to definitively opt out of the social contract. It rightly stated, however, that it anticipated an extensive exercise in judicial review and that perhaps it was time to at least give a chance to the third branch of government to do its job in reasserting the rights of a minority. The Supreme Court was the final check in the system.

Immediately after ratification, MPA was challenged in federal court by multiple states and plaintiffs. The nine justices of the

Supreme Court took up the question of the constitutionality of excluding people based on their genetic makeup. Among the challenges posed was if such a provision could withstand scrutiny under the fourteenth amendment's equal protection clause.

As both sides proceeded to make their case, the country watched on edge as if at any moment they'd become helpless participants in a head on collision. The dread was palpable even for those who weren't avid followers of current events. For some, it was as if they had their whole house destroyed, except the bathroom while they sat on the john. Nothing was theirs anymore. The water tasted different. The communities no longer seemed welcoming. Beams of sunlight no longer felt radiant on the skin. They penetrated more like daggers to the head. What was off exactly? What was disrupting these daily reprieves? It certainly couldn't be reduced to a case in the Supreme Court. Something else was happening, but what? Was it a recent development or had it just become more noticeable? Was it an international phenomenon or limited to the US? Whatever it was, one theme appeared to cohere all the disparate experiences—confusion. People were confused not only with what was happening, but there was a general muddling of the mind—a process of being pulled apart, an untetherment from what they once knew. For some, they asked, "Is this even a country anymore?" For others: "Who am I? What is even real?"

7

Different shades of green whisked by infusing the rental car with warm piney earthy scents. Eggers breathed it all in with window down as he drove west from Boca Raton as if taking hits off a nebulizer. The moist heat of the air did him well, especially after his most recent viral bout fought in the dry chilly tomb that is the Capitol.

With December having come and gone and the new year a fleeting memory, he wondered why he didn't leave the city more often. There was a time for work, but there was also a time to smell the foliage. And for Eggers, that time was passing and passing quickly. Being now forty-eight years old, he didn't know what happened since turning forty. He just knew he had to grab onto every moment, like now, before it completely slipped through his fingers. Besides, who really knew how many years one had ahead of them? Who knew how fast the night was over and when the bill finally came due?

The sound of his phone's navigation cut into his head space. He followed its direction by turning into the first strip mall that came up between the trees. "Destination arrived," the woman's voice said as Eggers saw the cozy little café on the corner called Kat's—the place where they agreed to meet.

It took time and patience for Eldridge to finally come around. The calls and emails were well timed almost always coinciding with a new story of unrest that made the headlines. And sometimes it felt that when Eggers had made two steps forward with Eldridge, he then had to take two steps back. Eventually, he could sense a real change in the man. The guard in his voice came down.

What propelled his persistence? While another journo may have given up, Eggers felt he had to push on. The fact was that he found himself in a unique position, ever since meeting Peter, Clint, and now Kristi, he felt himself being drawn in by whatever touched this study. Everything connected to it appeared rotten. Nothing about it seemed genuine—it was like an actor drawing too much attention to himself on screen, and Eggers could see these scenes standing out like a blooper reel. Even with these violent outlashes labeled under the misnomer of protest, he could only see them for what they really were. No one could tell him what was crystal clear before his very eyes because protests they weren't. Protests urged correction. Protests implied a system needed fixing. What was happening now was something entirely different. What was happening now was unfocused indiscriminate rage craving ruin. It was nothing short of rebellion against a system with nothing worth saving. There was no solution except for Souvarine's in Germinal—destruction at whatever cost. Fuck it all. Sacrifice. It was a reversion to some base desire of primitive man. The murderous legacy of the war tribe perhaps. So, as Eggers understood it, it was vile, and he thought he saw exactly where it was headed. Exposing it to the public was not a choice but what he had to do before the malignancy grew—before too much of the public would be lobotomized by the same emotion.

Eggers possessed something else, which he wasn't about to share, that caused him to push Eldridge. He had the recording given to him by Peter and Clint. There was nothing more valuable than hearing the responses of a drunk man to the violence erupting on campus. The inflection was unmistakable—the contempt. Eldridge hated the response. Whatever high he got from the recognition of his study was being undone by the rioting rabble. Perhaps that was the whole excuse to flood himself with drink. The conflict between his ascension and the pull of some semblance of conscience must be hell. The amount of pressure he must've felt, to have to release even the shallow confession that he did, had to be enormous. *How much more relief does he still seek?*

Putting the car into park, Eggers surveyed the lot. It was quiet, but it also happened to be after three in the afternoon, well past the lunch rush. There were sparse cars, and no one was sitting outside. Eldridge had alluded to the fact that there was danger—not only from the recording but reaffirming it in their last conversation. That was the whole purpose of why Eldridge wanted to meet here, away from the university. With all that had been happening, Eggers believed him, but to what extent, he didn't yet fully know. As for now, he felt safe in this public place—being a comfortable distance away from the city and campus—being away from the common misbehaving scum.

He opened the café door to the cool air inside. There was only a total of three patrons. A couple sitting toward the back and a man in the middle facing the door. The man was undoubtedly Eldridge—not hard to recognize from online photos.

Eldridge's eyes nervously followed him over to the table as if having second thoughts about today's meeting. *No. No you don't,* Eggers said mentally, donning a smile to put him at ease.

"Nice to finally meet you, Professor," he reached out his hand to Eldridge who reciprocated, his face flustered with worry.

He sat on the other side of the table gauging his mood— wondering whether his date was going to suddenly bolt on him. He noticed the almost drained latte and the barely touched mozzarella caprese sandwich. These weren't good signs. He wouldn't have been surprised if he suddenly ran out of the place knocking over a few tables and chairs along the way.

"Thank you for coming," Eggers said fully understanding the irony of how much he invested into this meeting himself.

Eldridge nodded.

"I can't help but see that…*you're afraid*, aren't you?"

Eldridge started trying to shrug off the notion.

"And that's okay," Eggers followed up as if he were the one being the psychologist.

The professor leveled a very serious gaze at Eggers indicating some offense taken by the comment. "If you're using that word to imply that I'm paralyzed with fear, I'm not," he corrected imperiously. "Like the rest of the animal kingdom, that happened to do them a service, I'm in a heightened state of danger awareness."

At first, Eggers responded only with a good-natured smile. It said, *I understand why you said that*. It said, *but let's not pretend anymore*.

"I didn't come to split hairs with you Professor. I can just imagine with all that's going on, that a white professor, even the one who brought racist genetics to the forefront, is going to perhaps be a little nervous about how he's perceived in public from now on. That's all." The jibe was a strategic one. It called to mind the present situation and the motivation for Eldridge wanting to meet with him in the first place. It landed perfectly.

"You don't understand at all if you think I'm nervous about some worthless baboons."

"Careful," said Eggers looking around facetiously.

"They're brainless seething parasites! They've never thought about anything longer than two minutes!"

"I'd say that's, at least, not comforting knowing they're still around."

"They think what they're told to think—do what they're told. Now they need to be told to fuck off and die, perhaps—" Eldridge's voice petered out, as if deciding better on the matter. He ended the thought with a different trajectory. "Leave campus at least."

There were so many questions to ask already, not excluding the reason for the deep-seated underlying special resentment Eldridge had against the protestors, but he knew he had to get to the heart of the matter. The time was ripe that his energy investment paid dividends.

"If that's not the real danger than what is? It's time you told me what is lurking out there for dangerous white men like ourselves," Eggers couldn't help himself making another dig at the man's research.

Eldridge hesitated before answering. His movements portrayed a man on the verge of a decision. Do I leave or do I stay they seemed to say. Can I trust this man? Instead of making a resolute choice, he decided to hedge. "There's a lot of what you could call overzealous people interested in the science."

"When you say *people*, you mean Ray Foundation, right?" Eggers sighed in the asking, feigning exhaustion at Eldridge's continued efforts to avoid revealing what both men knew.

The question momentarily struck Eldridge dumb broadsiding the academic with a level of candor that was much harder to deflect in person than over the phone. He was choosing his words again carefully when all Eggers wanted was a fixed point that he could count on—settling an ongoing suspicion for a good part of a year.

"Just say it already. No one's around. Simon Ray and his foundation. They're the danger. With all their power and influence with their political capital put into this, they want their investment to be safe and that…that's a natural concern."

Eldridge didn't answer looking at the table instead. He didn't say yes, but he didn't have to. Egger's shook his head in his stead trying to make the requisite eye contact to assuage any remaining reticence of validation.

When his intentions rose from the table, Eldridge still refused to look him in the eyes. Instead, he peered over his shoulder unfocused as if in the act of recollecting.

"The science is still good," he summarized after a while. "The fact is that these things cost money and the money didn't change the results."

"Of course not."

"It didn't." Eggers could see the little flash of anger directed at him for his remark. "I never liked the man."

"So you came to him or he came to you with the idea?"

"He was interested in a paper Gerry and I co-wrote theorizing about the subject. He wanted to know what went into an experiment exploring if there were any merit in the genetic basis for bias modeling."

"So, he came to you and Jersey about it?"

"He knew about Jersey's work, as they already knew each other."

"They knew each other?"

"Yes, at fundraising events. You see, they have similar interests." Eldridge now looked at Eggers as if he were accusing him of something.

"That doesn't look good."

"Nothing to do with politics does."

Eggers reflected for a bit hanging on this one point before going back over what he said earlier.

"But, why is it that you don't like Ray? Why don't you like him after funding all your research? Hasn't he put you on a short list of who's who in Psychology of Today?"

"Psychology of Today?" he asked with some disdain. "Ray is an activist and now he is—I just want nothing more to do with him. I'm still glad to have been able to do the study, but thanks. Now he can kindly fuck off."

"Like the protestors?"

"Exactly."

"Because he's responsible for the protests?"

Eldridge gave a toothy grin without saying anything. Eggers thought he read the whole expression as easy as a for sale sign. He was impressed by his insight.

"So, this whole thing is theater? Staged to garner support?"

"Not the whole thing no. A good contingent is also independently invested."

The thought of how it all happened came to Eggers' mind. For a good part of the year, the seeming stupidity and puerility played out in the streets as if it were all organic. Then again, what was even truly organic? It was assuming that human beings were somehow removed from natural processes. It somehow made more sense now. Drawing attention to the university as a place of learning—an oasis of free thought and inquiry was now subjugated by another idea—an idea that had to be smuggled into the very foundation of the same system that was pre-critical along with its founding tenets. An idea that could take control since the others, in a sense, were contentless. And what place was better to both force submission and draw attention than the cozy university itself being conquered by young soldiers for change? What a compelling fight it was—good versus an embodied scientific evil—an irresistible undefeatable narrative. If Eggers was right, it wasn't just another fraud, it was an amazingly well-thought out plan, ingenious in its subtleties. But, some things still didn't add up.

"What's even in it for these young people? Money?"

"Money?" Eldridge chuckled at the simplicity of such an idea. "No, money is only a small part, these people may as well have cut off hands. They're Ray's dog soldiers—true trained believers—no questions asked."

The more they talked, the more crazy Eggers realized it all sounded. This was not even to answer the question of what the ultimate motivation was for Ray. More money for the billionaire seemed way to absurd a notion. Was he a true believer as well? If so, in what exactly? Though Eggers sought to get a broad understanding of what was really going on, it was rather all high speculation at this point. When it came down to it, none of it mattered in his world unless Eldridge had something more.

Eggers took a deep breath in and then out. "This is a lot."

Eldridge drank the rest of his latte letting Eggers finish his thought.

"This plan…mass conspiracy…how do you know about it? I imagine you have something to substantiate what you're saying." Eggers indicated skepticism in his voice.

"I do have something" Eldridge said decisively.

"What?" he asked, thinking of the little fruit gleaned from Kristi's data cache and preparing himself for even more disappointment.

"A file on Ray."

"That would corroborate everything?"

"No." He leaned in closely though there was no one in the vicinity. A barista was taking a customer's order on the other side of the café and the couple had already left.

"After Gerry and I decided to take the money from Ray to do the study, I wanted to know more about the man who was bankrolling us. Certainly, an intimidating character the one time we met in person and even with Gerry already knowing him, what he ended up telling me was very little—only what you could find publicly. I needed to know more—anything compromising or that would tarnish my reputation, so I independently hired an investigator, ex-FBI. Not cheap. Two hundred an hour plus expenses. I spent nearly twenty grand of my own money to know."

Eggers listened intently, speculating at the possible resources an ex-G man could access that he couldn't—only being sidetracked in making a rough estimate of how much time he had already put into his own investigation and what that could amount to.

Sighing, Eldridge cut himself short seeing Eggers' distraction. "Listen, I'm willing to part with the file. You won't be disappointed with what the investigator found."

Puzzling at this, Eggers asked, "What's in it?"

"Ray's not who he says he is. He's changed his name and moved around for a reason. The investigator found an old address in Trinidad and Tobago. The details of which are complicated but documented within the contents of the file. But once on the island, rather than finding his roots, he discovered a trail of mayhem everywhere on the heels of a man the locals shrouded in superstition. Now they're only glad to be rid of him."

"Mayhem?" Eldridge repeated as if he'd never heard the word before.

"I'll give you the file with the understanding that there is no connection to me. You have to rediscover and verify the source material for yourself, as if you discovered it firsthand."

"You're saying Ray is a criminal?" The journalist pressed to better understand the quo part of the quid pro quo.

Eldridge again laughed as if it were an absurdity like a mathematician being told one and one makes three. "I don't think criminal quite encapsulates the scope of what's going on here. It's like calling Magellan a seaman. There are so many active murder investigations surrounding the coming and goings of Osiras Ram that it was an open secret that officials in Trinidad were covering for him—being paid off from a purportedly inexhaustible fortune."

"Osiras Ram?"

This is the second time the professor looked at his interlocutor like a complete oaf. His fleeting expression revealing a marked disdain for his slow-wittedness. Before it became too apparent, however, he caught himself and clarified. "His real name, yes. He wanted to make people think he made his money in the market when in fact he was already enormously wealthy. The how isn't exactly known."

"Incredible…and you still took the money from his foundation?"

A smile pressed across Eldridge's face with evident irritation. "I don't think you're listening very well Mr. Eggers."

"Sorry. Please explain it to me like a grade schooler." He made a playful grin hoping to lighten the intensity of the conversation.

Eldridge sighed again before responding. "The money was starting to be used before this information fully surfaced. The investigator told me of the address and the need to go to Trinidad to continue. I thought with all that I'd already spent in finding out, I should see it through to the end for possible damage control if anything."

"Can I see it then?"

"Yes, if you agree."

"To not reveal my source? Never do unless they want me to."

"And not to come after our research."

"What do you mean?"

"No more hit pieces on the research. Like I said, these are two separate issues."

"How so?"

"The science is undeniable. The scientific community has already spoken on it. Leave the research alone. As far as exposing, Ray, that's your business. At your own risk."

There were so many things to address, Eggers' head was almost swimming. *One thing at a time*, he told himself. But, as inconsequential as it was, he couldn't let lie the last point.

"Professor, that's not true. It has not been decided by the entire scientific community—only some. A Declaration of Concerned Scientists…"

"*Hokum*," Eldridge interrupted bitterly. "From the beginning, Barton clearly has had a vendetta against me that I don't wish to entertain, but the paper is simply bunk."

"I'll leave that to the experts to figure out," Eggers hit back all to ready to wield the refrain as a weapon for himself.

"I'm the one with expertise."

"And I'm not expert enough to start putting one expert over another."

Eldridge eyed him with bemusement as if not sure how to respond to this conundrum. His well of expertise was of no help either. He waited momentarily for some saliva to build up in his now very dry mouth effectively killing the former dead-end topic. He began slowly, quietly, "I think those are very reasonable conditions Mr. Eggers. Don't you?"

Eggers thought it over. He didn't want to feel beholden to this man in any way and neither did he wish to compromise his own integrity.

What was Eldridge's motivation here exactly? Was it to provide him with a red herring to protect his study from further criticism? Was it to make Ray somehow pay for his crimes? Perhaps it could even amount to his own selfish offense at Ray and his foundation's damage to USFL that was now spreading to the rest of the masses. And why not a combination of all three? People were rarely reducible to one. Whatever the case, Eggers wasn't going to be fully amenable. Eldridge was motivated enough.

"If what you say is true…that is, if there is nothing significant to come up to contest your theory, I agree. I won't cover it," he offered knowing full well that's what he would've done even without the disclosure.

With his eyes staring off momentarily in deep thought, Eldridge suddenly came back to the present. "Very well," he concluded. "I'm confident there won't be anything remotely significant to cast it into doubt."

"I'm glad you're that confident."

"What I'm not so sure about is *your* confidence, Mr. Eggers."

"Have you seen me in an interview lately?" he cracked trying yet again to cut the tension in the air.

"Are you confident that you and your loved ones are safe?" Eldridge asked him with eyes locked on Eggers'—without the slightest registry of his latest quip.

"I don't jump easily."

"This thing's nothing to do with easy."

"Why's that?"

"If you start really looking into Ray with a public audience, he's going to start looking into you."

"Okay," Eggers enunciated cooly suggesting that this was by no means unfamiliar territory to him.

"Just remember that if you decide to do something with this story, you pave new roads on your own. I never met you. And you'd do well to take care."

"What's he going to do with a public figure like me? If he does anything, it will just cause more people to look. Most people don't want to do that."

"Do most people kill?" Eldridge asked with a hint of a broken smile across his face.

"You keep saying he's dangerous—a murderer, but what direct evidence do you even have that he was involved with anything? What's even the murder rate in a country like Trinidad? Maybe these are coincidences."

The broken smile lingered on Eldridge's face for a moment longer. *You have no idea*, it said. When it faded, his words followed.

"The investigator, the one I hired through an agency…I didn't elaborate but he *was* noticed by Ray," Eldridge mused now looking through Eggers rather than at him. "He entered the little supermarket he frequented in Brooklyn in the middle of the day. Video surveillance showed another man following him close behind. A confrontation ensued, and after a brief exchange of words, the man lunged at him with a knife. He was viciously stabbed eighteen times in front of multiple witnesses…so…yep," he acknowledged Eggers' piqued look. "Bled to death over his basket of tomatoes and sausages…and do you know what the investigation agency said that the police found in the backpack of the man they caught?"

Eggers shrugged his shoulders.

"Multiple knives along with a tied baggy of what they, at first, thought must've been food or some hallucinogenic mushroom. But, when they opened the bag to check it out, few held on to their lunches. They were pairs of human nipples. *Nipples.*" He emphasized it again as if saying it once wasn't enough to accept the reality. "All with varying colors, ages, and sizes."

Eldridge now fully had Eggers' attention. He knew There wasn't going to be any more jests from here on out.

"Whose nipples were they? No one knew. What were they for? Mementos? Trophies? The man never said, and the police never found out. But, there was something else that the man had on him that soon made it clear why the investigation agency had to notify me about what happened in the first place. It was the man's identification—a passport. And do you want to know what country's crest was imprinted on it? Sure enough. The last country the investigator visited. Trinidad and Tobago."

8

Peter sat absent-mindedly before his monitor far from the topic presentation that Gemma delivered through Zoomer. She had gone on for twenty minutes and Peter lost the thread ten minutes ago. His new thought process started when he reflected on Gemma's smartly dressed white button-up blouse and grey coat. It wasn't that he had found it especially attractive though Gemma was an attractive woman. Lindsey Cunningham, who hadn't missed a class of his from the beginning of her time at USFL, had dropped this recent one. And as much as her comments could verge on irksome naivety, he had to admit that he now missed her innocent digressions. Now it appeared that Gemma was the one to don the more formal attire in the spirit of their sometime classmate.

It was from here that Peter's mind branched into different avenues of inquiry related to Lindsey's recent departure. While he liked to remind himself of the remaining doubt about the reason she left, his better sense felt some certitude as to the cause. When it was discovered that he helped author the "Declaration of Concerned Scientists" that was being heavily criticized in the headlines since being brought to the limelight by Senator Norbert's speech, naturally, discussion of the topic came up during a seminar. Yash was the one who questioned him about his and Professor Dumfries' involvement in the authoring of the statement. When he admitted to being one of the original fifty-three academics to vote on a final draft at a conference they held in Phoenix some months ago, Lindsey, unlike her usual garrulous self, remained absolutely silent throughout.

It wasn't hard to see what Lindsey's opinion of him had become from her open shares and usual conformity to the popular media's portrayal of things. The negative commentary about the declaration and its signers was relentless. Every tactic was used to make them sound discredited despite no direct dispute with any specific point made in the declaration itself. Instead, the new a-science label was being employed against anyone that had a similar or even somewhat sympathetic viewpoint. This subsequently led to many calls for the firing of the some one thousand seven hundred signers of the declaration. Fortunately, to Peter's knowledge, no institution, as of yet, gave in to such unprincipled pressures.

With the thought of Lindsey leaving for the sake of an imaginary consensus deeply vexing Peter in that she gave up on him despite their good rapport, he recently noticed that, like her, Johnny Pearson had also been out of character. Today, like the last few meetings, he had his camera off and barely said a word unless prompted to do so. *Was he angry about the declaration too?* It didn't even occur to Peter at first that any of his students would be angry or upset even if they disagreed with it. While the discussion had Yash and others gripe about DCS' tone, they didn't raise any further objection. That was largely how he'd expected it to play out. But, now that Lindsey was gone, he could see the one reaction that he underemphasized was silence. It was a tricky one. For silence could be as innocuous as indifference or of a much deeper feeling. Those greater depths, in the light of history, had always been a concern for Peter. It was the realm of intransigent belief beyond reason that really bothered him. At least one could say that the silent usually had reason enough to recognize it for what it was, that is, beyond the tongue's ability to be of any service to it. The fear was in those smart enough to keep mum was that their reason too had to bow to the same chimera.

This vision of another student, one of his best, being subservient to this irrational beast grated on Peter for the rest of Gemma's talk. If one such as Johnny, a very careful student in nearly every comment and paper he produced, could be taken in by such lunacy, then who was safe? If there was any hope at all in saving one youth's mind from being hijacked, Peter decided he had to at least say something, anything.

"Thank you, Gemma. Please post it so we can leave you feedback. Before we adjourn, are there any questions?"

His offer hung in the air for a moment as he stared at the black frame with muted mic symbol. Underneath read the stark white letters, "Johnny Pearson."

"Camila, you'll be up next time, so we'll be very much looking forward to your presentation. Johnny, would you stay after for a moment?"

The session attendees rapidly exited, as Peter stayed—not really sure if there was still a person there on Johnny's end.

"*Johnny?*" he reached out as the last few of the Hollywood Squares suddenly became one.

There was a long pause as Peter waited for the voice behind the name.

Finally, the mic icon switched on with a tired voice filtering through the speaker.

"I'm here," Johnny said.

"I thought we could just have a quick chat if that's okay with you?"

"Yeah, it's fine."

"Good. I just saw that—" he started before stopping himself abruptly. "If it's okay, could you turn on your camera?"

A dimly lit room was revealed. The camera pivoted to the thinning face with bulbous bags protruding from under the eyes. Peter's voice and manner changed right away. He was surprised he didn't notice the emaciating face from sessions before. When he tried thinking of the last time he saw Johnny, he figured it must've been well before winter break. Seeing someone as one box of many, important details like these were being lost.

"I haven't heard you contributing to our discussions," Peter expressed with concern. "So, I had to find out…if there was anything wrong?" In reality, Johnny's face said it all. *Tell me something that's right*, it said.

"Everything's fine," Johnny voiced hearteningly, his tired face incongruous with the utterance.

Peter waited for more. At some point, Johnny was going to have to address the face he saw staring back at him on his own screen.

Barton waited patiently, attentively. He was letting him know that he was there for him, and it didn't matter that it was thousands of miles away between Tacoma and Palm Gate. He sat there no longer just as a professor, but as a fellow person.

"I'm a little tired," he murmured in a light strange voice trying to fill the quietude with something.

"You are," affirmed Peter nodding his acceptance.

"Need more sleep," he expressed with conviction.

"You're having trouble sleeping? Are you feeling more anxious or do you have more stress than usual?"

Johnny looked at the camera distraught by some inner turmoil. Any moment, Peter wouldn't be surprised by the introduction of tears.

"Yes," he admitted, eyes shining with a more palpable glisten. He swallowed. "I may be leaving campus…leaving school after this semester."

"Leaving? Really?"

"I've been thinking about a leave of absence for a while now…"

"I see," Peter said wondering if he was even going to mention it if he hadn't brought it. "Well, that's not always the worse thing. It can give you time to sort out some things."

"I'm not sure I'll be wanting to come back."

This coming from a student who was extremely talented— someone he wanted to see in the field—someone who he was even comfortable with calling a colleague one day, caused Peter's stomach to feel completely empty.

"Well, you shouldn't be making that decision now. You have time to think about it."

"Yeah," Johnny agreed—again spacing out to recall something else.

Peter saw the troubling signs. He saw the deer in the headlights look—fatigue, depression, confusion, and disconnection. *What happened to Johnny? What trauma befell him while Peter was away?*

"It seems," Peter began again attempting to make it okay in exposing the haunting specter troubling the young man, "that something happened that you don't want to talk about. Is that it? Did something happen on campus? Is that why you want to take a leave of absence?"

"Thank you for your concern, Professor, but I'll be okay."

This response annoyed Peter with the real possibility that Johnny would never tell him even though he really believed he could be of aid to the young man. But, there was something else too, and he didn't want to admit this selfish motive. He really had to know whatever it was. With institutions seemingly in collapse, he felt like he had to bear witness to it all as if he were Gibbon himself alive during the Roman Empire.

"Okay, I just want you to know that you can tell me if you ever want to share. I mean I'm not telling anyone else or doing anything about what you have to say, but what happened may not be as bad as you think and sometimes it's better to have it out—to have someone help you process it. Ya'know?"

"Thanks Professor, but I'll figure it out."

"Are you sure?"

The next line of Johnny's was something Peter could never forget as long as he lived. It falteringly and painfully came out. "I just don't think I belong here anymore," he delivered.

Peter felt a great sense of loss as if an essential piece of him was being taken that he didn't know he needed. *If students like him were being discouraged, who were going to be the successors of the old university patrons? Were their new incentives the same as the old?* Peter had some idea, and it scared him. *If the incentives weren't right, who were going to be the most attracted to institutions anymore? Who but the most fawning and vile would seek it and happen to thrive in such a place? While the disease spread, the other animals fled, and the scavengers gorged themselves on carrion.*

Red. Last Gift of the Dead.

1

Jennifer came back to consciousness startled by strident echoing shrieks. She tried blinking the blur out of her eyes as she sought relief for the poor creature that suffered nearby. The dim light took some getting used to as she turned herself on the hard stone slab that she found herself. She was naked with her wrists and ankles clamped with cold steel. Her flesh was dotted with archipelagos of goose bumps and her limbs shook with the warmth of the drug now wearing off. At first, she reacted by trying to pull herself into a ball for warmth, but the hardened unforgiving steel dug-in and she had no recourse but to lay there exposed.

The shrieks had died and were followed by indiscernible mutterings that came from the glowing dim light on her left side. Her blurred vision still prevented her from making out just what awful thing was happening to someone nearby. She hoped this wasn't real. She hoped that it was a nightmare within the drowsy throes of sleep, but the starkness was too great for that, and it was becoming starker still. Her mind raced for an explanation trying to find some stable ground—the last thing she remembered lucidly, but it was hard going as she heard the screaming start over once again. Between each breath of screeching there was also something else. A repetition of the same line. A pleading. A prayer? She wasn't quite sure as it was spit out so loudly and frantically in response to whatever terrifying act was being perpetrated. "Omnoahrast! Omnoahrast! Omnoahrast!" it said. It was a voice that was about to dive under the frigid water and had only a moment for breath. Then the voice suddenly gave out to a grating creaking sound like a swarm of creeping rats in a feeding frenzy. It continued on that way for a moment as her eyes better adjusted to the moving shadows in the distance. As she studied whatever was transpiring by turning her head to the right, she heard another voice. This one she was quite sure was a man. "Fuck! Leh go!" he said. What followed was a reeking wave of shit and piss that caused her to turn her head all the way to the left just to try to prevent herself from vomiting.

Then she started to remember. It was as if the sheer pungency of the odor acted as a sort of smelling salt awaking her from her former narcotic induced stupor. At first, there were only fixed glimpses of reality. A time shouting in a crowd next to her friend D who was smiling at her shouting too. An acquaintance throwing a brick at a police car and everyone laughing at something said— something she didn't remember. Then there was the redolence of sweat and alcohol within the cramped quarters of a darkened bar downtown. All of these she knew were recent happenings flashing in her mind with no connection between them. They were images in a puzzle with no medium. And with the urgent need to find meaning in these incongruous moments to help her understand the dire situation she now found herself in, she carried on sometime with no progress. While the thought to yell for help did occur to her, with the person screaming in pain nearby she was careful not to draw that same unwanted attention. It was only when that same voice from earlier came back with the prayer, did she start to gather how she may have come to this place.

She had met D in the lobby of the Hotel Leonardo in Little Harbor. D, or Dorothy, was one of her best friends since they went to university together. Since then, with both sharing a keen interest in activism, they'd both joined the Anti-Hate Alliance, a non-profit organizer of demonstrations set on stamping out endemic racist structures. It was that very morning when they met, taking a light breakfast from the hotel restaurant, they'd entered into the crisp cold of AHA's latest protest.

They felt it was a great success. After swallowing a mystery pill with other friends they had met with from AHA, they marched from Little Harbor to City Hall with the streams of crowds waving signs, shouting, and disrupting what they called "a racist sewer of a city." It was exhilarating. It was empowering. Opposition was shouted down and stripped of signs. The racist police presence was finally made to feel uncomfortable just the way they did daily in the same streets. Admittedly, there was a little violence acted against these contingents that tended to happen with such movements in general, but they all knew these amounted to very little when compared to the systemic lynch mobs occurring throughout history.

By the time that evening came, they were exhausted from a full day's work. Not only were they hungry and thirsty, with the weather having warmed during the day, they were also sticky with dried sweat. Talking over what was to be their next move, one of the lead organizers told them of a trendy underground bar nearby where they had planned to congregate with other activists as a kind of victory celebration.

A handful of them went together north on Saint Paul's. After some blocks, they turned left on a side street hearing the chatter coming from the front of an old attached brick building. The horizontal sign hanging out in front marked the place as "Sweet," which she recalled someone in the group mocking at the time. But, when stepping down into the bar area, she had remembered liking the place immensely. There was a small towny feel and a cozy atmosphere.

There were perhaps twenty people there already with two tables being saved in the corner by a friend of the organizer. When they sat, immediately there was a tray of tequila shots ordered which they all clinked and imbibed in a fury. From that time, the crowd in the bar only grew with many more shots to come.

She remembered the warmth pulsing through her body after the fourth shot with people telling war stories and laughing when ever more activists had managed to pull up chairs and squeeze in at their table at the organizer's suggestion. That's when she remembered seeing a friendly looking man with a camo-colored cap take a seat next her and D. He was introduced by one of the organizers as Jack from BLL—a foreign org that she heard of but never quite remembered what its acronym meant. He looked young, mid to late twenties, handsome, and wore a charming smile that Jennifer remembered distinctly.

When he opened his mouth, the Bahamian style accent wooed her still. As the next round came, when Jennifer politely declined, she remembered him holding his glass smiling as if waiting for her to do the same.

"No," she laughed. "I'd enough for now."

"But maybe it hasn't 'ad enough of *you*," he said with such a tone and look that she remembered spitting up laughing not quite sure why.

He continued motioning to her glass with his. "The spirit can't be left alone. It needs a body and the body needs it." This was followed by silence as if everyone were trying to understand what he was getting at. He furrowed his brow as if offended by something and lifted his glass once more. There was sudden fear of being disliked by this man. It was as if a sudden need arose that she had to please him no matter what. "You cannot deny the spirit. Not on a night like tonight," he clarified as if this settled it once and for all. Everyone including D stared at her to see what she was going to do.

She took the glass and he put on his best smile again bringing her relief. She didn't want to have to see that other face of his again. She mirrored his cheers and poured even more of the burning liquid down her throat.

From there things really kicked off. The drinks and jokes flowed. She remembered Jack ordering a drink for D and her that could actually be enjoyed, one called Under the Tiki Hut, with Chareau, rum, coconut, and pineapple. It tasted wonderful and when they weren't experiencing the firework of flavors in their mouths, they were cracking up from one of Jack's many witticisms.

The night was riding high and quite frankly they didn't want it to end. It was only when most of the crowd left and with Jack heading to the restroom that she realized she may be too blitzed to get up. And what was worse, just holding herself up from falling into her new drink, she noticed D was practically passed out.

When he returned, she was on her phone searching for available Youbers in the area and that's when he offered to give them a ride back to the Leonardo. At the time, it seemed like the best bet. He was not only already known in some capacity by the group, but there was also the simple fact that he was a foreigner, and in their circle, foreigners were almost by definition, good. To say no to such a good-natured offer was not only uncouth but it reflected poorly on her and the very person she knew herself to be—the person that she wanted to prove to him that she was—to prove to him that she didn't have any fear of going with him at all—that she herself was, in spite of her appearance, one of the good ones. Here was yet another opportunity to demonstrate her true virtue—to show her belief in justice. The only thing that could make the night complete would be to document the trip for all of her friends to see. Maybe they could even get a little laugh at seeing D so far gone, but then there was the matter of just getting her into a vehicle.

She held D under the arms as he went to get his car to pull up front. She recalled not liking his stopping twenty yards short of the door but didn't complain as he got out a little winded while helping them over to his black SUV. After helping D into the back seat, he opened the passenger door to let Jennifer step up and fall into hers. This was when he turned his back to her looking over to the bar as if he forgot to pay the bill. From where they were, all appeared quiet. No one was lingering outside. The protesters had long since fizzled out since the city imposed another curfew. She didn't expect much police activity until they got closer to Little Harbor. Time seemed to stand still as he appeared to ponder over something.

Only when she was about to ask what the matter was, did he whip around eyeing her with a smile that wasn't the one that graced them before. It was a mischievous face pull. She stared back at him questioningly with fear flooding in faster than the pull of a vicious rip current on a puppy. "Can I get anything else?" he asked stepping closer. As her brain was muddled with paralyzing fear, he pulled the syringe from his pocket and plunged it into her thigh hard pushing the plunger down almost immediately. She grabbed at his hand weakly trying to remove it, but the warm liquid was already streaming in. It was only seconds before she lost consciousness.

Breath appeared to reenter the suffering creature's lungs in one pronounced blood-curdling scream. "I'm not racist! I'm not raaaaacist!" The once incoherent sounds now culminated into words that she recognized as the creaking started up once again. This time, she turned her head and held her breath to behold the truth she didn't want to believe—to behold the person behind the voice.

Her eyes slowly adjusted to the lighting as the sweaty back musculature of a shirtless man turned a club wrapped in rope around the hanging body. His taught sinews strained as he slowly twisted the wood causing the body to jerk around as the rope tightened creak by creak. All the small frame could do was moan indescribable pain under the pressure about her abdomen. Terrified, she felt nauseated as she released her breath and filled her lungs again with shitty air to see if her deepest fears had come true—the fears that she had tried so hard to deny.

The limp face of the small frame slowly flashed into focus by the flames—blinking into existence what she had suspected, the terror of the familiar in the unfamiliar. D was the one being tortured. D was being squeezed into pulp by some beast of a man. With the way his muscle worked on her relentlessly, she was surprised her friend was even alive enough to belt anything out anymore. Perhaps this was the end and the contents of her bladder and bowels attested to this fact as it dribbled from one of her legs onto the hard floor making Jennifer's own guts wrench in bouts with nausea due to the stench.

"Please," she managed weakly in tears. "Please stop." She turned to her side to cough up vomit before seeing if the man even noticed. That's when she saw the two red dots in the blackness that she hadn't seen before. How could she have missed them? She didn't know what to make of it but hoped it was a sign that her appeal meant something—that it could possibly affect what was happening to her friend. She could only think to make it weak and pathetic enough to not turn that same rage inflicted on her friend's body on her instead.

"Please stop. Please stop." She said it louder when she collected herself and the man finally did. As he let it go, the stick unwrapped, loosened suddenly and hit the ground with a smack. *Thank God*, she thought. *Make it stop. Make it all stop.*

She saw D's body slowly inflate and deflate in shallow respirations while the man made his own much deeper and fuller. She was still alive. There was still a chance she could intervene before it was too late. What was she to say? The words weren't coming.

When he appeared to catch his breath, the man slowly stooped down to take up the club once again. There was no time. He was going to continue unless she said the right thing. It didn't matter anymore—whatever it was to make it stop, and since she had no idea, she spewed anything and everything that came to mind. She questioned. She begged. She dropped names and monetary figures. She even appealed to religion that she didn't believe in.

The man only stood with his back to her quietly as the red lights beamed on. She wasn't quite sure, but she thought they were even brighter still. Maybe someone else was listening to her after all. Maybe it was some kind of remote viewing or recording device where the man would be signaled once she revealed what they wanted. Besides that, she couldn't imagine what this was all for. *Were they some black activists that saw them as racist infiltrators to their movement? Why else would D have to try to convince them?* Maybe they told her before the torture began. This line of reasoning made sense and suddenly she seized upon it.

"Sir," she said in her small voice again. "I think there's a mistake. We're not the people you think we are. My friend and I are good people. We only wish to serve your—we are trying to make things better. Please see that."

This caused a crackle to echo through the cavern. The man began to sway a little back and forth as he squeezed on the club. She couldn't believe it. After her pleading, all she could do was to make him laugh.

"I'm not wha—"

"You disgust me bitch," he growled between puffs of laughter. The familiar voice shocked her into silence and she listened to whatever the once friendly voice was going to say next.

Jacques turned around with a menacing smile that revealed nothing of the warmth it projected from the bar. It was a hideous daze of hatred fueled revelry that appeared unquenched from its handling of D.

"Why are you doing this?" She tried to open the same channel of communication with the man with the once friendly smile—the man who had charmed them with drinks and jokes. She could see right away, however, that this sometime human being was not responding in the way people do. It was like trying to have a conversation with a crocodile whose jaws were clamped around your neck.

He clapped her across the face with the club without warning. Only glancing her head, he followed with one thump after another. She tasted blood before starting to drift again into nothingness. The last fleeting thought she remembered before one of the club's final descents was that this was it. She would be no more and that was okay. Everything was going to be alright after all.

When Jennifer slowly came to with the help of a whirring sound, memory poured back faster than before. Her head hurt and she quivered from the dry cold air. The thought of her thirst and discomfort immediately gave way to a renewed fear and dread as the nearby ominous sound of something out of a machine shop purred intermittently. It was then that she cursed life knowing this recurring nightmare was set to continue. This wasn't just talk or the high speculation that largely filled her life with friends since her time at university. No matter how much she refused to believe it or what people might've said about its near impossibility, this was really happening to her. And to her greatest despair, nothing could seem to change it.

She turned her head to see D's body no longer suspended nearby. Instead, next to her, stooped Jack over a portable battery plugged into a circular saw that he appeared to be making adjustments to. That was it—the rotary sound that helped awaken her. And now, with little else to do, it was her time to scream. She put as much of her body into it as she could using the little room left in the metal clamps to throw her chest forward into projecting all of her terror into an outward peel of life's remaining noise. It echoed through the massive cavern back at her as if it were the only sensible response possible to such a statement.

Jack now brought the circular saw up to the stone slab holding it between her legs as she writhed her limbs frantically if only to relieve the immense pain that was about to follow. He revved the saw and stopped and revved it again as if toying with her before laying its long cold guard over her clitoris. She shook and screamed to no avail. He took his time appearing to adjust the length of the retractable blade. It was at this point that she saw the red orbs bigger than ever. She now saw what they really were. They were a part of a profile of a very tall body standing back from the slab. And while the shape of its presumed visage made little to no geometrical sense for a human, she clearly saw that she was the object of their speculation.

She wanted to die quickly. She wanted to pass out, but she felt that the eyes wouldn't let her. In fact, the worst thought still came to her just as the circular saw started its horrible teeth toward her center. "I deserve this. I'm. just. no. good." She poured these last tears of despair just before resistance found the blade.

2

Clint traversed across the expanse of the park for the second time that day. Thankfully, he didn't have to do it as much anymore but what he wasn't so thankful for was having to teach an Introduction to Psychology course again. He couldn't say for sure, but it appeared the department wasn't so keen about his relationship to Barton and his signing of the DCS. His usual Abnormal Psychology course, that he had taught for over two years in Dorfman, had now been given to Garretty. As of now, Tuesdays and Thursdays consisted of tending to two sections, one morning and one afternoon auditorium class on the far side of Peckhart.

What did it really matter anymore, he thought bitterly. *Until they could remove the contingent of activists from campus, nothing was going to be made right.* With a hope remaining, he was willing to play along in the trenches for a while until they saw the error of their ways in going along with the screamers, as he now liked to call them.

It was at this point that he passed one of the screamers' main outposts on the park. This was the worst part of his walk. It was a well-organized pavilion now surrounded by signs and a rotating staff that wore signature black scarves tied about their necks much like a boy scout neckerchief. They shouted or chanted slogans intermittently to passersby at the major fork in the park's walkway.

Even as he kept his distance, he heard their slogan and sighed as he hurried to Peckhart to avoid the rain as much as to not have to see this branch of the people's temple now working on campus with the consent of the administration. "Res-komun! Res-komun!" he heard them shout faintly through the breeze as some students sounded it back. Only, due to his intellectual curiosity, did he come to ask them what the strange cadence meant. "Racial Equity, Community, Unity" one member of the new guard told him proudly only to look sour at his disrespectful scoff.

Taking a closer look at the signs neither engendered any additional sympathy for their cause either. "If you hear something, say something," many of the signs read having a reporting station set up under the tent for those who violated, or were at least accused of violating, equitable norms of conduct. These signs now grew on the campus like weeds and each day it seemed he noticed yet another sprouted in a new surprising place.

Another sign he noticed consistently, getting his dander up, was demanding "Genetic Testing Now!" The absolute ignorance and acceptance of having such a policy being paraded around a university campus in the United States was enough to cause him to have to yell at a new administrator in the Diversity Equity and Inclusion office. It was a wasted effort. The woman there lamely claimed students' rights to freedom of expression while denying that those same views reflected the opinion of the university.

None of it was good, and it only appeared to get worse. The screamers were not only assigned to a certain area, with ever more frequency, Clint witnessed them walk the campus like a new commissioned patrol looking out for any new offense to report. Among the psychology faculty, they called them hall monitors in recognition of the apparent further infantilization of each successive student body.

Joking aside, it was really starting to wear on Clint. The aggressive symbol of a trident on the black scarves started to grate on him at an ever-increasing rate. Its celebration along with the now evidently stupid new saying of "Res-komun" was pushing him to make the bi-weekly venting call to Peter more frequently.

The wind rose and Clint felt a few large freezing drops surprise him with cold as some landed on his neck taking some breath with it. He increased his pace passing the covered Peckhart statue whose tight drapery still managed to billow in the strong gusts.

He didn't know what offense it had committed, but he remembered having a discussion with a student about the covering over Henry Nordrick right after the graffiti had been removed. The administration didn't yet know what they were going to do with it but talks about tearing it down and replacing it with something more *up to date* had been circulating, even the idea of giving it to an interested donor. The student posited it as an example of the idea of the Jungian Shadow of the university given the negative unwanted aspects of the historical figure. When Clint questioned him what those negative traits happened to be, the student laughed at the professor's apparent ignorance.

"Well, he was racist…and is quoted as promoting ideas like the inferiority of certain peoples even involving himself in eugenics research," he snickered looking around at the other students as if asking, *isn't this one dense?*

"Where are you citing this information from? A Readit page?" he asked with some venom at the kid's wiseass attitude.

The student wore a continuous smug grin. *Get a load of this guy*, it said. "Uh, I didn't look in the Encyclopedia Britannica if that's what you're asking." This brought some tittering from the audience that surely only aggravated Clint's hypertensive condition.

"I doubt Professor Nordrick was perfect, but he was nothing of what you say. He was a scientist, a philanthropist, and if you did your homework, an anti-segregationist. To my mind there is no reason to do anything with the statue except uncover it, maintain it as he helped build this university into what it is today."

The student laughed again. "Professor, it is well documented. He used the n-word repeatedly and had structures built on campus to accommodate segregation. This isn't disputed anymore."

Clint had no idea what he had been referencing and imagined that he referred to the word "negro"—not necessarily being derogatory in that era. In any case, they had strayed from the topic, and he knew what this was. He knew better than to further engage. This student was the type more interested in giving in to argument as some kind of sporting exercise than discovering facts. These emotional highs only caused further digging in and more wasted words—for words were all they amounted to.

"I think you're mistaken, but I'll check my facts and you check yours. But, just imagine, if you will, if we started pulling down every structure or discounting any work done by imperfect people. Wouldn't that be everywhere and everything? It's a non-starter."

"Imperfect?" The student posed the last word as if that were enough to win the crux of the argument, as if Professor Dumfries offered a bait and switch.

The rain was now pouring hard on him as he rushed for the entrance to the auditorium. His remembrance of the twerp's self-satisfied grin was more unpleasant than the rush of cold water drenching his head and back. If anything, it was freeing, relieving him from the burden of his thoughts.

When he reached the overhang leading to his class in Peckhart, he pulled at his sports coat to shake off the excess rainwater turning to see the grass of the park being battered by the torrent in undulating strips. There was a hypnotic quality to the way nature played upon the green canvas. It was enough to make him forget many of the artificial human impositions now prodding at him as if by a failing acupuncturist. For the given world, including him, weren't having any of it, anymore.

He watched as students were driven from the cold wet field, even the screamers in the pavilion had to abandon it for better cover. There was nothing for them to say anymore. Fortunately, no amount of word surgery could compel them stay there any longer.

3

In front of the mirror, she turned her head at different angles critiquing every feature. There was much she didn't like about what she saw. She didn't like the early signs of crow's feet. She cursed many times those stubborn infectious wrinkles lacing her eyes to the rest of her face. Ever since comparing herself with other girls in high school, she also had a rather low opinion of her lips, dreaming one day of growing plush full ones—ones like Angelina Jolie had in the movie Wanted. It wasn't that her mind superimposed on those big fleshy cushions on herself, it was that she really felt they were a part of her, at least, in the dream world. She remembered feeling proud to part them seeing them as she faded in and out of different scenes—a mishmash of borrowings from both real life and film. Back and forth she switched from first person to third—seeing herself with confidence, with true power, yet unknown—seducing an old crush throughout. It was such a disappointment to wake up—to discover something missing. Then again, feeling wasn't everything.

She did have her qualities. She had her naturally long lashes. She still had a nicely shaped nose that didn't protrude nor flatten on her face. And then there were her C sized breasts that have drawn the attentions of various men at work or in passing. Yes, she believed she still had something to offer in the sex department. She only wished that the man she was seeing now, not yet in any official capacity, would notice these features too, or at least, hint at his noticing.

She proceeded to pencil the outline of her lips in the reflection—making small carefully connected lines over its curves before following up with the light rose color lipstick that grew on her after trying the dozen or so samples at the mall.

The process wasn't just satisfactory by the end-product, she rather enjoyed the application itself. There was something calming about the ritual. Maybe it was the art, the precision, and the focus it took to establish the look she really wanted. And then maybe it was the outward manifestation of her taking control at a time when she felt so afraid and so weak. Only if there was something like that— something that she could apply to the rest of her life, she knew she'd be set. Maybe not happy, but at least normal again. Absent the poisoning effects of dread spoiling the all too fleeting joys of life, who even knew? For now, when alone, the simple application of lipstick brought her from the depths of its crushing influence.

Kristi pressed her lips together a few times to make the finishing touches scrutinizing her work carefully. Overall, she wasn't unhappy with the outcome. In fact, this time, she believed that she nailed it. No concealer necessary.

Next, it was time to try it out, so to speak. She put on the best smile she could muster, but it was clear that she wasn't really into it. It came out awkward, almost screwy in its forced presentment incongruous with the rest of her face. So, she put on some more, trying on different looks to find out what she was going for. They were better, but none of them good. Maybe they would convince someone, but they weren't convincing her. She thought for a moment and had an idea. Lifting her blouse and dropping her bra, she flashed her bare breasts at herself in the reflection. A naughty capricious smile impressed her face as she stared at herself in lipstick with her perky breasts jetting out. Not exactly what she wanted, but there was that missing element. Authenticity.

The little playfulness had brought it out, and it worked for a little bit before the effect wore out. Now she was back to her serious self—blank, no semblance of a smile left, like readying herself for the rubber glove treatment at the doctor's office. She hated it. She hated that it reminded her of what happened—what had befallen her and her friend, Yunnie. *Maybe I should just go naked.*

But that thought too wasn't funny—wasn't welcome. It reminded her too much of the naked women she saw in Ray's paintings—there milky white bare bodies tinged in bluish light. And while she wasn't and couldn't have been pregnant at the time, that placid vulnerable look that they all shared, she also identified in the woman in the mirror.

Kristi's phone rang. "Patrick."

"How's everything? How's the new job?" he spoke over a reverberating voice in the background making some announcement.

"Good…Where are you?"

"Fort Lauderdale boarding back to D.C. I just wanted to tell you….I spoke with someone I believe you'd find interesting—someone from the university."

She knew what university. Detective Gonzalez had since shared that the DNA found on the knife left at her apartment by her attempted kidnapper matched multiple victims from the Youhaul Killings at USFL.

"I see," she acknowledged simply waiting for him to divulge what he could.

"This seems to confirm everything you suspected."

The voice took over. In a moment, that was all there was, just her and the sound of Patrick's voice.

"Apparently Ray's a dangerous man Kristi—a really dangerous man—almost legendary in his own country. In fact, I think there's a lot he could say about the man that he left out," he said softly, incisively into the receiver giving her a chill that made small hairs stand out on her neck and arms.

She tried to respond with the words "I know," but mouthed them inaudibly.

"I've a lot of information now. This is going to be a big story, much bigger than the one we ran about Yunnie's disappearance the other night," he said with an uncharacteristic monotone. "I know you think that your new job, your new place is safe, but I think it may be a good idea to start taking extra precautions."

There was something that prevented her from speaking. The night at the old apartment replayed in her head—the thin knife plunging for flesh, homing for her vital organs seeking a new path for blood. *Had Yunnie received the same treatment? What if the man was successful and drugged her the way he tried to do it with Kristi? And what if…?* She couldn't imagine that deranged smile had any modicum of human understanding—nothing like mercy could occur to someone like that. The very menace stimulated him. It seemed to be some kind of fulfillment of a vicious revenge fantasy. And now that she thought of it, with those paintings of Ray's pregnant nudes in certain poses, she didn't want to speculate what sort of depravity could be on the mind of someone in his employ.

"Kristi?" he said diffidently. "You still there?"

"I'm here."

"You're going to be okay. You just understand that there is a likely history with him and—" he paused listening to the next announcement. "I've got to board."

"Yeah, I've got to work."

With this reality confirmed, the prospect of going into the hotel where she was hired as concierge had given her a renewed rush of dread. There was a reimagining of scenarios whether unlikely or fantastical that could result in her executioner finishing what he had so ardently fought for. But before she let this fear continue, she made great efforts to have her rational self take control again—to have it dampen the hysteria of some kind of mystical denouement.

"I understand. I was hoping we could get together and talk more about this…"

"Yeah, let's do that," her voice had perked up at the prospect surveying herself in the mirror again.

"How about tomorrow night eight o'clock? Same place?"

"You mean the diner just off the boulevard?"

They had already gone there twice, but it was the last time that she remembered having a distinctly pleasant evening—having some recollection of what it was even like to be normal again—staying up until one in the morning eating pie and drinking coffee laughing together about the trivial. It was something she was eager to repeat no matter what the grim news. She wanted to laugh again and maybe, just maybe, something else could happen too.

"Yeah." She agreed trying not to sound too eager.

"See you then."

She put down the phone continuing to examine herself one last time now wearing her hotel's name plate. "Kristy," it read, technically misspelled, but she didn't mind too much. It was going to be another long night. It was going to be another night with extended periods of solitude, and when she had given it some thought, some strange macabre curiosity built within her. The idea was that it could even be her last night alive. The way she saw it was at a distance, and from here it wasn't so scary. She entertained the idea and could ask herself if she would ever see Patrick tomorrow night. She could speculate on the feeling of what it would be like to never feel real love from a man again. *How unfair that would be in the scheme of things,* she thought. And *what a waste of life.* But when she thought again of Yunnie, she realized that wasn't just speculation—a distant possibility of many. That was a flesh, muscle, sinew, and bone reality still hunting for her.

4

"Every day, university life resembles more and more a smorgasbord of anti-scientific nonsense," Clint chuckled into the computer camera without mirth, as if he was soon to be driven to the insane asylum.

They were filming a segment of Peter's weekly podcast, Psyclips. Peter watched from his home office as Clint answered a viewer's question that had soon escalated into a tirade.

"It's one damn thing after another. This study is bogus— perhaps something a layman may miss—but absolute bullshit. But now with the proliferation of racial justice studies, we have entered upon a world of mass hysteria based on a false assumption—being that everything is tainted by racism…"

"But—" Peter tried interjecting a moment, yet Clint was on a roll.

"Appearing to be the basic postulate everyone is working from. And I tell you what, I'm tired of it. When I start reading a paper now, whether it be a colleague's or a student's, I'll see the assumption and know what they expect me to do—just sit comfortably along for the ride and accept it whole hog. And I'll tell you what—I'm not doing that. I'm not comfortable with it. I'm going to have to ask them to prove it like anything else—using the scientific method with the same level of rigor that's expected from every other assertion."

"Well, they're going to say," Peter found his opening. "You probably know what they're going to say. They're going to talk about inequalities—everywhere inequalities in the data—inequalities across the board in every single discipline—proving racism," he smiled at his good-faith attempt playing devil's advocate.

Clint collected himself as he heard where Peter was going. It almost seemed a bore to him in mounting a response, as if at this juncture, he had heard every retort from the other side.

"Pointing out inequalities in everything is like a child suddenly noticing the jagged surface of a smooth ball when looking at it under a microscope. The person who expects everything to be totally equal across the board has never lived in reality, and we would appreciate if they'd kindly remove themselves from the field of science. I mean…" His eyes wandered off the screen as he laughed to himself. "I wonder what we are to expect next—a future study of the inequality of wishbone breaking at Thanksgiving dinner? How whiteness is inextricably linked to being the winner of the greater part?" He continued to boff.

Peter joined him adding, "or their preference for white meat."

Clint was sauced and laughing a lot, not so much with glee, but repulsion. He was repulsed by the idea of such weak people. His laughter was a mockery for their little doings—their false friendships. How pathetic, how weak were those who couldn't say no to the race game. They couldn't stop placating it with false declarations, pledges, oaths, or stop indulging those who told themselves a fairytale about the whites who lived in trailer parks in the woods at the center of plagues and other evil machinations against the helpless black city folk. It was time to stop the fantastical thinking. It was time to stop mentally placing people into camps. And maybe, just maybe, one day they could see him as he really was—no longer treating him as a handicapped Eloi in need of coddling.

When the talk for the camera ended, both friends fixed up another one of their preferred beverages to share across cyberspace. Peter set upon the scotch he kept in the cupboard well out of sight and reach of his short father-in-law, a recovering alcoholic. The few chips of ice he added were more about the temperature than watering down the potency or flavor of the drink.

Clint was in an altogether different mood, lately making himself a Manhattan with Rye. He even used a special stir stick as the finishing touch spreading out the maraschino cherries.

Both friends offered a cheers by lifting their glasses toward their cameras proceeded by the intake of deep drafts. There was a simple existing momentary contentedness that the alcohol helped to infuse. Peter took a few more sips considering the latest Psyclips episode and what he was going to propose next.

Even in the middle of recording, he knew it was going to be yet another success. He knew it would likely garner at least a hundred-thousand views within the week just like the last one did, and he knew why. It was Clint who stole the show. He happened to be his most requested guest, and despite some of the much more popular academics that ended up joining him, the magnetic personality of his friend—deep voice, giant features, and distinct erudition and humor were irresistible.

He was more than satisfied with the podcast and liked the way his social media presence was growing, but in the end, he wanted more. The reason for launching his channel in the first place was to make the public more aware of the current state of Psychology, especially given the outrageous methodology in the Eldridge and Jersey study and the news' largely one sided take on the matter. But he thought he had made a consistently good case already of how the conclusions of the research didn't actually map onto reality. Now there appeared to be another even more pressing issue though he had been reticent to address it, and his ongoing contact with Eggers continuously attested to that fact.

There was an urgent need to expose the activist Simon Ray and his foundation. Though it wasn't a topic of psychological research, the organization responsible for the study and stoking the flames of the resulting chaos, needed to be called into question. The public needed to be warned. And while he knew that Eggers already agreed to do a whole future episode on the topic, he felt time was running out. The MPA was being lobbied by the same organization, and with the track record it had, more insanity was likely on the way. But how was he supposed to address what verged on the political? What were the dangers exactly of navigating this narrow passageway that could not only result in some kind of litigation, but could even bring himself physical danger? Who knew what these powerful men were even capable of? Whatever the case, he found staying silent on the subject unworkable. It was as if its proclamation were as necessary as having to exude sweat in a Finnish bathhouse. His conscience had been needling him now endlessly, and he couldn't just let yet another opportunity slip by.

After Clint gave a deep sigh swirling ice around his glass while reclining in the comfy chair of his study, Peter made a couple big swallows of scotch. The resulting euphoric rush to the head was just the boost he needed to lift him from the drowsy spell that was taking over.

He leaned forward from his leather ergonomic swivel chair (costing him nearly a thousand dollars upon arrival in Tacoma). "What did you think?" he asked almost rhetorically—wanting Clint to return to a more garrulous mood than he seemed to be at present.

"I think—" he began before tilting his glass to his mouth all the way up until the ice rattled. "I'm going to get myself another. What about you?" he asked upon finishing.

Both left to refill before reconvening in front of the camera. Clint landed himself back in his chair with a whumpf.

It was hard for Peter to get used to his father-in-law's little makeshift office, but at least it was quiet on that side of the house, and with the new chair that was relatively comfortable. Still, seeing Clint in his own office, he did miss the house in Preston Heights. It wasn't that there was no other nice place left in the US to raise children, but it was their dream that he missed most. Margery and he wanted to raise their family with the ideal house and neighborhood to do it in, but now that dream was no longer the same. It was tainted. Margery had just given birth to their new child, Samantha, and here they were thousands of miles away from that ideal. So seeing Clint in his own home, reminded him what it was that brought them to Tacoma in the first place. You'd think that distance and time would be enough to squelch the anger. But it was still there where it only grew. Indeed, it was thriving into a different animal altogether—an animal even more difficult to control. Peter was practically possessed by it. Given what he already knew, it drove him much further than what good sense would dictate. He was putting it all on the line, but informing him of that fact was akin to warning teenagers of STDs before sex. Sating the fire now burning in his chest like a burgeoning wasp's nest caused him to overlook what would have been patently obvious to most.

"Thank you for doing this again, my friend," Peter said abruptly as to continue the conversation. "They absolutely love you. You should think about doing your own channel."

"How do you know it's me they love?"

"The comments. Most of it is about you. You're just so damned likeable."

"No."

"We can't even do an episode without someone mentioning you. That intellect, that charm."

"Stop it."

Peter snickered. "I mean it."

Clint took a moment to survey the face in the screen before him. There was something in it problematic, something that he was deciding about. After a silence, he spoke. "Then why aren't you happy about it? You look like you just came short of bronze," he said before taking another pull on his drink.

Making an effort with an affected grin, Peter didn't disagree.

"I should've known that I was being dissected…" he said as the mask he wore lifted some. "There has been a lot on my mind. Well, a lot about one man in particular."

As Peter said this, Clint looked up at the old photo of his father, whose face remained unmoved by the events going on right before him. He could almost feel the power of those lively magnetic eyes directed at him—working something in him. They were telling him what he'd told him at sixteen after less than stellar reports from school. *You got to be the best man you can be. Every. Single. Day. If not, you're squandering your life!* He placed his wide hand on his massive chest, as his eyes continued to blaze at his son in the passenger seat of his immaculately kept DeVille. He remembered those eyes, two tiger's eyes the way they were illuminated within the caddy's spacious tan cabin. The fervor they emanated wasn't anger—rather conviction. The way he said it bored into him. They were delivered as if he were finally sharing the monumental undertaking of a man—one that permitted of no compromise.

Clint managed a response. "I can imagine…since our talk with Eggers, I've thought about the man too."

Peter stared at his screen wondering if his friend was really interested in discussing the subject. He proceeded, "I do wonder what stakes are in these fires he creates. Why does he even create them? I mean, why not just retire to a nice private island somewhere?"

"What like Trinidad? Boredom," Clint offered into his drink as he took another sip.

Peter chuckled before imbibing too. The temptation came again to just forget about it for now. Leave it to Eggers or other media types brave enough to take up the subject. *Hadn't he done enough as it was? Didn't it cause a lot of grief for him already?*

"I wonder," he started thinking aloud before he formed his thoughts, "if we should do an episode on Ray Foundation and the man himself." The alcohol was clearly having an effect on his filter. The way he wanted to pose it was supposed to be much more appealing, but it came out simple, flat.

Clint's eyes widened as if the old man were coming at him about something else now.

"You know," the tenor of his voice rattled Peter's speaker as Clint's revelation came through, "I was just considering the same thing."

5

Hands were touching him—people he knew—people he knew of. They were pressing on him. Every so often a face could be seen through the tangle of arms and hands—someone complicit. They knew he could barely breathe. They were slowly suffocating him.

At first it was his colleagues. Then it was his boss before many of his close friends contributed. They were pressing on his head, his eyes, his nose and mouth—everywhere off and on where there was room. And the pressure was mounting harder and harder.

He tried to throw his head from side to side to escape the jungle of feelers from attacking him, but his attempts were futile as ever more emerged from a space too small to possibly contain their number.

Despite his best efforts to break free, his legs and arms wouldn't move. It was only through great effort that he was able to suck in enough air as if he had to do it through a straw. Either he was dying or this was hell. The latter possibility, no matter how small, whirred his mind into a panic. *He had to get out.*

He saw yet another face. Simon Ray's giant head peered into this cocoon of human limbs to look at him as a specimen inside. The horrible bulbous eyes were filled with orange marble—colors bleeding into different shades. They dissected him thoroughly. They made him want to hide or at least shield himself from their terrible witness.

When he could do nothing but helplessly be subject to their regard, the hands pressed ever further into his face as if all by Ray's decree. They pushed and stretched with unremitting force testing the very integrity of his skin. It pulled and twisted in such a manner that after a time, he didn't know the difference between his face and the beginnings of their hands.

The figures soon became discontent. At first it was slow, jerking his head this way then that, but then it developed into almost a panic. The arms were trying to yank back from his face as if caught in a flytrap, and in so doing, they were separating his skin from his skull in all directions. It was stretching to the point of failure. He was becoming a hopelessly disfigured product of jerking arms pocking his face like many tongues through bubble gum.

When he screamed out at his hopeless malformation, his head came up out of the horrid dreamscape—out of the sticky drool and sweat that had formed over his folded arms that had acted as his pillow on his office desk.

It was amazing just to be able to breathe again. He took deeper and deeper breaths as his eyes adjusted to the fixtures about him and their consoling permanence. The nightmare appeared to be over.

"Thank God," he said to himself before running his hands over the sweat of his face into his hair. Everything was okay. His skin was still intact and hadn't been tampered with. Nobody was smothering him or staring at him with burning eyes. It was just him in his simple office, but for some reason, he didn't feel just fine. Not yet. Something from the dream seemed to remain and unsettled him.

Looking at the clock, he propelled himself up knowing he was supposed to meet Kristi soon. He had to see her. And it had to be tonight. Just the thought of their meeting managed to dampen the thickening dread. The thought of her warmth, her magnetic presence was what he needed right now. Tonight, the worst option he could imagine was being alone. Its mere prospect weighed on his chest delivering an icy chill shooting through his limbs. *Was it the case that everyone merely feared dying alone and did the demon of loneliness himself also have a hand in facilitating that outcome?* Tonight, Eggers didn't want to find out.

Entering the corridor, the fluorescent artificial light struck his eyes harshly and the faint hum of their power buzzed at him almost mockingly as he strode down the empty passage. He knew this part of the building vacated quickly by this time and that the night crew was taking over.

He rounded the hallways passing many of the dark offices, even entering into one of the open newsrooms. How uncanny and eerie it felt that no one seemed to be around—not even so much as a distant vacuuming to indicate the presence of life. He longed just to meet one normal face with normal eyes acknowledging him with a friendly hello or goodnight—to be seen as a human creature—to be treated with dignity—not some object for exploitation.

While he reminded himself the dream wasn't real, he needed someone to verify it for him. He needed their eyes to replace those incomprehensible orange marbles. For despite his repeating to himself that they were only phantasms, products of an overactive mind, they were still stubbornly fixed in his head. Their weight bore down on him. He felt them ogling him even now. It was as if they had to continue watching him do this plodding little dance ritual before moving on.

By the time he reached the elevators, he finally felt some relief in spotting a security guard. The man appeared preoccupied with something on the monitors behind his station, but it was refreshing to know that he seemed to take his job seriously. Having seen the man before, greeting him from time to time, on this occasion, he was a little disappointed in himself that he didn't know him by name.

"Have a good night," Eggers called out to the pudgy beard as he approached the elevator shaft.

The man's eyes peeked up to see him before reverting back to the monitors.

"Night," he replied.

While the elevator progressed, he couldn't help but wonder at what so captured the guard's attention. It was something he wished to ask about—maybe not directly, but how would he even do it without embarrassing himself? No matter. The elevator arrived.

He stepped aboard feeling some reservation about leaving the relative safe company of someone normal.

But, the elevator doors closed and as the lights flashed on each floor passing by, he quietly counted down the number.

The elevator stopped. The doors opened to a darkened hallway. He waited with anticipation. At any moment, he expected a dark mass with pearly eyes enter the elevator staring down into his—that perhaps they'd make him believe things—horrifying, absurd things that never were. That upon seeing them, there was no coming home again. There was no return to solid ground.

The doors merely closed this time.

He reached the ground floor. He knew he still had one more hurdle. He had to venture the wide space of the garage without meeting that figure his mind dredged up. *It was* going to be *okay. The security guard was monitoring him, wasn't he? He'd do his job in the end if something happened. Like what? What would a lone security guard even do? Would he get there in time? Would the police make a full investigation? Would the case just end up like all those mutilated women? Like the man who attacked Kristi?* If something happened to him, he had no faith in the system to do a thing about it. That was just not how it worked. In this town, there were people who could do things to you, vile things, with impunity. And deep down he knew he could just as easily be another forgotten casualty.

On the way to his car, he avoided the columns and stayed to the center of the lane. He was only twenty yards away still imagining someone rushing up to him, but he resisted it, dismissing the thought as part of this horrible headspace that he created—a remnant of the dream.

When he started fishing for his keys, his heart nearly stopped from a movement of shadows that scurried in the light before the elevator. He paused like a terrified herd animal looking back to the shaft to identify what the possible threat could be. The elevator didn't open or close. There was no movement despite swearing that a figure passed a row of cars in the distance from the corner of his eye. He cursed himself—an idiot spooked by his own shadow.

He threw his bag in the car before switching on the ignition. He adjusted the heater, took his phone out to send a text to Kristi then stuck it in the cup holder and moved for the gear shift. That's when his heart fluttered again with the illumination of headlights of a parked black SUV coming from over by the elevator.

So what, he thought. Maybe someone was there. It was someone working late like himself.

"Go fuck yourself," he said to the person in the SUV and pulled out from the space.

As he swiftly rounded down the exit ramps of the garage, he heard the buzz from his phone in the cup holder. *Kristi.* At the garage's base, he took it out to check the message. "It's ok. 8:30 then," she wrote.

Headlights came up quickly behind him. When he looked in the rearview mirror, he was almost afraid that the big suburban would smash right into him before stopping.

What's with this fuck? He took a squealy right out of the garage. "Goodbye dickwad," he said before focusing on the road ahead.

He knew it was time to check his own paranoia. The stresses from his research on Ray were clearly taking a toll on him, and he recognized that it was time to get back in touch with reality.

"Get it together," he said to himself a few times as he tried reigning in the red alert response that his mind was in.

By the time he pulled into the diner, it was 8:45. The loud base from the electronic music tracks he listened to were a good distraction from the traffic and the palpable anxiety he felt earlier. He now sensed some dignity regained after feeling almost like a little child frightened by a monster in the closet. Tapping to the rhythm of the music on the wheel while drifting through the bumper-to-bumper commute, had put him back into the zone—the realm of regularity, predictability, and complete control.

Even with this reprieve, as much as he made it a point to himself not to do it, he couldn't help but to check back in the mirror for the vehicle he saw from the garage as he began navigating the large parking reservoir abutting the diner. *Of course, he wasn't followed*, he told himself. *And what if he did see a black SUV? What then? Would he freak the fuck out? Was this how it was going to be from now on? Hell no.* He couldn't give license to anymore of this nonsense. It was time to put this dread behind him and be the rational adult he knew himself to be. As a matter of fact, that was just the person Kristi needed him to be right now, wasn't it? That's who he'd be for her, and in a few minutes, he'd turn on the switch to be stable Pat once more—the prize-winning journalist who people actually respected.

Sitting at one of the small booths for two people, Kristi waited for Eggers by scrolling the news. It had now become her daily routine to browse the articles for missing or dead women—something that had been obsessing her since inspiring Eggers' friend to do a piece about Yunnie's disappearance. Not only was she looking for possible clues in Yunnie's own case, but she was looking for any attack that would stand out in the ways hers did. Unsurprisingly, any sighting of a Caribbean man abducting or murdering women in the area under mysterious circumstances wasn't forthcoming. Even the mere use of the word "black" to describe someone was a faux pas. Nevertheless, she labored on for anything resembling the well-planned invasion that happened, even if reading about the disappearances could only help her to better internalize her own experience, which it did.

She saw that this week had a number of sexual assaults and murders as she checked the dwindling crime sections of online news media containing the most limited particulars on the subjects. From time to time, one case would interest her enough to do further research and could even warrant it being recorded in her notebook that she kept in order to bring to Detective Gonzalez's attention later.

She now had over a dozen cases written down, but thinking of the number of bodies recovered from the Youhaul alone, only one of which was now identified by the molars of Deborah Haugh, who knew how many cases would ever be closed? Would she ever get closure on what happened to her friend?

Thinking of their recent appearance on WNT's Jane Doe story, she wondered if Yunnie would ever want her own mom and dad to know about what happened. Perhaps it was more humane not to share the sheer horror suffered by the victims in their last moments. It was better not to know the true ending of a story like this. For Kristi, however, it didn't matter. She needed to know and felt that it was her responsibility to bear all possible anguish that came from knowing the facts.

When she started doing this, she first had to admit her surprise at how little was covered about these tragedies anymore. It was almost as if they were purposefully keeping things vague about the facts on the ground. It made you wonder if people didn't really care as much anymore. Tonight was different.

While nothing caught her eye in the usual places, a major story was looming. Headlines showed a photo of two young women, one showing a cute pert smile and short blonde hair next to a taller, darker haired friend both embracing for the camera. "Missing Friends with a Higher Calling" the headline read. The caption elaborated that both had disappeared in the aftermath of Baltimore's March for Change.

The article seized her. It was like reliving the loss of Yunnie all over again. Her breathing became shallow as she weighed every word of it from time to time reverting back to the same photo of the two together. The authentic joy in both faces was distinct. It wasn't just something planned or doctored up to present on some social media account. The light wasn't quite right for that, and their faces were a little too goofy to be the typical blemish and soulless postcard types uploaded for the masses on places like InstaGrat. Kristi stared recognizing something of what she and Yunnie had in the small snapshot.

With all the uncanny facts satisfying her: the planning, the location, the political association, the genders, there was very little doubt in her mind about what happened to these two. That unreal terror they must've felt at being so suddenly and ruthlessly attacked was something Kristi knew. There was only but a moment for herself to register the fiery disposition so potent as to still feel its effect almost a year later.

The most baffling part of the article was the lack of answers. How was it possible that more wasn't known? Wasn't there, in fact, a whole slew of witnesses on the same night in a crowded bar together? How could it be that no one knew more? Cameras are practically everywhere. Couldn't they at least track some of their movements? Their phones perhaps? Indeed, what was it about this case, hers, Yunnie's, and the others that kept them cold? Were officers that incompetent? Did no one wish to reveal a thing to the authorities? Even for her level of cynicism, some of her most basic assumptions about the system were dissipating fast, and the emotion taking up residence, replacing the interim discomfort at their displacement, raw contempt.

It was there, in the biting depths of such a state, that Eggers found her. He could see not all appeared to be well as she stared off at a place of havoc in the window.

"Kristi," he said.

She turned to him and her expression immediately changed. She hugged him tightly and he reciprocated. When their eyes met again, he asked her what was wrong. She had to tell him.

"Now there's no way that this isn't him too. Tell me it's not fucking him! Those detectives can fucking tell me!" Her face flushed with anger and her eyes with tears. No one was arguing with her. He let her blaze with emotion that boiled over. Everything that had made sense to her a year prior had fallen apart. The whole reason she sacrificed was to work at a place like Ray Foundation. It was the reason she had never married—why she moved away from family—how she justified all her hours put in. The whole idea of having made it to such a politically well-connected organization with a noble cause was the reason she did it all. And that reason killed the one friend she had, and it almost killed her, too. And if this weren't enough, she was treated by the police like a lunatic. She had told Patrick as much. It was as if no one could think anymore. That, or no one cared.

Brenda, their cute, always smiling waitress brought the hot steak and eggs with fries and ahi tuna salad to their table. Eggers eyed the fattening dish regretfully as he didn't have much of an appetite. After drinking half his beer, he felt more than satisfied, and saw that Kristi didn't appear hungry either. It seemed that both ordered the exact same dishes as the time before, as if they could recreate the joy they shared by taking the same steps. Sadly, it wasn't working this time. They were both in a dour state. The only thing Patrick wasn't going to do was make it any worse by sharing his own lingering paranoia and gloom.

"You're right," he finally broke in resolutely as the food remained untouched. "What I've come to find is that despite what colleagues tell me—despite what I've been telling myself about this type of story, I can't help but see something bad, really bad, staring me in the face." He went on at length to expound all the details of what Eldridge told him and of what the private investigator wrote before his death. To his surprise, every new detail he considered revelatory at the time, didn't seem to move Kristi at first. She processed it all listlessly, as if in a trance.

He could see that she was listening, but when her eyes began to water, he stopped himself. "What is it?" he spoke softly, gently indicating that everything else could wait.

"I don't know," she choked out a sob of frustration. "What to do. I feel so useless." The tears trickled down her face as she tried to fight them back. Eggers reached his hand out to hers and when he grasped it, squeezed reassuringly. She held it back weakly.

"It's like I'm watching the world being deconstructed, and I can't do a fucking thing about it. I just exist to see every piece being removed with agony—like someone with no real hope."

Eggers listened as he now put both his hands around Kristi's small cold lifeless one. It was as if it were communicating its weakness—its surrender and he took it to encourage it—to resurrect its spirit.

"No one can stop him. He's gotten away with everything already. What can I do? I'm nothing."

"We're going to ruin him with a story that no one will be able to ignore anymore."

"They *have* ignored him. He's probably earned them too much."

"No, the public won't be able to stomach it. They will have to do something when the outrage grows."

"They can just wait it out until something else outrages them. They can act like they're doing something but do nothing in the meantime."

"Kristi," he whispered as his eyes connected with hers. "We can do this. It's happened before. It's a given that those in office don't want to move when their comfortable. But, we're going to make it *real* uncomfortable for them. We're going to have an investigative story that scares the living hell out of people. It'll get people to start demanding action from do nothing DAs and all the royalty sitting on that hill. We'll make them start earning their seats again."

"Scare? I'm the one who's scared. When this starts happening, you think he won't come after us? No one that matters has any interest in stopping him. They don't even try. You think someone like that will stay there hand against a threat?"

"We need to be careful until the story gets out. Then it would be too stupid to come after us. We should play it safe until then."

"I'm not sure if that's even true."

"Well, it is," he said good-humoredly. And we're going to be fine in the meantime. You keep a low profile as you've been doing. No one knows where you are."

She took her hand out of his and touched the tears at the corners of her eyes.

Her lack of an answer bothered him as he looked at her more intently. "You can believe that can't you? That all will be well?"

"I want to believe. I'm dying to believe."

"That's all I mean—"

"But this is—this is more than just about belief. My belief is not going to change anything. It's not going to change what happens to us—what happened to Yunnie."

"I think it has a lot more power than you think," Eggers said with the best reassuring smile he could muster.

"Do I have to believe that the power of belief works too or is belief on this occasion enough?"

Eggers' grin remained, encouraging her to put on her own despite watery eyes.

"No one is sure of how or why it works," he spoofed in a bad documentary voice. "It just does."

"Oh, is that just how it is then?" she expressed with some playful sarcasm. He didn't answer her. The way her eyes gleamed with the half smile in that moment struck him dumb by how beautiful she was. Something about it caused his heart to ache with desire at the stunning aura she gave off. There was such a freshness, such a rawness to it that there was nothing to do other than wholly surrender to it—to embrace it. As her person captivated him, she drew in her eyebrows as if skeptical at his demeanor.

"What is it?"

"What?" he said with the same dopey gaze at her.

"*That* look."

"This look?" he pointed at his face.

"Yeah, that one," she said grinning wider.

"Because."

"Because…?"

"Because I can't stop looking at you."

She shyly ran her fingers through her hair as his comment threw her off guard.

"But I look terrible right now."

"No, you don't."

She rubbed her eyes some more then proceeded to reciprocate his affectionate longing.

"Thank you."

There was no more hiding from each other. In that moment they both knew this was more than the look of friends.

When she excused herself to the restroom, Eggers felt his heart throbbing inside his chest. The amazing feeling she instilled in him brought him back to life and his appetite along with it. All he could do was dig into the cold meal before him—gorging himself as if some unseen evolutionary mechanism just kicked in.

It was in moments like these, if asked, one could admit that fleeting moment of happiness elusive as the end of a rainbow. But Eggers was riding too high to reflect—seeing only the good things that lay ahead for him on the horizon. It was one of those instances when good feeling and optimism produces a myopia that looks past dangers ahead toward the one unifying experience more consequential than any other. Any outsider with experience could see what was transpiring.

Jacques could see it too, from where he was. He snacked on trail mix fixedly watching Eggers' every bite. He had parked a couple of rows back still able to catch the show with the SUV's elevation over the other cars between. As both men ate, Jacques was the altogether more ravenous with his dinner—carelessly missing his mouth with more and more nuts and raisins crunching down fast as he threw ever more into his noisy gullet. It was almost as if he were racing against Eggers in a childish display of supremacy.

When Kristi re-entered the booth, Jacques stopped his sloven feeding frenzy and crunched the remaining nuts in his face more slowly. A trace of a smile grew across his lips as her figure adjusted herself on the bench. She looked slightly flush in the face and refreshed. Eggers smiled at her form buzzing with energy. He grinned with his mouth closed full of food as she adjusted herself regarding him with her own silly smirk.

"Wow. You *were* hungry," she said to him teasingly.

"Still am," he managed to say after gulping more down. "What about you?"

She pulled her plate slightly back from his gorge fest, as he chuckled trying to hold the food in.

Jacques almost appeared in on the joke himself sporting his own satisfactory expression if not bordering on the obscene. His hand took the knife from the door pocket and pressed the button to hear the satisfying click of metal revealing the glint of the new thin long blade. He proceeded to run the tip along his arm with enough pressure to cause a mark but before breaking the skin. This is what he liked—the feeling of its virgin sharpness that, even with sharpening, would never quite feel like it did now over the course of its long life. The discernible pattern he pressed into his skin was like a distant mountain range. One *V* followed another as he ogled Kristi through the windows.

6

After they had finished the recording and signed off, it was in the early morning on the east coast. Peter was tired, but with the possession of the over two-hour discussion session now on his hard drive, he felt he had became steward of a radioactive weapon. The risk of its deployment could very well blow up in his face.

He pulled out the three hundred seventy-five milliliter flask of Wild Rooster he had stashed in the back of his desk at the beginning of the week. *That should do it*, he thought. *That should be enough to put his ass to sleep tonight*. The cap made that satisfying snap of no return as he twisted it loose and guzzled down a few strokes before previewing the upload. He paused at certain points to judge if he wanted to edit out certain parts but wasn't very picky. Everything they discussed about Ray was not only incisive and on point, it was positively evocative.

"*Okay, okay*," he repeated under his breath after the preview—beginning to fill in the final details before the upload.

Hovering over the title prompt, he heard a tap at the door before it popped open. "Honey?" He turned to see Margery looking over his shoulder curiously at the flask before the computer screen. "Everything alright?" she said in a hushed tone.

"Yep, everything's good," he smiled at her as best he could. He understood what she saw—not everything was exactly honky dory right now. They already had the big fight about he and Clint's jaunt to campus nearly a year ago and after their rendition of the 1812 Overture happening one night, the drinking alone didn't seem worth it right then. She looked far too sleepy for that.

"She's asleep. You still going to be a while?" she queried nonchalantly as if the bottle had just disappeared.

Peter sighed, "yes, a little longer."

She came up to him and gave him a peck on the mouth before retreating back to the door. He knew what she was going to say next.

"I'll be in bed. She'll probably be up in an a few hours."

"Let me get it this time. You sleep."

She dismissed this without a second thought. "It's okay, I've got it."

As she limbered off, a working title came to mind. He was sure it was just cryptic and provocative enough to draw the attention of the typical viewer. He read it over a few times before deciding that it would do. The production was weak compared to so many other popular channels and it was a little drawn out at times. But, wasn't there a certain beauty in that?

He took another swig as he saw the task bar complete. He stood unsteadily and opened the top right desk drawer fishing with his hand into the back corner. Before listening for any sign of anyone outside the door, he produced a little key and inserted it into the center drawer, just under the computer screen. Within, he carefully removed the black 9 mm Berretta. He released the magazine to feel the weight of the ammo still inside and then inserted—clicking it back into place. It made him feel a little better.

7

Eggers' neighborhood was as still and dead as a remote cliff face. While the cars and houses with well-groomed lawns could indicate signs of active life, there was a stale thick air hanging heavily over the inhabitants. Someone could have mistaken it for having been rampaged by a recent plague if it weren't for the fact that they'd see movement begin again within a few hours. But, then again, that wasn't quite right. Something of this stifling blanket would remain in more active hours. Something of it has been there for a while. It was the new norm—persisting across the vast circuitry of roads, highways, and internet networks connecting other like neighborhoods of the first world, and just as if cleft-lip were a new feature of each newborn, no one dared point out these dying clusters of white matter. Within this broken space, one activity, however, was thriving.

Jacques was sure having a good time watching. Parking some blocks down underneath a large oak, he eyed Kristi and Pat obsessively as they entered his house. He knew his business and was content to wait for now listening to a lively steel drum percussion classic as he snorted the magic white dust from the back of his knife—now illuminated neon by the dash light. There were plenty of more hits where that came from if necessary. Half a kilo bag sat in his console if he needed it to stay awake. *Yes. He could do this all night if it were required of him to finish the work he had started.* But, to call it work wouldn't fit exactly. To call it a job would be an insult. Sure, it required expending an enormous sum of energy— time and expense to take the required "beeches" out. Certainly, no easy task. But, *he* had made Jacques see that all differently now. He made him see something in himself that he didn't know was there. What this was—wasn't a nine to five grind. It wasn't at all just a means to an end—to a nice steady paycheck at the conclusion of a long day. It *was* an end. It was art. He was finishing a masterpiece.

Kristi and Pat didn't quite make it to the bedroom. Pat poured the wine and they sat quietly imbibing on the sofa. The meeting of each other's look hardly garnered a moment of reflection as she instinctually swiveled onto him like a saddle kissing him ferociously between gasps as she felt his hands cup her from behind. He proceeded to slide both hands underneath her sweater and bra to find both breasts as the saddle of his lap only rose. In that unplanned awkward timing and position, she unbuttoned her pants having to make a couple of goes at it before getting them undone. Now it was largely up to her dance partner, who knew the next steps well. He shifted her onto the sofa twisting from underneath. When her hungry eyes met his again, he dropped his pants to the floor and she followed suit with her panties without hesitation— drawing him in. The result was a fury of fleeting minutes that couldn't be helped in the heat of desire just begging to be quenched. They lay there together half naked in a daze—replaying how they found themselves in that compromising position.

It was a great relief for her to finally have that moment together—to forget about all else and live in the present—to enjoy a simple moment of pleasure no matter how transitory. She didn't know what would happen to her or to them now that they had broached this point in their relationship, but for now, she was okay with that.

Absent his characteristic grin, Jacques viewed the short-lived spectacle wedged between the window and a bush. Overpowered by the cold curiosity of a hunter, there was something else to the face—the slightest of flares—a flutter in the cheeks.

"More wine?" She asked after gulping down the rest of her glass and leaning against Pat's shoulder.

"Why not," he said expertly filling both glasses without making her lift her head.

He gave her the filled glass and took up his own before clinking them.

They sipped silently before she revealed what was in the forefront of her mind. It began as timid murmur, despite their recent familiarity, developing slowly into demand.

"I…thought we'd…could we…Let's go again," she said worried that she wouldn't sound forthcoming enough to meet her need.

Pat smiled encouragingly, ready for a second engagement partly sparked by the aggression peeking out from underneath her façade. He started to kiss her again and she put her hand on his chest to stop him—half laughing with pleasure at his eagerness—not to reject him so much as to set her condition before continuing.

"I'd like a shower."

He laughed, "You'd like a shower?"

"I need it," she smiled playfully.

"We're just going to get dirty again," he chirped back teasingly.

"I know it," she shot back pecking him on the lips.

Jacques made several trips back and forth from the Cadillac to snort some coke and await whatever signal had failed to appear up to that point. He listened to some more Calypso classics while cutting tiny crosses into his arms and noticed the irony taste on his tongue. That was when he looked himself in the car mirror to see the stream of blood running from his nose. He could have mistaken it for a mild cold, but the thing was, he couldn't even feel his face. Licking and brushing the fluid with the back of his hand, his blood ran onto his pant leg.

"Focking cunnie!" He spit out angrily subduing the end of the slur.

He reached over to grab napkins from the glovebox. With napkins in hand, he pinched his bleeding nose for a few minutes—checking the mirrors and the neighborhood as if someone were sneaking up on him in such a state.

When he felt it was coagulated enough, he removed the napkin and looked himself over again in the mirror.

"Cunnie," he repeated laughing to himself.

His chuckling trailed off.

"I'm not done yet," he told himself flatly as if to a dog that would stay. "I'll be the one to decide when it is I'm done."

He watched his person in the mirror take another whiff off the edge of the knife, the powder disappearing into the vast dark void of his nasal cavity.

It was at his favorite vacation spot off the beach in Porimão, he stroked with great ease into the deep water parallel to the rocky barrier cliffs looming over the span of the bay. Never had he been so far out and with so much energy that he entertained the idea that perhaps he could go on like this forever. *Yes, he was immortal, indeed. Who could say otherwise?*

As the shore got further away, so did his familiarity with his surroundings. The cliffs were more jagged and craggy than he remembered towering over the tadpole of his person as he continued to plough through the chop foot by foot.

What of those people who dared swim the Atlantic? He was on his way to Africa at this rate. On and on he carved through. It was at some point that he stopped himself—as the cliffs never appeared so high and peered down upon him with their powerful teeth as if in a mocking smile—stunning him suddenly at how scary his relaxing late afternoon exercise had become. He was nowhere near the beach now. Panic began to seep like venom into his bones.

Scanning along the shore, all he could see were rock and…there was something else too. What he thought at first was part of the stone face was a darker figure, tall and extensive. It took his focus from the waves to what stood on a cliff not looking out to sea but, in fact, regarding him from that perch. He knew it was staring at him. He even knew its identity. The orange glare from the eyes appeared in the shadow formed by the late afternoon sun. His recognition paralyzed him, choking him as he stared, dropping beneath the surf unable, despite his distress, to avert his gaze from Ray's penetrating eyes. Life was leaving his body as waves rippled above. A brief reprieve would come after the peak of a wave, a fleeting breath, but he could tell that it was all to no avail. He couldn't stop his descent, and he believed it was Ray. Ray was in his mind, somehow doing this to him—disabling the very use of his limbs. The how was unimportant. He was about to die.

The glassy disturbance of water was still penetrated by the height and breadth of Ray's looming presence. With a final bon voyage to the surface above, he held his breath as he made his final plunge under the waves. There was no more hope. His cold descent into the abyss was assured. All he could do was look up in agony for want of air.

After moments that felt like an eternity, with pressure of a sunken ship's cabin ready to burst at a point of weakness, he let go exploding to draw a final breath of salty water in one deep draft of panic. When he felt something like a burn of salt into his lungs, he awoke.

Pat jerked his head up awkwardly, exacerbating a painful crick in his neck and gasping for breath. He straightened his back on the bed holding his neck as the pain eased. Laying completely still, recovering from his self-induced asphyxiation, he picked up on Kristi's own respirations next to him.

It was good to suddenly be back in the ordinary and to hear something familiar—something alive in the house other than himself, someone to share his space with, which he could now admit, always scared him in the past. He could get used to this. Maybe this was a good thing. Then again, he should probably ask himself the same question in the light of day. He should reevaluate when the influence of his nightmares subsided.

What was with this image of Ray he had held onto? Wasn't his subconscious mind ready to move on? It was another dream sequence as clear as an early morning run. *Where was all of this coming from?*

Dreams, he knew, weren't reality. Yet, there was still something to them. There was something in them that his mind had recognized, whether he was fully aware of it or not, something very real. And that is what disturbed him now. He knew Ray, even being only a man, was not the type to underestimate a threat—no matter how small. If he wanted Pat dead, he had the means to do so, and who knew what games he could play to tear people like him down—into submission—to make him, if not literally drown, somehow dead financially, politically, socially. Hence came his fear of being followed earlier. Hence came his fear that he was being watched right now in his very own home.

Was it that outlandish? What was it to a man like Ray to surveil him? Wasn't it an absurd notion—a regular conspiracy theory that should be dismissed immediately. It seemed neither worth the time nor the investment to bother. On the other hand, Ray's world wasn't his. If money grew on trees that you owned, as surely as investors threw it Ray's way at the slightest whiff of success at Atta Capital—not only was there the means to actively seek threats, there was the accompanying discretion to sometimes deal with them no matter what kind of publicity it could garner. What was a good PR firm for otherwise?

Pat could accept all of this, but for the fact that nothing had happened to him yet. Wouldn't Ray have already pounced on him by now? Wouldn't he have taken him to task through his hard-ass boss just waiting for an excuse to assert himself? And if Ray had anyone watching him or tailing him, as he was quite attuned to the possibility earlier, he certainly would've noticed.

There was a palpable tap at the window, like metal on glass. Pat's heart felt that it had just burst in his chest—breaking his train of thought to be fully in the present. His neck crawled as he listened further laying frozen into place. Almost nothing. His now heightened senses picked up on nothing but Kristi's muffled breaths. Perhaps it was only a bird as they were sometimes wont to do, thudding into the window like a human mistakenly stubbing a toe on a corner wall. He pressed himself to his feet quietly gliding over to the glass without disturbing Kristi.

He listened carefully now right behind the blinds daring to hear another sound on the glass yet too cautious and fearful to peak out. There was something. A slight tap barely audible and then a…hiss. There! A hiss, it keeps coming through the window. "What the fuck…is that," he said under his breath now smelling a faint artificial tinge to the air.

His head became dizzy and his arms tired. *No.* His anger at both being afraid and the necessity of action caused him to finally yank the blinds up. Stumbling into place, he saw the outside tube extending from a tank squeezing through a slight gap made in the window.

"Kristi!" he now shouted.

Adrenaline pushed him to throw open the window despite the strength of his limbs retreating. It all seemed to happen in slow motion. As she stirred, the figure stepped out from the side of the house with a ball cap and white teeth showing in the ambient moonlight. What he had in his hand only came apparent in the following moment as his flesh shuddered to the floor. How the two cartridges from the stun gun managed to ply into his chest without him noticing its initial bite, could have been due to the adrenaline and or the gas. Whatever the reason, he was done like a spent firecracker, body collapsing fast. Consciousness fought but then drifted out like dandelion seeds in a gale.

8

Eggers felt a dull pain in his arm as he came to out of the void only to soon descend back into it. Time seemed illusory—either flitting by quickly or at a standstill. His awareness faded in and out only allowing him for momentary glimpses of passing blurry lights emerging from darkness along with the intermittent thump of concrete.

When they stopped, he noticed his body being carried from under his arms, but it wasn't enough to shake him from his induced torpor. While he hadn't completely lost the idea of the looming danger, all he could do for the time was witness the slow build up to some horrifying doom. The plane he was in was crashing ever so slowly and it was only a matter of time before he would inevitably hit the ground. There was no time to think clearly. There was nothing he could do now. Here he was a mere creature in the jaws of whatever fate imposed on him.

A frigid air and waft of his own piss rudely awoke Eggers from his sleep. It must've just happened, the warm pee finally being released from his bladder streaming down his left leg to the floor. His shorts were drenched but at least warm. A solitary dim bulb hung from the center of the dark room revealing the full naked body of Kristi tied down to a long thick wooden work bench at the center. She was immobile, seemingly lifeless. The sight of her illuminated flesh struck him with raw terror.

Pumping like a steam engine, his head was dizzy as he heard his blood vessels pulsating within his skull. The display he was set to watch was too much for him. The stripping of her body while here he remained clothed was exacting, purposeful. The gruesome pallid light already violating, to him, what was inviolable. The affection he felt was now being probed. The sheer audacity to display the object of it in such a vulgar way was unspeakable—slapping him with one message: *nothing was truly inviolable—not anymore.*

His mind raced with regret. *How fucking stupid he had been. How arrogant.* To think he was safe and could ensure the same for Kristi was sheer delusion. To think that his fame as a journalist would somehow shield him from the machinations of a true manipulator of the system was a testament to how warped he had become in his D.C. bubble. The little awards for journalism he had accrued and the praise he had denied openly, yet internalized, had done him a great disservice. Now what ungodly fruit was this that he had grown for himself and was forced to consume.

Ignoring the pain, he tried jerking the braces that held his hands and legs to the wall. Knowing that the effort would probably prove futile, he worked at it anyway for what could have been hours. He even felt at one point that the metal was beginning to budge as he used the force and weight of his body to jerk left then right pausing from time to time—breathing out the pain as quietly as he could.

"Hello…is anyone there?", a voice suddenly paralyzed him—croaking out into the darkness. It was a crushed voice hard to recognize from the tremulous fear. Kristi then began to sob

"*Yes.*" Eggers tried whispering projecting strength and comfort. "I'm here. Stay calm. Stay quiet."

"*Pat!*" More tears followed from Kristi in both happiness at them being together and sadness at their shared fate.

"Yes," he repeated that also indicated for her to shush down her voice. "Nothing's going to happen—."

"No. It's Ray." She silenced him with the self-evident fact before continuing. "We're going to die." She wept at it all. There was a pouring out over herself, Pat, Yunnie, and every woman who found themselves where she was now. There was nothing else to do.

"It's ok. It's ok." Pat could only say when it wasn't. His own tears formed dribbling down his face.

A squeal of metal pierced out from the far side of the room. A small flame flickered towards them with echoing footfalls accompanied by a thin shadow of a figure.

Kristi choked back her tears heaving in deep draws of breath.

When the figure entered closer, Eggers recognized him from the house. The camouflage cap with that outré toothy grin was unmistakable, suggesting the possibility of some permanent mental infirmity.

He walked over to Kristi as if inspecting his own handiwork. As soon as she saw his face, her terror became overwhelming.

"Oh God no—no!" She could barely talk anymore with the shock. Her greatest nightmares were coming true. He had come to finish the job.

"What do you want?" Pat angrily barked at the man to try to at least distract him away from Kristi.

Jacques regarded the other prisoner before looking back to Kristi. He snapped shut his zippo.

"You chook him good beech," he snickered as she lay paralyzed with fearful anticipation.

Frantically pleading, Eggers ceded everything in his first offer. "You want to know about the story don't you? You want details? You want sources? I'll give them…whatever you want…"

"*Big man ting,*" Jacques interrupted Eggers as if he had heard all of it before. "You goin to give us everyting."

Eggers looked around the room wondering who the us was. That's when he noticed the two red dots glowing in the back of the room. What he thought were only wall fixtures were moving, focusing, regarding all.

9

It was late, but Marcus was up and ready. When he heard the knock at his townhome residence in Georgetown, he didn't hesitate to answer it.

"Hey," a woman's voice cooed to him on the doorstep from under a hood. He let her enter. She removed the covering—her straight black hair shined and the prodigious non-public smile only he knew beamed.

"How nice of you to pay me the visit, Senator."

Susan breathed a laugh at his feigned formality. She always liked being called that even though she knew he was merely being snarky.

"Dry wine please."

"White?"

"Of course, you know what I like," she said as if his playfulness was already spent.

"Coming right up."

He brought her the chilled glass of chardonnay as she made herself comfortable on his red velvet sofa. He sat down with her as she held the glass and sipped expressing her delight.

"Mm. So good." She smiled at him and he smiled back.

"I aim to please," he said coldly.

"Mhm," she sounded.

She didn't mind him like this. That was partly what she came for. They were alike in many respects. One of those respects was business matters. They had to be addressed right away.

"Ray's enthusiasm for PMN is still great and his appreciation has not waned."

"But—" she preempted his remark.

"Yes, but," he emphasized, "it has not been implemented much in practice. In effect, a law that is not enforced isn't a law, Susan. That is *not* what we've been backing."

"That part, Marcus," she said testily after her last sip, "isn't something I can control. You know as well as I do. These things take time to be reviewed, implemented, and fully accepted."

"Not true. You are partially responsible for enactment. You must investigate where it isn't being followed and apply pressure where necessary."

"Doug, the president is working with people and they're confident that we are on the right track. As far as making its impact bigger, that's where you guys come in, isn't it? You have to raise hell with these kids. You have to get them moving and fighting where the older generations are too busy worrying about their mortgage and retirement. That's how to get this off the ground quickly."

"It's happening," Marcus indicated confidently, "we have no problems there. Ray just wants to move this along and know all the parts are working together. This is a collective effort after all."

"On the hill, we've never been more aligned perhaps in the history of this country… whether the people are ready for it or not."

A moment of quiet reflection followed, as she took another sip and wedged herself better into the corner of the couch. Even with her black nylon stockings riding up her skirt overlayed by a long fleece coat, she still appeared cold.

"How's Ray anyway," she broke the silence wrapping the fleece around her torso a little tighter. "It's been a while since I've seen him."

"He's…busy, busy. I couldn't even tell you whether he's in Mexico City or Sydney and vice-versa tomorrow."

"The usual."

"Yes."

"So, what about you?" She eyed him with interest in a suggestive manner.

"Me," he said as if he were guilty of whatever she implied. "Let's see…I…had to fire another employee."

"Really? Yep. Her heart just wasn't in it, unfortunately."

"How did you handle it?" Susan asked, eyes intoxicated by the drink and whatever he was to say next.

"What I said was: thank you for your service, but we must part ways due to lack of shared interests."

Susan moved closer. "What did she say to that?"

"She said…oh what was it…something like, *how can that be. What did I do wrong?*"

"And you said?"

"I was very pleasant to her, but at some point, I had to tell her, not in words exactly, imparting in other ways, *Look, it's over. You couldn't keep your mouth shut. I'll give you another chance with the non-disclosure and if you know what's good for you—wanting your severance, you'll keep it shut from now on.*"

"Really? Was it that serious?"

"No, she was low level—giving some details to a reporter."

"That's good. And how close to her were you…were you like this?" Susan moved over to him placing her hand on his thigh."

"Not at all," he grinned.

"But what if she was…what would you do if she was doing what I'm doing now."

"Nothing."

She pushed up against him with deep breath tonguing his mouth with wet animal ferocity before withdrawing. "And that? What if she did that?"

"Not much."

She stood up not bothered by the cold at all now. She pulled down her blouse revealing her breasts to him squeezing them. "And this?"

"Better."

"Is it now? You like these? You wouldn't want her to leave now."

"Let's see what happens."

She drops her fleece and pulls her skirt up teasingly showing the panty-less surprise underneath.

"Wait," he says.

"Let me have a better view."

She grabs the ottoman and stretches down tossing up the skirt to reveal to him what he wants. Her prominent round hourglass figure was now showing him its full majesty. After a moment she feels his warm body behind her working. She moans at first quietly but the rhythm changes and she begins to whimper. Long had she waited to feel him again.

With blurred outlines of the room taking shape and a mouth that felt like it had been filled with concrete mix, Clint fully emerged from sleep soon wiping the tears from his eyes. He was sitting forward in his comfy chair processing the disturbing images scorched into memory from the mysterious dream realm before pushing himself up with arms on thighs. Dizziness ensued and he had to steady himself on his desk avoiding his half empty glass of whiskey that was already partially spilled there. A discernable layer of nausea could be felt bubbling up, but in the closing of his eyes and stillness, the wave passed.

One feeling that wasn't going away, however, was the seeming import of his oneiric journey. Fear. What a potent shade that had somehow crossed with him into the physical conscious world. If the purported phantasms of sleep were less real, how did they leave him with such unforgettable impressions. How could the bite still leave teeth marks? The acknowledgement of improbabilities wasn't enough to assuage his doubts. He had to see for himself.

The door slowly creaked in upon the snugly wrapped figure upon the bed. She lay still within the comforter and between the chiffon pillows. Her breathing steady and her face untroubled. Clint couldn't imagine Giselle right now going through the rollercoaster ride through hell as he just had. It was enough to just see her alive and well. He did the same with Daniela who even caused him to chuckle at her more erratic splay upon the bed compared to her sister.

He took the oversized glass from the cabinet and poured himself whole milk—a little remedy he sometimes used to stave off the imminent hangover. *What if*, he wondered, *his dream were reality?* He didn't like entertaining such thoughts, but it came to mind anyway as did the headlights of passerby on a dark country road. *That would be it*, he thought. *He'd go mad.*

He laid back down in bed next to his wife who looked so much like their daughters as she slept. Watching her, laying that way for a long while, his stomach slowly settled in a way that his mind never quite could.

Through soul piercing screams, Eggers roared his futile protest as a short thin man donning scrubs, skullcap, and surgical mask was performing a procedure upon Kristi's abdomen. The doctor's scalpel carved into her belly like an X-ACTO through canvas. Everything about his demeanor was methodical and unhesitating—a chef in the kitchen. To him, she was just fish on a cutting board.

There was nothing else to be done as camo hat stood by expressing some satisfaction—lips curling tightly about his dentate maw. As the doctor came in with his surgical tray ready, little did Eggers know that what he said made little difference to the final outcome. But while that was always a distinct possibility Eggers placed it in the back of his mind, he had to try. What other choice did he really have? So, he gave camo hat everything—all facts, all sources, even, as shameful as it was, the new address of Peter and his family. The desperation and immediacy trumped all.

Some relief only came with Kristi's passing out in pain. Still the sound of the surgeon's sticky fingers probing her exposed organs—scooping one globular mass out before the other caused him to retch and cry out in horror. Tears coursed over his face as the purplish liquified contents of his stomach simultaneously shot out of his mouth.

Jacques snorted out a laugh only momentarily glancing up from his phone. It was one that not only said he didn't care about Egger's pain. It was an open mockery of it.

Slowly, with bated breath, Eggers recovered albeit with vomitus at the corners of his mouth. He dared to stomach the sight of Kristi again, but this time, watching puzzled as the doctor began sewing up the incision that he made as if it all were a legitimate medical intervention from the first. Everything appeared calculated, sterile, even professional. The way that he peeled off the plastic film from the gauze bandage was thoughtful, meticulous. Eggers stared on as the doctor wrapped the wound absorbing the blood—too shocked to react outwardly to the overabundance of stimuli—stimuli that were sufficient for a lifetime. Still, the two spherical organs that sat in a distant collection tray gleamed in the unnatural light. *What the fuck was all of this for?!*

His eyes wandered now as a catatonic, an addict's stare into a flashlight, viewing it all as if it were a world that had little or nothing to do with him. The probing red orbs had brightened in the distance. No more could they possibly be light fixtures or some ethereal visual effect. These were physical and dialed in the way a cat's luminous eyes may behold a pedestrian at night. Their suspension in a relatively small head with wide attached husk was now undeniable.

Eggers eyes shifted to the body momentarily trying to see what the mass before him saw. *What was the fascination?* Could he zero in on the same feature of this figure's inspection? He now examined the details one by one. The lower abdominal suture, the vaginal region, the missing organs and the strange expression on Kristi's incapacitated face—almost Mona Lisa-esque in its presentation. Searching disembodied himself, it was as if this somebody before him was no longer the one he knew. She was just a specimen of their observation and what had just occurred was indeed a remarkable transformation. What had happened was a true unburdening. Laying there before him was a captive set free— something ascended to a higher state—a new unparalleled freedom. What could be more desirable or even admirable?

That moment of out-of-body reflection was broken like a spell when Kristi's seemingly peaceful respirations were interrupted by her sudden cry out in agony. "Please God, make it stop," she pleaded. "Pleeeeease!" Her voice pierced through the room.

That is when Eggers returned to what he knew. He returned to the undeniable pain and despair of the present and the futility of making it any different than it was. He turned his head away from Kristi's agony to meet the gaze of those red quasi-living orbs that had, at some point in his mind's wanderings, changed their focus to him.

His limbs were paralyzed with fear. Held in that milky red stare, he felt fetal—exposed and completely helpless before the powers that be. *Don't look,* he told himself, before averting his eyes. *And don't fucking lose it. Don't you dare.*

What the fuck had he been thinking? A lot of nonsense. Accepting first thoughts, childlike and unreflective. Manifest absurdities. Yet there was a certain pleasure in it all, wasn't there? Bending the knee—being the bitch. There was. It was a certain letting go before the chaos. It was as if to say there was no more need to struggle. The abyss is bad, but the toil against it is only worse.

She's depending on you, fuckhead. Everyone's depending on you. He mouthed these lines with eyes closed trying to block out the other thoughts battering his resolve. Peter, Clint, the young women, and all of those naïve drones were at Ray's mercy. What could one even do against such a man, such a force, indeed, a true nightmare?

With the wailing of Kristi stiffening his resolve, all he could think to do was confront those red eyes in a flare of defiance. In shifting his regard, immediately he regretted it as his body jerked at the triangular mass looming down on him and Kristi. Those bulging murky reds found his once again and as if by an invisible tether reaching out and grasping him by the spine, he was theirs. His mind was pulsing at the same rhythm as the patterns that were distorting the lenses. Like on a soapy bubble, his thoughts whirled in incoherent inanities. His grasp on everything was slipping. Tears blurred his vision of Kristi, a moment of lucidity, before being swallowed in a tide of anomie. He was hopeless and useless— letting go and letting everyone down. *Come for me. Come oblivion.*

12

In the late morning, the faint chirp of some solitary birds called out as the cool air warmed, sun briefly unimpeded by cloud cover. Sipping his double espresso, Peter was deep in thought over the email before him. A troubling thought occurred to him that gave him pause. The idea that he was at a pivotal moment here and he could somehow blow it, ate into him. *What if this were it? Was this not the midlife everyone dreaded?* Like it or not, how many more moments like this could there be? Even the fact that this was somehow the middle wasn't guaranteed. *Could this moment define him?* If the maximum positive impact he could have in the world were dependent on his next couple of moves, how could he know? He couldn't. One wrong move, he was checkmated, but if he struck out another way, even with the slightest variance, he could somehow win, whatever that looked like.

Sounds over the birds broke into his meditation. Roger passed by his door on the phone with who he guessed was Daniela again. It sounded as if Margery were in the kitchen with one of her parents while the baby was probably drifting off again in the nursery down the hall.

He picked up his phone and pressed Pat Eggers' name. The more it rang, the more Peter worried he was interrupting something. While they had talked before at this hour, he was still cognizant of those type of mornings—the kind where all the bells and whistles of a funhouse were buzzing around in your head. With the pace Clint was drinking last night, he didn't want to disturb him just yet, just in case that's where he still was, so he was trying Patrick instead.

He heard the generic message of the voice sounding like a wife ready to bite her husband's dick off. "Please leave a message."

"*Pat*. Nothing *too* pressing. Clint and I made another episode last night. Looks to be gaining a lot of views. Over fifty thousand already…" he smiled to himself knowing Pat was going to hear that in the remainder of the message. "I know we should've probably run it by you first. It was in the moment type thing. Maybe you want to be on the next episode?" He paused again thinking if there was anything missed—anything he didn't mind being recorded. "Anyway…take care of yourself. Talk soon."

He hung up and hesitated before closing out the email that he was about to compose to send to Eldridge. He wanted to run the idea by Clint and Eggers, first.

He downed the rest of the coffee and got up dizzily before steadying himself. Slowly, deeply, he breathed in and out. "It's always something," he whispered. "You got this. You got this," he encouraged himself quietly.

Down the hall he slinked, only hearing a little movement from downstairs. Everything was very still which he considered a nice reprieve. When he came to the baby room door on the other side of the house, he peered in to catch a glimpse of that fleeting innocent bliss only found in the young, especially the newborn.

"Wha—?" he shrunk back at the sight of a figure in the middle of the room.

Roger was on a video call with Daniela showing her what she also wanted to see—the baby Isabel. Peacefully, she lay passed out with mouth ajar in the crib.

They all quietly relished the tiny breaths of the infant. Daniela gleamed a smile. "She's gorgeous," she mouthed as Roger steadied the phone's camera the best he could. Peter affectionately squeezed the back of his son's neck which caught him off guard. His attention distracted between the call and his dad. When Roger left, Peter kissed his daughter's big round forehead. Lightly touching her chest with his palm, he felt her little heartbeat thudding with life as his eyes watered with pride.

Out in the hallway, he overheard his son and Daniela's conversation.

"When are you guys coming back?" Daniela questioned between laughs.

"When Kim Kardashian grows a third ass."

"What?" she chuckles. "Where did you come up with that?" she asks, trying to control her outbursts.

"Nothing. Just something I heard on InstaGrat." He follows with a laugh of his own. "My parents say we'll go back when its safe again."

"Safe? When will that be? Is anything ever safe?"

Here, Peter stands just outside Roger's room who sees him put a finger over his lips.

"Good morning," he says quietly.

"Good morning, Dad," Roger says more quietly.

"Good morning, Daniela."

Roger turns the camera so that she can see his dad.

"Morning, Mr. Barton."

"How are you?"

"I'm good." She smiles sweetly as she waves from the screen.

"And how's your dad? Is he up yet?"

Her smile disappears. "I think he's still getting up…?" She looks off camera.

"Well, ask him to call me when he's up. No emergency. Would you?"

"Yeah, okay."

"Thank you," he says before leaving the room.

As soon as he does, he just overhears Roger ask. "Your dad still isn't up?"

"Yeah…thas what I'm saying. Since you guys left, he doesn't do anything anymore."

"What do you mean? *Nothing*?"

"Yeah…we used to go out and do things." She hesitates as if she's already said too much.

Roger glimpses down the hall to verify that his dad has gone before closing his door. He proceeds to give Daniela the thumbs up indicating it was now safe to speak freely. She smiles.

"I mean he goes to work, comes home in an unhappy mood, and reaches above the fridge for his whiskey, pours it, sits in front of the TV for a while and checks out."

"Yeah, our dads can *drink*."

She laughs at this. "I knowww…I spoke with my mom and sis about watering down the liquor so that he wouldn't get so drunk sometimes, but she said he would notice."

"Yeah, I bet he would. Dad would too. When you're a pro drinker, you must."

Roger then continues in a hushed tone. "Dad doesn't do much else. He holes up in his room doing his classes and then makes trips to the kitchen to take another drink before and after doing the conspiracy podcast."

"You ever listen to that?"

"Yeah, I did once but it was really boring. Fell asleep listening. It went on about the university and who is behind all the protests."

"Me too. It was like two hours about that. One episode connected it to the Youhaul Murders though. I could barely sleep when I heard that one and didn't listen again."

"*That's* what's different now," Roger asserts, "that day at our old house."

"*Hey*—I thought we'd agreed not to talk about that anymore," she cuts in.

"I know but the constant drinking. The fear to go out. That was it."

Daniela appears to be lying down looking up at the camera before her eyes drift away as if in remembering. Her face winces at the thought.

Roger continues, "I know. It's still hard to believe that happening right in front of our house like that."

A sour look lingers in Daniela's face before she looks back up into the camera. "Let's not talk about it."

The bike race ending with that noxious liquid—the foulest odor Roger ever smelled was skipped over in his head as well. He didn't want to remember either. They couldn't even open a window in the house at the time. His mom was lighting scented lavender candles every night well after the crime unit largely cleaned up the spilled contents of the truck.

"I wonder…"

"What?" she asks if now going back on her previous request.

"…why."

She coughs out her disgust. "Because he's a freak monster. What else?"

"I mean do you think he's a sadist? And why particularly women?"

"Women never liked him. They teased him in school. He's got a small penis. I don't know."

They both laughed at this.

"But, why show what he did like that? Was he just disposing of the bodies? It seemed like he wouldn't care about being spotted in the wide open like that with a danger of being caught."

She chuckled at this speculation. "You think that he really thought this through when someone like that doesn't seem to be thinking right at all in the first place?"

"He did have to think over it somewhat. How have the police still not caught the bastard after all of this time?"

"They have new leads. They'll catch him. And one way or another, he'll fry."

"You sound so sure."

"I have to believe that yes."

"But do you think he was making some kind of statement?" he said while typing *Youhaul Killings* into the search bar on his computer.

"Like what? *I really need to get laid by someone willing?*"

Roger didn't laugh as some of the articles and pictures flashed across his screen—some depicting the street they used to live on. There was also a story speculating about the disappearances of numerous women that followed. They exhibited not only the faces of Deborah Haugh and boyfriend, Mark Dempsey, but other pretty faces including Jennifer Sterling and Dorothy Frazelli from the March for Change. Apparently, the latter had their teeth recovered from a Youhaul along with more bodies in front of long-time senator of South Carolina, Christopher Norbert's house. The cameras were on in the front yard, but apparently, were of little help—only picking up blurry figures in the night. The vehicle itself was stolen from the driveway of a family that were to return the truck after a move from New Jersey.

"Like?" she repeated now more seriously with a little heat—seeing as how he was now distracted by the computer.

Still glossing over the articles he managed, "He wanted us to see these women as what they're not."

Her eyes lifted from the camera confused over the strange order and choice of words that seemed to be the last ones she was expecting. She asked him what he meant.

"What was spilled onto the street."

She frowned clearly revolted by the mention of the substance. "And what about it?"

"Maybe that's just want he wanted us to see."

"See what?" She was clearly frustrated she still couldn't discern his exact point.

He directed his attention back to the phone's screen where her dark lively eyes waited for him to enlighten her why such a despicable act could occur. They may have as well asked him why was there not only evil in the world but why some events surrounding humans seemed to reach above nature—so unspeakably dark that their very existence makes little sense not only in the human world but in the world of animals alike.

"I don't know. It's just a thought."

"Just tell me." Her eyes were piercing and adamant.

Roger looked uncomfortable in his own skin for the first time in their conversation. The thought was perhaps best unsaid but now he saw that she wouldn't take a refusal.

"I don't know for sure. It's just ya'know speculation. But, perhaps…that's what he wants us to see—women, maybe not just them, maybe just especially them, are nothing more than… spillage—not individual human beings—they are just one soupy nothing—and," he managed before she was able to express her full horror at the idea. "He begs us to believe him. For some reason, he has no choice but to try and convince us."

"Oh my God that's so gross…so awful."

"I know," Roger said almost as if in a dream. He now thought and talked about it at a distance—in a safe zone, as if the events they had witnessed never happened, at least, not to them.

13

The room's light flickered on and off as easy as did Eggers' mind. Thoughts that weren't his bombarded his consciousness as he endured Kristi's ongoing mutilation. Other times there would be darkness and the sort of rest where either he would be flung into the dream world or, when he was lucky, into dreamless void.

Only they dictated what he was to see. When the operating light was on, the doctor would cut into Kristi some new inventive incision on her torso that defied explanation except to induce blood, pain. Kristi would scream, pass out, which was then the time for the doctor to apply more bandages and inject IV fluid.

He didn't know what day it was or how a person could have spilt so much blood without death. All he could do was watch without knowing. All he could do was yell, spit, and cry.

At some point, the red orbs in the distant dark faded away and so did the growing number of bent thoughts worming around in his head save one last notion. It nested there and he was struggling against it. In it, Kristi was more of a canvas of paint strokes than victim and the doctor an esoteric artist. This was nothing other than an exhibition and Eggers, one of the spectators. He was captured by the final master touches of red erupting on the milky white. The flow of paint formed viscous pools of life—of surrender sucking him into an ever deeper contemplative mystery. It was not until the light came on again that reality started to seep back—welts still impressed by its distinctive sting.

When he heard that squeaky cart of tools pushed by the doctor once again, he emptied his entire diaphragm. The scream was potent enough this time to see the doctor regard him and spit out a laugh at the absurd noise made, as if by a lonely cat.

His dry throat gave all that it could, and he ended his outburst in a fit of coughing. The scream was not only for Kristi but to refocus his own mind. He needed his rational self back. He needed the journalist that saw the facts, unaffected by trauma induced delusion.

In this moment of clarity, he thought of a new strategy—maybe not a winning one—but with the disdainful laugh of a clearly failed physician, it suggested an opening which he could affect.

When his breath returned to him and his choking coughs came under control, he found himself in a forced chuckle as if he were contributing to the present asylum.

"You're nothing but a fucking peasant," his voice penetrated just audibly enough for the immediate company. While Jacques looked on unphased, for some reason, this gave the doctor enough pause to cause him to hesitate before he began cutting again. He stayed his hand, scalpel held ready for carving. Why did this have an effect unlike the invective he delivered so loudly earlier? The novel choice of words? He didn't know, but sensing the weakness, he didn't hesitate to seize the opportunity as a hawk swooping in to clutch wounded prey.

"Yes, you. *You.*" There he stood. "You're a poor fuckup, aren't you?"

While this got Jacques' attention as well, the walking medical malpractice seemed to ignore him making another incision that quickly filled with blood.

"I'm talking to *you, you*, the…," he forces out more laughter, "*Doctor.*" He ends with the title as if it were a punchline—a mocking epithet.

The man continues cutting, more slowly, but cutting all the same. Does he see a slight tremor in the hand, a mounting frustration in the body movements? He believes he does.

"Knock, knock Doc, whose there? It's me."

"What are you even doing here?"

"You're a poor little cockroach, aren't you? Yes, I see you for what really you are."

"You're not even fit to live in the world of men because…you're a roach."

"See, you can't even make that cut. Poor little roach. What a fucking loser…"

On he continued, chatty even-toned, as the doctor appeared more rattled—cutting perhaps deeper. Was his arm shaking? Was he…? He was pissed.

Then he delivered the beginning of the coup de gras, not only for Kristi, but mercy for himself as well.

"Doctor, time to play. Doctor, time to play," he repeated in a sing-songy cadence that concluded in a whisper. "But you're a roach…yes you're a *COCKroach.*" Again, he sang it, and again.

"Shut the fuck up! Shut him up," he finally turned to Pat in a distressed face that protruded from under the mask. The reaction for him was sheer satisfaction.

Jacques finally sprang into action punching him furiously in the head with the sudden and rigid motion as if a brick had caught him. Yet dizzily he came to resume his taunts and even managed a laugh. The doctor now lifted his scalpel as if to use it against Eggers.

"I can't do this…I'll fucking kill you, too!" he dared Pat to continue—bursting with a fury only a life of suppressed trauma could develop.

This time Jacques not only caught his head but included Pat's body too—battering away as if he were a stationary kung-fu practice doll. Amazingly, he remained conscious seeing the life blood of Kristi, the life of his beautiful woman, substantially leave her.

Now that he was in the doctor's head, he was hard to get out. Yes, he could do something too on that battlefield.

As the man and Jacques waited to see if he was tendered up enough to stay quiet, he peeped again.

"Not you," he forced out as the fish was still on the line. "No, no, not you…," he directed this time at Jacques.

"You're no roach." Blood left his mouth as he managed a smile, a nasty smile that may have competed with Jacques' own. "I know what you are. I can see it in my mind right now. I know…"

They waited for his comment. "You're a little shit beetle." This time it was Jacques to shed his cool guise to present rage at his disruption. He disappeared into the darkness accompanied by a shriek partly in frustration—a war cry.

Pat laughed and laughed. The doctor couldn't continue without knowing what Jacques was to do. There was a smash of glass and a momentary quiet. Kristi was no longer heard either. But, just as he thought he may have run off, out of the darkness Jacques came, fire axe in hand. At first, he swings it down connecting where the neck and shoulder meet. It's a glancing blow slicing slightly into Pat's right pectoral. While still gruesome, he barely even feels it—the shock dampened the pain.

"Little sheet beetle!"

Jacques shouts at the taunt with resurged fury and starts to hack consistently at the same blood spurting crack in the neck plunging further and further into less resistant muscle. Pat's final thoughts come. *Kristi, here we are. Our exit. Don't worry, Be at rest now."*

Jacques finishes his hacks until Pat's head is only hanging on by strings of skin and tendon. It just dangles there as they look on while it glares back with dead vacant strapless goggles.

When they return their attention to Kristi's body, they don't realize it at first. She's looking up at them as well, eyes drained. No more tears to come. Ever again.

14

Detective Gonzalez wheezed deeply as he closed his eyes to rest them. It was a momentary reprieve given the incessant ringing of phones and chatter around him.

"Gonzalez…Gonzalez," Brennan called to him.

"Yes," he answered the detective after opening his eyes.

"You okay? Maybe you should sit this one out. You look like death."

"Nope," a hint of the familiar affable smile grew on his face. "I'm only his garbage man when he throws a party."

"Well, if you go home, there'll still be garbage when you get back."

"No," his scratchy voice said with another smile, "it's our mess this time and I want to clean it up now."

Brennan took another look at the man. *How does he do it*, he asked himself, *stricken with plague yet still radiating.*

"He's here," Brennan answers Gonzalez's inquisitive look to which Gonzalez nods.

When the two men reached the front of the station, they see Clint waiting for them. His face wears a drained expression, as if he had been up all night worrying. Brennan thinks he could take a page from his partner.

"Mr. Dumfries, I'm Detective Brennan."

Clint stands and shakes the hand Brennan offers.

"Gonzalez," the detective introduces himself. "I'm sorry I'm a little under the weather," he says as Clint reaches out to shake his hand too.

"Thank you for coming. How was the flight over?"

"Fine," he says flatly, "I've another back this evening."

"That's okay," Brennan said recognizing the concern, "we're going to get you back in time. We'll go to the interview room."

They walked down the hall into a bare space—only table, chairs, and two-way mirror. *Interview room? More like interrogation room*, Clint thought as he stepped inside.

They brought him the diet coke he had accepted along with a couple of notebooks and files. Brennan sat next to him and Gonzalez across.

When they saw that he wasn't going to be the one to break the silence, Brennan started.

"We appreciate you coming. We thought an interview, possibly a formal statement in person could help the investigation," he said, looking to his partner who nodded.

"From the phone conversation, we understand you and Mr. Patrick Eggers are friends."

Clint shook his head as if to say, *let's get on with the formalities.*

"When was the last time you spoke with him?"

"It's been almost a month ago now," Clint looked up trying to recall. "Perhaps a couple days before Peter sent that email to him."

"Okay so it was that Thursday," Brennan wrote a note to himself.

"Yeah, maybe."

"And what do you know if anything about the woman he was with?" Gonzalez rasped as his partner wrote.

"Woman? If he had one, he didn't tell me about it," Clint looked puzzled, as Brennan continued to write.

"Look, I need to stress to you both, Detectives, stop whatever it is you're doing and listen carefully," he said imperiously, rudely if he hadn't made use of their titles.

They both looked at him curiously.

"As I said on the phone, he was doing a story, very provocative story to many people, powerful people. If you want to know what first came to mind when I was told of his disappearance, it was that fact." Clint hated how it sounded, but it had to come out, one way or another, whether long winded or concisely, he had to tell them and he preferred it plainly.

"I imagine you believe Simon Ray had something to do with his disappearance?"

"I'm certain enough to take the time to come here and tell you face to face like this."

"That seems a little presumptuous at this point, doesn't it?" Brennan followed. "Many people subscribe to conspiracy theories these days when it's much more likely that he took a month's escape to Mexico with his girlfriend without telling anyone, maybe even getting hitched while there?" He smiled at the thought.

"If you really believed that we wouldn't be here, would we?" Clint's answer silenced Brennan. His smile faded away.

"Have you looked through Eggers' office and home? You must have found some things he was working on? There could be a latest draft? A file? I mean, was there evidence of anything being searched?"

Gonzalez and Brennan suddenly sat very still.

Brennan started again cautiously. "There is an ongoing investigation which included searches, yes. What I want to know that could really help us, was if you have ever seen this man around?" He pulled a photo from the folder of a man sporting a playful grin for his mug shot that had to be quite memorable for the processing officer at the time.

Clint looked it over.

"His name is Jacques Bouvier. CCTV captured him leaving Mr. Eggers' apparent girlfriend's apartment building. He's already wanted on different charges including kidnapping and assault. While on probation, he disappeared."

"Don't know him or of him," Clint took a second look at the photo before deciding he didn't ever care to see that face in person either.

Clint was growing increasingly frustrated. He decided to save them all a lot of time and cut through the bullshit.

"We made an illegal recording…Illegal in the state of Florida, at least. I don't know about here…"

Both detectives now didn't dare stir as Clint proceeded candidly. Leaving out the small embarrassing detail of them breaking into Blanchard Hall, he spilled it. Eldridge had been found drunk in his office, and that's where they recorded a confession of sorts. The detectives gobbled this part up, captivated as he related the savage protestor who smashed the windows of Peter's car and the coincidence of the Youhaul murderer leaving the truck of victims' bodies right in front of Peter's home. He capped his telling with Eggers' ongoing criticism and research into the foundation—all starting with that first scathing WNT interview with Peter.

"Now Detectives, tell me that these are all just coincidences. Are they all just disconnected events in time? I think you know better…Maybe you're not willing to admit it. Maybe you can't?" He let the question linger.

Detective Brennan looked to his partner again who now gave a slight nod.

"We weren't originally assigned to finding Mr. Eggers," Brennan admitted reluctantly. He continued after a listless pause, "We were helping a woman, Kristi Connor, to find her missing friend, Yunnie Lee. After being attacked once already, she herself has now gone missing…For a while there, we were hopeless. We had no leads, that is, until we discovered that her clothing and wallet were found at another missing person's house, your friend Mr. Eggers."

"So you're saying this woman is gone too? Are you kidding me? How many more people have to go missing until you do something about it? For fuck sake, *do something*."

"Please Professor, let me finish so you have all the facts. We didn't have to share this information with you, but we think more people involved should know."

"And we're not even telling you this now. Understand?" Gonzalez added.

Clint nodded calming himself with deep breaths.

Brennan continued, "Apparently from the credit card info, they were at a diner before they went back to his place. At some point, and it's still being pieced together, the window was breached. Whoever took them somehow knocked the both of them out and dragged them through the house to the outside. It must've happened in the early AM."

"Okay and what are you doing about finding them? Why are you telling me all this?"

"Kristi and her friend did work for Ray Foundation."

Clint grimaced. "And there you were just trying to sell the idea about going to Mexico? It's always a fucking exercise in debate."

"We still want to leave open the possibility for an easier explanation," Gonzalez chimed in with his scratchy throat, "before entertaining more of this theory." The effort drove him into a new round of coughing.

"You think it's about time that this *theory* be taken seriously? What do you think?" Clint tartly boomed over the sick man. "What did this woman Kristi think? Did you listen to her?"

This time they both didn't need to answer. He saw the look all over their faces. They looked like mutts warily approaching a stranger on the street, tails between their legs. Now, he realized what this was, they may have failed Kristi, but they were doing everything they could to somehow make up for their error. They wanted to be able to look at themselves in the mirror once again as good cops.

"Was there evidence of a search or of things missing?" Clint asked again, certain now that they would oblige him with an answer.

"His desk drawers were turned out and his computer was taken is all we know of. His office files seem intact."

"Oh thank God. Thank God. Please find what he had on Ray Foundation and secure it. You need to—have you gone to the FBI? This has to be interstate—all of the killings. This has to have federal crimes written all over it."

"That's the good news," Brennan offered, "we reached out to them, and they've indicated they're interested in getting back with us on this. *This* is *good news*." His last sentence was a reassurance that seemed to be in response to Clint's sour face.

"They'll be able to sift through the evidence. There's a sizable amount collected from Eggers' office. Whatever crimes have been committed, they'll help us get to the bottom of it," Gonzalez assented.

"But that could take time, what are you going to do to find them now? Surely there has to be cameras, witnesses…"

"You have to understand—"

"You mean to tell me there's nothing? Twenty-first century tech and nothing."

"We are doing everything we can."

"We've told you what we know, Professor," Gonzalez answered with his red sickly face.

"Take this to Ray Foundation. Interview the people there. You must have a close relationship with Metro PD. Interview Ray, himself."

"You don't understand, Professor, this isn't academic freedom over here like you have. Not even close. We have a boss and he wants this all done. He wants it gift wrapped for the FBI to decide how to proceed. We won't be able to do something like that."

"Then what *are* you doing? If you're telling me you're done, what am I doing here?"

"Not true, not true. We're not done. We're waiting for the FBI to step in, but we are still trying to find them both. We're not giving up."

"But why? Why tell me?"

"You have a family, Mr. Dumfries?" Gonzalez reverted to his typical *mister* now that he had to stress a point.

"Yes," Clint said.

"If you're right and the truth of the matter looks to be closer to what you discuss on that podcast of yours than a simpler explanation, you need to watch out—not only for yourself—but for your family. Lay low. Maybe consider taking a long getaway together. And I would advise the same to your colleague, Professor Barton," Gonzalez managed to croak through without a cough this time.

Here is where Brennan added his own warning. "You have to think Professor, Kristi was hiding and they found her. Aren't you still there at the university? How hard would it be to find you? Or even your friend, Barton? What would be the odds of them hunting you down too, given your newfound public persona? I'd say pretty likely."

Clint sat there starting to think if it were a mistake coming. He left the family at home. *Would they even be safe? This woman, Kristi, died on their watch. How could he live with himself if anything like that happened to them on his watch?* But, then again, why would they pursue him when it seemed antithetical to their very cause? He remembered part of the reason why he stayed in Palm Gate in the first place. He wasn't a target. He wasn't white.

Once he squeezed inside of his compact rental, Clint called Peter. Eager to hear the news, he picked up after a couple of rings.

"Hey."

"Peter, it's not good."

Peter stood up from his work desk.

Not skipping out on any of the grim details, Clint told him what the detectives revealed. At points in the story, Peter aired his own anger and frustration at the handling of it. At the officers' warning, he could only laugh.

"Thanks a lot for all your help. I'll just go run and hide now instead of you making an arrest, God forbid," he snorted.

Clint didn't laugh. "Maybe he's right," he mused. "Maybe you should think about changing homes again just in case."

"No, I *did* my move," Peter responded with a brief flash of anger. "We feel safe here. Roger has made friends at his new school. Margery's making up for missed time with her parents. We're good…but, what I do worry about is you, my friend. I'd worry if I were still there near campus."

"That's the thing, I don't think they're after me. They never were…besides, we've been here through it already—the campus unrest—the murders—the continued tensions. If they wanted us, they would've tried by now."

"These people are professional. When they mean to kill again, they probably will. No doubt Eggers was going to run that story and to expose them better than we ever could. And I'm confident with this woman as his source—having worked at the foundation—he had an inside view…I hope to God they—"

"Let's not speculate on that now. We need to think about what *we're* going to do."

"We need to work double time getting the message out. Interviews. We need to start working with other channels. We could continue with academics who signed on to the Declaration, but also branch out to more popular ones—more mainstream internet personalities…"

Clint clicked the car's AC dial a few notches left as he thought of the daunting task ahead of them. He decided, *yes, despite recently telling his wife he'd cut back, he did need a drink at the airport after all.*

When Peter's brainstorming ideas tapered, Clint said his peace. "You know I'll do it. But, I must tell you that I don't have a good feeling about any of this."

"You think I do?"

Clint finished as if hadn't heard the refrain, "I'd say, be careful, but it's too weak and too causally used. I'm sure Eggers was careful. So, I say to you, shoot to kill, my friend, if ever in doubt about you or your family's safety, shoot."

15

The American flag slumped against the pole in the sultry stale windless air before the tall colonnade of the Supreme Court building. Marchers paraded signs along its fence with trucks from news agencies from around the country and world ready to report the moment the court's deliberations were released. The constitutionality of the provisions of the Minority Protection Act was finally to be decided.

While many protestors questioned how the court was to rule, they also questioned the smell. Was it from a broken wastewater pipe? A rotting animal in the sewer? Whatever it was—it was positively rank, and the heat only cooked the aroma into the air further. Many begged for rain's mercy rather than fry in wait. Others just resigned themselves to fry, as they knew their cause to be just.

Like the protestors, remote viewers anxiously waited, watching the live coverage.

Peter sipped a beer before the stream on his computer, Clint sat on the sofa before the TV with his daughter, Daniela, whose curiosity was now piqued, and Levy looked up at the screen while doing his vehement hip thrust exercises at the gym. The last of these, whose skintight spandex shorts left little to the imagination as he flexed his glutes in the air, lifting the weight from his pelvis, could have been considered obscene if everyone there wasn't also so preoccupied by the historical event on the TV.

The breaking news screen cut into the coverage to play the dramatic music that kept the viewers frozen before their devices in anticipation. Here it was—the moment of decision all had been waiting for—fearing, hoping, arguing, fighting for democracy. And out came the verdict.

"MPA Constitutional by Split 5-4 Decision" read the headline across the screen. "Democracy has spoken," LNN's reporter declared as the camera panned to a select crowd cheering.

What a great story, many thought while others sulked in silence. Levy himself had sprung up from the gym floor and gave out his own hurrah pumping his fists as if his alma mater had scored the winning championship touchdown.

Into the wee hours of night, different talking heads opined after quoting from the ruling's text. "Arguments against, concerning the Fourteenth Amendment, ignore the whole intent and purpose of its passage at its post bellum inception." The Fifth Amendment objection of "not being deprived of life liberty or property without due process of law is consistent…Even with having satisfied due process at its congressional ratification, liberty has never before been construed as right to employment under any precedent."

But what did it all mean? Did it really matter when the result felt right? The full reaction to the ruling, however, was yet to follow.

Days elapsed before the quiet members of the public made their own statements across the nation descending on capitals and Capitol. Online organizers called people to action to repeal the dangerous law that would compel companies with one-hundred or more employees to kick some of their workers to the curb. They now mandated any superior, with the thoughtful exception of those members of the executive board, to have blood drawn in order to weed out Chromagen carriers.

In an abundance of caution, with most company leadership duly agreeing, possible oppressors could no longer wield power to underpin a system of prejudice against the darker races of society. If any disagreed, however, they were mum, as a company found out of compliance would become the new project of the IRS, an object of a new progressive tax that could turn the stomach of even the most minor owner of capital. Seemingly by design, only the mass of middling workers and their families were in the position to dare question the machinery anymore.

Police and national guard were soon ordered by the governors and President himself, to break up, what he called the "reactionary rabble." This, of course was the nicer epithet, as news agencies, including the nation's leading news organization, LNN, marked the protests repeatedly as "anti-scientific" and "inherently racist." Clashes between the protestors and authorities were cited by lawmakers, especially Senator Dembier, as reason for laws with broader scope to tighten down on dangerous anti-democratic elements.

Soon counter protestors who had flooded into the nation's campuses a year before also joined the fray igniting new conflagrations of violence that saw hundreds of deaths nationwide. Weapons such as the police grade flashlights, batons, bats hammered through with nails, razor blades, swords, M-80s and even guns contributed to a new level of brutality. Months of chaos played out like this before legislation was finally enacted that allowed the freezing of accounts targeting the purported leaders of unrest. Only then did workers start returning to the grind, afraid to be left, like some of their colleagues, destitute. Their only consolation being the government's false reassurance that no one knew their Chromagen status for certain, that is, until tested.

Those determined by the test to be actual Chromagen carriers were recorded within a national registry being deemed chrome-plus and non-carriers, chrome-minus. While some companies allowed chrome-plus workers to still fill in entry level roles, others decided not to take the risk. Too much was now hinging on public perception or the prospect of future law.

In anticipation of the paucity of employees from its own citizenry, a new program for fast-tracking work visas was quietly put in place by the US government. Now workers could arrive from almost anywhere in the world at the drop of a hat, attracted to the sometimes very generous move-in bonuses, without needing to take the test. Best of all, they were hired at a fraction of the cost.

The only problem, as if an afterthought for Uncle Sam was the ten percent of the population now deemed chrome-plus, who still collected unemployment benefits. What were these people to do? No one had a good answer. Yet congress, President, and his administration had consistently good press at how much they had accomplished to stamp out racism. Wasn't the US economy, in fact, booming with low inflation and companies, by and large, flourishing? As a matter of fact, the problems ancillary to the ones already dealt with would be, the President claimed, "addressed all in good time." The registered chrome-plus population, therefore, awaited their next instruction with many even finding hope in the President's message, going so far as to agree to their own racist tendencies and restrictions. Still, there were others, and while their discord ran deep, they chose to wait for the right moment.

In a relatively short time, the country had seen radical structural change. Some questioned how it all happened and why the rest of the developed world seemed to follow suit. Answers ranged anywhere from the tendency of the state to take control of its population to more mundane reasons such as the climate precipitating rapid migration. Many news outlets did choose to run the latter story despite the already very public information about the new work visa program. Besides, the edits on the news segments were superior to the written word in every way and when in contradiction, they won out for some, every time.

Who could argue with that catchy musical jingle preceding that handsomely cut TV personality speaking pure truth, anyway? Their suits simply weren't tailored to lie now, were they? Who could question those smooth words when delivered with the kind of confident snobbery exuded by those high off the smell of their own laboring rectum, when one might like to try on the air for themselves? And even then, what if they did lie? Why not? What did it really matter? What good was truth when these gorgeous scenes were clearly a cut above it all?

<h2 style="text-align:center">16</h2>

The audience stood and clapped warmly, some even whistling through the auditorium, as Professor Jersey made his way on to the well-lit stage following his introduction. Next, Professor Jeffrey Tompkins, Professor of Psychology of Pennsylvania University, joined him after the moderator provided a brief bio garnering his own moderate applause. The first of the night's boos did, however, moan through the din as both Peter Barton and then Clint Dumfries were announced. Once they settled into their chairs, the boos died away to a deadening silence as one of the most anticipated live internet spectacles in the nation commenced.

It was finally happening after two different reschedules following multiple protests and threats on the California University campus. But now the "Chrome-plus? What can be ethically done?" debate finally began. Even tonight while they entered the arena for verbal sparring, members of the student body and others tried to cross barricades and police check points outside. Fortunately, the auditorium, Mills Hall, as planned, provided a well-insulated environment to appropriately house the academics and spectators for the controversial talk.

The moderator cut into the silence and some of the tension felt in the room as the pairs of men sat on opposite sides of the stage not looking at each other. Jersey looked as if he swallowed something acrid while condescending to be in the presence of such men—even men that came from the same institution. This, the moderator quickly seized on joking that, "Despite how this looks with these people present, we are not, in fact, currently at the University of Southern Florida—that's just so happens to be where this all began." Clint and Peter smiled at this, but Jersey retained the same sour expression.

"For those who don't already know," he playfully lifted his eyebrows, "the question for tonight's debate is projected on the massive screen behind us. It is up to our guests how they choose to interpret the question and what systems of ethics to consider. One man of each opposing side will present an argument for twenty minutes, then the other will offer a five-minute rebuttal. After such time, there will be a thirty-minute Q and A where I will ask questions and take some from the audience. Finally, there will be a vote, instructions and access code will be provided on the screen, to see how each fared during the debate."

He looked to both sides. "Is everyone clear about the rules?" They nodded.

"And a warning, to anyone who chooses to interrupt our speakers, I understand passions are running high when it comes to, perhaps, *the* hot-button issue of our time, but conduct yourselves here with dignity," He proceeded to eye the audience gravely. "We are here to win with argument what emotion has failed to do. So, please, keep that in mind before doing anything brash. You will be duly escorted out if you cannot conduct yourselves civilly. Thank you."

Silence ensued as Jersey paused austerely at the podium arranging his notes.

What followed was twenty minutes of firing non-stop verbal shots at the "misinformed, anti-science spewing, gentlemen."

"Never has science been so under attack, as it is now," he ranted. "The audacity of these men to capture vulnerable youths on that despicable channel is horrid—not to mention unethical."

At this, Peter only smiled. The free advertisement of his podcast and the vitriol it had inspired was most welcome.

The tirade continued with a lambasting of those who didn't accept the evidence of the genetic basis for racial animus, not failing to cite the ninety-five percent scientific consensus.

"I must ask, what makes you so much smarter than an overwhelming majority of scientists?" he directed at Peter and Clint. "And there isn't even one bone of Biology between you two," he said earning laughter from the audience.

With the adroit skill of a rhetorician, Jersey proceeded to state his welcome of the MPA and even thought it was a necessary step to the right treatment of minorities only adding, "to my mind, the chrome-plus people are not being treated inhumanely, but rather, I think, with compassion."

Failing to work this into any ethical framework, as the rest of the speakers would also neglect to do with their positions, he ended with one dire warning spoken as if from a parent keen to do the spanking. "Anyone not brave enough to accept a new course of history—a history enlightened by the bold tongue of science, will be rendered outside of it." The line failed to land the way that Jersey had hoped, yet in leaving the podium, he did earn a delayed cheer for his overall performance.

Peter was the next to speak. "You know it's tempting," he smiled, "but I'll have my colleague directly address Professor Jersey's accusations, as we have our own prepared argument."

To this the moderator turned on his lapel's mic nodding. "Yes Professor, do save some of the lightning bolts for later."

"I like how the debate is defined behind me. *Chrome-plus with a question mark.* I like that," he turned his head to look up and point at the projected letters. "To this first question my colleague Professor Dumfries and I reply, *no.*" His laugh followed the audience's. "We agree that it is a something, but what it is—is like finding a face in the moon. It's not science and let me add that I say this as a Professor of Psychology—not Biology. It's based on the false premise that bias testing can prove racism. It doesn't. So, there is no need to go any further, but if you do and you do accept this first big assumption, then you decide to combine this false premise with having AI determine similarities in DNA sequences of individuals who didn't do well on cognitive bias testing then bam! You get the genetic basis for racism." Peter paused to look over to Jersey to aim his speech more directly. Jersey faced straight forward, and with the exception of a subtle projection of a clenched jaw, appeared nonplussed. Then, at length, Peter carried on criticizing the many other worrying details of the study. He named it "black box science" agreeing that real science *is* under attack and that it is indeed offensive that something so false could be foisted on the people so shamelessly as an actual law to live by.

"There is no question that such a law fails every ethical test. It is based on patent untruths…I would go even further and say this is not about ethics so much as meeting the minimal requirements of justice that humans and some nonhumans have understood about fair treatment—a much more visceral and basic level of understanding even before a philosophical level…"

Peter didn't notice but Jersey's temple artery was now protruding. It was like Peter had just slapped the man across the face.

"So why are we all here? Why all the drama? It's not enough to say that some people stand to gain from exerting control over others and so they do. The people need to want to latch onto something first—something controversial—something edgy—but the truth isn't always like that. Race has been that kind of topic—an issue that can boil the blood inspiring more hate than any other. Using this with a pliant public that appears to be suffering from a sort of Stockholm Syndrome capable of accepting any justifications repeated often enough, we now have this persecutory law, and worse, every day it becomes normative, acceptable. In fact, they're talking about more measures against people who have done nothing wrong. What started as a pretension against racism is leading back to eugenics. It's like just throwing out the baby and ignoring the bathwater, like claiming to be a pacifist with the proviso of surviving by slurping up the blood of dead enemies…"

"Fascist! Free the black race! Final Freedom!" a member of the audience could tolerate no more, shouting along with other buzzwords and phrases that were hard to distinguish from the many outbursts of the crowd. Peter waited patiently for security, who earned some claps, to escort the heckler before continuing.

Slowly, he started again, as if the spectacle of the protestor spoke for itself. "I ask, therefore, for the sake of these people, people I'm sure many of you know by a great deal of real evidence, as good people, for their sake, for the sake of the soul of this nation, repeal this law and enter it into the tome of history to die."

Unlike Jersey, who now appeared to be cleaning his teeth with his tongue, Peter's introduction earned a thunder of applause that resonated even well after he joined the others in his seat on stage. With anonymous polls online already rolling in, the majority said one thing. So far this was a blood bath. And their respective comments sections mercilessly throttled Jersey for his aloof stage presence and lackluster opening. If his side didn't turn it around soon, there was no question of who were going to be the winners tonight.

Clint was next to be called up.

Standing there, dwarfing the wood fixture by his large size with his tailored navy-blue pinstripe suit, textured teal tie, he demanded some attention, and when he began with his deep thunderous voice, all of it.

Thanking everyone for holding the debate not excluding his opponents Professor Jersey and Tompkins, he thanked Eldridge, who had been absent, adding that he was the next major contributor to the study. What he failed to mention was that Eldridge had been missing for months now. No one close to him had any idea where he was. This was a little prod at Jersey, Ray, and whoever else knew what really happened to him, especially after it had become known that Eldridge had communicated his reservations about his research to several individuals from independent media.

He seemed to wait for some response or outburst at his mention of the man. There wasn't one, so he cleared his throat and took a sip of water—taking his time to deliver that uncomfortable burn.

"What I found particular…particularly interesting over the course of this debate, is how Professor Jersey continues to dodge any points that we make about his study. All he seems to do is go on about this ninety-five percent consensus, which is not what he is making it out to be. This figure does not include the area of Psychologists and Biologists who never pronounced on the question of if racism has a genetic component. It is only from the papers who have made such a pronouncement, on something that many scientists in the fields of Psychology and Biology disagree with in principle from the get-go. Such a question is too complex for a definitive answer at this point. Whether genetics, environment, or events determine inclinations or disinclinations and to what degree, we have no idea. And to attempt to wrap it all up into a nice easy bow of an affirmative or negative is plainly fatuous and irresponsible." Clint took a moment, with arms pressed on the sides of the podium, to deliver the seriousness of the point to his audience—almost daring someone to question it. "I say to those who still, despite ignoring these facts, go on to answer such a question, that you aren't scientists and should cease to be taken seriously—perhaps losing any academic position after investigation by an ethics board." At this juncture, Professor Tompkins was the one to show a little rush of blood in his cheeks with red blazing around his spectacles. "The only ones answering such a question are not motivated by facts and reality but the easy money from grants to explore what they take to be an *exciting* new area in the field. If their answer just so happened to be negative to genetic racism, do you think the spigot of money would remain on...? Let's cease this talk about science altogether because this isn't a question of science.

"Let's talk about the damage already done—about the MPA and the threat it is to this country. It's a downright embarrassment—the like of which has not happened since Japanese internment camps in the second world war. Professor Jersey has said that chrome-plus people have been treated with humanity. Really? How is that? When you take away their very livelihood in order to make them dependent on the gracious teet of the state? The state knows no humanity. It's cold. It's uncaring. The state depends on us to make sure it does anything good at all...So what are they doing by removing them from society? Racial justice? Is that it? Is that what they are saying? That's a joke for anyone who's put any thought into it. But that is what Ray Foundation and many of the supporters of this law are claiming. Well, what is justice then? What good is the phrase when by using it, you make the word meaningless?

"And…Even if these people were potential racists, which again, the science says nothing one way or another, justice is not punishing them for being a potential something. There is no person I know of convicted of a potential crime. We don't even pretend to regulate what someone may simply feel about another person or group. If I knew anyone who would be arrested in such a world, it would have been my late Aunt Helena or just Auntie, to us…We don't talk much about dear Auntie…You see Auntie," Clint changed into a lower gear—the gear used more for a fireside chat rather than debate. "…loved to eat butter pecan ice-cream. When she would take out the gallon tub from her ice box in summertime, my sister and I'd be so excited…" Clint looked over the audience wistfully as if seeing it materialize before him. "Yeah, that was her favorite thing in the world. Paradise to the taste buds. But you know what else Auntie really liked, many, many things. But *whites*, not so much." Peals of laughter could be heard throughout the auditorium, but Clint pushed on to finish his point. "So best to lock her up until she recants? How about firing her from her job and isolating her? Maybe then she would've started liking white people more?" More laughing continued. "So don't pretend for a minute to have anything to do with justice. Just don't. You aren't doing anything remotely just by imposing this monstrous law. Refrain your lips from speaking a word so noble for now you are the one who is the violator. You *are* the oppressor."

Clint finished up his rebuttal with a bang earning the most applause yet. Tompkins tried to sit a while longer to let the applause fizzle, but the moderator urged him on anyway.

It didn't take long to see that Tompkins wasn't quite the person for the job. His points were simple and yet he belabored them as if the audience would never be able to understand them without undue assistance. First, he mentioned the ninety-five percent of scientists. They were trained scientists just like he and the other members of the debate. There was no reason to trust them any less in the war of money when he was sure that many donors were also giving generously to Barton and Dumfries' one-sided podcast. Second, it isn't at all that surprising that racism has a genetic component just like alcoholism does. Just as the penchant for alcohol runs in families, racism does too. Just as there can be a tendency or inclination toward something, there can be a tendency or disinclination away from something. Last, as almost an afterthought, he said the law was not a moral judgment such as imputing guilt on those falling inside its scope. It was, as the intent of the law made clear, "out of an abundance of caution."

He earned a polite clap before taking his seat sensing with the others that his rebuttal had rather been a dud compared to the flare exhibited by the prior speakers. They were good at this, and he had just filled a vacancy in a card of a different league with fighters that have long been slogging it out. Nevertheless, the match wasn't over. He knew he still could—he had to—make a comeback to show he could contend here, as he desperately wanted his own ascendance into popularity with the concomitant book sales and guest appearances. This could be the only opportunity left. It nagged at him that perhaps he only had less than an hour of fame remaining.

The moderator then took control of the Q and A that followed—trying what he could to zap the stuffiness out of the room with his dry wit. He had some success in putting his interlocutors more at ease, yet that there was still no love lost in the room, a body language expert had no need to comment.

"I want to really zoom in on a salient point I think made that was never addressed by the opposition. Professor Tompkins said that some being chrome-plus is akin to being alcoholic in that it also runs in families. Is that not a distinct possibility and showing that this is a scientific question after all? What do you say to that? Professors Barton and Dumfries, could you or your colleague address this possibility?"

"I'll answer," Clint said forthrightly twisting his class ring at the time. He stopped. "Alcoholic studies are based on actual data—consumers of an excess amount of alcohol. Cognitive bias tests are not necessarily indicating biases—not to mention racism—in the way that drinking too much alcohol is, by definition, an alcoholic. No, it just doesn't work at all," he shook his head as if agreeing with himself.

"I don't think that's a correct characteriz—"

"Wait your turn Professor Tompkins. You'll get a chance to respond."

"I don't think you really want to say that anyway…even if the science was clear that there was a genetic predisposition to racism, we don't lock people up with a predisposition to alcoholism or keep him at home because he could get drunk and run someone over. It is an insane proposition as it is insane what we're doing now. The MPA isn't about science or safety anyway. It won't keep anyone safe and doesn't really pretend to do so. Do you know anyone who considered someone black to have to take the test? It's not happening in practice with the presumption that they won't be racist anyway. If it really indicated racism, why isn't everyone taking the test? Maybe they're the ones worried about being considered racist by excluding blacks from the workplace?"

"That's not—not true," Tompkins got out—this time without objection from the moderator. "All are tested for the Chromagen markers regardless of race—"

"Well do you know any black person who was excluded? Please tell."

This putting Tompkins on the spot had him visibly uneasy as if he were searching with his feet for a thick layer of ice as he heard it crack.

Peter laughed it off after a few seconds. "He doesn't have anyone in mind." He meant it more as a hand of mercy, but Jersey took it as a further slight and he was already seething.

"If I may, I'd like to know why Barton is so interested in this particular subject of science. He appears to be on this incessant crusade to show that the conclusion couldn't possibly follow and is absolutely certain of it. Why would that be?"

The moderator waited not wishing to interrupt such an open challenge.

"I'm sorry. What are you trying to say, Professor?"

"I don't know. What am I trying to say?" Jersey said with detectable mockery.

Peter smiled. "Are you insinuating something about my intentions?"

The audience didn't move and neither did anyone else. Clint looked blankly at Jersey waiting.

"How do you not know of your own potential biases? As you know, every good scientist should weigh them in whatever professional endeavor or else remove themselves totally from the conversation."

"Are you saying I could be racist, Professor?"

"Well, your words, not mine…" An exasperated sound could be heard out of the audience. "Are you?"

Peter waited a few seconds to respond. He rather expected this challenge and relished the moment.

"Well, it's funny that you should mention that." He nonchalantly removed something from his folder of notes that he had placed under his chair after finishing his speech. "Ah, here it is…Wait…It seems to say, why yes," he nodded after taking a moment to peruse it, "I'm chrome-minus."

There was a disparate applause from the audience. Jersey and Tompkins sat silently managing stoical faces. Clint let out a belly laugh that he was holding in, and the moderator couldn't help breaking character as well.

"Would you like to see it?" Peter held it out to Jersey who didn't seem to be in any hurry to look.

"So…does that answer your question, Professor Jersey?" The moderator held back another laugh just behind his smile.

"That's all well and good that he got tested, but it doesn't really answer it, no," Jersey spoke with noticeably less passion in his voice.

"But, it seems that it does at least allay some suspicion that you had. Does it not?"

Tompkins felt his usefulness slipping and needed to help his team with some counter. "It doesn't because the test doesn't rule out racists. You can be racist and be chrome-minus all the same. Going back to the alcoholic example, there can be many other factors outside of one's genes that can lead one to alcoholism when one doesn't have the typical genes of alcoholics. Racist ideologies and tendencies can develop growing up in a racist household or having an influential friend or family member, trauma that an individual interprets with a racist lens. Endless possibilities really."

"Okay, so, if that is all true, what are we to make of this law where a lot of people are not at all racist and are excluded from the work force? Doesn't that highlight the point that Professor Dumfries made earlier? How can that be just?"

"No, no, no, not quite," Tompkins indicated with some frustration. "As we said, it is out of caution that the law is in place and there is good reason for it when there is a high likelihood of problematic behavior from an individual who tests chrome-plus. Also, do keep in mind, that they are not actually excluded from the workplace. That's not what the law does. It removes those who test chrome-plus from leadership or managerial roles only—eliminating a lot of the workplace racism and employment discrimination that has continued to haunt our nation. It is a good start to finally break us free from the cycle of this contemptible systemic force."

The moderator appeared to weigh Tompkins' words with some confusion before opting to have Clint respond. "Let's ask Professor Dumfries. What do you make of these claims?"

"No need to respond," Clint said confidently, "more of the same guff."

"You don't wish to defend your colleague?

"What's to defend? I know him very well. He's a friend. And we went in this discussion from how important this research is to how it doesn't really matter in the end. You'll never be able to disprove to these people that you're not the literal embodiment of Goebbels. Meanwhile, they have yet to prove anything they have said. It's a waste of time, but I'm glad that anyone watching can see what this really is."

"Peter, won't you confirm that you're not a racist at least?"

Peter laughed. "What good would that do? I have taken the test haven't I, and they won't accept that. I'd prefer not to be clipped and have the side of the internet against me to use it as evidence that I am. They'll say something like, *anyone who has to say that proves that they are.*"

"So, you refuse to say it because of some people on the internet?" Jersey gibes with a smile.

"No, I won't," he confirms not at all bothered by Jersey's outward malice. But, I will say that isn't it all illuminating from what has just been said?"

"What's that?"

"Professor Tompkins said this is *a good start* didn't he...? He isn't denying it that there are more laws to come. It will never be good enough."

"But what would that be? What's a good start?" The moderator began asking Tompkins, but Peter offered an answer.

"There has already been discussion from certain politicos to have a law that mandates testing of embryos with the understanding if they turn out to be chrome-plus, the women carrying them will qualify for a free abortion service, all paid for by the taxpayer."

"You're sick!" Tompkins hissed.

"Is that a no?"

"That's just whacky—a conspiracy theory."

"There've been multiple public speeches. Anyone can find videos of it if they look. Hardly a conspiracy."

"Enough!" Tompkins started laughing awkwardly, looking to the moderator as if he were certain to agree with him. The whole look came across as deranged and was to be popularly clipped, shared across the internet.

Tompkins had his day of fame in the end. The video feed showed a side that more popular media didn't want people to see. It showed power bleed. Of course, its influence would be considered rather minimal compared to what was to come. Many spectators were soon to be gorged on views beyond their imaginings—views they could never quite unsee. In the moment, however, at this, the audience didn't even make a peep.

As the debate made the final transition to the audience Q and A, what was happening outside Mills Hall was spiraling into chaos. Police were repositioning to fight off the onslaught of swarming activists who had successfully ignited two police cruisers with many more in their sights.

One squad of police came upon three protestors smashing out windows of another cruiser. They showed their guns, subdued the suspects and were being arrested. The thugs' masked faces were planted firmly into the hood of the car and asphalt as the officers cuffed them. But, with their being led back to the detainment bus, they were quickly overcome by a large hoodlum band rushing in with bats and Maglites bludgeoning officers and grabbing their friends. The officers fended off their attackers the best they could by pumping pursuing assailants with 9-millimeter rounds as they retreated to the entrance of Mills Hall leaving their cuffed suspects to the mob.

Breaking news of the event scrolled across screens "Unarmed Protestors Shot by Police at California University". Many channels cut into scheduled programming to the live feed of the mayhem. Cars were on fire and the police now congregated behind the perimeter fence as objects were hurled over at them. Rocks, bottles, canned food, locks, and many other heavy substitutes were raining down. Even with all of this, it was only the molotovs conflagrating on two officers that organizers finally decided to pull the plug. While they wanted to show courage in the face of mob rule, with the risk of a fire to the hall full of people, they knew they had to end it.

It was the middle of a long student monologue directed at Professor Jersey starting each sentence with "ya' know?", the moderator cut in to announce the early termination of the event due to a nearby fire. Everyone knew what that meant despite its neutral framing. Some already saw the carnage playing out silently on their phones. The members of the black bloc were at it again and they were intent on finally silencing the right-wing propagandists.

Peter and Clint warily eyed the sea of black behind the perimeter fencing. They were battering it with their bodies. Some climbed over as others continued throwing projectiles.

The call was made. Cops had killed two of their own, and now they were descending on the event fast, seeking revenge.

Some drivers were trying to leave as thousands packed the streets and allowed little to no movement. They broke windows and pulled out drivers and their helpless riders. Others took this as their cue to plow through if necessary. They drove into the bodies of limbs at a slow but steady speed hoping that mob mentality could learn. Instead, they flattened dozens, even carrying unwitting passengers who were riding on the hoods and roofs before being flung off at turns. The mob fruitlessly tried running down many of these offenders falling to the ground, cursing, helpless against the twentieth century marvel of the combustion engine.

"Not this again," Peter said to Clint who shook his head at the stunning stupidity of it all. Peter was indeed glad he wasn't driving at the moment, especially after the year long legal battle he fought for running over protestors at USFL.

He quickly surveyed the area homing in on a weak point in the throng. Others from the debate were threading their way to the other side of campus seeming to give up on the idea of retrieving their cars for the night. "Fuck the rental. Come on!" Peter urged Clint, who joined him a double time to safety. They huffed their way across campus with deja vu on the mind. They thought the days of finding it necessary to sneak in the shadows of universities were over. They were wrong.

17

The media framed the night's debate as rightly provoking the wrath of the public. It reported the facts. The activists were shot by police without proper restraint causing the deaths of two protestors and multiple injuries. The right wing was out of control with anti-science propaganda. Professors Clint Dumfries and Peter Barton of University of Southern Florida were by no means experts, but at the same time, should accede to the rest of the scientific consensus.

The pressure was palpable. Members of congress from both parties were equally disavowing not only the police violence but both professors who sparked the rage filled campus. They were abusing their first amendment rights, and the University of Southern Florida should take appropriate disciplinary actions against them. The platform they were using to spew their hate-filled garbage should forcibly take down their content as it both contravenes existing law and is considered an incitement to violence.

Senator Susan Dembier led the way in agreement even going a step further when she spoke before the chamber. "Democracy is at stake, as a democracy that cannot properly decipher the truth, is not a democracy but an aimless libertopia. We must protect scientific integrity for without it, we cannot protect our own people."

Many thought, that this was going to be a springboard for her frontrunner-ship in the coming election—comparing it to great speeches, Gettysburg, Freedom from Fear, or Liberty or Death. Her positive media hype captured much of the public's imagination, but on the other side of the coin, the negative proved equally magnetic.

Following the attack on the campus of California University, Peter's channel hit one million subscribers and the request for interviews bombarded his university email account. He couldn't keep up with all the demand and had to hire a remote working secretary full-time to handle it.

When the university received the request for leave of their most controversial tenured professor, who no longer wanted to split his time between his podcast and teaching, they approved it the same day. Peter was a free man, and the university was free to disassociate from him at a most pivotal political juncture. While they still received flak about Dumfries remaining, something about seeing the white man leave, took much out of the wind out of activist's sails who were pushing for a lot more than just a change of faculty.

Peter was to make a circuit around the country drawing public ire from many preprogrammed audiences but also an outpouring of support. Not all were affected the same by the popular exposés that preceded his appearances. In fact, many of the interviewers were thrown off guard by his positive demeanor and tact despite their deployment of verbal traps. Even with these engagements, he still managed to release new content with Clint's help. His celebrity only grew by saying those obvious things many wouldn't dare speak. It all came to the forefront.

With many reservations, the Senate's Committee on Health, Education, Labor, and Pensions had formally invited Peter to the chambers to be questioned about the effects of the MPA on the American workforce. As soon as the date was set, he revealed the good news on Psyclips with Clint. He told his audience that it was time to reveal the truth to the rest of the American people—people stuck in their bubble of media that he couldn't normally reach. It was unbelievable, he mused, the number of people out there who were being drubbed in the mind accepting manifest falsehoods every day. There wasn't much recourse for the other side, but to have someone push back, and maybe, one day, the echo would be heard, but in the mystery of the human psyche, no one knew who, when, or how. He elaborated, "But I imagine that something may not sit right with them one day in following the same source of the tune. Something abrasive enough…They're unwilling to dance or listen anymore. It may be a detail as small as a missed note or a blare from the orchestra. They're well on their way for life to be their own again. They can block out the noise and start living—*really* living."

Clint's reply wasn't so optimistic. "I believe you'll be heard only because it is a recorded event. And that's good. But they're there to discredit you—to deplatform you in a sense, just like they wanted. As far as the people watching, they'll only have time for your heavily edited responses that some drone will cut. Even then, viewers may not welcome your incursion into their lives. They may really *like* the loudspeaker telling them what's what. Some people don't desire the freedom you speak of. They want easy to follow directions and all you're going to do is disrupt their peace."

"I'll give you that—that some are going to be there to try their hand at demeaning me to the public and I'm prepared for that but, I think what you're forgetting is that there are some out there who do need me to speak for them because they're afraid. I don't think they would have called on me otherwise. There would be nothing to gain… I disagree with you that any considerable proportion of the United States or even abroad abjure their own freedom for the sake of the machine, in a matter of speaking, even though I admit there have to be some."

"But if I'm playing the probabilities," Clint thought aloud, "public humiliation has to be the goal for most of them. They need to squash the idea that there is not an infallible consensus behind stripping millions from their livelihoods. In fact, as I've told you before, I think they need to have a beaten down enough populace to prepare them to accept whatever's next on the agenda. They need everyone duly tenderized…And you're one of the only ones standing in their way."

A chill suddenly ran through Peter's spine and gooseflesh infected his forearms. He had been riding too high for too long. It was as if he had forgotten about mortality, his and his family's. What were they willing to do to them if they didn't have their way? If they had forcibly terminated millions, what wouldn't they do?

Clint may be right. Is this the reason for keeping him around? They still had a use for him after all—to make of him a foil for the rest of those who held any dissent in their hearts—a warning that said this is what happens to those who don't fall in line? But would they still risk his speaking out to a broader audience? Couldn't it invariably make new converts? There had to be more to it. Whatever the case, he was going in and going in prepared.

Before signing off, he thanked Clint and all those who supported them on the channel encouraging live stream watch parties to witness the government being held to account. "We're not going to stop fighting, and we'll win in the end because remember, when your weapon is the truth, there is no equal."

Viole-t.

1

The phone rang repeatedly. He had called earlier but Peter hung up at the start of the message. Here he was again, anger repressed, cussing into the phone watching the little one roam around the house.

"Come on…fucking…do something for fuck…Isabel! Not there!" he called out as his daughter made her way into the kitchen. He came behind her as she felt her way around the counter and stood before the stove knobs. She lost interest and moved on.

"Hello," a tired familiar voice answered on the other end.

"Gonzalez? It's Peter," he said with a smile.

Gonzalez answered without surprise. "Yeah, how're ya?"

"You know me. Fine. Yourself?"

"Do'ya know what my late mom said it was like being on the police force?"

"What?"

"*'It's not just any job, Memo*, I remember her say, *it's a calling*.*"

"And now do you agree?" Peter snorted, waiting for the punchline.

"She was absolutely right. Every day is a calling. Calling again and again and again. That's all it is ring, ring, ring. So what can I help you with Pete?"

Peter laughed. It sounded too good natured to be taken as an insult. "You might've heard that I'll be at the capitol in a few days."

"That's the word. Capitol police will be beefing up security to roll out the red carpet. Prepare for true royalty."

Here Peter wasn't sure if Gonzalez was taking a genuine swipe at him or not, but he didn't much care. He and Gonzalez had become friendly, frequently relaying news about the Youhaul Killings for some time now. It's a strange world how a murderer sometimes brings people together.

"You can thank the United States Senate for that. I'm there at *their* bidding."

"My thank you letter has been on its way."

"I sure would like to touch base with you while I'm in town. It's been a little time since I came to D.C., but how about breakfast first thing Tuesday? I have some time before the noon hearing."

Someone was talking to Gonzalez on the other end, and it sounded as if he were responding with his face turned away from the receiver.

His voice came back. "You say breakfast?"

"Yes."

"Tuesday, seven am?"

"Yep."

"You know when everyone here realizes I'm supping with his highness again, they'll get jealous."

"When you tell them, they'll only think it's you by yourself again. They know you're the only real ass around the department." They both laughed at how bad the joke was.

"I was going to confirm a few things, so I'm glad you're headed this way for once."

"Yeah, it's a long flight as a straight shot. Don't care to go much unless there is a very good reason to."

"I imagine I wouldn't either," Gonzalez agreed. "But I also wouldn't be galivanting about the country when a certain peace officer warned me to stay safe. I wouldn't be doing that either."

Peter laughed at the picture that occurred to him of being tended to by hot stewardesses flying around the country in plumes of smoke, as if he were a high-roller in the 70s.

Gonzalez continued in a more grave tone, "You still remember exactly what I told you after telling Clint?"

"Yes," Peter said with his laughter dwindling. "Be careful."

"No, what I said was, think about disappearing."

Peter wasn't laughing at all now.

"While I'm very glad to have gotten to know you, Pete, I'm saying that again now. You're about to go on the biggest stage yet saying, *hey look at me, look at me.* If I were you, I wouldn't be poking the lion anymore. I'd take my family and go somewhere. Far away out of the US."

Peter paused at this, suspended in thought.

"I'm just saying, you don't have to go through with this if you don't want. I mean you've done enough"

"No," Peter answered after another pause. "No, I haven't"

"Okay, Pete, just be safe, okay?"

"See you Tuesday morning Guillermo."

After hanging up, he thought through different scenarios trying to anticipate where it could all go from here. What were the probabilities? There were just too many variables and too little time. It was overwhelming. Life felt far too uncertain and there was far too much riding on it. That's when he heard the thumping down the staircase followed by crying.

"Shit!"

He ran to Isabel laying on the floor tears streaming down her face as she wailed louder and louder. When he picked her up, he felt her whole body shake with wails, as he rubbed her back.

"It's okay Belli, It's okay. Daddy's got you. *Daddy's got you.*"

2

At the James Darcy Library, the six flights of stairs up he decided to take as exercise brought him to the room where that day's seminar would be held. He entered the room, and his students were all sitting waiting for him as if they had been there an hour already. It was quiet but they were smiling. He returned their greeting then routinely withdrew some of the texts they were covering that day from his bag.

His two star students, Johnny Pearson and Lindsey Cunningham, were sitting side by side at the conference table, and he looked to them to summarize the day's readings as they were usually wont to do. He turned to the board to write their observations, but when he didn't hear anything from them, he gave them a second look. All were now looking their way.

Johnny appeared to be in sheen of sweat that hemorrhaged from his face onto his collar and the table. It was as if someone were emptying bottles of water on his head. His demeanor had shown great discomfort at his uncontrollable gushing. Meanwhile, he thought Lindsey too shared in his discomfort by proxy, but she looked to be suffering from her own malady. She sweated as with a fever and her face was flush. She groaned with some deep sense of pain. The rest of the students merely stared at Johnny with dead, helpless eyes.

Peter tried to find his voice, but he couldn't. Something prevented him from speaking at all. He wanted to ask them what was wrong. Then, he wanted to yell for someone to help, but he couldn't. He choked in trying to exercise his cords, but all he could do was hold his throat as he coughed. Finally, a strange shushing sound was heard and he thought that perhaps he was able to produce it. Straining his throat harder didn't cause the shushing to grow, so he regarded his students once again to see what it was. It appeared to be coming from Johnny.

Johnny's mouth was making some kind of chatter, but it didn't comport well with the rest of his face. It appeared to be against his will. "Shushishta, shushista," Peter thought he had heard with a most hateful expression—an expression of overt revilement. The mouth drifted to the side of his face, and when he thought it couldn't move anymore, it went to Johnny's cheek. It continued to express the same indecipherable words then moved on to his cheek bone, now even with his eyes as tears rolled down them. "Rashista, Fashishta, Rashishta, Fashista," the enunciation of the words could be better made out now as it said them, spit spraying from its gob. Johnny's eyes dared not move over to see what was speaking from his face. He was too terrified to move. Lindsey continued to groan only louder as she was too busy with her own problem to see what was happening to Johnny.

Finally, the mouth appeared over Johnny's eyes. "Rassista, Fassista", it said with its big nasty expression, now the whole orifice appeared to displace much of Johnny's head and his eyes rolled back into whatever remained of his skull. He fell back into his chair.

Peter tried to walk over to check on Johnny, but his legs wouldn't let him move. The fact was that he too was paralyzed with fear to go anywhere. All he could do was watch and try to yell. His other students were now laying back in their chairs. He didn't know if they were dead or passed out.

Looking back to Lindsey, he was stunned to see Lindsey now on the conference table crawling legs first toward him panting luridly as she proceeded to pull her dress up. Peter looked away in disgust.

"Professor," she said as if in the middle of death's grip itself, "I'm crowning." He didn't dare look as he was so horrified, but he knew what it was. Somehow, he knew. Coming out of her was a man with half his head clipped off. The bottom half of his brain was showing, and she screamed as she pushed. The piercing sound resonated into Peter's head. It vibrated in his own skull even after he awoke.

He and the bed were drenched in sweat. He just lay there breathing, recovering.

God, when will it stop?

3

"I don't see how you can believe any of that," Daniela laughed into her phone's camera as Roger withstood her barbs with a smile. "Why would they come all of that way? To probe us up the ass?" This got Roger and Daniela bawling with laughter. His camera shook as he tried to hold it up but couldn't.

"I am not saying that—not at all. *You* said it," he explained.

"Okay, then what is it?" she couldn't help the laughs from still bubbling up.

Roger got up from his bed wiping the tears from his eyes. "We don't really know. But it doesn't have to be little green men if that's all you're thinking. It could just be a terrestrial phenomenon we don't fully understand yet. It could even be an experimental craft."

"I think there are simpler explanations, but I don't know of any good ones that fit what people've been seeing."

"But why is it that *you* believe? I mean have you experienced anything?"

Roger shook his head. "No, but there's so much evidence from videos, documented experiences—with nothing to gain—only with the possibility of losing face. And that is just what people decide to come forward with. There seem to be way too many independent observers for it all to come down to nothing but a weather balloon."

Daniela looked away from the camera pondering over this. "I just think…that would be…"

Lowering the volume of the rock music coming from his computer, Roger scrolled though the videos that came across his InstaGrat feed.

"That would be incredible. To roam the galaxy on a starship…" She shivered with excitement, as Roger eyed her on his phone once again. "Would be so romantic…don't you think?" She smiled.

"Yes, as long as nothing goes wrong which it almost certainly will."

"I know. That's part of it."

She got up from her bed to peer out of her window looking at the exquisite expanse from the mysterious sparkles of light in the night sky.

"Where would you like to go?" Roger asked, imagining what his own interstellar journey would be like.

"After swinging by Saturn to see its rings, I could head for the cluster of three stars I'm seeing now. It looks so inviting from here. It has to be that much more amazing there. What fascinating discoveries there must be…"

Roger stood up and raised his blinds to look for himself, not that he really thought he was going to find the exact stars that she was looking at. The lights from the city really made it hard to see stars from where he was looking. He did notice a few, but his attention was soon drawn by the quiet serenity of the neighborhood in early morning. The cars were all parked safely in the driveways. Neighbors were all likely passed out from weekend wine laying before their screens exhausted by the demands of the modern world—not least the holding of strong opinions about any given topic. It wasn't a bad place that they had to move to, but he did miss the old house. He didn't know if he'd ever feel safe there again, but he remembered when he did. It was less dense with people and there were more stars in the sky to see at night. Perhaps he just missed what it was like before—before all the confusion.

"What about you? What would you like to see," Daniela asked, as Roger's eyes further drifted down the street. Something didn't quite fit, and it began to instantly nag at his psyche. What for most would have appeared as common to a neighborhood as an ornament to a tree on Christmas, didn't sit well for Roger.

"Hello? Can you hear me?" she asked as he further studied the move-in truck that sat parked curbside. He was pretty sure it would have to be ticketed by code officers. Was there someone moving in? He couldn't remember any sale. Maybe it was as simple as the moving of boxes into a storage unit. That happened often enough.

The side of the truck had no markings though. Even without the name Youhaul, it didn't make him feel any less comfortable.

"There is a strange truck I'm looking at."

"What?"

"It's a move-in truck that is parked in the neighborhood."

"Don't even joke about that…"

"I'm not."

"Well, what's it doing there? Is someone moving?"

"I don't think so."

Daniela waited quietly for Roger to report something as he continued to watch for anything else amiss. He knew, in all likelihood, his concern was silly. The chances that it was anything sinister were small, nevertheless his breathing had quickened and muscles tightened.

"Anything?" Daniela asked after another moment went by.

"Zilch," Roger said as if he were beginning to relax again.

"Do you know what you'd be looking for if it were…ya'know?"

"I don't know," Roger said still only half in the conversation.

"I've thought about it…and I can't say if it would've ever occurred to me something was off about that truck sitting in your neighborhood… except for ya'know."

"It's not dripping out of the back if that's what you're getting at," Roger said with a sardonic smile.

"Stop, stop, stop. No, no, no." She recoiled. "Remember we agreed not to ever talk about that again."

"You're the one that brought it up."

Roger sat at his computer and began typing into the search bar. He clicked on one of the pages he was quite familiar with by then—a page fanatical about all things Youhaul Killer.

"I know, but let's not dig up the specifics. I just—I can't anymore…what are you doing now?" Daniela only saw the ceiling from his camera.

"I wanted to…verify something about the murders."

"What about?" Daniela waited patiently as Roger scrolled on quietly. For some minutes, she could hear his clicking, clicking. It almost seemed too much. Did he forget her question? "So?" she finally asked when she heard a pause between clicks.

"I don't know."

"You don't know what?"

"It's a lot…the Youhaul Killer or killers may or may not still be killing. It's speculated that they could've changed their methods. Some killings are suspected, but they miss the trademark of leaving bodies in a moving truck for someone to discover."

"Just any moving truck or a Youhaul truck?"

"That's the thing, despite the name of the killer, they haven't all been Youhaul trucks."

"No shit."

"The good news is that, according to this site, at least, there has never been a known killing anywhere near the west coast…"

She breathed out a sigh of relief for him.

"And you have to figure if that's what the Youhaul killer really wanted, to come after us because of Dad—something political maybe—he would've gone for it by now. Nothing prevents him from doing anything. The speculation is that this guy is taken care of by world governments. There'd be no way they couldn't have picked up on some evidence by now otherwise."

"How can that be? Still, no evidence?"

"Well. Other than remains of the victims, some of them being the renters of the trucks themselves, nothing."

"So insane."

"Dad still seems to think that it is the same man behind the killings, you know the one, Voldemort, the one we agreed never to say the name of anymore, but I'm not so sure."

"My dad hasn't changed his mind about that either. But why don't you believe it?"

"The motivation doesn't make any sense anymore. There are countless times he should've killed, but he didn't. Enemies all over. Men. He doesn't seem to care about them so much. Also, random women, he kills. It's more complicated than the political. These may have just been events of opportunity or to throw off his true motivations…no…the killer's motivations aren't really known."

"I think we know he's a freak. Whatever else he wants, he has a thing for hurting women."

"Yeah, but he'll hurt men too, if they get in the way," Roger said while examining the apparent grainy security camera still of the killer walking away from one of the move-in trucks. The dark shadow could be seen more as a specter than as a man with its lack of definition. The only distinctive feature seemed to be a slight protruding brim of a ball cap.

He continued, "There've been multiple incidents where—"

A few seconds go by, nothing. "Where what?"

"Fuck—the internet's out." Roger tried disconnecting and reconnecting, but it wasn't working this time. The page kept saying that it couldn't be reached like one of the most bullshit of answering services. Usually when there were down times, he just made use of the 4G on his phone, but he didn't feel much like using the hotspot now he was still on the call with Daniela.

"Fuck it," he resigned himself to going without.

"Hey, watch your fucking mouth."

"Fucking make me, Fuck!"

"I'm going to and you'll be sorry that you ever got upset over something as stupid as InstaGrat."

"FYI," he said with playful attitude, "I was doing important research unlike you spending your whole life on social media."

"Research, my ass. There's nothing to find out online. Unknown. Unknown. Universe unknown. Hey, you think the killer is an actual alien? Like something from the movie, They Live?"

It hit Roger right then. Coincidences lining up. He got up from his chair to see something out the window that had nearly stopped his heart. The move-in truck was now parked on the curb right in front of their house.

Fear enveloped him. He could barely move as his spine felt anchored into place, but he managed with his lips.

"Daniela," he whispered harshly. She could see the instant change in his demeanor, "I think he's here."

"Who's there?"

"*The killer.*"

"Don't even play!"

"The truck moved. The truck *moved*," He explained with exasperation. Now she understood and her own face turned pale.

"My Gah—" She cut herself off covering her mouth.

Roger ambled over to the door as if someone had skewered him as a kebab. He listened intently for any sounds coming from downstairs.

She waited with him, taking his cue right away. Her neck crawled so much with fear that it felt as if a hand were brushing it at the nape. She could only imagine what Roger must be feeling.

"Go. Call the police. Wake everyone," she finally said with some restraint, her reason coming back to her.

He hesitated. The prospect of raising the alarm in panic when he wasn't absolutely sure, also held him back. No matter what he felt, it still seemed much more likely for the truck to be as mundane as geese swimming in the pond. And besides whatever the reality was, he wanted what was safe to be true. *Dammit, it had to be.*

"I'm hanging up. Call the police and call me back."

"Wait." He wedged his fingers in the crack of his door inching it open further and further with enough prowess as not to hear the whine of its hinges. A triangle of darkness penetrated into his room as if it were calling out to him. He stepped into it.

Coming to the rail at the edge of the landing, he peered down toward the vestibule half expecting some dark outline to be waiting for him. There wasn't any. All was quiet. He hoped for an ambient sound—any reprieve to disrupt the stillness, but he kept on waiting. Daniela too waited, seeing only darkness but listening keenly.

Roger crept slowly downstairs. He saw that the front of the house appeared secured. Seeing the truck in the same place outside the window, nothing had changed. He made his way to the back. Walking midway across the den, he suddenly stopped. Were his ears playing tricks on him? What was it?

A dull thumping a few times like batting out the dust from a car mat could be heard down the hall where his grandparents slept. In seeing the front of the house, his heartbeat had a little rest, but now it had ratcheted up to firing on all cylinders—thumping into his ears. His mouth was dry. He was at a loss of what to do. Were his grandparents up?

Their door opened. Roger hid behind the dividing wall to the living room, trying to control his breathing. Two figures came out one at a time. They weren't Nana and Opa. One had a slender arm extended by the long glint of a machete. The other with the cap casually carrying an automatic like it was a hand fan. It was almost too much for Roger. His fear was getting the best of him as torpor infected his limbs.

Seeing them coming, he knew he had to act but couldn't. *Move, goddammit!* He thought of himself as pulp just like those women. His family, nothing but pulp. They'd all soon become that foul smelling goop pouring from the back of the truck into the street if he didn't act right now. He squeezed both his thighs as if to push their on switch. It must've done something as he suddenly propelled his legs for the stairs. Avoiding line of sight the best he could, he spryly high stepped up them.

Swift by any measure, he still imagined they heard the pressure from his footfalls and were right at his back. He ran into his parents' bedroom. "Someone's in the house!" He made a shrill whisper across the room.

"What? what is it?" came from his dad who seemed awake and alert. Roger repeated it again before saying,

"Downstairs. They're here." His dad leapt up.

"No," his mom expelled almost breathlessly. Peter peered down the hall from behind the door.

"Roger, call the police," Daniela urged from the phone. "I'll do the same," she said before hanging up.

This signaled to his mom to reach for her device on the nightstand.

Roger knew there wasn't enough time. He flew from the room, but instead of running to the office with his dad, he entered Isabel's nursery.

He saw his baby sister sleeping under her blanket undisturbed, as if the very world itself were innocent. Taking her up into his arms as steadily as he could, he wrapped the blanket around her. He could hear her rouse a little with a half-hearted drowsy whine before drifting off again.

Crossing the hall into his room, he locked his door then entered his bathroom, locking it as well. He held Isabel to his chest, mindful of the pressure he was exerting, but still not as gentle as he should. His entire body was charged with fear.

There was yelling followed by the blare of gunshots causing him to blench.

Peter felt the warm torrent of blood leave his body as he slumped in the corner of the landing. He could barely grip his gun anymore, but he knew he had to hold on. He had to see his family to safety.

"You come here, you're dead! Police are on the way!"

He was confident he shot at least one of them, but one had also plugged him good in the rib cage.

"Cash, jewelry," one said in a thick Caribbean accent.

"You want money? Of course. Of course." Peter didn't know about the genuineness of their request, but he did know that the more he could stall them, the better chance they would all have to survive. *Margery had called the police. The neighbors hearing the shots were probably doing the same.* "If you let me, I can get you cash. I'll have my son open the safe and throw it over the railing, but you're going to have to—" A fury of rounds split through dry wall into Peter. He found himself making a sound that he shouldn't be.

The men came up the stairs. The man gripping the machete was also holding the top of his right shoulder, blood covering his hand.

"He's done," he said needlessly.

Jacques used his foot to pull Peter's hand out of the trigger guard of his gun while the other continued up.

Jacques was soon at the ready covering his companion's creep down the hall as if at any instant another member of the family would open fire. He knew he'd dispense the threat without batting an eye, but he also knew that was something best avoided. Otherwise, what were they doing there going through this trouble in the first place? Orders are orders and he didn't like good meat going to waste. Still, if the threat were a melee, and he held out hope there'd soon be one coming from the son. He knew the man holding the bloody machete could carve better in combat than a butcher on a carcass in an abattoir.

With bloodshot eyes bugging with adrenaline, warmth of the blood from his machete dripping over his hand as if empowered by enchantment, he passed doors one by one head cocked for sound. He briefly paused in front of Roger's door before thinking better of it. To the left he could see the door open to a crib. No movement. Too exposed. He continued with Jacques still covering behind, moving as a unit. The man finally stopped when he reached the end of the hall before the master bedroom.

When he looked up to Jacques, he was given the nod. One fluid movement was all it took. He kicked through the door, cracking both frame and door like a wafer. Margery trembled from the shock still holding the phone to her ear at the bedside in her nightgown.

"Phone fucking down, Jamette!" he said.

Terrified, she slowly lowered it with tears of defeat, someone still chirping at her on the line.

The machete was now held up even with her eyes as if daring her to resist.

"I'll give ya one chance beech. Thasset."

With his left hand he removed the steel cuffs from his pocket throwing them onto the bed. "Put these."

She moved her head ever so slightly as if to refuse but he interrupted her with his next words.

"Put these or kids die!" the voice menaced the poor woman into cooperating. He waited for her to snap the cuffs into place before reaching the chain and yanking her toward him. He threw her on the bed and snapped them tighter to the wrist as she whimpered like a helpless animal caught in a snare.

Jacques came in the room giving it a once over before taking control of Margery's body gripping down on the back of her neck propelling her out. He got her really moving after cursing and squeezing harder as her legs didn't want to give way. Soon she was crying so deeply, she barely made a noise as she was forced past her husband's riddled body.

The man with the machete lingered momentarily going back over to the nursery. He eyed inside the crib with bitter anger at what he found or didn't. With his cords of muscles rubberbanding back and forth he chopped at the cheap wood slicing off the railing and sending splinters flying everywhere. He growled in the destruction as if it were the very thing standing in the way of true satisfaction.

"Padna! Fuck out now!" Jacques yelled out from below.

He left but not without first giving Roger's door a thunderous kick as if to rattle those inside.

The baby had already been crying from the ongoing clamor but Roger did his best to distract and quiet her. He swung her in his arms as he whispered soothing words. The bang from the kick, however, sent her into a renewed fit. He sat her down. "Beli look." He showed her the disembodied thumb trick—concealing the end with his pointer. She looked on in fascination trying to grab at his fingers. It never ceased to do the trick.

He had an idea what was happening just outside the door, but couldn't know for sure and that doubt gave him some comfort. It was his duty to stay put to protect Beli. That's what Mom and Dad would want of him.

After the kick, there followed a lull. Was it time to check outside his door or was it all a trap? His brain blocked out his worst imaginings. It was all he could do to keep momentary sanity. *Dammit, where were the police when you needed them?* Indecision racked his brain as he paced.

It was only overhearing murmurs of a struggle from the front yard that finally shot him into action. Unlatching the window in his bedroom he saw what it was down below. His mom was now their prisoner.

She worked valiantly against one of the men as Jacques pushed her toward the truck. They had wrapped her mouth with some type of gag, but it wasn't enough to fully stifle her protests, and the cuffs did nothing to subdue her legs resulting in the man's gushing of expletives at their lack of progress.

There was not even a thought. There was no way he was letting them take his mom. No universe. Leaving Belli tucked in the corner of his room, Roger grabbed the first potential weapon he could think of from his bedside—a long native American fashioned jacaranda flute his parents bought him one summer visiting the Black Hills.

He hung his legs over the edge of the windowsill pushing himself off into the bush below scraping arms and legs alike but emerging unflagging, burning with all the anger a son could muster for his mother.

Jacques was already drawing up the truck's rear door with hand still grasping Margery's neck. Before Roger could pursue, the man with machete drenched in blood confronted him, huffing with rage at the sheer audacity of the child. He swung obliquely grunting hatred, as Roger evaded him circling around the lean murderous muscle.

At this point neighbors had come to see the madness from the safety of their own porches uselessly hollering at the spectacle making some allusions to police. It was then that Jacques had shoved Margery into the truck and despite her kicking, propelled her into the hold. He then jumped in himself, securing her by the waist before she could stand herself up. She was exhausted.

Roger kept evading the blade the best he could with no game plan. Whether it was the attention they were drawing from the neighbors or having caught a glimpse of his partner's success, the man with the machete gave up his pursuit withdrawing back to the truck. He took Jacques' cue from the back running immediately to the cabin.

Roger's heart dropped when he heard the engine fire up. "*No!*" he said to himself. His legs carried him faster than he ever thought capable of as Jacques took a couple of shots at him from the cargo hold as his mom screamed. While Roger envisaged bullets ripping through his body, he felt nothing, pursuing unharmed, unwavering. The door to the cargo hold was pulled shut by the draw chord closing off view of his mom and sinking his hopes that he'd ever see her again.

"Fuuuuck!" he yelled pulsing with blood. He jumped onto the passenger step and ripped open the cabin door. To his surprise, it was unlocked, but nowhere near as surprised as a former hunter becoming prey.

Roger seized upon the initiative—going to work on the man's skull with the jacaranda. While using one hand to drive, the man used the other to block some of the blows. Whump. Whump. Whump. Three landed squarely one after another on the dense rock of a head.

Roger felt hope. He felt he was tenderizing the goliath as the man's attention was divided between him and the road. He was looking more sluggish. Maybe he was seizing up from the impact of the jacaranda. Roger intended on finishing the job and not stopping until the man was completely immobile, *dead*, *pulp*. That's what he wished to make of him. Only then could he figure out what to do about his mom being held hostage in the carriage. *Yes, it would all work out somehow. It just had to.*

The thought had barely formed in his head when the man caught the flute suddenly, almost effortlessly, tugging it away in one sudden movement, as if he'd been toying with Roger the whole time.

It was then his turn to beat Roger, and he did so mercilessly. Again and again, Roger heard the hollow clock of the wood bounce off his head, with every hit, blood pattering from the man's arm onto his face, and unlike the man, it only took a few for Roger to be stunned into helplessness. He lay there across the seat in a haze, barely conscious, before the next blow came, finally turning the lights out.

4

On the sofa of the living room sat Jenelle and Daniela holding each other, red faced with spent tears. Giselle looked on with empty dreariness from a barstool near the kitchen. Clint stood in his robe seeing all but not fully processing.

When Daniela woke everyone to tell them what was happening, Clint felt it was one of those recurring nightmares he kept having. Nothing was really happening to his best friend and his family. Nothing was proven fact.

His wife did well to find the number to the police station in Tacoma and make the call. When they received one back from a detective, they held their breath for the worst. This was no mere nightmare. They learned of a struggle including the deaths of an elderly couple and a man fitting Peter's description.

The new revelation firmly knocked the wind out of Clint. He felt dizzy, faint. He remembered just seeing his friend on video call. He hadn't looked so well in some time. He was ready to do his duty for all the world to see. It was their time, and nothing was supposed to ever take that away from them. After giving years of service to the cause of science, it couldn't just all be for naught.

He found his legs falling before him as he slowly floated into his office. There was enough light to see that photo of his dad— looking at him, through him, even now, across time. This is when Clint did what he had never done before. He fell to his knees putting his arms up before him on his recliner instinctually.

What came next though, he didn't know. What was he even doing? He didn't believe in anything. With eyes closed and hands folded together he breathed in and out, in and out. He felt utterly alone.

5

They stood in the driveway of the white suburban home that had been bombarded with police vehicles including the mobile CSI unit's van whose crew was still inside.

Detective Gonzalez and Brennan waited for the FBI special agent to arrive. Tomlinson had been the lead investigator of the Youhaul Killings for over six months and had included both detectives on the task force authorizing them to travel with him across jurisdictions to scenes where the killers had appeared to have left their dregs. This time, however, no one seemed to have held any doubts.

It had been quite a ride already, but over their time together, both city detectives grew weary of Tomlinson who only appeared to be dragging his feet on the investigation. Even now, his running late told of a lack of professionalism if not downright apathy. A look of biting agitation now managed to permeate both detectives practiced faces of neutrality.

For Gonzalez, of course, it was much more than that. There was a keen emptiness as well that could have been mistaken for a hellish hangover from the night prior, but his partner knew better as did others in the department. It was the loss of a friend and being party to a fruitless investigation that may have prevented it. He clenched his jaw looking at the house of horrors before them while Brennan sipped a steaming Styrofoam cup of coffee.

Watching many uniforms come and go from the house, "*there*," Brennan said finally seeing a white Kia sedan pull up curbside without entering the cordoned off area. He had called it right, Tomlinson soon exited the rental taking his coat from around the seat and pushing his arms through each sleeve. With his big dark eyebrows and large nose, one could see why someone might've chosen him for the job, even putting him at the head of such an important investigation. It could have been a look of determination, diligence, or conviction, but he knew better. He knew by now that it was all a front. He was an FBI man, and it was all about looking the part.

"Officers!" he called out to Gonzalez and Brennan, "we're running behind." They rendezvoused with him to the front of the house. Showing his badge to the managing officer outside, they met another local investigator waiting for them just below the open window from where witnesses say someone had leapt twelve hours earlier.

They shook hands somberly introducing each other. "Let's see where we stand," Tomlinson summarized staying true to form of getting in and out of the scene as fast as possible. After each utilized the protective plastic shoe covers, Tomlinson asked the investigator to lead the way.

Inside the house, Gonzalez's breath seemed short. He felt life sucking dread whenever stepping into a new grisly scene.

The detective gave a provisional narrative walking from room to room commenting on blood spatter and rounds that had entered walls, as they took notes. The bodies had since been removed, but photos were referenced whenever Tomlinson wanted a look. Gonzalez forced himself too—seeing the lifeless twisted up corpse of Peter, like a thrown-out marionette, lying on the staircase. He was glad that no one seemed to notice his face. He turned to clear the accumulated tears at the corners of his eyes.

They started at the back room where the first murders had occurred, both of Peter's in-laws had been stabbed and chopped up with a long blade. The killers had taken the couple by surprise as both died in bed even taking the additional step of decapitating the grandma well after the coup de gras. Their bed was now soaked through with brown as if someone had splashed a brimming bucket of caramel drizzle over the bedclothes and surrounding carpet.

The local detective continued a general narrative as they observed the broken door frame at the back of the house. "After cutting the security and phone lines, they pried open the back, as you can see, even leaving the crowbar here," he indicated a marker placed on the floor. "That's when they proceeded to take care of the Weisses. Those upstairs, must have heard a scream prompting a call to 911 and Mr. Barton's exchange of gunfire with one of the assailants."

They drifted upstairs hovering around the landing observing with little commentary. The demarcated outline of Peter's body with his weapon and casings were surrounded with many splotches of dried blood appearing as if they were preplanned Rorschach images that shrinks tend to show patients. Along with the various neon stickers indicating the different entry and exit holes of gunshots, one could almost mistake the whole display as a tucked away exhibit in some contemporary museum of art.

Gonzalez's guts had enough of the avant-garde. He ascended the rest of the way up the stairs while they lingered. After momentarily peering into Roger's room and the master, finding them unremarkable except for the open window, he stepped over debris taking a closer look at the decimated crib. Wooden shards and clippings feathered the floor in the astounding aftermath of nursery become rage room. He stood there pondering the sheer barbarity of it all before the detectives entered the room themselves aghast at the mindless destruction. Nearby, lay a Kermit-the-Frog doll covered in a layer of white splinters and shards as if it were a Muppet Christmas special.

"Thank God, the baby was saved, at least. They had the foresight to hide her across the hall," the Tacoma investigator tried couching the scene in a positive light—failing to make it look any more inviting.

Gonzalez stared at the man as if he looked for him to continue. When he didn't, he asked his first question since the beginning of their walkthrough.

"And what about the mother and son? Any leads?"

His face already told him the answer, but he still waited.

"The truck with the mother and son had been abandoned just outside of Spanaway. Too much heat for them to continue on in it…"

"Ya'*think?*" Gonzalez's voice now spiked with emotion. The detective eyed him to try to better deduce his meaning, as Brennan recognized in his partner that dark side that peaked out on occasion. You mean to tell me they can't find a mother and her son? Her husband having to engage in a firefight? Neighbors watching a full feature film, and poof, they just disappear!?" Anger, frustration, and something else, a hint of a sob, one of despair could be made out from the veteran detective. *Was this what law enforcement has become? Is anyone even capable of a job anymore? Were they all so lazy, stupid, corrupt?*

Brennan patted his partner on the arm as Tomlinson and the Tacoma detective focused on the debris to avoid the gnawing discomfort from the outburst.

They completed their tour and reconvened outside. Little was spoken except in whispers between Tomlinson and the local detective to keep Gonzalez out of it. When they removed their plastic shoe covers, the detective finally looked at Gonzalez straight.

"Looks bad doesn't it? They're here to kill…I imagine just like in Arlington…How long's it been now since it started?" Gonzalez only stared at him wide eyed. "Anyway, I hope we have better luck than you did." The deliberate slight after taking offense was there, and Gonzalez didn't have a response. He didn't care to. He knew he had failed far too many times and wasn't leaving himself off the hook.

"Over here detective," Tomlinson signaled to Gonzalez to a part of the yard that was devoid of evidence markers. Preparing himself for the federal scolding he knew he had coming, he took a breath and followed.

First, verifying they were nearly alone, Tomlinson let it out while trying to maintain his inner voice. "And what the fuck was that?!"

Gonzalez looked at him and said nothing.

"You made me look like a total asshole for bringing you! A total asshole!"

Tomlinson studied Gonzalez's face intensely trying to find anything to latch onto, but he couldn't. All he could do was blather some curses under his breath before ending with a sigh.

He continued more measured, "Look, I heard Peter was kind of a friend of yours. I understand that. I've had friends killed in the line of duty, so I thought I'd be doing you a favor in bringing you here…but I shouldn't have done that. I see that now."

"It's not just Peter. There's—" He thought of Kristi. But he didn't mention her. He could still see the distress in her blue eyes when she first came to him. She deserved better. He could've done better. "There's a lot I've lost over this case." The voice sounded almost pleading.

"And that's okay, you've done your time, detective. You've had a lot of great insights…But, as with all things—things go on. We're going to have to carry on without you."

"But, I can see that—"

"You *can*, right? After what just happened, we must do what's in the best interest of the case, of the team. It's also for your own health. You gotta look out for that."

"Who's replacing me?"

Tomlinson let Gonzalez see his eyes glide over to the local detective, indicating who without saying.

Gonzalez noticed the other officers talking on the far side of the property. He saw Brennan scanning over different areas of the yard with the local lead. The cool wind gusted through the branches of bare trees. He waited for it to finish, understanding the decision was going to be final, but he didn't want to fully lay down—not just yet.

"Ok, I got you. I see where you're coming from. I just wonder if there's something I could wrap up for you before I go."

Tomlinson waited as if he could be gracious after all.

"Let me close out the other side of the investigation."

Looking confused for a moment, his face slowly turned to sheer annoyance.

"No, no, can't… *Wait*. What other side?" Tomlinson stopped himself mid-sentence.

"Give me access to all of Eggers' files—"

"No, fuck no, conspiracy shit again—"

"What would it hurt to have another pair of eyes?"

"No!" Tomlinson started turning his back.

"How can you overlook Ray Foundation when all the victims seem to be connected? It seems unthinkable not to at least consider it."

"People online see all kinds of shit. They use numerology in Time Magazine to pick out names of their future sons."

"The dossier, the recordings following Eldridge's disappearance. These can't all be coincidence."

"Eldridge is an unrelated investigation," Tomlinson said as if it dismissed everything said before it.

Gonzalez stood there trying to get a read on Tomlinson. He had held something back for months just to try to get him to reconsider the possibility, but nothing had worked. Now that it was just the two of them, he noticed something new. It was in Tomlinson's face, even if it were the slightest hint of it. It was glaringly human in the chink of his continuous facade. As he was now walking away, there was some shame there.

It was time. It was now or never. "You're never going to consider the possibility because you can't. You simply can't. Can you?"

He waited for Tomlinson to respond but instead the G-man just stopped.

"Someone told you to lay off, right? The FBI has certain untouchables and he's one of them, isn't he?"

At this point, Tomlinson turned about like a drill sergeant staring a recruit straight into the face—locking onto Gonzalez's eyes with his own. "There's something…something your *beaner* brain needs to understand…"

Gonzalez was so thrown off by the racist comment that he felt he'd been struck.

"And that's when to Shut. The. Fuck. Up. Do you understand? The fuck right up. Do it now or *never* again. *Understand?* Clear out!"

When he turned back to the house leaving Gonzalez behind, he could barely make out what Tomlinson said next. It was to himself under his breath. He must've registered that he went too far and now wanted somehow to justify it. "Can't you see I'm trying to help you for fucksake," he trailed off in the breeze.

6

He crashed, awaking into space as a bold indictment to unreality. His eyes were blurry, mind muddled, head aching, but he had finally landed at his destination, and the more he saw there, the more he wanted to curl up in his bed's comforter like he did at age five, as if it would make the scary world outside suddenly disappear.

A vast speleothem filled cavern with fire torches lining the walls sprawled everywhere around him. His mother stood tied to a thick stalagmite drooping forward in the ropes, but still breathing, likely passed out from their long dope filled journey. Likewise, his own arms and legs were bound to a stony fixture of his own.

It took almost no time to come to grips with what had transpired in his last moments of consciousness. Now he felt a distinct empty torment of the guts and a bitter metallic taste in the mouth. *What was this? Was this dread?*

How was this really happening that he and his mother were soon to be turned into melting corpses at the bottom of some cheap rental? And more importantly, what would happen well before they added whatever ungodly agent to their lifeless bodies? Anyone with a mind had some idea. He was old enough.

Faced with the terrifying prospect of any sudden appearance from that distant recesses outside the torchlight, Roger went right to work. With the hope that the resonant hiss of the torches would conceal the sound of his movement, he wriggled, this way and that, pulling at his restraints, testing for any sign of give. They wouldn't budge. He tried repeatedly, but the effort seemed fruitless. His arms soon became burnt raw from the nylon and his body full of sweat. The brine from his forehead started eating into his eyes.

He stared at his mother catching his breath. It was hard to wrap his mind around all that she'd been to him. Her hair draped down covering some of the stony face he had come to know from the depths of his earliest childhood memories. Later he saw that same brow, eyes, and nose in the painting Bouguereau's Priestess of Bacchus, with that same youthful energy. How could it be that this slim woman carried him nine months, granted him life, raised and loved him, with those same caring arms, holding him, feeding him, embracing him on birthdays, comforting him as a child when he was afraid? And now deciding to do it all over again with his sister. It was incomprehensible how one could deprive the world of such a one—a continuous giver of gifts, a locus of human existence.

As she hung there helpless on a stone stake, he thought of how the cycle of life had come full circle. She cared for him over the years, seeing to his every need as a helpless infant, but here he was now, infant, no longer. He had to find a way with every string of muscle and teaspoon of marrow, to protect her.

With his breath even again, he was prepared to throw himself back into the effort. This was it. All or nothing. He'd have to watch his mom tortured and killed, or he'd at least go down fighting for her. If someone got close enough with one free hand, he'd take the man's eye. If not, he might even be able to propel his neck forward enough to crash his forehead into a face.

Commencing again his strange dance out of his ropes, he suddenly stopped himself better regarding the stalagmite his mother was tied to. He noticed how its jetting up from the floor looked more rickety than solid. It wasn't even standing straight up but arced and twisted more like a scoliotic spine than a spike—nothing like the marble pillar of a temple. If anything, it seemed thinner, more brittle, and he gathered that being in the same vicinity, the one he was tied to was roughly the same. He'd been going about it the wrong way.

He now rocked his body back and forth utilizing all the physiognomy he could, the muscle groups of his back, his stomach, hips, and even bending his neck forward before jerking backward. He tried not to injure his head too much against the rock, and after suffering from some miscalculation, managed to maintain a steady rhythm.

For what seemed a dauntingly long time of pressuring his body against the stalagmite, not sure it would do anything but waste time—time that could be better spent trying to come free of the rope, there was hope. He thought he'd felt the slightest give and that drove him on to greater efforts. It was his will against the stubbornness of the sedimentary, and he pictured he was winning the fight. He would make it bow. In an instant, he heard the crack at its base that sent him falling backwards. His stomach felt it reached into his diaphragm before hitting the floor. The rock fractured into multiple partitions.

With the back of his head battered, he still felt high, adrenaline had kicked in. The ropes were now slack at his sides where he quickly and easily slid them off. Cognizant of the echo the crash had made through the cavern alerting anyone nearby, he knew he had to act as flawlessly as possible. Every second counted.

He went right to his mother's bindings. She stirred as he tried untying them, but the knots were too tight. Technique number two it had to be. He put his arms around her tightly. She murmured something indistinct. "It's alright. I got you mom." This time, mostly using his weight and strength of his upper body, the base came free after a few shakes.

Setting his mother down, he pulled off her rope and saw that her eyes were now open searching their surroundings with confusion.

"Mom, we have to go," he whispered. It didn't seem to register. "*Mom*," he waited for her eyes to focus fully on his. When they did, his face made plain the urgency. "Time to go." Her look showed understanding, assent. "Can you stand?" he asked helping her to her feet. She stood feebly as he now wild-eyed scanned their surroundings listening with the intensity of in-season game.

He heard sounds of movement reverberating off the walls from the far side of the cavern.

First picking up the pointy fragment of the stalagmite, he guided her with his hands scurrying off the path of torches into the dark recess of the other half of the chamber.

The sounds kept coming closer, and he knew it was decision time. If whoever it was, were to find them missing, who knew how many he'd alert to hunt them down? If he could prevent that at all from happening, now was the time to act. He squeezed his mom's shoulders as if to tell her to stay put—zipping crouched along the floor to reach the next large stalagmite and then the next.

When he looked back, he noticed his mom was following his lead with the same motions albeit more slowly. He tried motioning to her with his palm to stay put, but it didn't have any effect. She ran from one cover to the next trying to catch up to him. Given the darkness impairing any kind of visual communication, Roger gave up. The sound was too close. It was time to focus on the threat directly at hand.

Paralleling the torch lit path staying in the shadows, they were like mice making their way from one source of cover to the next until a shadow appeared out of the darkness. Its features came into focus—that same ugly gaunt face and sunken apathetic eyes he saw in the truck's cab, a fresh bandage now wrapped the wound on his arm.

Hatred burned in Roger's chest as he watched the former machete wielder that had put his lights out in the truck idling down the path lazily. This time, however, the machete wasn't with him. A gun was holstered at his side, as Roger now supposed that his role had shifted from butcher to sentinel.

Roger waited behind a wide stalagmite as he passed. As soon as he did, he crept toward the path. He stalked closer to the man, coming from behind, stalking him just as he supposed he and the other goons did to countless women. How much pain, how much carnage came from this one cracked out islander? Too many. Roger planned on ending it.

When he glanced back, he saw that his mom knew of his intention. He thought he could just make out the flailing of her arms as if to wave him off, but it didn't matter. This man had to be stopped.

Gripping the stalagmite tightly, gritting his teeth, he jolted, as lightly on his feet as he could, down the path to the man's back. And just as he turned, Roger drove true—plunging the makeshift dagger into his solar plexus. There was a rotting exhalation of air leaving the man's lungs as Roger forced it up behind his rib cage. The man's hand had dropped to his gun but nothing more. Hot blood shot from his chest over Roger's hands.

When his victim started making guttural noises, Roger pulled out the makeshift knife and tried to strike the neck, grazing repeatedly off muscle before the point found its target in the membrane just below the Adam's Apple.

Red zonked out eyes, doubtlessly influenced by some depressant, stared up at him in disbelief as Roger forcibly pulled away the man's weakened hand from his gun.

His mom came out onto the path seeing the stream of tears from her son's eyes trying to comfort him. "I'm okay," he said shaking her off as he was trying to remove the gun from its holster. It took some effort to finally get it out, discovering the snap on the slide cover plate.

He examined it carefully, getting a sense for its weight in his hand. There was a time when he shot his dad's handgun with his mom at a range under supervision, but it had been so long ago that it was as if he were feeling a real gun for the very first time. "Here," his mom held out her palm asking for it. He cautiously handed her the piece.

She pushed the magazine release. It slid out from the handle with smooth metallic friction. "It's full," Roger whispered. "Yes," she agreed. She pointed to the safety. "To fire, push, point, aim, and then pull the trigger, but don't put your finger here," she said indicating the guard, "not before you have the target." He nodded, as she searched his face for understanding. "For now, I'll use it, but just in case." He shuddered at what lay ahead.

They followed along the path in the dark, mom leading the way with gun at the ready. At any moment, he expected someone to emerge from the shadows, grabbing them.

The cave was high, deep, labyrinthine, and if it weren't for the line of torches lighting the way, escape would prove impossible. *It seemed more than an inconvenience to bring them all this way. Why even go through the trouble? There certainly had to be better options to execute people.* So many questions were cycling through his head but no answers. They lingered there as they passed through foul smelling chambers with spent torches and fragments of stained rope without comment. Coming across any new scene that suggested some foul practice only quickened their pace.

Climbing through another wide passage, they found themselves in the precarious situation of having to navigate through a narrow recess. His mom hesitated looking back to Roger as if to say there was no other choice. She held the gun out before her as she maneuvered through the jagged limestone. With their breath held through some of the blind bends, they were soon rewarded. It was a smaller cavern, but fresh air blew on their faces as the fire of the torches billowed through an opening in the rock.

They heard the flushing of an agitated sea, a breeze relieving their nostrils of the lingering stench of the cave as they found themselves at the precipice of a cliff.

"Where the fuck are we?" his mom asked as she studied the coastline.

The line of torches discontinued. A dark desolate rocky shore curved to the left on the side of the promontory where they now stood. A faint light shined from a large structure above the cliffs.

Where would they go? Knowing swimming these waters was far too treacherous, they found a small indentation in the rock that seemed to start scaling the cliffs. It was subtle, but Roger noticed a well-defined step a few yards away. Before that was a barely passable incline. A fifty-foot drop into the jagged rocks below for anyone who didn't make it. There had to be another way—a better way. *How did they get their incapacitated bodies into the caves in the first place?*

They weighed their options, They decided taking their chances falling into the rocks and surf below was a much better prospect than to ever be recaptured for whatever murder ritual awaited them back in the cave.

Before making the initial leap past the quagmire, his mom grabbed Roger and took a moment to hug her son. He felt her body quiver and realized she was weeping as he held her back. She sniffled as Roger stood a little confused why she chose to let it out at that moment. "Be careful," she concluded with a final squeeze.

The grueling walk up the trail led them onto what appeared to be an enormous colonial estate. The massive three-story house may have been occupied by a Vanderbilt or Rothschild given its level of grandeur. It also might as well have been a museum standing with its mostly dark vacant rooms. Yet an incessant flood light exposed the immediate vicinity including three vehicles parked in its roundabout driveway. The property was wide open yet starkly unwelcoming. A wall topped with barbed wire surrounded its significant acreage. A guard house stood in the distance before what appeared to be the entrance gate. The light was on. They could be hunted any moment.

Roger and his mom stayed in the shadows moving immediately away from the trailhead along the cliff's edge. They were exhausted and thirsty from the climb, wanting to stop for a breather, but pushing on with the looming threat of being seen.

They made their way on the outskirts to what appeared to be a guest house—the only cover just out of range of the floodlight. They tiptoed onto the porch that faced the oceanside. His mom was at the ready. The pistol's muzzle she pointed at the door.

Roger tried to look through the windows for any sign of occupancy. There was nothing—no light, but the drapes had also been drawn. They were taking a big risk being there, but what other choice did they have? They were desperate. With their bodies aching and spent, they sat on either side of the door to rest. It had already been a grueling strain—not only the killing, the hike, but the persistent fear that at any moment, they could be taken, bound, tormented for as long as it took to satiate some sick fuck.

Now with the breeze and the waves as the only sounds, the spot gave them a much-needed reprieve. If not for the knowledge of the absolute horror inflicted on those having doubtlessly screamed their lungs out in the caves below, it could be considered an ideal, peaceful getaway. It was for someone.

"Look," Roger whispered quietly, tapping his mom on the shoulder and pointing to the other side of the property. A substantial dock extended into a small harbor with several vessels tied up there. "There has to be a way down."

"I know. I see," his mom breathed, already trying to discern any details she could glean at that distance in the limited moonlight.

Roger waited for further commentary. He could hear her rapid huffs as he scanned the area with her. At any moment, he felt her breathing would slow, stabilize now that they had rested a while. It didn't.

"There has to be…", she said between pants, "a smaller launch we could get into…something easy to untie and get going."

"Where do we go?"

"Away, far away."

Roger didn't mean the long-term plan, but only once in the boat. He didn't bother to clarify. There were a lot of ifs in between.

"When?" he asked after another pause.

"Give me a few more minutes." Roger heard the continued hyperventilation now realizing she was terrified. She was already working herself up for their next move.

The moment didn't improve. Beams of light shined over the guest house causing Roger's heart to sputter and his mom to raise the gun back up at the ready position. As the light beams brightened, Roger snuck to the end of the porch from the side of the house where the light was coming. Before reaching the corner, he dropped down in the prone position—crawling to get a better look, as he heard his mom angrily air her disapproval.

When the lights shifted direction, he poked his head out to see the SUVs entering through the gate and up the long drive. To his great relief, they were turning, heading for the main house. He dropped back to where his mom sat, beginning to tell her what was happening, but as they heard car doors slamming in the distance, his mom was now the one to pop her head on the other side. He crouched behind.

"What are they doing?" he whispered after no report.

"People going into the house. Some discussion."

"And?" he asked impatiently.

She suddenly dropped back with a gasp running into Roger. "What?"

"Two are walking away from the house."

"What? What are they doing?"

She looked back to the marina and then began investigating the house, checking the windows. "Check there if there is a way in."

Roger didn't mention the fact that it still wasn't verified no one was home. He tried lifting the other window, but it wouldn't budge. Then he walked over to the door and turned the handle. It opened. Of course, on a property with security detail, why not?

They crept into the dark living room and deadbolted the door. The only light within appeared under a painting in the center.

Ducking behind the sofa with his mom, Roger waited for shouting or someone trying the door—preparing himself for the shock, he bided his time fixating on the unusual painting. It took no time at all to decide there was nothing of beauty in it. It may have been what they call, expressionist, but it was also disturbing to say the least. In the foreground, an androgenous figure laughing with undue mirth was leaping in some remote mountain range. A thin waterfall, the only aesthetically pleasing part of the piece, ran down a taller distant mountain into unseen crevices below. Not mentioning the fae-like theme, that wasn't to his taste, neither did he like the fact that the person was completely and unnecessarily nude and with neither male nor female sex organs. The painting screamed that it was trying to be something that it wasn't, and he'd say good was one of those things. It wasn't a far stretch to see that this place was owned by whoever wanted them there, and he was one cracked up bastard. Maybe his purposes were multiple for taking them, but now, seeing this, it didn't seem as personal as he once thought. He took pleasure in this shit.

The more he analyzed it, the worse the painting got, as seconds felt more like minutes. It had been too long for nothing to happen. If they knew they were there, they would've come by now. He could see his mom's greater distress at the uneventful wait than when they first entered.

"Go see where they are." She indicated with her head at one of the side windows as she held the gun steady on the front door. He peered through it unable to see anything. He proceeded to the bedrooms to try the different views, glad that their original assumption that the house was empty was now a certainty.

He finally found a view. No one was in front of the mansion anymore. Instead, two lines of flashlight led a pair of shadowy figures to the shoreline. One had a massive duffle bag that required some effort to lug along. *Gifts.* He imagined what kind of horrors it contained. It would take a little while, he decided, for them to reach the caves. That's where they expected their associate to be—where they expected *them* to be—at their complete disposal.

Roger came back into the living room to tell his mom the situation. She breathed out a sigh of relief lowering the gun she had propped on the back of the sofa. She stood there turning inward, considering their next move.

"Let's just go—to the boat. You can drive it. I know you can." She had to know he was referring to their time spent on the lake with her friend's family in Sheboygan, but to this, she didn't say anything. From her expression, he could picture that her mind was running through scenarios and not liking any of them. What was her reservation?

"Mom?"

"Okay, okay, we'll try for the dock, even though I don't know if there'll be one that I can drive. We don't even know where we are..."

"It's our best shot. They're coming for us—"

"I *know*," she replied in frustration.

They ran across the groomed grass in the direction of the marina. The wind blew on their faces as the heavenly bodies appeared ready for battle—stacks of clouds in broken folds of orange and reddish hues.

Roger was winded, the muscles in his legs achy as if battered repeatedly by a two-by-four. How long was it to the marina? It felt in that moment they could have been suspended in eternity.

As the slope rounded away from the mansion, with almost no cover, he realized it would take no time for them to be found. *At any moment, they could be overtaken. Then what? A gunfight of one versus ten?* Roger didn't like odds of that scenario very much.

While the different gambits played out in his brain, the dock was now well in view. Its owner had the works. A mega yacht at the end of the pier they'd seen from the guesthouse, a good-sized yawl, a couple sport fishers, but other various smaller craft were also tied at the ready.

With their every step, the sky brightened along with their hope, as they entered the wooden staircase leading down the steep incline. In his excitement, Roger rapidly stomped his way down in rapid succession. He was a little less than halfway before he noticed his mom was well behind. She was now hobbling, trying her best to catch up but each step looked more painful than the last. Roger raced back to help.

He saw what loomed from behind—what they'd been fearing all along. A foreboding convoy of vehicles crested the hill. Two Black SUVs accompanied by three ATV escorts were making short order of their lengthy trek. The hunt for them was now on.

The unwelcome look of surprise on her son's face compelled his mom to witness it for herself. "No," she commented with almost a whimper. With her forehead already furrowed with sweat, she went back to work trying to quicken her pace. "We'll make it!" he yelled to her. No reply was given, as all her concentration went into the painful trudge down.

Finally landing on the same step, he stood beside her as she tried different arm positions to best lean on him. With her hand on his far shoulder, they commenced the stepping with Roger calling out "one, two, one, two" to coordinate their feet in an unwieldy dance of survival.

It was hard going. Roger soon realized he had to slow down the cadence significantly if they didn't want to crash the rest of the way down. They had a few close calls as they stumbled to the next stair but managed to stabilize.

As soon as their feet hit bottom, his mom released him to manage the last twenty or so yards on her own. Roger tried resisting the urge to look back but couldn't help himself. The ATVs were taking circuitous routes to avoid rocks and an incline that was sure to cause rollovers. The others, who he gathered came out of the SUVs, were now running downhill.

There was something else. Out of place, on the hillside in front of the vehicles, was a shape he must've missed on his way down, the shape of a small tree. When he fixed his gaze on it, however, it sent a chill straight through his spine like an electric jolt. It was no tree. A large man lurked there as rigid as the stone cliffs themselves. And what was he doing? It was hard to see. *Was he looking at Roger?*

I see you. There is nowhere to go. Give up, he seemed to say with inscrutable confidence. "Go fuck yourself raw," Roger responded under his breath. Despite his defiance, he felt the uneasiness creep in. His hope, his optimism wavered. *Did this man know something they didn't? If they happened to secure a boat to get away, could they make it, or would it all be for not? With all the resources at their disposal, was this all in fact, recreational?*

"Roger!" his mom called to him from the dock. He rushed over to the long steel skiff she was already hauling in by the line. "In," she told him. He hopped inside right away sitting down on the bench in the middle as she herself got in at the stern.

She put the gun on the thwart next to her before lowering the outboard's prop, pulling out the choke and squeezing the pump.

"Alright," she told it as if she didn't want to hear any complaints. With one hand leveraged on the outboard's cowling and the other on the draw chord, she pulled decisively. It rumbled momentarily spitting water and noxious fumes. She tried to give it more juice from the tiller, but it soon sputtered out. The combustion cycle had died.

"No, fuck you, no," she spat at it reaching for the chord once again.

Roger watched the men, guns drawn, close in on the dock. One ATV was now plowing along the shore, and it was sure to reach them first.

When his mom pulled this time, it ended up being an off-balance weakened draw causing her to stumble rocking the boat. But when should stood for the immediate follow-up, putting her body with coordinated effort into yanking the chord again, it turned the engine over true.

A large plume of smoke billowed in the area as she tried releasing the boat from the dock. Un-cleating the line, Roger didn't know if she saw what was coming. "Mom! *Mom*! here! here!" She just got it off as the man stalked up the dock in the four-wheeler. "Pull this up!" She tapped her hand on the line to the stern anchor with relative calm. She picked up the handgun from the bench without hesitation and fired with a loud resounding bang. The man on the ATV must've never seen it coming. He immediately jumped off the vehicle hitting the dock and rolling, splashing into the water below.

Watching, Roger still managed his task through the action, successfully pulling out the anchor and clanking it down under the seat. His mom switched the gear into reverse and pulled away from the pier, gunning the motor enough to throw Roger down into the boat. They had almost crashed into shore, before she adroitly flicked the gear back to the forward position pushing the tiller hard, swinging the boat away from the marina and leaving a good wake along with the fumes of smoke to choke on.

At this point, echoes of gunshots rang out. His mom tapped her hand on Roger's back as if to tell him to lower himself into the skiff. He did a little, but was too captivated by seeing his pursuers, including the giant man on the hill. He saw that the large body managed to step down some of the long staircase, as if he were still prepared to welcome his guests there at the dock. It was only now with the sun higher in the sky that he saw who this man was. Yes, he recognized him. There was too much discussion between Clint and his dad for him not to know. It almost surprised him that he didn't realize it right away, but then again, even the way he stood there barely seemed human.

He saw where his mom had positioned the gun next to her and decided to go for it. She was too busy handling the skiff through some chop to stop him. When he took it up in his hand, his mom's face exuded fear of what her son was to do next. The best that he could, he held the gun straight, other hand steadying underneath, lining it just above Ray's head. *It's time to end it all here.* As small as it was, this may be their only chance.

"Don't!" his mom shouted above the noise of the motor just as the gun jumped up from Roger's hand in another ear popping blast. He did it a few more times, as his mom urged him to stop, adjusting his aim each time for the globular target on the shore. She finally let go of the tiller altogether to grab hold of his wrist. He knew then it was time to stop. It was useless now anyhow. They were too far out. Besides, there was a need to conserve ammo. Their escape wasn't over.

His mom eventually turned the skiff along the coast. She made it a point to steer closer to the cliffs which Roger supposed was to prevent any larger vessel from getting up close. He wasn't sure it was enough. Knowing what he knew about Ray, it wasn't hard to imagine multiple ways for him to catch up with them. He could imagine, if not having other boats in pursuit, a helicopter could suddenly appear overhead.

It was far from over, he knew. They needed luck, providence maybe, but the good thing was there was hope. He had hope, and no matter what, he wouldn't let Ray kill that.

It must have been half an hour rolling through the surf as the skiff planed along. They had been searching for any sign of civilization, any sign of sanctuary, and were yet to find more than a sparse number of houses situated near cliffsides. And though there were freighters in the distance, they were still a long way off to be of any help.

At this point, Roger thought it had to be the rays of the sun with its incessant attention that caused his mother's face to flush red. It took him a few takes to realize that wasn't the case. Her chest was heaving erratically and he could see tears drip down her chin. He scooted back to see what was wrong.

"What? What is it?" he asked loud enough to overcome the engine's roar. He thought she had seen something of concern, or worse yet, that her own hope had left her.

She shook her head, as if she didn't want to say, but he insisted. "Please tell me." Again she refused but also couldn't stem the tears from falling as they both looked at each other—knowing there was no more use trying to hide it. She finally cranked the engine down to tell him what the matter was. He leaned in.

"I didn't want to say back there…I wanted to wait until we were all the way in the clear."

"Tell me."

Her tears started to pour anew.

"Mom—"

"Your dad's dead."

"What?"

"I saw him. I saw him," was all that she said before choking out more sobs.

"Dad?" Roger said simply—uncomprehendingly.

"Yes."

It took a moment for it to sink in before Roger's own tears formed. He thought from the start that they'd make their way back to him. That he'd be waiting with Beli in his arms so happy to see them—elated that they were all well. Now he knew that just wasn't to be.

He sat next to his mom hugging her along that remote seemingly endless coastline that appeared less and less like anything resembling home. Wanting to say something comforting, something reassuring, his voice failed him. Instead, they sat there for another moment rocking in the surf in silence before she wiped the tears from her eyes and gunned the engine once again. And they continued their way—just the two of them in a stark, uncertain world. The wind was picking up. The small craft bobbed up and down working against a relentless tide.

7

The still pond before the museum house on the edge of campus was placid, the lot virtually empty and Clint liked it just fine. He sat there in his car with his coffee that he made English adding to it from his emergency office whiskey flask.

Following the teaching of his last course of the day, he was only too eager to leave the bustle of campus, pockets of protestors buzzing about this inanity or that. Today, he even saw a new contingent on the park with the signs, "Liberate Southern Florida Now."

Apparently not recognizing him as the infamous enemy he had become to their causes, one student had handed him a leaflet about the petition for the university to join the Chroma-Free Campus League. In solidarity with other universities across the country, it explained the CFCL's dedication to ridding academia of unsafe environments. Its first stated policy was to have university admission contingent on genetic testing effectively barring entrance to chrome-plus students.

At first reading it, Clint couldn't believe his eyes. He couldn't believe they were pushing for something so bafflingly dipshit dumb that he had to read it again. Yes, someone really took the time to put that into print and distribute it at an institution of higher education. It caused his chest muscles to tighten, heavy perspiration, and stomach pains. Only upon leaving the main campus was he able to start to evaporate the dark cloud that enveloped his mind and lingering bodily complaints.

He began reclaiming his peace. Now even looking at the very spot where he had restrained the deranged man that had attacked Peter's car, didn't disturb him. He reminisced. How high-spirited Peter and he had been that day. How invigorating it was to manhandle the mindless thug into submission, seeing him put into cuffs. The fact that the youth was soon released from jail, doubtless to make his next societal contribution, didn't at all spoil it.

Many fond memories of his friend haunted him. While it had been months since his brutal death, he was always right there on campus—there outside the door of his office, with a coffee in hand walking along the park or down the corridors of Blanchard Hall, being the paragon of an uncompromising academic, a terrific family man, the kind of friend very few will ever have the pleasure of knowing, of being right there in the thick of it with you whether it be at the lowest hell or highest Valhalla.

It was at the eulogy that he tried to impart this and more. Words needed to be said, to witness, no matter how many people had shown up to the wake. It wasn't many, and with Roger and Margery still missing, what remained were distant family and friends. The sole survivor, baby Isabel, cried then slept in the care of Margery's brother's family, who did their best to act closer than they were. Garretty sat in the back.

When he was invited to take the floor, Clint did his duty to share the life of his friend, but seeing those in the audience, he wondered if anyone had really listened. Many appeared to move restlessly in their seats as if eager to leave, and he supposed with this kind of tragedy, they really couldn't be blamed.

The next steps for himself and his own family were going to be difficult. Jenelle and the girls had discussed it with him at length. After what happened to Peter and his family, after the hopelessness in Gonzalez's words over the phone that they would ever be able to hold anyone accountable, they agreed it was time for a change.

They didn't see it exactly as escaping, or worse, giving up. That's certainly not how he defined it. Rather, it was framed as an overdue family vacation—a time to forget past sorrows and time for new beginnings. And while their dad wrapped up the semester, putting the house on the market, settling accounts, he was later set to join them.

The plan was to move to Cat Island for a year and see how it went. They knew it would take time to settle in and adjust to a different kind of life. It would be a while before his family could feel safe again. It would take a lot of ocean air—a lot of beach, maybe a storm or two. But all the same, they had to do something different. They had had enough.

There was also something he knew that he must do before that time. He owed it to Peter, and if he didn't, he'd end up regretting it for the rest of his life.

He took his case from the backseat, opening it again for the flask of whiskey he deposited there. He emptied the rest into his coffee cup—not wanting Jenelle to see him drinking during the day, especially as he promised that he'd been cutting back.

Outside, the sun heated up the crisp, cool air, as he stood over the pond sipping from his cup. He roamed around it, taking in the different views, and eventually even walked up to the museum itself to see what it was all about. He never knew, even after a decade of passing the site. It may just be his last opportunity to discover what it was. He tried the door. Locked. The small sign on the glass was barely visible due to the glare. "Krikpatrick Homestead Museum Closed until Further Notice." *Renovations? Staff shortage?* No reason given. *Too bad*, he thought. The vision of living on such a remote site long ago greatly interested him. Without a university, student body of thirty thousand practically at its doorstep, it must have been a relatively peaceful life. Mosquito ridden, for sure, yet still serene to him. Peering through a porch window at any extant antique furniture of the old household was when he noticed a small sign in the right corner of the window. "Designated Safe Space," he read aloud then laughed. "Safe," he repeated the word scornfully.

He sat on one of the porch rockers thinking, considering the next decisions and many possible futures that lay ahead. There were too many. Contingency upon contingency. One trajectory leading to another. What was trajectory anyhow? The arc of history? We are but dilettantes pattering about our presumed trendlines completely in the dark. For trajectory was one thing and path totally other. Only after the fact, was the connection even made between the two—to necessarily harmonize them for our own benefit. Two mere data points were considered while holding our breath. The first meant so little; the second meant everything. The latter totally subsumed the former. Not only did it conquer, but it razed, pillaged, and salted its assumed territory. The actual future was everything. Events made present could smack the face or even grasp the heart still—the price irredeemable.

Whatever happened, he had to ensure his family was okay. He had to believe it. It was the only way he could keep moving—to keep acting, hoping for change.

But the concern of what world they were to live in was really the same. When he thought of his father, he couldn't stomach the possibility of his daughters having to sublimate superior ability to their skin tone. What was the purpose of sharing a participation trophy in inane cultural preferences that could just so easily turn back the other way, except to deprive them from meeting real fellow movers and shakers of the world? It not only mocked his accomplishments—it insulted the very idea of merit, of the true wonder of discovery in science—a testament to nature's dominion. If they were to bow, it wouldn't be to the new social hierarchy, but to the universe, to reality as it really is, as it is really lived. Safe it wasn't, but genuine, marvelous, powerful, especially crushing to all these little people denying its preeminence.

Clint felt a distinct chill shoot up through his back as he imagined what it would be like in his confrontation of Jersey. It unsettled him on the wooden chair. Drowning the rest of his drink, he crossed his arms as if to keep more heat inside of his sports coat. It wasn't long before he thought about buying another flask.

Yes, he decided. *One more*. The sting of conscience needed to be assuaged, as it pierced him from multiple fronts without mercy. It even nipped at him about the future drink that he knew he wouldn't deny himself.

The chair creaked its complaint as he pushed up with the arms, forcing his weight out of the chair to stand. Through the trees he looked back toward the main campus. The rabble was doubtlessly still mindlessly pushing someone's cause for lack of anything else to believe in, and past that on the other side of the park lay Nordrick Hall where he imagined Professor Jersey poking about his office, tapping away at the keyboard to keep the distortions alive. *The hack.*

We'll see what true beliefs remain after being put to the test, he told himself. *After the smelting, we'll see what's metal and what's slag.*

8

A youth with a lab coat and goggles had someone in tow likewise fully garbed, exiting through the door to the anteroom. Beyond lay the laminar flow hoods occupied by the students and post-docs surrounded by beakers, chemical agents and reagents busying themselves with the tedium of micropippetting and remixture.

When they came into the room, the man following blenched as he saw the giant emerge from the corner. The wide body miniaturized the space, standing almost a full foot taller than himself.

Jersey didn't bother removing his PPE, he only had his goggles repositioned above his head as he stared wide eyed at the figure before him. Seeing his fear, Clint relished it. *Yes, you should be afraid,* he told himself. *Surprise, dickhead.*

The student saw it too. He searched his professor's face as if to ask whether granting Clint's request to see his fellow academic was the right decision in the end. Jersey's face softened and he gave a slight nod to the student as if to say it was, despite revealing the gaping chink in his facade.

"Professor Dumfries, how may I help you in the Biological Sciences?" The tone was rich with import. It poured out with deep-seated enmity and resonated with the pitch of an open jeer, but he supposed that in front of the student, he could later deny that interpretation. To Clint, it was a manifest snarl.

The student entered back into the anteroom after Clint gave him a steely look, and he could see Jersey's reticence at being left there without him. But, he wasn't one to openly protest this confrontation. No, he was too proud for that.

Clint scanned over the room with the row of unoccupied computer terminals with concomitant data storage and processing units and through the window into the clean room before taking a step towards Jersey.

"Why, I've come to see your raw data from the study, as requested."

Jersey laughed at this with disgust. "Why would I want to show you?"

"You could make me a new convert. I want to be convinced. I still want that."

He chuckled coldly, "All you've ever wanted was to discredit me. That's all you're about."

"You know that's not true."

"Get the fuck out of my lab before I have security drag you—"

"Shut the fuck up!" Clint had slowly positioned himself between Jersey and the window, his body blocking the view. He pulled the pistol from the breast pocket of his long coat covering his suit beneath and pointed it at Jersey who stood amazed at the bold threat of violence staring at him through the hole of the muzzle.

Again, there was fear that Jersey tried to shake by a forced smile. "Ha ha, you've gone berserk. You're a fucking right-wing nut. You'll be fired before going to—"

"I said, *shut up*." He had already locked the outer door, but knew there wasn't much time as someone was bound to come in from the lab. "Now where's the raw data?"

"Or you're going to fucking shoot me? Yeah…"

"I'm going to shoot you," he agreed flatly. Clint slightly angled the barrel up and down Jersey's body as if to say it could strike him anywhere. There it was again, that shimmer of doubt in the professor's face, his eyes following the barrel like a viper to the flute of the charmer.

"I'm not showing you anything," Jersey said recovering himself.

"It's just you and me now. Peter's dead. His family missing. I want to know it all. I want to know what's behind the curtain. What's behind the slaughter? You're a part of this. I fucking know you are. No, don't shake your head like that. Your denials are useless to me, but I know they are your first defense—for everything. As a dog barks, you'll deny. You may not always know why exactly. You just will."

Jersey stood there silently with a grin. His face pulsed at the dog comment, but otherwise he waited. A sheen of sweat glistened over his receding hairline and the faint souring of deodorant, of metallic body odor just beating out the fragrance was palpable even at the distance he stood away. Clint felt seconds tick away and Jersey knew it too.

"Look at all of this," Clint directed his head at the extensive facilities that had only been added onto since the published rag. "What a waste…you aren't fooling me. You may have the whole world taken in by this alluring, make believe story. Ray told you and Eldridge what to do and loaded you with millions giving you the name recognition you thought you deserved, directing every step of the way. He tells a whore open up, and you do. He eliminates anyone who opposes. How does it feel to be fucked by the devil?"

"Cut the shit!" Jersey interrupted him against his better judgment, but the temptation of pride rippled beneath. "Ray's a visionary and knows how to extract value. That's all. Eldridge isn't here anymore to set the story straight, but I'm here telling you—"

"He told me alright. In a drunken bender, he told me how scared he was. And what did they do to him? He just so happens to disappear when he starts telling the truth. He meets with Eggers and disappears along with him. How convenient."

"Coincidence."

"Just tell the truth once in your fucking life."

"That's—"

"You're scared," Clint says with a smirk, as if to say he is a useless coward. "I see it now. You'll never speak truth when you know he'll just as easily make you disappear too."

"Truth? *Truth*?!" he repeated it as if the very word itself were an absurdity before mocking it the second time around. "The only truth is what fills the void. That's all there is," he said with disgust. "That's the *truth*!" He delivered the word this time with such a vitriol as if the very word itself were a meat by which he could shove down Clint's throat and make him choke. He was out of breath and Clint merely studied him as he recovered.

After a long moment of Jersey's defiant glare locked eye-to-eye, Clint laughed. "I expect nothing less from you. It was always a means to an end, really. And that's all. There are no raw data. There's never been. There's nothing to look into. It's a scam you peddle. Nobody will know for a time, but that's what you are, and nothing will change that—Nobel Prize or not. It will be exposed and rescinded. The truth will wait stubbornly—"

"Hah!" Jersey spat. "What astounding naivety….to think history something other than it is. Let me explain…there'll be no great reveal." He reverted to whispering smugly, slyly as if at the same time injecting venom into a wound. "As a traitor, you'll be an adopted member of the race of Hatti. Does anyone remember the Hatti? The Hittites genocided them on the Anatolian plains. Who were they and what they stood for—erased from record—left with name only. And that's all you'll be a part of—some obscure footnote. What do they mean now? What does a name mean? What does anything mean as subjects to oblivion? It's my time now—our time to do what we want, to shape it precisely the way we want."

Clint put the gun back into his coat and approached the door now that he saw that he had spurred the necessary rise he wanted out of the man. Whatever he was going to glean from his empty threat was already had.

"You're going away."

"Probably not." Clint responded pertly, turning his back on Jersey and leaving him with the echoes of his booming laugh.

"Laugh. There is no stopping what's coming to you…to your family."

Clint didn't know what to make of that. Jersey may have meant prison time, but he wasn't sure. He considered turning around right there and then, blasting him for the suggestion, but he knew he couldn't do that. He had a family and more than what he expected on the voice recorder in his inner coat pocket. He had what he needed—the tacit admission that the study was a lie contrived by Simon Ray who funded it. Who could make use of such an indictment of gross institutional power yanking an enchained people by an insidious premise—a falsity only now being subject to a refractor test years later. Only after prolonged poisoning, where the body adapts, can one think it medicine. This person had his work cut out for him.

The journalist, Paul Higgins of WNT, former colleague and friend of Eggers, picked up the story after he'd reached out to Clint to find out the details of what his late friend had been working on. It had to be the biggest story ever with the biggest risks, Clint warned him. But, Higgins didn't bat an eye when he revealed to him the full haunting details from the beginning—the story of bad science justifying a captivating idea, of the highly impressionable, of power hungry forces making a move, of a serial killer, of Simon Ray, Osiras Ram. It had not only been the ending of his friend Eggers, but it was also that of so many others. And many unknown. Others who weren't just numbers. Individual human beings who deserved to live—far more than mere instances of demographics, as flesh for the meat-grinder. It seemed that Higgins understood this too, and the details of the conspiracy sucked him in right away. Of course, he could help and have the recording after Clint clipped the first half.

He hoped that it was all going to be enough. *But, was it? With a story this big, was it ever going to be? Would there ever be substantive proof? God, it had to be at least something.*

He exited the building with some haste. Getting into the car he had parked in a handicapped space in front of Nordrick and speeding off without incident. His first errand was to send grandfather's hand-me-down gun to its watery grave in the homestead museum's pond. Then after he took the flight from Fort Lauderdale to D.C. to meet with Higgins, he would be in the air again for a twenty-four-hour run with transfer in Santo Domingo to meet his wife and daughters on Cat Island. He would call them on the way to make sure they were safe, as Jersey's last words caused the pit of his stomach to feel barren and incapable of assuming food, but he had prepared his wife for such a contingency. She was on high alert, and he trusted her maternal instincts.

How eager he was to hold her and to see the warm mirth in the smiles of his daughter's faces once again. Just meeting with a man like Jersey made him feel covered in grime. It was time to wash himself clean, time to be free of being one of the standard-bearers for science and truth and hand it to others in what appeared, for at least one side, unlimited warfare.

It was decisive. If he lost his family, he'd have nothing left. He had to be saved from that future. But what if they won? What if they had their way? Wouldn't they be lobotomizing the world— imprisoning the mind in stories and categories suitable for their own ends? Would life even be worth living? He dared not consider it. Not just now. He had to take a load off first.

9

The door's keypad glowed a rich gamay color carving a small window into the darkness. Having used his phone's flashlight for guidance, he now opened his messages to retrieve the passcode, and proceeded to press each digit, resulting in high-pitched beeps ending with the pound sign. With the satisfying response of a green light and unwinding churn, the deadbolt was released, and he entered the roomy Caribbean bungalow.

In this early morning hour, it was dark. Both the living room and porch light were off, but Clint surmised Jenelle was still getting used to the new house, simply forgetting to turn on what had been automated in the former.

He spoke to her before leaving D.C. "It's okay," he said to her protest of trying to meet him at the airport. He told her they'd have breakfast together in the morning, hopefully after catching a few hours of sleep himself. There had been a long delay, and she knew not to wait up as he was able to prearrange a long-term rental—its key left in a lockbox at the airport.

It was almost comical he thought as he stepped inside his new, sometime, home. What was this journey of a code to a key to a code to a code that was the key? It seems that this was the exact essence of life itself, mysteries revealing ever greater mysteries that only an ever-expansive unknowable future could reveal as it shook hands with the present. In that same vein, he hoped they could be happy at their future time spent there but was anything but certain. In fact, his drive to the house down those pothole-filled roads from the Podunk airport in that Podunk town had him second guess their decision more than once.

Still, the air was different. With his window down during the drive, the smell of salt from the sea filled his lungs and with the faint rushing sounds of water up the sands of the beach, it relaxed him. It was what he was really looking forward to. He and his family could walk those sands, ride those waves, snorkel that shoreline and firmly be in the present without fear of what was to come. Maybe it wasn't the life they had been used to, but it could be the very impetus to a more grateful existence. For wasn't that what life should be about—not with money or recognition, but with gratitude that made every breath of air oxygenizing every cell, fresh, salty, and crisp? With all that had occurred, Clint believed it now—gratefulness—toward whom or what, he couldn't define exactly but somehow knew that in the act of belief itself, everything would be better. Life would be transformed each moment to what had been lost in the bustle of modernity—to sheer triumph over circumstance. To reference the beyond, connecting it to this very moment, was a different way forward and Clint was firmly ready to take those steps. It charged him up. It was the first time in a long time he could say it. He felt good.

His finger found the light switch along the wall and the strange orangy incandescence of the old ceiling shade and bulb flashed to sprinkles of blood-spattered walls. A pool of it had drained out from Jenelle's lifeless body lying on the dated upholstered sofa. She had been bound with mooring lines, hands and feet, another gagging her mouth, but still managing a stare up at whoever entered, anguish and humiliation at any witness happening to find her naked body there. Her breasts, exploded peaks of saturating brown, had gushed from the strange puncture wounds around each zenith.

Clint was so struck at the sight, he could barely breathe, barely move at something so ghastly that he wanted to wake up now. But, he knew his mind could never have constructed it in his wildest nightmare. The distinct shades of colors, gnawing perceptions overpowered him at once dictating to him that, as much as he wanted it to be, this was no mere dream.

He began to sob, and the contents of his stomach began bubbling up as he stumbled into the far wall—catching himself yet falling down all the same. Tears and vomit were coughed up onto the wood floor. "Rayyyyyy!" His mind began to flare. "He knew he had to get up. *Rayyyyyy!*" A fever of rage was building, and he knew he had to accept it, harness it to find his daughters. He had to act now, but his body wasn't done purging yet. His own fluids covered some of the far-reaching blood specks of his wife's.

Footsteps thumped against the hollow of the floor up to where he knelt, finding him as if he were facing east in an act of early morning worship. Belted out chuckles breathed down upon him from the walker, and he pushed himself back onto his knees to see that he wasn't there alone. Through blurry eyes, he saw the gaunt silhouette of a man who simply said to him, "sod sack of sheet, sod" before continuing to express a noise that clearly wasn't from any genuine sense of humor. It was only there to salt the wound of his gaping heart.

Barely did Clint take another breath before he roared—lunging forward as quickly as a big body like him could do, grasping the man's leg and pulling it up into the air, slamming him down in a strange unconventional judo. His body thudded hard against the mahogany and Clint began battering down on the thin hyena face. There was no thought. It was pure emotion, and as quickly as it showed itself, it was soon terminated by a jolting shock to his nape, inducing his whole body to seize up like sugar clogging a combustion chamber. Clint could just make out the sulfur stink of his burnt hair as his head was then attended to by a steel toed boot. All he felt was the sudden and repeated pressure of the blunt force on his skull. The pain was another matter. They would have to catch up soon, too soon, like old friends in a funeral parlor, as his vision faded to neon shadow. Pinpoints of light danced before him. Vibrant stars led him through to a blanket of uncompromising night. He was ending in a place he tried his best to avoid. He was now about to make his final plea to whoever, if anyone, cared to listen.

Black. All Colors Left Intact?

1

The engine whirred in the dark as metal clanged faintly in the distance. A light flickered on causing Clint to come fully awake again, and like before, he was able to see the extent of serpentine structures of metal piping around him slithering in and out, up and down, penetrating the dark along the diamond plated walkway.

From his first waking, Clint didn't doubt based on the sound and sparse red light of mechanical fixtures that he was in the bowels of some massive vessel underway. He had already spent hours there, and even thought he'd heard just above the din, voices in the distance. Could they be his Giselle and Daniela, comforting each other, wondering as he now did, what horrible denouement could be in store for them, or were they even still alive? Had they already been taken like their mother and now haunting whatever meagre life persisted in him? He didn't dare explore that question too much, as he knew he needed to be fully collected. Desperately, he needed to find out what happened to them and strike true as soon as the opportunity showed its fleeting face. If his worse fears were realized, he knew one of the people he'd exact that revenge on was his very self.

His arms were cuffed to a solid vertical steel pipe he had since tried to break by yanking out with the force of his body mass. The stubborn alloy was insistent, unforgiving as were the cuffs on his wrists. He felt the pain shooting through the bruises there with open abrasions stinging with sweat, yet he continued. He did whatever he had to—no matter how seemingly hopeless.

Still working the pipe with only a slight dent to show for it, he called out to the voices. It was to no avail. The chattering continued unabated by his entreaties, making him wonder if they were even voices in the first place and not some ambient murmurings of the ship itself.

Footfalls suddenly rattled across the metal floor causing him to perk up ceasing the struggle. A silhouette of a slender figure emerged in the distance. It didn't take long for his stomach to ache in sheer aversion for this creature. Its inhumane tittering crawled across his skin electrifying his limbs with pulsating voltage. The battered face confirmed what he already knew as it briefly showed itself in the light beneath the brim of the same camo cap that welcomed him to his new home.

The grisly grin was still there, gleaming whites that appeared to persist even through shadow. Clint was glad to see some of the fruits of his earlier work—bruising across the cheeks including the closed shiner and split lip. It wasn't nearly enough. Some accomplice had ended it only when he'd just begun.

Jacques read the odium in Clint's face with pleasure knowing there was much more of it to come. *Did he think it was bad now? He didn't know what pain was. No one knew until the end and when that true sweetness finally emanated from his body, there would be nothing left for him but a useless husk he'd have Jacques dispose of. What did this man think he was doing here? Did he think he was special? A respected adversary? Compared to the girls, he was mere seasoning.*

"Look at ya," he reveled in power at the bound hulking man. "Boss' happy at ya—so happy now that he wants to thank ya. A true honor what you've brought him…" Jacques trailed off in a laugh as he stood regarding Clint partially obscured in shadow.

"You mean Ray. I know who." Clint clenched his jaw.

This response surprisingly caused the first frown Clint had seen in the man.

"You don't know sheet, chup," he said before resuming the smile.

Clint was glad he could cause a reaction in the man and hoped he could rattle him enough to make a mistake.

"I know what you are, what you're trying to do."

Jacques didn't say anything.

"You're race traitors—reworked Uncle Toms now programmed to kill their own. I salute you, brotha," Clint's guts wrenched as the words left his mouth.

Again, Jacques said nothing giving Clint the idea to continue.

"You're not—"

A flitting shadow passed that ended in a sudden crushing force to Clint's face. Only after did it bite him with pain—pain that he couldn't rub out with his bound hands.

"Stupid fucking cun thinks about race," Jacques scoffed to himself. "You chup fucker."

Clint noticed what it was that hit him pointed at him now. The pistol was leveled at his heart. "We tell *ya…what* to say." Jacques gripped his hand under his chin. "Ima from beech's cattle cunnie. I do what I told." Jacques squeezed his mouth with each word as if to compel him to talk as he caricatured a voice. Clint shook off the hand from his face, as Jacques further mocked him. Again, the laughs came as Clint fantasized about seizing him and the new sounds he'd make while breaking his windpipe.

When his chuckles finally died, Jacques produced a key ring. "Now you'll be a good steer…real…I'm taking you to see your kin. Boss' keeping company."

"Where are they?"

"It'll be an honor," he spewed acidly ignoring the question.

Getting behind Clint, he unlocked one cuff with the gun firmly pressing into Clint's back as if to be crystal clear what would happen if Clint didn't cooperate.

Jacques stepped back at the ready as Clint rubbed the freed wrist.

"Left," he said to Clint peremptorily. When he didn't react right away, Jacques snapped. "Left! Fruit of a cunnie!" Clint felt the drops of Jacques' spittle hit his face and neck before turning as he was told to a corridor with a dog hatch. He stepped inside to another long passageway as Jacques trailed him closely giving one-word directions.

The workings of the ship buzzed ominously as the metallic crunch of their feet busied themselves along the tread plate. Clint's heart seemed to throb ever harder in rhythm with their steps as he felt each yard closer to a vague nightmare he had once had. The exact details, he couldn't remember but the vague deja vu of doom caused cold sweat to drench his chest and back. As little weight as he had put into such premonitions, he put a lot into them now. His whole body was a believer. He knew that whatever was about to happen, he couldn't let it. The window to act was fading fast.

They must've been on the other end of the ship by the time Jacques said something new. "Here," he indicated toward one of the corridors. Clint repeated the same word in his head. Here, yes, *here*. Stepping through the inward opening dog hatch, he hesitated as if he stumbled on the other end.

"You cun!" Jacques shouted right before Clint attempted to weave his body behind the hatch. A deafening shot rang out cutting into Clint's side as he flung all his weight backward into the door. It caught something before the frame. An agonizing wail followed with a clack of metal on metal. When Clint tried to force it home anyway, it sounded as if twisting off a roast turkey leg. He continued to put his weight on it as he crouched to find the pistol on the floor. Gyrating his body against the arm in the steel door as the man echoed in agony, Clint only wanted to find a cripple on the other side.

By the time he opened the hatch door, Jacques lay on the floor screaming, frantically grabbing at his crushed appendage. "Cunnie! Fucking Cunnie!" he squealed at Clint with all sorts of indiscernible invective. His legs moved as if he were running, but he was going nowhere.

Clint held the barrel of the freshly fired gun against Jacques' cheek burning the flesh there, giving the man something new to complain about. As much as he enjoyed watching this beast who killed his wife now clutch at his busted wing, his daughters needed him. He just hoped this necessary gamble didn't cause Ray to kill them already. The gunshot had to have been heard, but it wasn't time to second guess himself. It was time to act.

With the barrel of the gun, Clint proceeded to beat Jacques' head into the metal floor, fully intending to finish what he had started hours prior. Each successive hit mingled his own blood from the grazing in his side with Jacques' hemorrhaging head. Every rattle of metal added to the sizeable pool that flooded underneath them. In it, the camo hat now sat drenched many shades darker.

The skull gave way with a final crack making Clint want to wretch, but the feeling soon subsided. He picked himself up off the floor cradling the wound at his side while his right still held the gun. He rubbed the blood from it onto his shirt while catching his breath. Its action looked unimpeded and the safety was still switched in the fire position. He was comfortable with firearms, having used them for protection most of his adult life. *Just aim then pull.* The four-hundred-foot pounds of force behind the nine-millimeter round would do the rest.

3

Something is behind this hatch, Clint gathered. A faint high-pitched bleating rose over the ship's hum causing Clint to feel a distinct icy chill through his bones. He tried to swallow the bitter chalky metal residue—the only moisture left in his mouth, but all he did was contract his throat. He tried waiting, listening for some indication of what lay on the other side, but minutes passed without change. All there was—was that same stirring whimper where the more he heard it, the more he was convinced it wasn't from the ship like before. It was human. Images of his two daughters being hurt in unspeakable ways compelled him to action, opportune or not. Whatever lay on the other side of the door, Clint had to face, whatever the consequence.

Slowly, he turned and pulled back on the wheel handle. With gun drawn, the metal hinges offered some complaint as he pushed into the dark chamber before him. The door swept in with pistol trailing for the first sign of a threat. Light poured from a source on the other side of the compartment and when the door had largely completed its course, he stepped over the bulkhead to see the two bodies with arms suspended by chains from the ceiling. Daniela and Giselle stared into the darkness at their visitor, faces seemingly pale, broken. The very source of radiating positivity in Clint's life, faces that so many times were beaming with joy were now perturbed by dread. The sight immediately stabbed at Clint's heart.

They were speechless, rapt in terrifying anticipation. Could they even see him? Nothing indicated they could. In fact, Clint had to stop himself from calling out to them. Everyone in the cavern expected him to come through that door only with camo hat just behind, but with the enclosed space and bad lighting, how could they even know? "Ready," a heavily accented voice uttered from the darkness. The outline of a thin figure to Giselle's right was now fixed upon by Clint's darting eyes.

He fired at the center of the target without hesitation. The sound crashed through the air flashing a harsh light as thunder at ground zero in the dead of night. As if in stop motion stills, Clint saw the body that was formerly standing now fallen to the floor, but in those same glimpses, his eye had caught an opaque looming mass on the other side of the chamber. Training the barrel on it immediately, he let the gun loose in rapid succession.

The gun jumped just as he did when more and more of its physiognomy was revealed to his disbelieving eyes. A rounded triangular mass, almost the width of an SUV, was bearing down on him, beams of orange swirls staring at him from its neckless head. Falling back to the other side of the room, shots continued to ring out. *Hadn't he struck it? How many times? God what the fuck was happening?* Crack, crack, crack, the gun spit its fury, flame blooming from its muzzle yet failing to impede its stride. It only grew. It was upon him.

Spending his final round at the abomination, the flash revealed its frontal features. The leathery transmogrified face between man and chameleon towered over him, Ray's likeness somewhere latent in that horribly deformed visage. Facial ridges ran from the tops of dead orange eyes meeting at a small protrusion where its nose had been. From its would be neck sprouted miniaturized frills fanned out in aggression. While its short disproportionate clawed feelers held next to its puffed torso, the mouth was agape splayed with jagged fleshy teeth breathing its horrible burning sulphury hiss into his, as its serpentine tongue peaked at him in excitement.

What happened next, he couldn't know for sure, but in the darkness, he was struck in the head with such a sudden devastating blow, it was lights out. The last thought was that he was being yanked through space and time, as if wormholed into another dimension.

4

Clint came to in pain, whimpering, and darkness. His whole body protested, especially his head that felt exploded via arial bombardment. The cuffs that had remained on his hands were now fastened to the lower frame of a steel cargo shelf. He sat before his daughters whose arms remained shackled, chains hanging limply from a support beam. Daniela was the one crying.

"Daniela honey, I'm here," was all the words Clint could find to say at first—not like it was much consolation.

"Daddy! You're alive," she gushed forth with a renewed fit of sobs.

"Dad!" Giselle brightened through the dejected demeanor.

"*Wait*," someone stepping from shadows on the other side of the room said with such fervor that it jolted them.

Though the man looked like the henchman whose brains he recently bashed-in, he could see that it was someone else, and the anger in his voice was palpable.

Clint looked over to where he shot his comrade, seeing the shape still lying there where he'd put him. *Really? Was he mad about that? Look at us here, look at what you've done to me and my family. And you've a right to be angry?* Clint continued to muse about the pin brained man and what he could do to him.

"Where's Ray?" he asked studying the man in his own imposing voice. He knew there was an opportunity that involved getting under this man's skin—to challenge him before Ray returned. Never did he want to see that grisly presence again—not in the remotest dreamscape.

Within the darkness he heard the answer. Dread filled the pit of his stomach like a liquid at the sound of rending metal accompanied by a waft of burning chemical drawing his attention to orange orbs that swiveled toward them. They then focused bright and full upon Clint. There were no pupils, just irises flaming bright and swirling with madness—oranges, yellows, and reds.

"Mr. Dumfries," the pitch rivaled his in depth resonating in the very marrow of his bones.

Seeing the bodies of his daughters, standing the furthest back their chains would let them, shuddering in abject fear, he tried to swallow back his own. Despite everything in his body freezing up, as if playing dead during an animal attack, he knew he had to resist it. He had to do something. He had to speak, but the words weren't coming.

"To be with us, brings me no pleasure," it said with eyes suggested something else.

Clint's mind frantically sought the right response—anything that could give them a chance.

The eyes then directed toward his daughters. "My poor, poor children…All is useless. All suffering. When you come into the world, everything stacks against you. No one is for you. If anything, they want your space, your livelihood. They only succeed where you fail. They live fully where you fade away and die." There was a long pause as if to take in the moment—to breath in the air even if it reeked of oniony body odor and a tinge of coppery blood.

"And here you are now come…to me," it said at last.

To this Daniela responded with a bloodcurdling scream, "Help! Please God, hellllllp!"

She continued on twisting the chains and turning her body away from the awful stare while Giselle seemed to be in an exhausted resigned state of doom hanging limply with turned away sunken eyes.

"*Ray*, if that's who you really are, *nothing* of what you say is true," Clint felt he found the right words and stated them for his daughters' benefit as much as for himself—to shake them free of the fear.

The flames of the eyes rekindled their intensity on Clint now.

"Truth is but a word. To what purpose does it hold when it evaluates everything—being itself evaluated by nothing?"

Clint ignored the further deception—the attempt to deflect. "We were never victims, until now…We're—"

"*Cease!*" Ray's timbre commanded, and Clint shut up immediately. He wanted to finish his thought, but it was like he didn't know how anymore. His speech and ideas were lost to him. His mind was being overloaded by other words and images— foreign intruders barraged his consciousness choking him of any independent mental movement. A condescending smirk of Peter's. A formerly unperceived slight from Garrety drinking coffee together. Students everywhere eyeing him, judging him for who he was—for what he was. Whatever the time and place, whoever the people he was with, they were now no friends of his. How could they be?

They were only set out to destroy him—parasites intent on undermining his work, seeking to override him—to ignore his interior self—to disappear that inconvenience from existence only caring to make mere mechanical use of his bone, muscles, and sinew, a ventriloquist with its dummy. Who knew what lengths these vermin would go to continue to smother his very personhood from language with their maliciousness—smearing, deprecating, limiting him to what they would impose—repurposing him into a perfect automaton—reducing all his complexities to sheer utility. Without even considering him a substrate that anything nominatively human could inhere, he could be sliced up at any moment as if on a charcuterie board, and without a second thought, divvied out to only those truly worthy of nourishment. The invasion of his thoughts was full on, and while in the beginning he resisted—pushing against their cynicism, their malignancy, his will was fading fast. His mind was weary. He was giving up because it felt good. To go with the stream for once was almost freeing. And behind each idea was a great force—almost irresistible power. Resentment, hate, egoism. He felt them all now exponentiated like never before. It felt euphoric, godly. And if there wasn't a faint sickly undertone, it had to be the perfect drug. But, then again, what drug didn't have its side effect?

His mind was whirling while his eyes didn't fail to witness his daughters. Their eyes rolling more and more off kilter, jaws dropped, strings of spittle dripping down from their mouths. Were they experiencing the same thing as he? Were they crushed by this tsunami of emotion?

That's when he saw it out of the eye of his daughter Giselle—a single tear flitted down to the floor as if trying to conceal its necessary escape from the prying eyes of the world. Its fall was what bought him some freedom of the spiraling nosedive of his mind. The mind raping was partially interrupted. Whatever was going to happen, he couldn't countenance this anymore.

"Girls," Clint said breathily almost through an echo, a shadow of his voice's formidable presence. "I want to tell you something…something about your…grandfather…" The wound in his side had largely coagulated saturating through his shirt, it still nipped at him. And with his head covered in a feverish sweat, limbs shaking from a chill that wouldn't depart, he pushed through.

"He was…extraordinary…a man who built everything with his hands," he continued as a man wearing a surgical mask and gown proceeded to wheel an instrument cart just before his daughters.

"Everyone who knew him loved him and he had a lot of love to give…the truth is that…he'd have been so proud of you girls….*so proud…*"

To this, Ray's irises seemed to swirl ever faster, brighter as if fighting every word.

"And your mother…" Clint faltered but forced his vocal cords to action, "she had the hardest time with the pregnancy. Everyone pushed to give you up…but we wouldn't hear of it…We're so happy to have had you…You're the greatest blessing that a man could ever know…I just wanted you to know that."

Tears poured forth from Giselle and Daniela's eyes, as a look of occupancy had returned to them. They were listening to what their father was telling them. Something in them had pulled them from their trance, puncturing through the warped words and imagery to the actuality of their lives.

Thoughts of happy childhood memories took their place. Toddlers with their dad and mom playing hide and seek together— Dad comically stooping down behind a tree, concealing nothing of his giant shape provoking seemingly endless fits of laughter, the thrill of licking the sweet batter from their hands after helping Mom mix it for Daniela's tenth birthday cake, squealing sounds of joy of sisters and Mom through every drop of the roller coaster, Dad bellowing his equivalent from a car behind. So many memories. Moments reminding them what could so easily be forgotten. One simple truth, while things could be otherwise, they matter. They're loved.

"Whatever happens, girls, remember who you really are. Hold onto that—no matter what happens, what you're told to believe. You know who."

At this, Clint could just see the outline of Ray's horrible trans human face hover above him in the darkness. A sound of the highest pitch, just within the range of human ears, had been intensifying from its center of mass. The sight was so disturbing that even the surgeon couldn't move. Fear and dread captured him. He could no longer fulfill the purpose to what he had been paid so handsomely. After a spell of shuddering, the instinct for survival finally freed his feet. He ran overthrowing the tray of utensils which clanged to the floor in a thunderous crash.

Clint knew he had to keep going. He had to keep talking—ignoring this ungodly cosmic hiccup.

"My daughters! My angels…God, that's the truth… We'll be okay. In the end, everything will be okay—"

A sudden sound pierced the chamber, a guttural snarl. With a face suggesting illness, Ray's maw shot a straight jet of textured red light into the wall behind Daniela and Giselle searing the haul of the ship with immense heat and accompanying hiss. The strange vomitus that behaved less like liquid and more like pure energy exuded such noxious fumes and smoke that Clint's eyes and throat felt assaulted by an onslaught of tiny embers. The cloying sulphury, ashy, stagnating bile like odor was not only displacing the oxygen from the hold but attacking tissues as if aerosolized venom.

Clint hacked and hacked trying in short intervals of puffing at the sparse clean air that remained—witnessing through watery eyes, his daughters dying of the same biting suffocation. All he could do was yank at his cuffs futilely humbled more and more by the facts of circumstance.

Ray's henchman was now keeled over on the floor experiencing a coughing fit of his own. Having inhaled a greater part of the toxic vapors from where he stood, he tried finding his legs but failed when his retching fit started all over again. The face that had before flushed with anger was now flowering from pink to crimson.

They were dying and nothing could be done about it. Clint's chest was now filled with a distinct heaviness. Every breath was an agonizing process of glass into the lungs then out. No more did he keep his stinging eyes open. Instead, he focused his mind, preparing himself, doing what he could never do before—making a plea to that higher power—to the loving mind at the center of the universe believed to be ready to swaddle together its children at the end of their trial. He distinctly recalled a undergraduate student once asking him in his office, did he believe in such a power. The answer had been easy then—so easy, so concrete. No. He said it dismissively. He said it proudly. So what did his act mean now? Did it mean he believed? And what did it even matter? What kind of purity test was he supposed to pass at this point? What did he have to prove to anyone anymore? He simply made his petition.

Seconds turned to minutes like that suspended in the moment—
the longest moment of his life.

The sounds abated then ceased to be replaced by a steady roar.
Opening his eyes, Clint saw they were still alive. The stream of red
had disappeared along with its lurid author replaced only by the
cool saltwater splashing into their bodies—a fortifying solace
amidst the torturous cloud of putrefying air now dissipating. The
water sent the henchman down after nearly finding his bearings. To
his astonishment, the force flushed the man right at Clint's feet
who surprised himself at his seamless reflex of scissoring his legs
around his torso from behind. The man grabbed back at Clint's
hair even elbowing his ribs, but nothing would break him free of
Clint's powerful haunches.

"Lemme go!" he threatened, as if he still stood over him in a
position of power.

"Unlock me!" Clint growled into the man's ear.

"*Lemme go!*" he repeated as if the second time would certainly be
the charm.

Clint proceeded to clench his jaws around the man's ear and
wrenched fiercely at it. The man screamed trying to headbutt and
swat Clint's face away before a small piece came free.

Spitting it into their communal pool of ocean water, Clint
restated his request to his suffering prisoner. "Unlock these cuffs or
we die with my teeth in your neck."

Clint let the man produce a key ring from his belt. He steadied
his hands while guiding the man to the keyhole. His daughters
looked on wide eyed as the man blindly reached behind their father
to undue the lock. After a few frustrating fails, just as soon as his
arms had been bound behind him, they were locked around the
man's throat. Clint opened his legs standing the man up only to
plunge his head under the water. The protests were garbled, stifled
as the man tried again and again to resurface, but the more he
struggled, the more Clint bowed his weight on top of him. It didn't
take long for the man to give no struggle at all. Lifeless, Clint let his
body slip below the water to the floor.

He wished he didn't have to do that. He wished he didn't have
his daughters witness him kill anyone in all its primitive brutality.
But, he'd also wished a lot of things. There could be time to come
to terms with that—to come to terms with all of this—their loved

ones lost—the destruction of their safe world of categories. There could be a time to say sorry, a time to heal, but right now wasn't that time. Right now, was the time to live. And if they still could, they would like never before.

5

Dressed in a smart pantsuit of pink zinfandel adorned with pearl necklace, President Dembier beamed at the participants with ingratiating vigor standing patiently by the podium waiting for her Press Secretary to finish the day's agenda. It was a look anyone could tell that she knew too well, indeed, the very look that helped her win the election. With her cheeks puffed out like immaculate marble hills, her lips spread wide to make room for porcelainlike incisors and canines, she showed her confidence if not invincibility. It spoke more words than anything she was about to say. And for the unaccustomed, there was a vacant glee about the intention of the eyes, for the more discerning, however, it was much more specific. There was something familiar—a sense of belonging—ownership—a claim made on their object—straddling somewhere on the line between the rapture of a lover or outright dominatrix.

It was now her turn to speak. Her time to enthrall. She paused before the mic holding that same hypnotizing stare on her audience, the room as well as the world of screens captivating countless tired faces lit up by blue light. The moment was long, but she bided her time well with hidden excitement, deciding before proceeding that, yes, this is it. This is everything. This is all she's worked for—all she's deserved since birth. Here she was, from helpless victim to ascending to the pinnacle of power, deigning to speak—not so much as their president—but as their new world deity. She knew she was the closest thing to the second coming. Her believers were ready to absorb her every look, every word.

"Thank you everyone for being here," she said to an audience as quiet as the grave. With photographers told to refrain from taking shots until the end, nothing could be heard stirring even so much as an erratic pen stroke.

"Our nation, standing on a precipice of great progress, seeks a future free of those difficult life decisions plaguing our world, free from the toil of everyday work, carrying unwanted pregnancies, of having to put bread on our tables, free to express one's affirmed gender, heal from disease, to raise and educate children, to stamp out the ever-present evil of racism in whatever new manifestation it takes. These are not the times to run from such problems anymore or to close one's eyes hoping that these great travails will somehow disappear tomorrow. We must boldly tackle them face on without the shackles of the past to constrain us from a necessary brighter future—a paradise of our making. That is the platform my campaign has run on and that is what will happen during my presidency. With people having known the choices before them, they have answered with a resounding yes to our message. They have shared the vision—our hope. Therefore, acting out the great dictates of our people, I have moved forward with the intensity and velocity never seen before in our dark and storied history. We have brought forward bills of great change that answer our calls—for equity, justice, and their much-needed oversight. Bills, without which, there would be no breaking out of our close-minded deep freeze. The first of these, I'm proud to call the Economic Valuation and Inequity Act. It will establish, the long overdue, Department of Economic Valuation possessing the broad powers necessary to monitor and mount a response to the complex sticky inequities inherent in our endemic structures. The appointed head of the department will lead a team of expert analysts to map out a future that works for our people—not on the behalf of the monied interests of corporate profiteers. Next, having given the people fair compensation and food on the table, we need to ensure justice for our most vulnerable. And while we have paved a path that leads away from tyranny with the success of the Minorities Protection Act, we will seek to bolster it with the Federal Chromagen Disclosure Act. It will expand the protections now afforded most workers to all workers, securing ongoing funding for further invaluable research in this nascent field. I look forward to completing the structure that my predecessor, despite being from the other side of the aisle, has started, as the final piece is timely. The last, and dare I say, my proudest piece of legislation, as both President and mother, is the Mothers First Act. How long has this country pushed and pushed, with great distress, to have women finally be able to terminate unwanted pregnancies? The answer is: *far too long*. We are doing what none of my predecessors would dare do. We are codifying abortion rights into federal law." Some mild applause could be heard from the room, turning the heads of some reporters to see which of their colleagues broke standard protocol.

"Yes, this is an exciting moment. Women will have the capability to abort a fetus for any reason at any time she deems necessary and completely free." More claps could be heard and even a gauche whistle from the back of the room.

"When I said bold, I meant it. We are here now at a crossroads with this being certainly one of the most astounding moments of our time. We are pioneers discovering a vast new landscape ahead. Who is not ready to discover what waits for us beyond the horizon?" She looked over the room smiling confidently, acting as if anyone at any moment could challenge such sentiment despite its rhetorical context.

"Of course, unfortunately," she continued with a derisive nod. "There are ones who don't wish to go there…and you know who they are…While some may have minor reservations, others outright reject our proposals. They don't wish to follow the arc of history, pushing back on anything they see as a threat to their oppressive narratives. They are naysayers. Agents of despair. They sit on their mounds of riches thwarting the very democratic will of the rest of the nation. They cause us to wallow in self-seeking stagnation rather than the all-embracing warmth of collective cooperation. And what do I have to say to them? I'm here to say to them, okay. That is, okay, now stand aside. You'll have what you want. You'll be on your own from now on. For what else is there to do with such saboteurs of change? If they are not wishing to come to see our vision of a powerful United States, they can finally be cast out to roam freely. For we cannot destroy the whole batch because of some bad actors. We cannot let them transgress our very freedom. So here I am laying the case before the people—who can apply the necessary pressure on their representatives as needed. Let's finally get the job done, as there is nothing more to fear. It's time to remove these chains that bind us forever—releasing ourselves into the ever steady ever sure hand of institutional progress. And I look forward to seeing that grand future ahead. In fact, I can almost see it now, and I believe you're catching a glimpse of it for yourselves." She paused for effect. At that moment, a still of it was captured by an authorized photographer to be long memorialized. It was powerful—mesmerizing. The look of a convicting will.

"Put these bills on my desk and they shall be signed into law," she concluded with electrifying gravity that stirred something in viewers. It projected unwavering intent. They were more than mere words. They were loaded with energy. Like a magnet, they caused something in them to bend—to bow—to soften the will like clay. It wasn't so much an order of command that removes choice, rather, it was a refreshing sentiment facilitating a need to cooperate, as freeing as a rainstorm in the dead of desert.

The speech was stunning. The room was predominantly awed by the new Madame President's apparent altruist purpose and charisma. When her Press Secretary informed them that it was time to take questions, it almost seemed that no one was going to ask any. It took a long moment for hands to appear with the Secretary first calling on the correspondent from LNN.

"Madame President," the woman addressed nervously as Dembier smiled knowingly like they were the best of friends. "For those Americans—"

"*People*," corrected Dembier right away.

The woman gave a slight wince and look of confusion before agreeing. "For those *people* who aren't the naysayers, as you call them, but the many with minor reservations, how do you win them over to your side when there are many politicians with good intentions that don't see these bills as the path forward. How can you keep them honest?"

"Thank you for your question, Carly. I have a very simple message for them. If you have good intentions, prove them. The people want action. As of right now, this is the only path forward and all you have to do is say yes, this one time. All I ask is for them is to try it. Once we put these structures in place, we can see how they work, and if they don't work, we can always remove them or improve them with further legislation. This isn't rocket science. It's a new path forward. And in the end, I think they'll do it. I really think they'll do what's best for the people."

"Nancy," the Press Secretary said pointing to the young WNT reporter in the fourth row. Conferring her notes, she rose from her chair. She wasn't about to tow the line like her colleague was. She only had one shot at this. There were so many questions to ask, and she knew she couldn't ask them all. She settled on three and remembered to breathe.

"Madame President, as you know, these bills have been widely criticized throughout popular media. A lot of the criticism has seemed to focus on your hallmark Mothers First Act. Capitol Review's David Sedecker described it as greatly missing the mark and conservative podcaster Our Time with Melissa Walker says it is, quote, "comic book authoritarian". Many are even now using the moniker the Mothers Never Act as they claim it directly inserts government into women's affairs by incentivizing abortion rather than motherhood. They specifically discuss a subsection of the bill that requires the healthcare provider to have, quote, "video documentary evidence of the abortion's completion" which they claim stands in the face of the very medical privacy concerns the constitution engenders. My question, therefore, is, first, how is this not having the government interfere in a mother's choice to have an abortion. Second, what is in place to address medical privacy concerns when video documentary evidence seems to be the antithesis of one of the most private acts. Third, couldn't there be a gentler softer means to having abortion rights in this country?"

President Dembier listened good humoredly without a hint of disturbance in her face. And taking her time, her response appeared to be composed, thoughtful even. Only did Nancy herself swallow hard at seeing something in the eye contact the President made with her. Behind those eyes something in them screamed to her— her future judgment.

"I don't know about all these critics. Who are they exactly?" the president asked playfully to some laughter. "No, I welcome their concerns. In fact, I'm glad you asked…What they need to know is that the Mothers First Act is the culminating response to years of meddling with women's rights. It is the holy grail that we have so longed for that comes down to the mother's choice. In the end, no one decides but her. The government is just there to support that decision—whatever it is."

"But childbirth or care won't be provided for by taxpayers?" someone called out from the audience.

The Secretary saw who it was and stepped toward the mic. "Please let Madame President finish. Wait your turn." She stared wide eyed at the offender as if they uttered the worst blasphemy in the holy temple.

Dembier's demeanor remained unchanged. "This legislation is only the beginning, but to answer the question about the provision. It is the oversight necessary to ensure that the services the government provides are unequivocally being carried out properly equipping only those stakeholders, who are there not to share medical information but rather protect it, to monitor the possibility of exploitation, malpractice, or fraud. The latter of which tends to happen at the great cost of taxpayer dollars. In this way, it really is expanding women's privacy virtually guaranteeing these medical procedures are privately being carried out by good faith actors—"

"But how does that make sense?" came from the same offender. "Why do they have to document something so private?" The room interrupted in disparate voices who had seemed to be so well behaved until then. An infectious boldness poured forth from various members of the press in the form of questions that begged answers—questions that when withheld, disturbed one's conscience and deeply in the viscera. It was as if they were passengers on a transatlantic cruise keeping mum about the ship's listing underwater or police failing to interview a murder suspect whose clothing is saturated in blood. Secondary considerations had to yield to the obvious, to the concrete. They had to discharge what they pretended to ignore—the very truth their senses imposed on them. How could they even sit still for another minute playacting, degrading themselves to bottom of the barrel thespians when they were supposed to be better than that? At least, some of their number thought so—the ones who lashed out at the dais. The rest sat back passively protesting their colleagues, assuming their positions.

Continuous calls for a return to decorum could be heard between outbursts. It carried on for a full minute before the Secretary put an end to it with a hateful disposition and accompanying voice like a cantankerous feline.

"Wait your turn!" the Press Secretary belted. "Sir, if you cannot wait your turn, you will be asked to leave!"

The rabble in the room settled down again to a hush. The Secretary gave the reporter a daring look before nodding to the president the go ahead.

"Madame President," she said.

Dembier laughed with an awkward squeaky chuckle homing in on the man that dared defy her in the room. She knew who he was. Indeed, they'd remember him. They'd soon remember all of them.

"I think I've answered the question fully with history as my witness. I'll let women out there and their supporters be the judge as to the adequacy of my answer."

6

Johnny Pearson sat in the darkened room lit only by the computer screen before him. With the occasional trip to the bathroom or kitchen for a fresh diet coke, he busied himself answering the web's seemingly inexhaustible promptings.

This was every day for the graduate dropout. His routine was to start the day cracking that first soft drink and end with one. The only difference lately was that he had to start taking medicine. It came on suddenly while sitting at his usual place at the desk when pain burned up from his stomach clawing up into his chest. It felt sudden, sharp, a dreadful injunction that so aptly fit in with recent events. His family took him to the emergency room in the fear that his heart was giving out—that their son was finally crumbling under the enormous strain following his academic departure.

The visit to the doctor was the one good piece of news, however. There was no reason to fear the worst. It wasn't serious, and in taking him home, they almost couldn't believe it. They were skeptical and proceeded with caution from then on. Health had to take priority. There could be no guarantees about anything.

Popping his PPI pill in the morning, Johnny's day had proceeded otherwise as usual. When asked how he was that morning, he had made the characteristic forced joke to make light of a more serious question. "Oh, kicking names and taking ass," he said with a wan smile. It was another way to say he was okay, but his mom and dad were seeing something different. The established mental drain was difficult to conceal in his bleary eyes.

The worse change they noticed was that whenever they mentioned the goings-on of the world outside, there was an impressed apathy in his demeanor—a harsh reversal of the former passion their son once possessed about current events. Without wanting to alert him to their concern and inviting his further denials and resentment, they simply decided to remain vigilant checking in on him from time to time so as they could pre-emptively address their deepening dread. For their own sanity, they had to prepare themselves—to stay one step ahead of whatever lay at the end of their son's ominous trajectory.

Johnny's dad now stood behind him regarding the stooped gloomy figure who had taken on much of his adult features. Seeing that his attentions were seemingly locked on something of interest on the monitor, he couldn't help but feel a terrible nagging anger in his chest. *How fucking dare they force his son to dropout. After all that hard work. All that money and sacrifice. Goddamn them. Goddamn them all to hell.* His mind searched for what could be done to them—some way to exact justice. Could they sue the fuckers? Expose them? Make them apologize? Could they join a resistance? Could they destroy them? Yes, he told himself. For that's what he wanted with them in the end. He wanted to do to them just what they did to his son's spirit. He just really wanted them all to die. Show him a red button right now to make it all happen, and he'd push it. He'd end them without hesitation.

Seeing his boy's defeated stature day after day in that quiet dark room scouring the internet for employment, however, he could never hold onto the rage for long. It was always love and immediate concern for his well-being that soon supplanted all other emotion. What would Johnny do with himself in the end? How could he afford to live on the government's meagre allowance? What prospects did he have to buy a house or have a family of his own? There seemed to be no silver lining—almost nothing good to garner from the foreboding storm clouds he saw ahead. Indeed, that the future appeared bleak was an understatement, but of course he would never tell Johnny that. How could he when hope was one of the few positives he still had?

"That must be one really fascinating application," he said walking up behind Johnny trying to match the same jocular disposition his son put on earlier that day.

Unmoving, with his head being held in his right hand, Johnny was slow to respond. "Yea," he agreed barely, weakly. His father stood beside him to get a better look at what he was doing. Rather than the screen, he appeared to be looking at a notebook on which he had scrawled various notes and figures. Within the jumble of apparent usernames and passwords and other obscure references was a blurry series of instructions that he could just make out from the light of the computer screen. He read each anguishing word one after another. This was it, he somehow knew—something they had been waiting for. To say it was a surprise wasn't exactly right, but to see it expounded on paper in painful exacting detail still felt like the shock of a successive battery of bombshell blasts. All he could do was stand there by his boy in speechless horror.

Sensing his dad's now looming close over him, Johnny's eyes finally opened meeting his old man's. He saw what they knew. Without saying a word, their eyes both sparkled in the blue light— his dad's with hurt and devastation, his with despair and shame.

7

With deep constrained breaths like a manatee barely lifting its snout to the surface of the water for air, Gonzalez's snores reverberated off his tiny office's bare walls. After the going away lunch that celebrated his retirement, he was fast asleep in the privacy of his own office, and no one seemed to mind too much. In fact, almost everything was packed up in boxes anyway. The back table was loaded with reams of case files that he had designated for someone to take to Records before the end of the day. Of course, he had to have one final look at some of them before making the request, failing to mention to anyone that many he had illegally copied for his own private records and research. The Youhaul Murders, Kristi Connor, Peter Barton, Clint Dumfries, Ray Foundation and its architect—he needed them all.

Nothing was going to make him forget, not even a chief hell bent on silencing his push for reopening the case. It had come to a showdown with the powers that be. Either he shut up or he retire. He decided on the latter. Besides, what case could garner his full diligence and attention when he always saw Kristi's face everywhere he went. No, he wouldn't be able to forget that vacant helpless plea for protection—protection that he failed to provide in the end. But, his fight would go on. It would happen outside of those limiting walls. And maybe the full facts could be discovered and even published without the interference of the appointed tow-the-line sphincter clearing cowards that stood in his way. So, fuck the chief. Fuck the FBI. He'd ally with the investigative reporter Paul Higgins and a growing movement of independent thinkers who were only beholden to the way it was and not the way that was safest or best for career advancement.

Gonzalez woke with a start as his former partner, Detective Brennan touched him on the shoulder. "Huh?" He looked up to see Brennan's smiling face. "I see your keeping busy."

"Oh yeah, yeah," Gonzalez started to come to life from the torpor induced by fried chicken and mashed potatoes and a second helping of vanilla celebration cake.

"Only about one hour left on the clock."

"Oh, is it? What's happening then? Nothing?"

"Another day of leads leading nowhere."

"Ah so the usual," Gonzalez chuckled.

"Yep," his partner affirmed.

The door opened. Captain Hartley, one of the youngest female captains in department history stood there eyeing the two surprised men suspiciously before deciding to speak.

"Detective Brennan, I need to speak with you."

"Yes, Cap," he said understanding it was only meant for him alone.

When he left, Hartley acknowledged Gonzalez with a forced smile. "Detective, everything coming together?" She peered around the room at the boxes, especially the ones containing files.

"Yep, I'd say its pretty much wrapped up by now. Just waiting on Records to come."

"Oh yes, we'll take care of that no problem. Let me know if there is anything else I can do, okay? We don't want to disrupt a well-earned retirement when it happens."

"No, thank you Ma'am. I think we're all good here."

"Okay."

She stepped outside and from their looks through the glass wall, it appeared to be a very serious conversation between Brennan and Hartley. In fact, Brennan's face had slowly turned from easy going to grave. The transition was striking. It was as if someone had just told him that someone had shit all over his living room sofa before dispatching the family dog. Gonzalez, feeling his beard with his hand for any spots of food remaining, watched with keen interest as the conversation unfolded.

When she departed Brennan, he glanced over his phone before re-entering Gonzalez's office.

"What's *that* about?"

Brennan looked to the far corner of the room as if he hadn't heard him at first. He came up close to his partner sitting on his desk before mustering a response.

"She said not to say anything to you," he answered in a hushed voice.

"Come on now. Out with it."

"I don't want to ruin your last day...I can tell you later," he said clearly uneasy about the new information.

"You know how I am. Now. Just tell me now. Don't pull any punches. Just the facts."

He turned to look out the window to make sure Hartley wasn't standing there watching, as he decided to continue.

"This is such bad timing, I have to admit...Paul Higgins is reported missing by his ex-wife."

"What?" Gonzalez said with some confusion.

"She had a key to his apartment when he wouldn't return any calls and after days of nothing, she found that while his car was still there, he wasn't. All his stuff unpacked. Nothing."
"That's all?"

"And blood."

"There was blood?"

Brennan sighed, "Yes, blood was smeared all over the bedroom's carpet..."

"What?" Gonzalez asked with an empty fearful stare.

As his partner continued to elaborate the details, Gonzalez stopped listening. He suddenly felt his age, his weight, and a sense of his true powerlessness. What was he even? One man in the face of unabashed evil. Doubt suddenly challenged his convictions. His hands shook as they further stroked his grays. To stand in the face of such a relentless force, to somehow weather these diluvian waters rushing over everyone and everything, how could he hope to remain in the end? Cold bit into his core spreading outward to his arms and legs. He shivered. How utterly alone he was and how feeble a life.

8

Flashes of light penetrated darkness. An enormous multi-screen display wall of the highest quality cycled videos, many of them ads for various products, cars, deodorant, pharmaceuticals—the kind most wouldn't even give a second thought to. Others were speakers: professors, senators, President Dembier, herself. Subtitles followed their endless talking points that had been rehashed for the public and would doubtlessly be again. Still, there were other screens—the ones connected to the surrounding speakers.

Occasionally through feedback boomed professionally toned voices—almost sterile in feeling. There was counseling, instruction, sometimes encouragement. There were directions to assistants to complete tasks along with the sounds of instruments clanging in trays, mild hums of suction devices, and all with the accompaniment of deep respirations. Though the video feed for these were of a poorer quality and fixed nature, they were clearly of a special interest to the owner of the setup, exceeding well over a thousand streams.

The viewer could see little of what was happening, but with a snap of latex gloves, the lab coats appeared to be doing the brunt of the work, elbows motioning back and forth, sometimes with a jerk. A cry. It could have been the most mundane thing in the world the way it played out. It could have been a streamer inviting the viewer to the world of sausage making.

With this incessant flow of stimuli, amazing spiraling colors permeated through the massive space like a glowing circulatory system of fireworks: reds, oranges, yellows, and the unknown colors between seemingly firing in unison with a life of their own. A viewer may have asked in wonderment: were they coming from the screens themselves or merely a reflection?

At some point there seemed to be synchronicity in the sound from the speakers. Even through all the thousands of disparate sounds. A woman's culminating breath then a whimper.

www.ingramcontent.com/pod-product-compliance
Lightning Source LLC
Chambersburg PA
CBHW020653110726
47901CB00001B/175